UNSTOPPABLE

THE LIFE AND TIMES OF A USED-CAR SALESMAN

RICHARD OCHOA

PAGE PUBLISHING, INC.
New York, NY

First originally published by Page Publishing, Inc. 2018

This story should be considered as a work of fiction, even though it is autobiographical in nature, it is subject to the writers own interpretation of events, and any similarities to actual people or events are simply coincidental.

ISBN 978-1-64138-489-6 (Paperback)
ISBN 978-1-64138-490-2 (Digital)

Printed in the United States of America

ACKNOWLEDGMENTS

I would like to thank my loving wife, Dora Ochoa. Without her faith and belief in me, my career would not have been possible. My friend and mentor, Michael Briscoe, who gave me the framework to build a successful career on. George Quinn, he who introduced me to the automobile business. The late Wendell Broughton, he who taught me how to close a sale. Kristin Garcia, and Felix Valenzuela who helped me tell my story.

There were many others who were positive influences, and friends I made along the way, such as the late Mr. Dick Poe, Dan Carter, Lewis Burfit, Joseph Bua, Phil Leone, Troy Duhon, Mike Kelly, Norbert Solis, Doug Turner, Sean Burst, Craig Stowe, Harris Henry, Augustine Vasquez, Steve Dautrive, Wayne Mariana, and the classy lady Ronea Wood.

This book is dedicated to all the men and women who toil on the asphalt lots, and in dealerships across the country. Your entrpernural spirit lives on, and is unconquered.

CONTENTS

INTRODUCTION

I share this story not because I feel my life has been so interesting, even though it has been, but I don't feel anyone has ever accurately depicted the essence of what it's like to be a car salesman. This has not been captured in a novel, and certainly not on film. No one except another true salesman could understand the joy, agony, fear, loathing, and ecstasy that could be captured in just one profession. If you are like most people, you drive by miles and miles of car dealerships in any major city and all you can think of is how much you dread the idea of looking for a car and having to deal with a salesman. I had a saved copy of an article published by the *LA Times* many years ago, from 1993. It read, "Car salesmen and women are assayers of true business, the core of the American spirit. They thrive on the asphalt lots expecting only what they earn on commission, nothing more, and would detest the thought of working for wages when they have the ability to go out and write their own paycheck. They thrive on competition and will accept any challenge, local or global, you name it. They are usually only loved and admired by their own family, close friends; if any exist, or each other, which is why they gravitate to their own kind."

This article was on my pegboard wall for over twenty years so that my customers would know that I was serious about myself and my profession, not another "fly by night," waiting for something better to come along. Only in the car business can one go from success, having your wife go out and look for a new house, and a month later wondering if you can file for bankruptcy while you look for a real job. I earned over six figures for most of my thirty-two-year career, often well over that number, and I made more as a salesman than I ever did as a manager. My career covered two states and three metropolitan areas, including the city of Houston, and the largest and most prosperous Chevrolet dealer in the country.

The first sales job I ever applied for had a management group that sent my application for a handwriting analysis. They said I was a total flake and should not be hired. They said I was a daydreamer and procrastinator, "one who would never amount to anything." The manager, a country guy named Dan, said, "I don't give a shit what they say. When a man can look me in the eye and shake my hand like you did, I know he can sell cars." Interesting to note that phrase, "I would never amount to anything," was the same thing my father used to tell me, right before he would suggest that I run away from home, because I was adopted (I wasn't really adopted). I had just graduated from Bible College, so I knew I wasn't so dumb. As for the daydreaming aspect, they have a name for it now, I believe it is called ADD. They even give kids prescription meds for it now. I wore this description of myself as badge of honor. From then on, I was determined to not waste time, to make the most of each day. And as for the daydreaming, I would use it to my advantage. I would envision a family crawling all over a fresh trade we took in, or a young guy buying one of our sports cars to impress his girlfriend, who would leave him for me when she realized he was a phony. I was never bored because my mind was working nonstop, and even when it was slow, I learned to entertain the troops with constant stories or jokes. I did a great impersonation of Howard Cosell, and I would use it to describe the day's events. Of course I learned to do this to distract the other salesmen as I maintained a watchful eye on the lot, so when I saw a customer appear on the lot, I was gone and would leave them hanging on, waiting for the story, while I had the customer.

This story is not "my how-to-do-it lesson" so that you too can go out and learn the joys of "pushing iron buggies." Or if you will just send me a token fee, I will make your "worthless" son or daughter into a used-car salesman, like me. My mentor, Mike B., who taught me so much about the business, and life, used to say, "You can go to any major city to 'skid row' and find tons of people with 'unfulfilled potential,' or you can go to the city morgue and see an example of someone who has 'finally given up.'" The fact is, people in all walks of life become "crapped out," they suffer from clinical depression, or a tough streak, a bad season, or a series of "bad breaks." No matter what you call it, everyone experiences it at one time or another, and how you recover, and pull yourself out of it, that is what separates the winners from the rest.

It has been said, "We have seen the enemy, and it is us." I spent a lifetime in the car business trying to defeat the enemy of myself, as the apostle Paul said, "I pummel my body, and subdue it, so that it may serve its purpose." I am not naive enough to think that I was the most successful car salesman ever.

I know people who have done better, but I did it in the trenches, like a career soldier who refused a promotion. Like the song says, "I did it my way." The song also says, "When times were tough, I ate it up and spit it out." There is a saying in this industry, "Could you make it if someone dropped you into an unknown territory, with nothing but your wits and the clothes on your back?" Well, I did just that. I not only survived, but I thrived and made a reputation for myself at every stop. Despite my reputation, I was ever careful not to toot my own horn; I let others tell most of the stories, until now.

I went from being a shy chubby kid with no ambition and no future to rise to the pinnacle of my profession, from a young man going to seminary school to become a minister to becoming an alcoholic suffering a devastating car accident and recovering from both of them, as well as a near failed marriage. With God's help, faith, and a positive attitude, I was able to overcome many of life's obstacles, most of them self-imposed. I prefer to think of my life in the scripture that says, "As a man thinks in his heart, so is he." This is a story of perseverance and self-preservation. To fully understand it is to experience what it is like to be one of the most despised, feared, and misunderstood characters in America, if not the world.

I have often wondered if people in Japan or China have jokes and stereotypes of used-car salesmen, or is it actually an "honorable profession" over there? In this country, a used-car salesman has become a punch line, a temporary type of employment for someone who has, unfortunately, lost their "real job." No matter your opinion, these stories are true; nobody could make this up. The names may be slightly altered, mostly because I don't have time to call everybody and ask their freaking permission. You will experience the laughter, the characters, the joys of victory, and the loneliness and agony of defeat. You are about to enter the world of the dreaded used-car salesman. "Buyer, beware."

Chapter 1
Post-KatrinainSouthLouisiana

It was September of 2005, just days after the devastation from hurricane Katrina. It was a tragic time for many—there were those who lost lives, home, and property, and of course, many who lost their cars. My specialty was helping others replace the cars lost during the storm.

I was working at a Nissan dealership in Metairie, Louisiana, where I had been *salesman of the year* for the last two years. After the storm, my general manager, Phil, called me and said, "Don't you dare go to work in Baton Rouge just because they are open and we are not open yet. You come see me, and I will advance you the money you need until we are open."

I lived in Covington, Louisiana, some forty-five miles away, where we, thankfully, suffered only some wind damage and no flooding at all. It was a scary time, as well as a time of great relief, where strangers even greeted each other with a sense of survival instinct like those who have overcome great peril and come out on the other side alive and grateful.

It was about four days before I was able to cross the causeway bridge to receive my seven-thousand-dollar advance, and about another week before, I was able to go to work, and when I did, I was twelve thousand dollars "in the hole" with my employer due to my advances. Other salesmen were sleeping in their cars at this time, but my boss exhibited faith in me and confidence in what I was capable of doing—I was determined not to disappoint him.

My friend and manager, Joe, "the Italian Stallion," had been busy buying all the cars he could get his hands on. There was going to be a great demand, and money was no object. Our owner, Troy, had even gone to Washington, DC, to obtain federal funding—his own form of an advance—and had come back with twelve to fifteen million dollars. The stage was set, the stars were aligned, and for those of us who already loved the business, we were about to enter car sales heaven.

Imagine a world where everybody needed a car and everyone had money to buy a car! There were people who got into the business at this time, and they made money, but for those of us who actually knew what we were doing, *the results were deadly.*

I remember the first sale I made after the storm to a slightly middle-aged man named James. He said, "I don't suppose you would have an automatic pickup for fewer than ten grand, would you?"

I told him, "In the first place, we do not talk price unless you are paying cash. Otherwise, it's a price range, or payment range, but to answer your question, there are no cheap trucks."

He said, "I have pretty good credit, and I can spend about three-fifty a month, but I have no money down."

After verifying his 760 credit score, I consulted with my manager to try and find something that we owned for under the book value. The reason for this is that the bank will loan 125 percent of the book value with a good credit customer.

We decided a Mercury Cougar would be ideal for him. We figured we could maximize our profit with this car once he came up with a little money down. Upon seeing the car, he said, "It is clean, but it's not exactly a pickup, and I was hoping for an import as well."

I said to him, "You are in luck! The car is a hatchback, which will carry more without having to pay truck prices, plus it is an import without having to pay import prices." Keep in mind, all this was said without having ever actually told him the price.

We soon came up with the plan to have James come up with fifteen hundred down, and we would make a nice "lick," or profit. I presented him a payment range that was acceptable, but the down payment was not something he had planned for. Having seen his credit, I knew he had plenty of "plastic" resources.

I explained to him how the banks were dealing after the storm, and credit card companies were automatically increasing people's credit lines since most people were waiting for insurance settlements.

After he signed the papers and paid the fifteen hundred dollars down for a car he really didn't want, he said, "Now that we are done, I just have one question—how the hell is that car considered an import?"

I opened the hood and said, "See here, it is the same motor as a Mazda 626. You have a Mazda in a Mercury Cougar body." I really hope it's true; I like to think so, at least. The result was about a five-thousand-dollar profit for the company, not including the financing, and about an eighteen-hundred-dollar commission for me: the first post-Katrina, but certainly not the last.

It was at this time that I met Doug, a black man in his late thirties. I would best describe him as "scrappy." He was one of the many who came to work with us post-Katrina. In my selling career, I seldom made an aggressive move without having an ulterior motive, so when I stepped in front of other salesmen to take a customer from them, there was only one thing in my mind that I had to do: make the deal! This served a dual purpose. First, it sent a message that I could do whatever I wanted, and second, it demoralized the competition! I have made lesser men quit over this, believe me.

I did this to Doug, and of course, I made the deal. When we were away in private, he confronted me. Now, I have been warned and threatened before, but he did something I had not experienced in many years. He put his hands on me. He grabbed me by the collar near my throat. Well, I don't even remember what was said after I knocked his hand away. People stepped in to break us up. All I kept thinking was, *He put his hands on me with impunity. Nobody does that to me.*

In the coming days, I kept thinking, *I should not have done that*, because at the time there were so many customers that I didn't need to do it, and it really bothered me. A couple of days later, I heard him bragging about our confrontation to another salesman, so I approached him. I said, "You know there is a little park close by. We could drive over and settle this, and nobody has to know about it until one of us has to go home because he can't work."

Needless to say, this move surprised him, and he began to tell everyone that I had challenged him. Well, I didn't need the publicity, and I already had a reputation. I just thought it would shut him up and put the incident behind us, but as it turned out, that ended it. And I acquired a fan! Soon after he was following me around to see how I conducted my business and calling on me to help him close his sales.

At the time (post-Katrina), I was in excellent physical condition; I had hired a personal trainer, thanks to my wife's business and bartering system—my wife owned and operated a day spa in an affluent area known as the North

Shore, about forty-five miles north of New Orleans. Being in good physical condition served me well at this time because the pace was fast and furious. There were so many customers and literally so little time because after the storm, many areas were enforcing strict curfews.

I do not want to give the wrong impression about my relationship with African Americans. I generally got along with them very well. I had attended college in Los Angeles and experienced working with them in Houston and El Paso. The thing is, many of them take themselves way too seriously. I mean, I am Hispanic, and I know more Mexican jokes than anyone I know. Some black people get offended when you ask, "What do you call a black man in a suit?" The defendant. Or "What do you call a black woman having an abortion?" Crime stopper. Or "Why are Mexicans not good at a barbeque?" The beans fall through the grill!

I get the world out of being politically correct, but people need to loosen up and learn to laugh at themselves. The real kicker was when I would imitate the great Martin Luther King. I would say, "Free at last, free at last, great googly googly, I'm free at last!"

Immediately black people would correct me and say, "He did not say that."

I would say, "Yes, that was his famous speech."

They would say, "That part is from *Sanford and Son*."

I would then ask, "Martin Luther King was on *Sanford and Son*?"

Most people understood that I was just kidding and laughed it off, but some would get angry and dismiss me as having a bad attitude. No matter. I suppose I was an equal opportunity offender who could take it even better than dish it out and expected everyone else to do the same.

I was in the middle of a sale where credit applications were required when a black man named Chris came in. Now my office was strategically up front so that when customers came in, mine was the first face they would see. Chris asked if someone could help him find a car for about five thousand. I asked him the usual, "Does it have to run? Or are you a mechanic looking for a fixer upper?"

He said, "Of course, it has to run, it is for my family, I have a wife and two kids."

I told him to give me a minute and I went and got three sets of keys and laid them on the desk in another office. I said, "This is it and if you don't have the money with you, don't bother looking because they will be gone by today." He said he had the money and I asked him to give me his driver's license as security while he went out back to look at them. I explained that I had to finish my other paperwork and after that we could test drive the one he liked best.

I finished my other paperwork and placed my other customers in the finance office then I returned to Chris. He had settled on a Dodge Durango so we took it around the block for a drive. When we returned he expressed his concern that the air conditioning was not quite cold enough. I said, "What do you want for five thousand? If I put that car in the shop to check out the air conditioning, they will run up a thousand-dollar ticket. Do you want to spend six thousand for a five thousand dollar car?"

Chris said, "No, sir! I best take my chances and take it just like it is. I can have my mechanic check it for a lot less expense."

I had just made two sales and about thirty-five-hundred-dollar commission in about three hours' time. On a day like this I could take a two-hour lunch and leave early, and I often did just that.

Now, this post-Katrina era had produced quite a cast of characters to work with. The automobile dealer owned five stores and ours was made up of a mad mix of all of them. There was Big Tony, a super religious, well-dressed black man. There was Danger, a semi-retarded young man—I named him after the character in the film *Million Dollar Baby*. There was the African Connection in the new car department: Three salesmen, one I called Motumbo because he looked like the former NBA player, a guy called Vander, and the Prince because he was related to royalty in Africa. The Prince held the position of GSM or second-in-command for the whole store.

One day I met a customer from Mississippi I like to call Redneck Ray. He was looking for a certain price range SUV so being that he was a retired older gentleman, I gave him respect and found him one for $8,995.00. I then allowed him $1,800.00 trade value for his old pick up. He said that the figures looked fine and he would gladly take them to his credit union the next day and we should have a deal.

I went on to explain to him that at this point what we do is "assume the

sale"—that is, we sign all the papers, have it all printed and send him home in the new vehicle in case the credit union wants to see it tomorrow, which was going to be a Friday. I explained that if he did not do this, the vehicle would not be here when he returned because we were selling cars at such a fast pace.

This was about the time it became weird. Redneck Ray looks at me hard and says, "Son, what kind of an idiot do you think I am?"

I knew instinctively where this was going so I said, "I want to get this right—what kind of idiot are you then?"

His expression changed and he said, "Why you little half-breed!"

I said, "Hey, I'll have you know I'm all breed, a full Mexican, which is better than being an inbred, any day of the week."

About that time my manager Joe, who is Italian, walked in so Redneck said, "Your man here just called me an inbred!"

Joe explained, jokingly, that he had heard worse. Red Ray said to him, "What do you know? You are nothing but a half nigger yourself!"

All this excitement soon got everyone interested. Big Tony came out of his office and other black salesmen's ears were perking up. By now Redneck Ray was heading with his keys for the door but his driver's license and registration were still in the manager's office. As Ray walked out the door he yelled, "You all are a bunch of niggers!" Joe and I had to hold these guys back from killing him.

By the time he got to his truck the Prince himself had reached him. The prince greeted him and said, "How are you doing, is everything all right?"

Ray's reply to this was a simple, "Fuck you, Nigger!"

It was not until about two hours later that a state trooper arrived and asked if we had seen a man fitting Ray's description earlier that day. We said, "Yes." The trooper said he was having lunch at the Denny's down the street when the man approached him and said he feared for his life to have to come back for his belongings. After we all had a big laugh, Joe gave the trooper the license and registration, and that was the last anyone heard of Redneck Ray.

Those African guys were something else. I used to tease Matumbo who was always hungry. I said he should go out back and invade a rather large ant hill I saw with a big straw—"Just like he did in the old country." I would often ask him if he ever ate a water buffalo or killed a lion. It was a good thing he had a sense of humor because he looked like he could kill a lion. He was big

stout fellow but a good guy as well.

His counterpart in the African Connection, Vander, prided himself as quite a lady's man. He was always bragging about scoring himself a new "concubine" for his little harem. I will never forget when I saw him after his vacation to Africa and I asked him how his trip was. "Did you have a good time?"

He approached me and got off to my side to show me pictures in his phone. He said, "You tell me if I had fun." The only thing I could see was the side profile of a black persons head, sucking on a big black pecker.

You could not even tell if it was a male or a female, so I asked him, "Which one is you?" I burst out laughing and soon the whole dealership knew that Vander may have been a mystery cock sucker on his own vacation.

You should know something about my laugh. It is funny and contagious and when I really get going, it's hard to stop. It has also been a sore spot for many. Men have had tons of fights or near fights just for "yucking it up" at some poor schmuck's expense. My own father could not stand my laugh and when I worked with him in his business, he would get so pissed at me that he would tell me to take the day off. I would answer him that I needed the money and he would say, "I will pay you to get out of here."

During this time we also had an Arab Connection, Abdul. I called him Ali Baba as in the forty thieves. He was from Jerusalem and was a heck of a salesman, almost as good as me, and that is saying a lot. In fact, at the end of the first month after the Katrina storm, the final sales' tallies showed our results were almost identical: we had both made the most money since the beginning of the storm, about thirty-six thousand dollars each.

The other person in the Arab connection was our new finance director from Lebanon. I called him Lou. He called me Samson Al Jabber because I had dabbled with hair growth products and suggested he do likewise, hence Samson. Poor Lou. He had suffered partial paralysis of his face due to a stroke and part of his face was pulled all to one side, with one of his cheeks puffed out as if swollen. The look made him practically expressionless and a perfect target for me. I would sit across from him and act like the fellow on Inside the Actor's Studio. I would say, "Show me happy, worried, confused, frightened, and now panic, followed by grief." His expression, of course, never changed— he had the same half-face swollen look. By then everybody would be laughing their asses off and all he could do is flip me off.

Often when I was working on a finance deal, I would barge into his office

when he was in a meeting with the general manager Phil and some bankers. He would try to brush me off to get rid of me and I would say, "Don't you give me that look!"

He would say, "What look?"

I studied his face again and said, "There it is. You did it again!" Of course by then, all the bankers would be enjoying a big laugh.

About this post-Katrina time I met Renee, an attractive salesperson in her midforties who became a good partner and friend—and quite possibly the best female car salesperson I have ever worked with.

We had a precision working tandem together. When she had a group of Spanish people with good credit, she had me work with her, and I got her help when I had some seemingly over-rated white folk with an over inflated opinion of themselves who needed her version of smooth. It didn't matter what direction we had to go, we played our own version of good cop and bad cop to equal a deadly combination.

One day when I arrived, she showed me a credit application by a Spanish couple with great credit. Now, it is a known fact that great credit and a big down payment equal a potential huge profit. The Esparzas were looking to trade in their Nissan Xterra valued at $7,500 for a late model Nissan pickup. When all was said and done, we made an eight-thousand-dollar profit, not including the financing.

A couple of days later when I was on my way to work, I got a call from my manager. It seemed I had a very important guest waiting for me.

The general manager of one of our top advertisers, a Spanish radio station, was waiting for me. His parents were the recipients of our big profit transaction. I gave him the song and dance of what a great deal we gave them and guess what? He believed me! But that wasn't the problem. It seemed his parents were going to greatly miss their Nissan Xterra, and would we be kind enough to find them another one to replace it with as soon as possible? I said, "You bet," and within a couple of days, I delivered it to the happy couple. This time we only made about a five-thousand-dollar profit on the sale; the result was about twenty-five hundred in commission each for Renee and I, and everybody was happy as could be.

I believe it was the following Saturday when "all hell" broke loose. Three Arab men were there looking at cars with another used-car salesman. They

were walking to the back offices when I heard one of them scream. It sounded like he yelled, "Allah Akbar!" After 9-11, you never know what to think, right? So I looked down the hall and over by the coke machine was the Arab guy on the floor, twitching and convulsing, like one of those fake wrestling shows where the guy is sent flying off the top rope. Immediately pandemonium struck. One salesmen named Jay, whom we suspected of homosexual activity because of his tight-fitting clothes, offered "mouth-to-mouth" resuscitation services. The man's friends said, "No" to this, of course.

Meanwhile one of the assistant managers went running to the busy Veteran's Memorial Boulevard with both arms waving franticly. I don't know if he was trying to find a cop or an ambulance on their lunch break. Thankfully, someone called the switchboard operator who called for 911 emergencies, but then she came over to check out the scene. Her name was Rose and she was three hundred pounds of black woman—her specialty was lunch or dinner. She yelled, "Let me through, I work at the hospital!"

A black guy named Brian yelled, "You work at the hospital cafeteria, bitch."

She said, "I don't work at a cafeteria, mother fucker!" This took place on a Saturday with crowds of people inside the building and outside as well.

By now I had taken my place on the front porch and was taking in the whole comedy of errors, laughing my ass off. I don't mean to laugh at someone else's misfortune, but I can't help it—I love slapstick comedy. My boss Joe came to me and asked me to cool it because by now the guy's two Arab buddies were giving me the stink eye for laughing at their friend's misfortune. Joe was really worried that they might come back and blow the place up. Yes, my laughter is that annoying, especially if you're on the receiving end of it.

By now people were coming up to me on the porch to ask me what was going on, like if I was the ring master of this circus. A woman approached me and asked if she should check out the patient, because she really was a nurse and she did not know if the large black woman was or not, and, get this, she thought she would ask me because it looked like I was in charge. I could barely keep a straight face as I said, "I don't think the big woman is a nurse. She just stayed at a Holiday Inn Express last night so she thinks she is." I had her examine the patient before the emergency crew arrived. It seemed he was allergic to Dr. Pepper, the building survived the bomb scare, and Jay had to practice his mouth to mouth treatment on someone else.

Living and working in the South was a unique experience for me. For one thing it was the first time I ever experienced any form of racism—after all, I was raised in El Paso which was 70 percent Hispanic. I went to college in Los Angeles, California, and I worked and lived in Houston, which was also a melting pot of people and cultures who learn that they somehow have to get along. I was shocked and confused the first time an irate customer said, "Why don't you go back where you came from?" I stood there thinking, *They want me to go to back to El Paso?*

Make no mistake about it, I was born in this country and I grew sick and tired of people asking where I was from. When I said, "Texas" they would say, "But where are you really from?" Once I had a customer who was working for the census bureau in the year 2000. I explained to him that I didn't complete the part of the form that asked, "If you are of Latin descent, where did your people come from?" I told him it was none of their damned business.

I didn't think they were asking Polish people or people from Russia what part of the Soviet Union they were from. So after a spirited argument with him I said, "I was born here, my father was a hero in World War II, and my brother made the supreme sacrifice giving his life for his country in Vietnam. I think I have earned the right not to answer these questions." I won the argument, leaving him and the rest of the room silent. I didn't sell him a car and I didn't care either.

When I first moved to Louisiana I was on the way to work and I had barely left my sub-division when I was stopped by a local sheriff. I was on Highway 190 in Covington, as I was barely beginning my commute. It must have been about ten in the morning since I had to work late that night. The sheriff pulled me over in my three-year-old Chevy blazer, and asked if I knew why he was pulling me over. I replied that I had no idea.

Then he asked, "Do you speak English?" I reminded him that I had already answered him in English, so the obvious answer was "Yes."

He replied, "Oh, a bit of a smart-ass, huh? Just answer the questions, son."

I said, "Yes, sir. What other questions do you have for me today?" He went on to ask if I lived in the area, if I was renting or buying my home, if I had auto insurance, and, of course, had I qualified for a driver's license in this country? The sheriff seemed overwhelmed by the fact that he had discovered a real live "Mexican" who could not only prove he was a citizen but was also a home owner in a nice neighborhood, and had auto insurance, too! I think he was so thrilled he probably wanted to take my picture for the local paper. Finally he said that I had cut someone off when I changed lanes on this busy two-lane highway. Well, I didn't want to argue with him even though there was nobody else on the road when I was driving. Instead I asked if he was going to give me a citation or just a warning. He shook his head in amazement that I spoke proper English and replied he would let me go with just a warning. He did let me go and then followed me to the toll bridge about nine miles or so. I made it a point to go the speed limit, and I did not change lanes at all.

CHAPTER 2
HOW IT ALL BEGAN

It was the fall of 1979. I had just graduated from Bible College that May and was supposed to come home and help with my dad's business, at least that was the plan. My father could only remember how immature I was during my growing up years and he could only imagine a world of frustration if we worked together now. But I had left Los Angles and moved back to El Paso and I was running out of options—jobs were not as plentiful here—I volunteered to work at church camp for six weeks. This was to see if I could be persuaded to go into the ministry, more or less to try and convince myself, but I became more convinced that it was not for me. I guess I was not that much of a giving person like I thought I was. I was also determined to prove my father wrong when he said I would never amount to anything.

When I returned from church camp, I found a group of people I owed money to with their hands out, ready for payment. I sold my car for just under a thousand dollars, an old Ford Maverick, with two hundred thousand miles, wrecked in the rear, and no windshield. My uncle George who sold cars was amazed. He asked how I had done it and I explained that was the amount of money I needed. My uncle said, "You should be selling cars." He picked up the paper and said, "Look, this Buick dealer has an ad for used-car salesmen, and they offer you a demo plan so you will have a car."

I applied and the rest is history. They sent my handwriting for an analysis and the manager was told not to hire me, that I was a flake. They said I was not going to amount to anything, just like my father had said.

The manager Dan, a country loving good old boy, hired me anyway. He liked the way I shook hands and looked people in the eye when I did—all those church services had paid off. I was a young, twenty-five-year-old, vocal, cocky, and ready to take on the world. I became a student of the game listening, watching and becoming a student of human moves. I tried to anticipate what a customer would do, even if they were with another salesman at the time. The crew was Jr, Jeff, Paul, and Mr. Brown who I re-named Mr. Magoo. Mr. Brown was an elderly man near, if not past, retirement age. He wore thick glasses and a fedora for a hat. He was a cold and calloused, veteran used-car salesman of over forty years, and I forced him into retirement. I could not believe how much I aggravated him with everything I did—my laugh, my jokes about him looking like Mr. Magoo. I really didn't even know I was the cause of his misery until the other guys started telling me that I was the reason he was going home for four or five hours at a time. I became an instant hit. I sold a car on my first day and was soon out-selling most of the other salesmen.

One day as fall was fast approaching, Mr. Magoo's hat was blown off his head by the wind. I ran after it and stomped on it with my foot. It was more instinctive than intentional but that day Mr. Magoo went home, and he never came back. I was really just trying to catch it for him.

Oh well, it became a sign of things to come. It became evident that one of my major talents was to demoralize and crap out the competition, and occasionally make them quit. Over the years there were countless numbers of salesmen who fell prey to this tactic, even though my first victim was unintentional. I became a good student who would ask lots of questions and observe the other salesmen in action, especially the good ones.

Jeff was a good one. He presented the case for his car like a skilled attorney. When the buyer asked him how much he would sell the car for, he would say, "As much as I possibly can." When they asked him how much they would receive for their trade-in, he would say, "As little as possible." This was a rather blatant approach that could not work for everybody. I used it on occasion, when I could get away with it. I preferred the look-dumb-and-act-stupid approach, like Colombo the detective. I would scratch my head and say, "I'll try, let me ask my manager."

I learned that there are as many different approaches to take with a customer as there are customers to sell. I liked to tell a joke, one of my dad's favorites: "You ask why do Mexicans have big shoulders and flat foreheads? The answer is: When they are in school and they are asked a question, they shrug their shoulders. And when they hear the correct answer, they immediately slap their forehead!"

The only bad thing about this first sales job was that we had to wait our turn for a customer—this sucked because I was young and I could run circles around these guys. The phone, however, was fair game and I became deadly on the phone. I also learned how to steal the calls. When a phone rang in another office, I hit 1-9 in another office and the call came to me. Sometimes the other salesmen didn't even know what had happened. They would call the operator and ask what happened to their call.

It was about this time that we discovered the Blind Date contest. This was a fun and peculiar way to show off your real phone skills with the opposite sex.

On the subject of sex I was somewhat of a novice, sad but true. Keep in mind that I had just finished studying for a life in the ministry—indeed, I was a licensed minister so I was not as skilled as the other more sexually active salesmen, or so it seemed at least. The college I went to was coed but we were strongly encouraged to abstain from sexual activity. I lasted for almost three years of abstinence from sex. The school I went to is now called Life Pacific College. It is associated with the International Church of the Foursquare Gospel. As students we were encouraged to attend and minister in some capacity at one of these various churches in the Los Angeles area. It was toward the end of my junior year when I had already decided not to pursue a life in the ministry, that I had my fall from grace.

Her name was Nicole—not really but I like the name—on a Sunday afternoon after church, of course. We went for a ride to the beach. This was my favorite date because of the price, plus it also gave me a generous look at her rather formidable physique. Things got a little steamy at the beach, and a little more after the sun went down. Well, I had to take a chance that my two roommates might not be home, and to my good fortune, they were at Sunday night services. It was over so fast I often wondered if it really even happened—but it had all right, and I knew it had.

Every Sunday afterward Nicole would come to me and hug me and cry her eyes out. I didn't know if her guilt was that strong or the sex was that bad! Later on I saw the film *Saturday Night Fever* and there is a scene where the girl lets three guys have their way with her, one after the other. The guilt of what she did kicked in and she started crying and the last guy says, "Great, how come with me she has to cry?" I still think of that when I see the film—I mean it was disturbing. I really wish I hadn't done it.

My buddy Robert went to the same church and would often ask, "What's up with her?" I thought of going to another church but that would really have been obvious. In retrospect it was still a fond memory when I thought of her pretty smile and her budding breasts.

But there was more to it than that. I learned in the coming years that whether you are closing a sale, or convincing a woman to have sex, or preaching while speaking to a crowd—there is no greater feeling than having someone bend and surrender to your will. There is little difference between reaching around a young woman while undoing her bra and sliding a purchase order over to a customer for them to sign. Either way you say, "Trust me, it's for the best."

The fall of 1979 was when the movie *10* starring Bo Derek came out. This was significant because every girl who called in on the Blind Date contest claimed to be a *10*. The contest had started on a country/western radio station. The female caller told a little about herself, her likes and dislikes, and what kind of date she was looking for. Afterward, prospective suitors, like me, called the station and acquired her phone number. Of course I did this at the request of the rest of the crew. They wanted to see me in action and insisted it was good practice for my sales career.

After numerous busy signals I would get through. I sang a little to them—I do have a pretty good voice—I told them a couple of jokes—girls love a good sense of humor—then finally I asked what they were wearing. No matter what they said (for example, "jeans and a tee shirt"), I gave them a long and juicy "Mmmmm." When I knew I had them right where I wanted them, I backed off and I said, "You probably have a lot of guys to choose from."

She would say, "No, I choose you. I want to go out with you!" I hate to brag but I always got the date! But the truth was the girl was seldom a 10 unless you were to divide by two or even three, but still I closed the deal, over and over again.

This is the way most of the dates went. The young lady told me where to meet her and what she would be wearing. When she asked what I would be wearing. I said, "Don't worry. I will find you." She would bring a friend and I brought my buddy Jr. This was to insure that we got along well enough to be alone. After a couple of drinks, our chaperones would leave us to our own devices.

I was very careful about becoming intimate with any of them. Keep in mind that this was not exactly the age of safe sex; however I had been celibate for the better part of five years, so I did know how to just say, "No."

The next day all the guys would gather around to hear about my date. So I would tell them, "We danced a little, made out a little and then I took her home."

They would say, "Is that all?"

I could tell they were somewhat disappointed, so I made up steamier versions—well, with one being rated R, and one rated PG. They could decide which version they preferred.

I learned then that car salesmen don't care if a story is true or not—just give them a good story, that's all. I found myself feeling the same way later on: embellish the story, make it fun and exciting, the truth be damned. But I did have some exciting dates. One girl asked me to meet her at a topless club where she was auditioning for amateur night and she was very attractive. After a few drinks, we made our way to my car, a demo, brand new Buick regal. We made out some and I sampled her voluptuous breasts. She then told me she wanted to have sex with me.

There was only one problem, and I could tell she wasn't into it, but why should I care, right? It felt weird. Like she was trying to force herself into it. It reminded me of a large, overweight salesman on his way to buy his fried chicken lunch when he is approached by a homeless man who says, "I haven't eaten in three days." The fat salesman says, "Maybe you should force yourself."

As it turned out, the girl had had mostly lesbian relationships and wanted me to transform her, I guess. I was not prepared for that kind of responsibility, so I passed. After all, in my mind a "Yes" is a "Yes!" I had closed the sale; I just didn't deliver the car.

Of course I told the R-rated version of the story to the guys. I thought I deserved that, especially since I had a standing offer from her to finish the job, and she called me at least once a week to remind me. I've learned that a particularly attractive woman cannot handle the thought of being rejected, no matter what the reasons are.

The only other memorable blind dates I had were also the ones when I refused my services, sexually that is. Her name was Velia and we went out on a Friday night. We danced till closing time and I liked her and thought of her as a very attractive, slightly older woman. The night had ended and I said, "Goodnight," but she would not have it—she had someone watching her kids and this was to be her night to get her kicks. I explained I was tired and had to work on Saturday at 8:00 a.m. She could not believe I was saying, "No" to her. I explained it was not "No"—it was just not right now. That Saturday was my turn to watch the bargain lot, a separate trailer on a lot with cash cars to sell for three thousand or less. Well, when she found out, she showed up, of course.

It went from "Let's test drive this one," to "Does this door lock?" Soon afterward she had her top off and was wanting me to check out the merchandise. Well, I am only human, so the next thing I had her *lying* across the desk while I explored the virtues of her lush mammaries. I am even reminded of the Barbara Streisand song when she sang, "Mammaries may be beautiful, and yet."

It didn't take long before the phone was ringing and there was knocking at the door. But I was oblivious to it all, that is, until the door opened. My manager Dan walked in. He calmly said for her to leave and for me to fix myself up because there were customers outside. I think he would have fired me except he got an eyeful of her chest and it made a helluva story to share around the dealership.

As a minister I had recently married my buddy Jr to his longtime girlfriend, and most of the people at the dealership had attended the wedding. After this incident, I was officially, and sadly, no longer regarded as the innocent young minister of the dealership. Later on, when I saw the movie *Used Cars*, starring Kurt Russell, I was reminded of this incident.

At about this time I met Kathy. She was a waitress and a student of modern dance. She performed with a dance company called "Viva, El Paso!" She was very attractive, with a profound sense of self respect that I found refreshing and appealing. We met when she waited on me at the restaurant, and I impressed her when I gave her a twelve-dollar tip for an eight-dollar lunch. I am no fool, you know! She also had some of the best legs and rear end I think I had ever seen. She claimed to have a boyfriend, but I didn't care because she went go out with me whenever I asked her. There was no sex involved even though we did have some romantic moments but having considered where this could lead, I decided it was best to remain friends. Part of this was decided for me when I met her sister—not exactly what you might expect—and her sister was looking for a car. Their father was a big shot officer at Fort Bliss, the military base in El Paso, and every time I took Kathy home and she mentioned her father's name, the military police at the gate would jump to open it with gusto and enthusiasm! Her sister settled on a used Mustang. If you don't know about Ford, it has been said that it stands for "fix or repair daily." Her father asked me to take it to the motor pool on base to have it checked out for her; I may or may not have intimidated the Puerto Rican mechanic who inspected the car. With her father thinking the car was all right, I sold it to them and earned about a six-hundred-dollar commission, and even though I was struggling at the time, I wish I had not sold that car. Being an older car there was no warranty on it, and this was not an era or a dealership where customer service mattered to anyone concerned.

Soon I was fielding calls from Kathy, and her sister, and their father. Even the mechanic on post was calling me—evidently the Colonel was making his life "a living hell" since he checked the car out for them. Naturally this meant I could not go out with her, unless we agreed to meet somewhere, which we did on a couple of occasions after the sale, uncomfortable as it was. I tried explaining that it was just bad luck: After all, I didn't build the car; they had selected it and even inspected it, for heaven's sake. But they would have no part of my explanations. As far as they were concerned, I had sold them a "shit box" on purpose.

By this time my once positive attitude at work had diminished. I could not wait to leave work every day, and I did not know how to cope with all the negativity. Consequently, my sales suffered and because I had "messed" with so many other salesmen when I was doing well, I hadn't exactly endeared myself to anyone. The potential for help or more of the training that I received before was now nonexistent. I was on my own and not experienced enough to see my way out of it. I was fell victim to being "crapped out." That spring when business is normally good because of people receiving their income tax refunds, I was so down-trodden that I quit my first car sales job.

I hated giving up the comradery, the income, and mostly the brand new car I was driving as a demo. The news soon spread around the dealership that I was leaving. Most of the salesmen were surprised or maybe shocked, but there was one who was elated. His name was Mario and he worked in the used-car department. He had been a wrestler in his younger days in Mexico. His professional name was "El Diablo Rojo" (the Red Devil). Of course he was much older now and almost 400 pounds as well. I used to do my Howard Cosell impersonation of him entering the ring, I would say, "In this corner, the heavyweight of the used-car department, Diablo Rojo himself." I used to pretend I was bouncing off the ropes of a ring as I would bounce off of the walls. I asked him stupid questions all day about his fighting weight or how he could wrestle with his tights all up in his butt or if he made the whole arena bounce when he landed on the ring mat from being flipped up in the air. He used to say that I must have majored in "aggravation" with a minor in "pain in the ass." When I told Mario I was leaving, he leaned back in his chair and said, "I am so happy!" I am not sure but I think I saw a tear roll down his cheek.

At any rate, I was gone from my first car selling job; I was down, but not out. It had served as a stepping stone, a sort of introduction to my car selling career. Failure can be a great teacher if one has the courage to admit they failed, the desire to learn from it, and the discipline to not make the same mistakes again.

A book I read helped. It was *My Losing Season*, about a college coach of a traditionally losing basketball program, like the one at the college I attended when I was on the basketball team as well.

I was determined to make it. I had an "I will show them," attitude and I went to the mall and took a job selling jewelry. This, of course, was short-lived because I was making about a third of what I had made selling cars, plus I was bored to death except for the entire selection of fine looking women working at the mall. And no surprise, I could not afford to date any of them because I was not making enough money. I also was not driving a fancy new car like I would have been if I was back at a dealership selling cars. But where could I go? Where could I go to learn more and prosper as well?

When I left the jewelry store after a brief forty day period, they said I was going to be in the Guinness book of records for being the first car salesman to ever pass a polygraph test, which was one of their job requirements.

While I was selling jewelry I had also applied at local, more stable employment opportunities, one of these was the gas company, El Paso Natural Gas Company. When I walked into their waiting room I was greeted by a gorgeous receptionist named Rosa. She informed me they were only taking applications for field engineers. I said that would be fine. She was pleasantly surprised by my response and said, "Oh, you are an engineer, are you?"

I said, "No, but if I read a few books on the subject, I know I can figure it out." She said she admired my confidence and the next thing we were talking about going out on a date, or at least I was talking about it.

Now I have learned a few things over the years, and one of them is never tell a beautiful woman she is beautiful because most of them have confidence issues, so your goal should be never to notice their beauty at all.

I had the day off, and it was late in the day, so I sat there talking to her. I said things like "In the right light, I bet you're kind of cute!" or "If you play your cards right, I just might let you buy me a drink." We were getting along quite well. She even had me look out the window at her brand new Corvette. Well, I didn't have one. I was driving my cousin's old Buick since I didn't have a car. Next thing I knew, we were at a restaurant having drinks and appetizers, and she seemed very attracted to me. We soon went for a drive in her new Corvette—she let me drive.

It was dark by now so I found a nice hillside where we could enjoy the view and make out. I don't know for sure, but I had heard while selling cars, that if you ask enough women if they want to have sex, some are going to say, "Yes." I decided to go for it. I asked her and she said, "Yes!" In fact she insisted we go to a hotel and do it right.

Well I pretended not to hear her and proceeded to try and have her do it in the car. I had her pretty excited and half undressed when she reminded me about going to a hotel. I decided to milk this as long as I could since I had no more money, and my lone credit card was well over the limit. I owed, I believe, $1,800 on a card with a $200 limit.

She was not going to do it in her new car, and I was not going to tell her I couldn't afford a room, so we had a Mexican stand-off.

The night soon ended with me driving back to my cousin's car and calling it a night. She was easily the most attractive woman I had ever been with, and I could have had her for myself for the price of a room.

I had met a beautiful woman and charmed the pants right off of her. This not only validated many of my theories, but my need to get back in the car business, and to be successful at it.

Most men might have been discouraged, but I was pumped. Not only did it validate my commitment to do well in the car business, but my game was so good that I had gotten that far with a beautiful woman.

Not only that, but if I had explained my situation to her she would have probably paid for the room—in fact she told me as much at a later date.

On that subject, I am convinced you cannot go back and recreate a romantic or even a special moment in time. This is why we are to cherish the great and magical times of our life, as they occur.

CHAPTER 3
MY NEXT STOP

I called my friend Ji. to see if he knew anyone I could see about my future in auto sales, and he recommended me to a man named Lou, the general manager at a local Pontiac and Toyota dealership. Lou hired me immediately. It was no surprise. He had an aging sales force to put it mildly. They were mostly retired military or on their second careers and not very hungry. I was starving in contrast. I was back in the business, driving a new car again for fifty bucks a month, or sell ten cars and ride for free. I was given a brand new Pontiac Grand Prix to drive. It was light blue with wire wheel covers, power windows, cruise control and a stereo cassette.

My job was now in the new car department—my only job ever as a new car salesman, and I was lean and green, but ready to learn. I practiced my craft. This was my job. I did everything I was told and listened to training tapes, anything to improve on my sales. I was always on the move, no more waiting for my turn with a customer. This was an open floor which meant I could have as many customers as I could handle.

The inventory was unique. We had gas-guzzling Pontiacs like the Trans Am which was wildly popular thanks to *Smokey and the Bandit* movies. This was, after all, 1980. On the other side of the spectrum, we had Toyotas. This was also the first time fuel prices had dramatically increased which made them very attractive and easy to sell.

I learned a new way to approach the beginning a new sales job at a dealership; I equated it with going into battle in a war. When you think of it, there are similarities: You don't really want to know the other men because one of you may be gone tomorrow, and it's all about self-preservation—every man for himself.

I know many salesmen did not share my point of view regarding this, but they were mostly followers not leaders, and not top sales performers. They were the type who sat in the back row in school and complained about everything, just as I had done—classic underachievers. I knew them well because I had been one most of my life, but not anymore. I could never understand how a man with a family to support could depend on sheer luck to pay his bills, or how he could leave early at two or three o'clock because it was slow. If you are in sales, especially car sales, you know more people are going to come in the evening, but I would hear them on the phone trying to set appointments for the afternoons when they were scheduled to work late. I studied the other salesmen as they provided examples of what not to do.

I was given lists of previous owners whose salesmen were no longer employed there. These were called "orphan owners" and they provided me great leads for my business. I was selling at least one or two cars a week just off my list. I would make contact and see if they had any needs or requests, perhaps a used car for a son or daughter to go back and forth to school.

I rarely engaged in the banter of the salesmen on the show room floor, but when I did, they would all tell me how useless those damn lists were, and how I shouldn't waste my time with them. About that time Lou would come to my defense and say, "He doesn't know any better, he's selling seven to eight cars a month off of those lists alone."

I was very aggressive and this bothered a lot of the old crew, but again, I didn't care. I was not there to make friends but to make money. One day I saw an older couple walking up to the front door of the show room, I didn't notice that Sam, an older salesman had opened the door to greet them. He stupidly opened the glass door toward him leaving the couple wide open for me. I stepped forward to greet them and shook their hands. As it turned out, the gentleman was a judge on his day off, hoping to buy his wife a new car for her birthday. They wanted to see the new Bonnevilles and pretty much knew what they wanted. The whole transaction took a little over an hour, and they paid cash for one which was on the showroom floor. When all was said and done I had made a $550 commission and was quite pleased with myself. About that time one guy Frank said, "Richard, don't you feel bad about stepping in front of Sam to get that sale?"

I said, "I didn't step in front of Sam, and if I did, he probably would not have sold the car anyway." About that time I had to jump out of the way of a huge fist that Sam had thrown at me. His hand shattered against the podium with a thunderous crash. Lou yelled at him as I went running down the show room floor. "I am off to lunch," I yelled back and I was gone.

This was also the time that I discovered the disco or club scene. The place nearest to the dealership was called Contempo's, a hot spot on the weekends and a real meat market. This made it a perfect match for me. I was making good money, driving a brand new Firebird and enjoying myself at night, especially on the weekends. I still worked hard but I played even harder. I had it down to a science. I carried a little cooler in my trunk. Inside I had beer and a bottle of champagne. I even had little plastic glasses for the champagne. I had no shortage of female company—it was almost too easy. As a salesman I was happy to get a "yes" response, and then I could decide what to do with them.

It usually started with a dance, a little conversation. I write poetry and can recite it and I also sing. It was often very easy to transition a lovely lady from the club to the car for a glass of champagne. Please understand I was not devoid of moral character, but I had been in church and in Bible school for a long time; so I was like a kid in a candy store. Or like a condemned man who gets out of the joint and finds himself at an "all you can eat buffet."

I was young and talented in many ways and I was having a blast! Part of me loved the challenge of getting a girl to do what she would not normally do. On at least a half dozen occasions after frolicking around with me in my car, the young lady would tell me, "I'm engaged to be married, you know."

One time after performing orally for me a girl said, "I'm getting married in three weeks, what do you have to say about that?"

I thought about this a moment and then I said, "Tell him from me, he's a lucky guy."

She went on to say, "I've never done anything like this on the first date."

I said, "This wasn't a date. I just met you at the bar, so don't go feeling bad or anything." Somehow, this didn't have the effect I was looking for. She called me an asshole and asked me to take her back to the Club.

The funny thing was stuff like this didn't even bother me. It was like customers at the car lot: some people said yes, some say no, some girls like you, then they hate you—it keeps life interesting.

I even had a run on the waitresses at the Club. At one point I had been with at least half of them. One night one of them named Linda asked me for a favor. She was getting out early and needed me to drive her across town for an errand, and she would make it worth my while. She was in her midthirties, and me in my midtwenties, so I guess she wanted to teach me a lesson.

She did that and much more; I had never had so much sex before or since. I worked out three or four times a week and thought I was in pretty good shape. There is no way to prepare for this kind of an event. I was so exhausted I could hardly walk the next day which was a busy Saturday and I was totally useless. Later when I saw her at the Club again she said, "Just think—that is only one tenth of what I know! If I were you, I would come back for nine more lessons."

I thought about it until I found out she was married to a guy in the army who had been away in Germany for a while. The way I found out was she actually sent him to look for a car with me. He said, "My wife says you are a nice guy and a heckuva salesman." Fortunately, in this case, I could do nothing for him which limited the time that I had to spend with him.

I asked her later what she was thinking, and she just laughed at me. She said, "You think you are the first guy I fucked to ever meet my husband?" I reminded her I was a licensed minister and she laughed even harder.

Aside from my lifestyle, which was tons of fun, I was actually getting really good at selling cars. It was October of 1980 and I was having a magical month. Everyone I talked to and every phone call I received turned into a buyer. I was on fire. My manager, Lou told me if I won salesman of the month, he would have my picture taken and put it in the newspaper, and we could even send a copy up the street to the Buick dealer I used to work for. He told me this on or about the twentieth of the month and it motivated me.

I still have the picture. I sold twenty-two cars and won my first Salesman of the Month plaque. Now I have boxes of them that I don't know what to do with. Needless to say, I carried that newspaper clipping around with me in my wallet for a long time. It was a great conversation piece when I met a new female companion. I had a vast repartee of dialogue from movies or books, even songs. I had so much ammunition that most females didn't know what to think or where I was coming from. I had a favorite line that I used from an Al Pacino movie. As he is bantering with a woman, sort of arguing with her, he says, "If you keep that up, you'll never get me in bed." This soon became a favorite of mine. I can't tell you how many women would apologize and say they did not mean to cross me. Of course to me, this meant they did want to go to bed with me so I immediately knew where I stood. It was so easy.

It was the fall of 1980 and winter was fast approaching. I had experienced the success of my first Salesman of the Month award. One day it was exceptionally cold and the weather reports were talking about an early snow. A young couple approached and I greeted them. The young lady's name was Celia and she was interested in purchasing a brand new Trans Am. She had saved her money and was thinking of putting down eight to ten thousand dollars.

I prided myself at being able to accomplish much, even on a slow day. Anybody could sell when it was busy, but it took real talent to make something happen on a slow day, and this was a very slow day. With her down payment she also provided the additional incentive of a potentially large commission on an exclusive product like a Trans Am. I always treated a couple with respect even if I had to fake it. In this case a jealous boyfriend had the potential to queer a deal by steering the woman in another direction.

He had nothing to worry about because with the threat of snow she was all bundled up with two sweaters, a coat and a hat. She reminded me of Rocky's girlfriend in the movie. It was so cold that the streets were iced and they were afraid to take a test drive, so I did the next best thing. I showed them an in-depth film of the car which had been provided to the sales department for training purposes. When I finally said goodbye I knew that I had a bona fide prospect, complete with her address and phone number.

Within a few days I called her as was my custom. I thanked her for her interest and asked when she would be coming by for a test drive. And then she surprised me. She told me that she and her boyfriend had been arguing and had now broken up, and the reason for it was me. He did not like the idea of her giving me all her contact information, especially when he caught her staring at me the whole time they were at the dealership. I said I was sorry about the breakup but buying a new car would go a long way toward helping her get over the whole thing. She said, "Don't be silly. I was hoping you would call that is why I broke up with him so that we could go out. Would you like to take me out sometime?"

Even though I had found a new sense of adventure and promiscuity, I did have a set of rules regarding dating customers. My rule was taking them out for a drink was okay as long as there was nothing intimate before the sale. In other words, after the sale all bets were off, especially since I had already earned their trust. So I said sure we could go out for a drink this Saturday night, thinking I would play it cool and then reel her in on the sale of the car and make a nice commission.

When Saturday night rolled around Celia surprised me again. Her bundled-up look was gone as were her thick glasses. She was revealing a stunning figure—in the old days it was described as an hour glass figure. I once heard a song that said, "She helped design the Coca Cola bottle." You get my drift. She was suddenly hot as could be, just like Rocky's girlfriend in the movie.

After a quiet night out we made it back to her apartment. When she was about to surprise me again she said, "Please allow me to change and get comfortable." When she returned it was with a see-through nighty, no bra and skimpy little panties, I watched TV and tried to ignore her for about ten or fifteen minutes. Then I broke my own rule. Yup, we got intimate, and boy, did we! I could not believe the transformation from our first meeting to the hunk of woman before me now. I could not believe my good fortune even though I had broken my rule. I had a helluva good time, plus I thought I could still convince her to buy the car later. My rule proved to be justified because I never did sell her a car, but it was probably a fair trade. Little did I know, my world was about to change, forever.

CHAPTER 4
MY ONE AND ONLY

My sales were going so well that I decided to upgrade from Contempo's to a better place to scout for eligible females. I began hanging out at a more upscale club called the "Smuggler's Inn."

One night before heading to Smuggler's, my friend Jr. invited me for a beer at my old hang-out, Contempo's, and that was the first time I saw her.

I remember reading in *The Godfather* how Michael Corleone was hit by a thunderbolt when he first saw his Italian bride to be. On this fateful night, it happened to me. She had a smile that filled the whole room, a long, dark haired beauty, and when she laughed, it touched me to my very soul, and still does to this day.

She was with a girlfriend who was wearing a hat—an unusual one, to put it nicely. And while I was admiring her and trying to find a way to meet her, just like that, she was gone! Of course I had to wait to pay the tab because, when Jr. invited you for a drink, it meant you were buying. He would always joke about how difficult it was to be him, a professional mooch. It was a rare talent indeed. He possessed an incredible talent for remembering all the bars in town who served free food for happy hour as he nursed his beer.

Upon paying the tab I set out to Smuggler's, by myself. When I walked in the music was just kicking in to prime dancing mode as the lights were dimmed. I looked around and I saw the hat, then I saw her. She was a senior at UTEP and worked at the Graduate School at the University. I learned this, of course, after I asked her to dance. She was not the prettiest girl I had ever met, but she was very close, and beyond that, she was vibrant, witty, intelligent and alive.

We became somewhat confrontational immediately. I remember telling her I sold cars and I soon produced my picture from the newspaper when I won Salesman of the Month. She said she could not believe I was carrying around pictures of myself. I guessed that with her attitude and inflated feeling of self-worth, she must have been an only child. She was amazed that I had guessed correctly.

It wasn't long before I gave her my favorite line, "You keep acting like that and you never will get me in bed."

To my surprise she blasted me. She said, "I had no such intention! You must think you are special! Who do you think you are?"

I retreated quickly before I really got insulted. We were having a good time dancing and bantering back and forth, but I had to do something about her friend—every time we sat down and talked, her girlfriend with the hat sat there listening to my pitch. I saw a friend of mine at the bar. He was the driver for UPS at our dealership, so I asked if he would dance with her friend with the hat to keep her occupied.

He did, giving me a clear opening to do my thing. As the music slowed down and we got closer together, she said, "When I get ready to leave, you can walk me to my car and I can give you my number to call me."

I said, "Sure," like I didn't care either way. Her name was Dora Guzman and the rest is history. We have been married for almost thirty three years at this time. I have always been amazed at the laws of probability that lead to the chance meeting and the possibilities of that meeting turning into a successful, long lasting relationship. That weekend we had our first date—she asked me to take her to a Christmas party at the Graduate School where she worked.

The party took place at one of the professor's homes and I didn't realize it at the time, but this was actually a test for me. She had convinced herself that I was an ignorant car salesman who needed to be put in his place by a group of sophisticated, highly educated individuals who would expose me for who I really was. Had I known this, I would either have not attended or felt a lot more nervous about going with her, but as usual, I was just hoping to have a good time. To her surprise her professors all liked me. They thought I was intelligent and engaging and funny. I remember I had them all laughing at my jokes. The highlight was that we played charades, and to her surprise, I knew quite a bit. I had knowledge of the Bible, I was well read, and, of course, I knew all about the movies. Plus I made the stuffy professors feel young calling them by their first names, Harry or Tom, instead of Dr. Jones or Dr. Austin. At the end of the evening, they were all saying, "Richard, don't leave yet. Stay a while longer, won't you?" I could not have been more impressive in her eyes.

A few things were about to become fairly obvious. We were about to fall in love and our courtship would begin in earnest, and I was going to have to make a lot more money. Fortunately, I was young and energetic enough to find a way to sell more cars, but the secret would be to make more commission per car, as well as selling more cars. I had already started to sell used cars more often because the customers were looking for a bargain. They could save thousands over the price of a new car, the financing was almost the same on either one, and it was 1981 and the recession was on. My new love interest Dora was about to graduate from college and I was about to graduate to a full-fledged, card-carrying, used-car salesman.

This would become a sore spot in our relationship for some time to come. As it was, she had a hard time telling people in her social groups and marketing organizations that I was in the car business. Imagine how she was going to feel telling them that not only was I a car salesman, but I was a used-car salesman with all the stigmas that accompany the career. I would catch her telling people like her parents that it was only temporary while I waited for something better to come along.

One thing I never understood was this stigma about being a used-car salesman—further proof that I was born to do it. Really, I loved everything about it. It required a certain skill, tenacity, perseverance and the belief that when you smiled and shook someone's hand, something good was about to happen. Shame is something that is not in my vocabulary. I didn't tolerate it from anybody, whether it was guys from work at happy hour not wanting to tell the women they met at the bar that they sold cars, or whether it was my new girlfriend not wanting to tell her associates that I sold used cars.

That crap did not fly with me. I was damn good at a job that was difficult and specialized, and I felt the only shame in selling cars was not being dedicated enough to be good at it, like so many others I had worked with in my short career. I equated my selling job to being a boxer with the power to change courses at any moment. It was up to me and I loved that element. I thrived on it. I would not be typecast by any pressure from society. I didn't realize it but I had acquired a fan base at the dealership where I worked, and one was about to take me under his wing.

CHAPTER 5
YOU LISTEN TO THIS OLD MAN

His name was Wendell and he was the used-car manager. He was in his midforties, but he looked like he was seventy. He smoked like a chimney, Camel cigarettes with no filters. He was super skinny, half of his stomach had already been eaten away with cancer. He was supremely confident in his world of used-car sales, and he took me under his wing and transferred me to the used-car department.

Some people would call him "corny," but I ate up his advice with a spoon. He told me, "Ochoa, you have a lot of talent but talent isn't enough. You have to be willing to pay the price. You hear of the great ones in any field or sport: how they work harder than anyone else, how they are usually the first to arrive and the last to leave." One of his personal favorites was Vince Lombardi and his winning statements like "Never sell yourself short, others will do that for you," or "Mental toughness is essential to success," and "Fatigue makes cowards of us all." My personal favorite was "Control the ball and you control the game."

This was never truer than in car sales. I will never forget when I first started working in used cars. An old cowboy tossed me his keys and said, "Appraise my car and tell me what its worth is." Three hours later I was in the middle of closing him on a car deal and he said, "Where are my keys?"

Of course old Wendell would just laugh his ass off, and he didn't just laugh. The only way to describe his laugh was like the old ZZ Top song called "La Grange"—a kind of perpetual clearing of one's throat, with a high pitch to boot. Working with Wendell was truly like being in the Old West—you could do anything to make a deal, or not. Sometimes he would send me in to a sale in progress—send me in on a difficult customer that another salesman was working with. Wendel would say to me, "Go make the deal or blow their asses out of here!" I could hear him laughing in his office down the hall. He loved the way I could insult the customer—after all, this was my world and I was ready for them.

The scary thing was often after I had insulted them to make them see the light, they often came around and bought the car. I was beginning to get a reputation around town. I would be at happy hour with my buddies from work and meet a salesman from another store, and he would immediately know who I was because I had taken customers from him. This did not endear me to any of them, but I didn't care.

I was falling deeply in love with my future wife and I negotiated with Wendell for time off. Her job after graduation took her out of town every other week and I wanted to accompany her often for a long weekend. I suggested to my boss that if I sold five cars by the end of the week (Friday), he should give me the weekend off. Keep in mind that a standard good month for most salesmen was ten cars for the month.

It was often a close call. Once on a Friday I needed one car to go and I didn't get a customer until it was almost noon. He was a young guy who actually was qualified to buy a car. Of course, he wanted a Monte Carlo, so I was selling him a Grand Prix. It was a re-painted piece of shit that the dealership had purchased real cheap, so if he went for the deal, I stood to make a nice six-hundred dollar commission. It was just him and his brother, commercial painters with the day off.

Before he would sign the papers he said, "I want my dad to see it."

Here we go, I thought. "Where is your dad?" I asked.

"Oh, he's here in the car," the young man said and his brother went to the car to wake him up.

I expected the worse possible outcome from this. The old man walked around the car, gunned the engine a few times, and ignored the huge puff of smoke that exuded from the tail pipe. Then, completing his examination, he said proudly, "It's like a new one."

Within the hour I was at the airport waiting for a twenty-dollar flight to join Dora in Albuquerque, New Mexico, for the weekend.

Somewhere about this time the store was purchased by a quality dealer. Mr. Dick Poe became the new owner and I enjoyed a long and prosperous tenure with his company, both at this store and his flagship dealership, the

Chrysler store. This would mean the world for Dora and me: a better bonus plan, better demo plan, better advertising, and of course, more sales income.

The year was 1981 and I was making a lot of money. To put things in perspective, a decent job for a college graduate was 15K to 18K a year. That's what my fiancée Dora was making as a recent college graduate in her first job. My first year selling cars I made about 30K; my second year, I made 42K. Once I heard the great football player Howie Long in an interview and he said in his rookie season of 1983, he made 38K. That's what I made in 1983. Of course, I would not want to compare checks with him at any time after that, but still it was really good dough, and in the middle of a recession too.

The thing about being in the Used-car department is that it is such a confined space that there can be no secrets. You know whose needy wife calls ten times a day and which guys the bill collectors are calling. Not me in either case.

We had a motley crew indeed. Charlie was a proto-typical used-car salesman. He wore an ugly toupee with different colors in it. I think the sun had discolored it. He wore tight pants and seldom wore underwear. He would sit there cursing into the phone with the vilest insults you can imagine, and then say, "Okay, bye, Mom." Unbelievable stories he told too, which confirms what I always believed, car salesmen don't care if the story is true or not, as long as it is a good story. He was full of bullshit, but was very talented in his own right.

For these reasons, I messed with him constantly. When he came in from waiting on some young female customers, I would say, "Do you think they knew you have a toupee? Probably not cause it looks so real and natural."

I often threw little jabs at him when he was with a customer only to see him erupt like a volcano, cursing and swearing. Then he went complaining to Wendell who would just laugh in his face. When we heard Wendell laugh, we would all laugh. This often drove him to drink, literally. He would leave, abandoning his customer, and go knock down a few drinks. Upon his return Wendell would scold him for being so stupid as to let me get under his skin like that, but he fell for it almost every day. Charlie really was quite a character and I actually felt bad and let up on him sometimes. Plus he was scary—not him but the people he associated with, a real murderers' row. Never before had I seen someone agonize over the "Wanted" section of the newspaper: whether or not to turn someone in for the reward money. I know this sounds crazy, but I am sure he started turning people in when they started Crime Stoppers and you can remain anonymous, because the thing he feared most was retaliation from the criminal element, which he knew all too well.

I brought my uncle George and his son my cousin Chris, to work at the dealership because of the better pay plan, plus the dealer where they worked was going broke. Chris and I used to march by Charlie's office with our hands behind our backs as if handcuffed while he talked to police detectives saying, "No, it wasn't me."

Charlie could tell a heckuva story, mostly about his baseball playing days, so I would say he had a huge advantage. He said, "What advantage?" So I pretended to take the toupee from my head and wipe home plate with it, and then proceed to a batter's stance and pretend to start swinging.

Everyone burst out laughing. Of course this infuriated Charlie. He actually used to ask Chris if he would intervene if he decided to come after me to kick my ass. Chris would calmly say, "Only if he's losing."

Sometimes Charlie got on a roll selling four or five cars in a couple of days, despite me getting most of the customers on the lot and nearly all the sales calls. Then I would take it upon myself to slow him down. We had a blackboard with our names and any messages we had, plus the number of cars we had sold. So one day I drew a picture of a man with a horse's mane on top of his head, swatting at a fly. Underneath I wrote, "Charlie's automatic fly swatter."

When he saw it, he immediately started cursing and swearing. I said, "Charlie, we have customers."

He said, "I know! They're with me, you asshole!"

"What made you think it was me?" I replied.

The poor customers were looking on in shock. They soon left and a short time later, Charlie did as well. It was a whole week before he sold another car.

General Motors had a very popular look at the time. It was called a two-tone paint look. This was very popular and a sporty look on many of the popular cars like the Buick Regal and our own Pontiac Grand Prix. As the weather got warmer I began to realize Charlie's toupee was also taking on different colors of its own, due in part to the hot sun, so guess what? I waited for him to get on another roll before I struck again. His business had picked up, so I went to work on a plan.

I visited with my buddy Arnold the parts manager and I got the name of one of the head honchos at General Motors. I told him my name was Charlie.

Soon one day I posted a message on the black board, telling Charlie to call this man at General Motors. It seemed someone named Charlie from our dealership had been calling him about making a similar paint that could be used on a fake head of hair, for a two-toned toupee look. Needless to say the man at General Motors was not amused since this was about the third phone call he had received from someone at our dealership named Charlie talking about this stupid hair coloring concept.

I actually was called on the carpet for that one. The man from General Motors called Lewis, our general manager, to complain. Lewis called me to his office to explain even though I never admitted to the deed, but everyone knew it was me. When I met with boss Lewis, he was upset that I had involved someone from General Motors, but when I told him about the whole elaborate scheme, he laughed so hard he almost pissed on himself.

Directly across the street from our dealer's used car lot was a very successful Chevrolet dealer, Courtesy Chevrolet, where my uncle Jimmy Ochoa worked as a salesman. He had been there for many years, and I had actually applied to work there before going to work at the Pontiac and Toyota dealer. The used car manager was a man named Sammy and he told my uncle he would not hire me because he thought I was too "young and cocky." My uncle Jimmy was very popular, in high school he had led his high school to a state championship in baseball, then later he won the world series of baseball in Mexico.

After that he was celebrated in parades in the streets of nearby Juarez Mexico, and when he went to a bar he seldom had to buy a drink. But even his influence could not persuade his manager to hire me, so he did the next best thing, he sent me a ton of referral customers. Since he was right across the street, I would watch him and when I saw that his patience was wearing thin with his customers, he would begin waving his arms and pointing my direction, soon the customers would appear on our lot with my name on the back of one of his cards. When I would make the sale, I would turn in a check request for a referral fee for 50.00 a "bird dog" reward fee. We usually took this to a local watering hole called "Tom's Gas House" for a few beers. He would often tease me that I was falling in love with Dora, because I would play songs by Julio Iglesias on the jukebox.

One day a young man drove his old pick-up truck onto the Chevy used car lot, and began looking at used Camaros. I watched as one of the younger salesmen waited on the customer, I could see he was having no luck, since he could not even get him to test drive one. Soon the young man came over to our lot and I went out to greet him. They must have had at least seven or eight used Camaros on that lot, and I had one black used Pontiac Firebird, and I began to show it to him. Soon we were test driving the car. It wasn't long before we were making a deal, without driving the young man's trade-in, Wendell agreed to give him 1500 dollars for it.

Soon after he took delivery of the Firebird I took the keys for his truck and went across the street to get the truck that was my customer's trade in. Uncle Jimmy went out to meet me and asked if I made the deal, I said "Of course I did!"

He began to tease his own manager Sammy, saying "See how smart you are! You wouldn't even hire him, and he just took a sale from right in front of you!"

The manager told Uncle Jimmy, "Tell him I will hire him now!"

My uncle Jimmy replied, "Too late now, he is doing so well over there, why would he come here now?"

Some years later my uncle died from a heart attack, and I was asked to speak at his funeral. I remember the church was so packed they left the doors open and there were even people standing outside, he was a great man.

This was the most successful era this used-car department had ever experienced at this dealership and Wendell the used-car manager was reveling in it. He was so full of himself that he thought he was above the law—by that I mean he believed he could do whatever he wanted to. If he spent too much on a car, he would simply transfer charges to another car that he took in on the cheap side. It sounds reasonable, unless you are the one selling the car with the fake charges on it and you work on commission for the profit of that sale. The good news for me was that I was his favorite and he didn't try to screw me too bad.

We always knew when it was Wendell's afternoon off cause we wouldn't see him for a while then he would call from his house after he was already drunk from his "tea glass full of bourbon." One night, on Wendell's afternoon off, I sold a super clean two-year-old Chevy Monte Carlo to an Army Sergeant. This car was so clean it barely needed a wash. I had worked the deal with the general manager Lewis. It was a nice profit that would pay me about nine hundred dollars if Wendell didn't mess with it. I took it upon myself to make Lewis a copy of the inventory card and I made myself a copy just in case, you know.

The customer was set to pick up the car the following day, so that morning Wendell called me to his office and said, "Too bad you didn't make any money on that car."

I said, "Bull shit! I know I did and if you try anything, I will go over your head. Lewis has a copy of the cost card, and so do I."

He was fuming by now—nobody challenged him at his own game. He said, "I will show you, mother fucker!" I didn't know what he was going to do but I was ready for him, that's all I knew.

I soon found out how Wendell was going to fix things. When Paul, the finance manager, came to inform me that my deal was approved, he said, "We may have a little problem." Wendell had raised the price by four hundred dollars—his way of setting me straight, you know.

I didn't care. I could just revert to my usual favorite pose, to look dumb and act stupid. After all the customer loved the car, and I hadn't changed it. Wendell did.

My father had a favorite joke: Why do Mexican's have big shoulders and flat foreheads?

Because when they are asked a question in school, they shrug their shoulders like they don't know. Then when they are told the answer, they immediately smack their forehead!

When the customer arrived, I took him to see Paul in finance. Everything seemed to be going very smooth. The customer signed the papers and the contract, and the only thing left to sign was the new purchase order with the price change on it. Paul had a habit of stuttering and stammering when he was nervous, so when he paged me on the P/A system, he was already stuttering.

When I arrived at the finance office, the customer, a rather large African American, was very irate. He said, "You raised the price on me." I explained to him it wasn't me but that cranky old used-car manager. Then he asked why I came up with some "half ass" reasons and I wasn't getting anywhere with him.

Running out of things to say I finally said, "Oh, quit being a baby!"

He said, "Baby! My ass! That's four hundred dollars you are talking about, man!"

I finally explained that Wendell never got to service the car and this was the normal cost of it. "But the car didn't need anything," he said.

I said, "Yes, but if it does, you have a year to bring it in at our expense." He wanted it in writing so I wrote it on the back of my business card. What the fuck did I care?

By now stuttering Paul had run to the front office to look for Lewis, the general manager. He thought for sure we were involved in a fist fight after I called the customer a baby.

The customer was happy and we were laughing and joking as he took delivery of his automobile, nevertheless Lewis was made aware of Wendell's antics. Everybody knew about Wendell, but now I was gaining a reputation as a salesman who could handle any situation.

One of the funniest things I did was to hang up on my own fiancé. Understand, I was very much in love with Dora, but I would do anything to gain an advantage over the other salesmen. So while they were saying their long goodbyes to their wives, or girlfriends, I would drop the phone and be out the door to greet a customer in no time at all. Whenever Dora brought this up to me, I said, "You like going out to nice places? Then that's the way it is going to have to be." And I might not talk to her again for another three hours or so, if I made the deal. Nobody dared to say anything to me about it because they did not want to be on the receiving end of my joking or teasing which had no end.

Wendell was so passionate about molding me into the best salesman I could be that we often got into heated arguments, often on the showroom floor, and then he would fire me. No kidding. At least once a week he would tell me to pack my shit because he was finished with me. I took a three hour lunch then I went back and immediately had a customer and soon we would be talking about making a deal.

Sometimes Wendell would say, "What are you doing here?"

I would say, "You really should stop firing me. It's getting old, and starting to piss me off."

One time we really got into a big argument next to the new car showroom and the GM Lewis heard us yelling at each other. He called me over and said if I couldn't get along with Wendell, I couldn't work there anymore. I was already upset about the argument and I said, "Fuck him!"

This time Wendell really got scared. He thought he was really going to have to fire me. He went and had a long meeting with Lewis and convinced him that we could work together. By the way, he also quit firing me. Years later when I was used-car manager at Dick Poe's Chrysler store and I had an occasion to go back to Wendell's office, the salesmen would ask if it was true that Wendell had fired me once a week. Wendell would chime in, "That's a man! I'd fire him and he wouldn't leave!" Our battles became legendary. I only regret that I didn't see him before he passed away. I still think of him with great fondness.

CHAPTER 6
MYWEDDINGANDANEWCAREER

The wedding was a humbling experience, to say the least, mostly because I was so in love and I felt like I was walking six inches above the ground. I was the big fish in a small pond and it was not enough.

The wedding itself went great. Our friends and family were all there and I was humbled by the well-wishes I received from all the men I had spent my days trashing. My constant goal was to be the best and to do so, I had to torture them into submission to get all the customers I wanted. They would foolishly try to corner me and ask if I really needed that many customers. They would say, "How many do you need?" and I would respond, "All of them!"

This created constant animosity between me and the other salesmen. My cousin Chris used to call me aside and say, "Do you realize none of the other guys are even talking to you because you are so aggressive?"

Well, I didn't notice and I didn't care. I was not there to make friends, but to make money. I had always considered myself capable of greatness. Some call it ego, but I call it motivation. After all, I was now a married man and I believed my wife and our lives deserved all the best.

My wife was constantly encouraging me to pursue a new career because she felt I was above all that. I think the truth was she didn't like the stigma of me being a car salesman and all that it implied. So I was constantly looking for new opportunities.

Following our wedding and honeymoon, we rented a new home, but somewhere in the back of my mind, I knew I would have to take a chance on a new career. If for nothing else, to at least prove to myself that I could do it.

The wedding took place in June 1982, and I had been successful the rest of the year. I was the top car salesman for my dealership but it had an empty feeling to it because I was still the biggest fish in a little pond.

As the year came to an end I began speaking with a company called Uni-lab. They were an extremely aggressive agency conducting multiple interviews in town. This was to be a career in outside sales that was said to be the best of the best. I was chosen out of sixty applicants to represent El Paso. They were starting a fledgling company of their own called Eagle Laboratories, basically a company that sold chemicals to businesses, restaurants, etc. At this point my yearly income as a car salesman was an estimated $39,000 a year, and they boasted to me that their top employees were averaging an income of $100,000 a year. So I accepted the position which included a $400 a week draw against commission and began my training program.

They had chosen me because they admired my drive and my competitive nature, yet these guys were amongst the most competitive I had ever seen. They sent me to Tucson, Arizona for a one week training that included video tapes of demonstrations, lessons on body language and patterns of speech, and role playing. It was an intense program, to say the least. After classes we played basketball or tennis and competed again. These men were fueled by competition. I loved the intensity and the training I received was one of a kind. It was the best decision I could have made. Not so much for the company but for the intense training I received which would help me later on in life.

They taught me how to identify a valid customer and how to ask closing questions and how to lead to the closing of a sale. This was immensely invalu-able because most salespeople try to sell everybody and waste their time on an unqualified buyer, someone incapable of making a decision. They taught me to make the best use of my time, and the most important thing you have as a sales person is your time. They used video cameras to grade our body lan-guage as we gave a presentation. Most car salesman have no idea about body language. The worst I ever saw were salesmen putting both hands behind their back in a fake disguise of humility. I always said that all they lacked was a blind-fold and they would be ready for the firing squad.

I took this training very seriously as I had left the positon as car salesman that was a job I loved. And I always knew I could take this training I was re-ceiving and use it to go back to the car business if things didn't pan out. But I was committed to do my best with the business and make it work. I was ready to take the town by storm selling chemicals for Eagle laboratories.

I was soon to begin my on-the-job training in El Paso with a manager named Allen. I had gone from driving a brand new Pontiac Firebird to my mother-in-law's 1969 Chevy Malibu. When Allen arrived in town to work with me, we made a startling discovery: our products were four to five times more expensive than our leading competitor. This, in itself, was not so bad if you could justify it by having a superior product. But we were in a border town in the middle of a recession, and even Allen found it difficult to sell.

I will never forget how he handled his business. This was a "cold calling" businesses which means that you are approach people unexpectedly. Allan had a way of disarming the people which was what we were supposed to do. It was called a "warm-up." You did this by telling them a joke or something funny or a story. It prevents them from tossing you out. His basic approach was telling them sexual stories of either the sex he was going to have, or had just had the night before. Of course, this was with the male managers. I never saw him try this approach with a female manager. He would soon disarm them and have them laughing or joking while he made his product presentation.

But even as good as he was, he had a hard time overcoming the dramatic price increase and shipping cost. His approach was to start high with a high priced order and then work his way down, and when they didn't agree, he would shame them into it and say, "Sign it, you little shit."

This was great training for me and a great example, but I inevitably knew it was going to be a rough road ahead of me. After he left and I was on my own, my sales were few and far between.

I was working hard, beginning my day at 5:30–6:00 a.m. and not ending till around 6:00 p.m. I was losing weight to the point that my clothes were literally hanging off of me. But I was still determined to make it work. I felt that if anybody could do it, I could do it.

I had to constantly report to the office my daily sales and actions. It had reached the point that my manager was giving me short term goals to strive for. My wife and I were in the process of purchasing our first home and I had borrowed the down payment and closing costs which totaled roughly $5,000. My days were filled with constant anxiety and stress as I tried my hardest to make this job work. I had been hand-selected by this company, received invaluable training, and I was putting forth the maximum effort I could, yet I was reaching a breaking point.

The breaking point came sooner than I expected, I went into one of our favorite restaurants located off of I-10. I had made sure to go around 3:00

p.m. when I knew the lunch rush was no longer there. I proceeded to approach the manager in his office. He was a large, middle-aged white man sitting behind his desk with his feet propped up, reading the paper. I approached him in a friendly way and tried warming him up by giving him free gifts of pens and calendars from my company. He looked at me from behind his paper in a condescending way and said, "I'm really busy right now and you are really bothering me."

I attempted to warm him up again by saying, "Come on, you're just reading the paper!" but again he told me that I was disturbing him on his free time. Please understand that the anxiety and stress that I was feeling every day was building up in me and at that point, I reached my max.

I responded in the only way I knew how which was to tell him, "If you think that bothers you, wait till I take you outside and kick your ass all over the parking lot!" Now I was the aggressor as I stood over him I said, "You think you can talk down to me? You think you can belittle me? I'm about to teach you a lesson on how to treat people!"

He was at least a foot taller than me but he wouldn't stand up. His face turned red and he begged me not to hit him. I had no doubt that with the rage and frustration I had building inside of me, I would have wasted him. But at this point, I felt embarrassed and humbled by this poor man begging me not to hurt him.

I soon made my exit and called the office to report what had happened because I knew he would be calling to complain. The managers took turns talking to me on the phone, laughing their asses off. They told me in no uncertain terms to take the paper work in, and tell him to sign it or I was going to kick his ass.

That was my last day at Eagle Laboratory. I was convinced that if those people could do the job better than me, then it was not meant for me. I had been with the company a total of nine weeks and that was more than enough for me—I was ready to go back to the car business.

My training with Eagle had been invaluable. I was so relieved to be going back to the business that I loved, armed with an arsenal of training that nobody else in the industry had. If I had dominated in the car business before, wait until they see me now, post "boot camp training." The only question was where to go, what dealership I should go to and make my mark.

So I asked some of my friends who had been in the business longer than me, where was the best place to go? To a man, they all said Dick Poe Chrysler, but there were so many horror stories about the place. It did however offer the best bonus pay plan and demo plan in the city. Most of the stories I had heard, I found out later were from loser salesmen who couldn't have made it there anyway; but I was determined to find out for myself.

CHAPTER 7
THE FLAGSHIP DEALERSHIP

At the time I went to work there, Dick Poe Chrysler had been in business for over sixty years. It was family owned and extremely profitable. This was in the spring of 1983 with a recession going on and Chrysler Motor Company stood the chance of going under at any moment. These were some of the fears of going to work there that had been instilled in me by others. They said there were oftentimes when days would pass before a customer would come in. One of the sayings was you could only see one or two customers a day and then it would just drop off into nothing.

What I learned was that nothing could be further from the truth; Dick Poe had an extremely aggressive and efficient management team, great advertising and a brand name in the city that encouraged customer loyalty. They also had acquired the Honda franchise that was now a part of the dealership. For me personally the stars were aligned. I had my training, my hope and dreams, my wife and family to support me, youth and enthusiasm and a will to succeed.

I soon learned that success would be no easy task; the sales floor was a veritable "who's who" of the best auto salesmen in the city. The top guy was Jerry. He was an older distinguished looking gentlemen type, with white hair and blue eyes. To me, he slightly resembled Paul Newman. He wore fine suits and sports coats and made no secret of riding his convertible Mercedes around the dealership as he smoked his weed. To this day he is the best salesman I have ever seen one-on-one with a customer, especially with the older people. His dialogue was almost hypnotic and he could convince a person of almost anything, even paying over price for a car. He would later be spoken about in a book titled, "Dirty Dealing" about the drug industry in El Paso. The book described him as an ex-con, a snitch and local con artist, and I used to infuriate him by asking him to sign his book for me in front of everyone.

Jerry had been salesman of the month for seven months straight before I began to work there, and in my first full month, I beat him. To show it wasn't a fluke, I beat him the next three months following that as well. He was not the only one. There were many great salesmen there but I felt that he would be my competition since he was the best.

Being salesman of the month didn't pay much. It was an additional couple of hundred dollars and a plaque, but it was more about the pride that came with being the best in the organization. How do you do this? you might ask. You don't just wake up and say, "I'm going to beat Jerry!" It takes self-examination, dedication and the ability to persevere through hard times. When you're the best, you receive all the accolades and praise from everyone in the dealership, but when you're the lowest, you get to "post the board."

We had meetings three times a week on Monday, Wednesday and Friday, and the finance managers handed out bonuses that were known as *spiffs*. These, of course, were paid to those who actually sold cars. Then the lowest two men on the board would have to get up and post the number of cars sold for the sales team, recording the salesmen's names, number of vehicles sold and profit generated by each one. And guess what? If they didn't sell any cars, they were perpetual board posters. This was a tedious and embarrassing prospect and some guys even quit so they wouldn't have to do it anymore. I did it once in all my years there and that was when I first started and I never wanted to do it again. One poor guy was an alcoholic and had the "shakes" so bad we thought he was going to lose his wallet from his back pocket. He quit after one day of "posting the board."

Some of the characters were hilarious. There was Al, a Puerto Rican guy. He had a crazy Cuban girlfriend who had actually taken a shot at him with his gun, and he was still with her. There was Carl, a redneck from Tennessee who was great with the military customers, especially if they were from the South. He wore the ugliest leisure suits you ever saw. There was Big Bill, a tall black Honda salesman who was a former basketball player. There was Steve, a good-looking Hispanic man who would pride himself on looking like "Ponch" from the show *Chips*. He was a real lady's man and *Casanova*. The funny thing was that whenever the money was passed out, everyone knew the guy's habits or dealings so they would shout out what he was going to spend the money on. For example, Al, the guy with the trigger happy girlfriend would receive thirty-eight dollars and everybody would shout out, "Bullets for Maria!" Carl, the guy with the funky leisure suits would get forty dollars and they would shout, "A new suit." For Big Bill they would shout out "the track." Then, of course, for Jerry who would usually get one hundred dollars or more, they would usually say a "dime bag or some blow."

Drugs were rampant back then. There was no drug testing and this was the Wild West. Later on the description they would use for me was Sioux Street. It was a restaurant-bar that sat behind the dealership and became my local hangout to keep me closer to work. The most feared man in the dealership was Mike B; he was the general sales manager, motivator and enforcer of company policies. Everybody knew that at a moment's notice, he would fire you without discretion including Jerry and me. There was always a saying that if you sold enough cars, you could go take a shit on the showroom floor and the manager would clean it up. This was a real paradox, because it meant if you were a real good salesman, you could mess up and say you were sorry, and even Mike would have to forgive you.

One of the things I did to gain an advantage was to go on Sundays. I didn't go necessarily to work but I would take a stack of business cards with me and my little dog, so that I was unassuming. Then when I would see customers out there, I would converse with them and let them know I worked there and give them my card. I'd also put cards all over the dealership especially on Hondas because they were like gold. So of course, my Mondays were usually very busy. I'd have people lined up or my phone ringing off the hook. It was not uncommon for me to sell four to five cars on a Monday. This created quite a controversy at the store and made the other salesman nervous that the dealership would start to be open on Sundays. In actuality they thought it gave me an unfair advantage by being there on Sundays. When they complained to Mike, he quickly mentioned in the meeting that if anyone has a problem with it, they should go out there and join me on a Sunday.

Once while selling a new Honda on a Monday after meeting the customer on Sunday, John the Honda manager mentioned to me that several of his salesmen were upset with me for putting my business cards on their new Hondas. I'll never forget the look on his face when I asked him if he had a problem with it. His response was "No!" So then I suggested that all those salesmen who were complaining about it should come over to the used-car building, line up, and kiss my ass. Of course, this was an open showroom so they could all hear me, and that was the reason behind the look on his face. The salesmen including Big Bill were all shocked that I had challenged them. I meant what I said and John told me later, "I know you're a pretty tough guy but it would be different if two or three of them went after you." I told him my answer was the same and that not only was I selling that car to the customer, but also the same customer would also be back next week to purchase another car! The customer did come back and purchased another new Honda for his daughter.

It's amazing how several people can be in the same place and see things completely different. On the rare moments that my wife would call me to see how I was doing, I would say I was busy. I was always busy, thank God. I had her trained so she would only call me once a day. I heard the other guys on the phone four or five times a day complaining to their wives about how it was so slow and they were getting ready to go home because it was so slow.

I learned that action creates action. I was always test driving cars or looking at our new inventory when people would stop me and tell me what they were looking for. I often drove a fresh trade when I went out to get a cup of coffee and people would see me and ask if I was buying the car because they knew it was a dealership car. I'd say, "No, I'm selling it, follow me back."

We even had a program going with the military. They would leave a deposit on a car but then they got shipped out. When they came back, they'd want their money back. If you were smart, you wrote it on the back of your business card. For example: $300 and that was the only receipt they had, so you'd tell them those were "stroker's fees." If they complained a lot, I might give them one hundred dollars back, but I would make sure and get the business card back from them.

I know for a fact that Jerry, being a human vacuum cleaner for money, would call his customers (mostly retired elderly people) to come in for a "radio upgrade." He would then charge them two or three hundred dollars and pay one of the mechanics to swap radios from another car for a radio similar to one they had. Two or three of those "upgrades" on a slow day and he was ready to go to the track.

On the subject of slow days, I believe it's all about perception. I once heard a story of two shoe salesmen who were sent to an island in Tahiti by the same company to sell their product. When calling the home office one of them reported, "I don't know how this is going to work. These people don't wear any damn shoes." But the other salesman reported, "We are going to need to order a hell of a lot more shoes! Do you realize these people don't have any shoes?"

Jerry was actually missing half of his index finger. The story was that he had gotten in a fight with another salesman at another dealership and the guy bit it off. He would use this finger as a pointer for effect with customers or in arguments. One day we had a big sale and I had an elderly couple waiting to go into the finance office. Jerry approached them on the showroom floor and began talking with them. They told him they were with someone but he didn't believe them so when I came to get them to take them to the finance office, he got upset. He turned red and started pointing his finger at me. I told him if he pointed that little thing at me again, I would shove it up his ass and, of course, it wouldn't have that far to go. Mike B was at the sales desk and heard the whole thing. He called Jerry over and explained to him that those people were already with me, but this only added fuel to the fire because the animosity of our competitive natures ran deep.

Jerry had a sidekick in new cars named Keith who was a country boy from Dallas that I nick named "Country Dog." He was a pretty decent salesman. I also had a buddy in used cars who was one of the few friends I had named Ronny. Ronny was an ex-con who spent six years in a penitentiary for selling cocaine. Still he was dedicated to the straight life now and I admired him for it. He was also a tough, no nonsense guy you definitely wanted on your side in a battle.

One afternoon Ronny and I went to Sioux Street for a late lunch and a few beers and Keith and Jerry were off at a table in the corner drinking. For some reason Keith came over and started messing with Ronny, calling him names and basically calling him out. I figured Jerry had put him up to it. Ronny was not the kind to be messed with or taken lightly, but he wanted to be peaceful and he told Keith to back off. But Keith had the liquor talking for him now and insisted they go outside and take care of business. So we all went outside and Ronny kept saying, "Don't do this, don't do this." Keith insisted and was dancing around trying to box with Ron. As soon as he got close enough to barely touch Ronny's face with a slight jab, Ron ducked his head and gave Keith a swift one-two-punch that practically knocked him out of his shoes. Keith staggered around like a boxer going down for the count and I started laughing my ass off.

Jerry's face turned red and he acted like he wanted to jump in but I was there to make sure it was a clean fight and I told Jerry, "You don't want any of this." Of course word soon spread around the dealership about the supposed fight and Keith was nick named "Glass Jaw" after an easy fighter from a video game.

The best salesmen in the dealership, of which I was included, were steadily making $60,000 to $75,000 and achieved *rock star status* in the company. This even included parties and so-called orgies set up by some of the women in the office. I often heard stories of Jerry and the other salesmen partaking of them but I never did. Some of the women would even come to me and flirt with me and ask why I would not come to their parties. Not that I was saintly, but I was newly married and I loved my wife, and the last thing I wanted to do was give these people an advantage over me.

But I did drink and Dora and I would go out to clubs and dance and have cocktails. Drinking became the biggest bad habit that I developed along with occasional gambling on a football game or two. Getting money was so easy. We had our regular meetings when we would receive our finance money, or you could sell your demo and get instant cash. Aside from that, you could sell an aged used car and often get an instant cash bonus for it. And if that wasn't enough, if I ever had a lapse of three to four days without selling a car, my general manager George or Mike the general sales manager, would call me in and offer me an advance because they knew I was good for it. This was unheard of because most salesmen were begging for advances and instead, the managers were begging me to take one.

During this time we went on many vacations but we saved most of the money from my wife's income while we spent most of mine. There was one January when Mike announced they would be giving away free vacations with the purchase of every car that spring. These trips were meant for customers and they included vacations to Reno, Anaheim, and New Orleans. The way it worked was you paid your way there and then the vacation package included the hotel, free dinners and discounts to places of interest. I immediately went up to Mike and told him that with all the money I had been making for the company, I would like one of each of the trips. I remember he looked me in the eye and said, "Okay, all you have to do is be Salesman of the Month for January, February, and March, and you will get them." But the key was all or nothing. I couldn't just win one or two months and get two vacations. I had to win all three months to get all three vacations. He had quickly reversed my intention of receiving a perk and had instead issued a challenge to me.

So I went all out and won all the next three months and all three vacations. We had a year in which to enjoy them. I took my wife to California to meet her grandmother who she had never met. I was also able to show her many of the beaches and hot spots that I knew of since I went to school there. Of course most of the places I was familiar with were from when I was a broke student. We also went to Reno, Nevada which included a side trip to the beautiful and scenic Lake Tahoe. On our trip to New Orleans, I remember eating hot dogs on a street corner of Bourbon Street and watching a jazz parade on Thanksgiving Day. Later we went to look at houses for sale and tried to imagine ourselves living there.

One of the characters in used cars had an incredible knot on his head. His name was Charlie and I nicknamed him "Charlie Longhorn." He was a former truck driver and a decent salesman. But that horn stuck out on the top of his forehead where his hair line was located. He wore a beard and often wore a shitty cowboy hat that I would say was to cover his horn. I often said he looked like "Pan" the mythical Greek character who was half goat and half man because of the horn on his head and his beard. I tormented this poor guy all day long. I had so many things to tell him about his horn. I talked football and how all the teams he liked had horns on them like the Longhorns and the Buffalo Bills. I asked him if I could borrow it to part the wind with it so I could be more aerodynamic. I called him *Cuerno* in Spanish, which means "the horn." All the other salesmen made fun of him as well, taking my lead. I used to ask him what would happen if you pushed it in real hard. Would it come out of the other side? Or tell him like in the movie, "Young Frankenstein," I know a surgeon who could help you with that hump. I even made up a story one day about his wife coming home and hanging a coat on his horn and then couldn't find him afterward.

The one thing he did for me was provide me with a thing known as "Black Beauties" which was a drug known as *speed*. A habit he had acquired when he was truck driving. Well, one thing I didn't need was more acceleration but it helped me sell more cars anyway. The drawback was when I drank and took the pills, I didn't feel the effects of the alcohol. This would soon be my downfall.

One day when I had a pocket full of cash, my friend Steve and I went drinking. We wound up at Smugglers which was the same place I had met my wife. The afternoon turned into evening and somewhere along the way I had lost Steve and I was by myself. We had been partying and buying drinks for some of the people we knew there, and then suddenly Steve was gone. The evening crowd was picking up and was becoming more of a dinner and dancing type of crowd. In order to go to the restroom you had to pass through the entrance. One of the bouncers stopped me and told me I was inebriated and would have to leave. I told him that I had my keys and some money lying on the table and asked if I would be allowed to retrieve them. He said he would go with me to the table where I had a full drink and I could stop to take a few more sips of it. He was being pretty nice about it and telling me that I could certainly come back at another time and be welcomed.

I accompanied him to the front entrance and was preparing to leave when I was stopped by another bouncer who was loud and arrogant. He confronted me and told me I had to leave when I was already on my way out. The nice guy was on my right and I had the belligerent guy in front of me. Somewhere along the line, one of them sucker-punched me, breaking my glasses and really pissing me off. I ducked my head and bull rushed the loud mouth in front of me, knocking him backward and bouncing his head off the floor. I soon had him by the hair, banging his head up and down on the floor. At this time I remember being hit from all sides. Probably two or three of them were taking their turns whacking me. I was soon slumped in the corner upright against the wall when Mr. Big Mouth came over to my left side, grabbed my collar and asked, "Have you had enough?"

I thought about it for a moment then I reached up with my left hand and grabbed his nuts and crushed them with all my might. I'll never forget the sound of him yelling bloody Jesus, but I wouldn't let go. This resulted in a lot more punching and kicking from all of them, and I soon found myself out the door, sitting on the porch. The nicer one told me I better get going because the cops were on the way, Well, I had no idea where my car was or how I could even drive in this condition so I ran down the side of the Interstate. I found myself outside of Denny's when a police car approached and the cop got out. To my surprise it was a guy named Blas that I knew. We had worked together many years before at a grocery store.

My friend, the officer named Blas, got me in the car and drove me to the other side of the Interstate. He said he was going to tell a story that I had been jumped by some guys who had just left me there. He was recommending that I be taken to the hospital instead of jail. He called an ambulance and they ended up taking me for emergency and kept me overnight for observation. The hospital called my wife to inform her what had happened, but she was so mad that she didn't show up until the next day. I felt stupid, miserable and ashamed for what I had let happen to me. And to top it off at five o'clock in the morning when I woke up, my mother-in-law was sitting there in the dark waiting for me. She had brought me food and slippers and said she was hoping I was all right. She never judged me or told me I couldn't behave that way. She just gave me love and support. I never forgot it and to this day, I would take a bullet for her. When everybody found out at work, they all said it was Charlie Longhorn who must have been hiding and waiting for me. Nobody really rode me too hard about it because they knew I wouldn't back down from a fight, but that would be the last time I ever took those black beauties.

It wasn't long after this that Charlie and I had a confrontation. He finally challenged me and told me to walk over to the Kmart parking lot where he was going to kick my ass. He said he had had enough of all the abuse I had given him and that he was going to teach me a lesson. So with the whole used-car department watching, we walked across the street, and to my surprise as soon as we got there, he told me to start something. I yelled at him, "You fucking idiot! I've been abusing you every day of your miserable life since you've been here. If there was a line, I think I've crossed it more than once! This was your idea and you made me walk over here so don't waste my time or I'll slap another knot on that silly little head of yours."

Soon I realized he wasn't going to do anything so I went back to the dealership and he became an even bigger laughing stock. His days were numbered after that and he didn't last very long. He was not only the object of my daily ridicule, but it was doubled when he called me out and he didn't deliver. I don't know what he was thinking but I have had my ass kicked by experts. Did he really think I was going to back down from Charlie Longhorn? No one heard much about him after that. I think he went back to driving a truck somewhere. My days of taking speed were over but not my days of fighting. There would be more incidents to come before I officially took off my gloves.

CHAPTER 8
A NEW USED-CAR MANAGER

Most used-car managers for me came and left without incident. They would either be caught stealing or proven incompetent. Dan was an exception. I called him "Dapper Dan." He had been the top Honda salesman at the Dealership and he always conducted himself in a professional and classy manor, unlike me. He was determined to bring that out in me and make me more professional. His way of putting it to me was that if you cut someone with a razor or a dull knife, either way they still bleed. He said this about the way I had of "slam dunking" a customer because I only cared about making the most profit on them. I didn't care if the car ran correctly or even broke in three pieces after they left the lot. Even though I was just interested in grabbing new customers, Dan tried to teach me that a satisfied customer would refer more customers to me. This was not an overnight process to me. It was something that I had to work on and it did not come easy to me. It was, however, the right path for me that would lead me to eventually become a manager myself.

I'm not the kind to take crap from customers and one day an unhappy customer of mine pulled up to the front of the building. He started yelling and complaining about the car he had just bought and how it would pull to one side and stall out. He went on and on finding fault with the vehicle. I got tired of hearing from him and I said in a loud voice, "Well, it sure looks like it took a real asshole to buy that car."

Everybody was out there including Dan. His face flashed so red I thought it would explode. Then the customer changed his tune and started saying, "Oh, it's a good car." So Dan stepped up and asked him what two or three things the man needed to be satisfied. When the man told him, Dan took him to the Service Department to get it taken care of. Dan came back from Service shaking his head at me saying, "We have got a lot of work to do with you."

For the most part I wouldn't have cared but for Dan, I liked him and wanted to change for myself as well as for him.

Shortly before Dan had arrived, we hired a new salesmen named Cecil. He was a rather large, heavy-set Spanish salesman with a super high voice. He sounded like an eleven-year-old whose voice had never changed. It was squeaky high. So needless to say, I had been mocking him and imitating him. Every time he spoke, it was hilarious and we would all imitate him, whether he was with a customer or not. This guy was no push-over and he was not used to being abused like that, but he eventually got used to it. But Dan had been on my case to back off and be more professional and have the others look up to me and I tried, I really tried.

One day at the beginning of the month, I arrived at around noon with a new sports coat I had just bought. Cecil was already in a bad mood because the other salesmen had been picking on him all morning on my behalf. During this time I had been riding my bike constantly after work for about 15 miles a day and I was in pretty good shape. So it didn't faze me when I walked in the door and Cecil punched me on my side. It surprised me more than it hurt me. I immediately went into my office and took off my sports coat and set my glasses on my desk just in case. He followed me and in his high pitched voice he said, "The next one is going in your face." Then he turned and went outside.

Now I was confused by his actions because I had just arrived at the dealership and I was already being assaulted. This was not a position I was used to. I walked outside to the front porch where Cecil was. I put my hand on his shoulder and said, "Cecil, have I offended you in some way?"

This time he punched me in the stomach. Again, with my conditioning, it didn't hurt me. It just pissed me off and I went back into my office and waited for Dan to walk outside with a wholesale buyer. As soon as Dan had walked around to the back of the building, I walked over to Cecil's office and I said, "So what is it that you want?"

He responded in his high pitch voice, "Whatever you want!" and he got up and started swinging at me. I immediately grabbed him by the hair with my left hand and I started swinging and punching him with my right hand. It's a funny thing when you have someone by their hair: Only you know where their head is going; they don't. I pounded him mercilessly with my right hand. He might have gotten a swing in but I don't remember. Then I released him to see if he wanted more and he ducked his head to bull-rush me. I caught him by his arm and his hair again and swung him around like they did in the three Stooges movies. I finally forced him to the floor where he landed on his knee. He was finished!

Then with one eye shut and unable to put pressure on his leg, he hopped over to his phone and called Mike, the general sales manager. He started whining, "Mike, Mike, Richard hit me in the eye and he broke my leg!" Mike came running from the new car department to find Cecil sprawled in his office, lying on his desk like a wounded pig.

Mike called for the porter to take Cecil to the doctor. Several salesmen helped put him in a car and they drove off. Mike then turned to me and asked, "Are you okay?" I said I was fine and Cecil had hardly landed a glove on me. He did tear my shirt, but that was all that I could tell. Mike told me to go home to change my shirt and come back so that we could go to lunch.

I lived very close by so it wouldn't take me very long to go, but then Mike then turned to the other salesmen and said, "If any of you mention this or even talk about it, I will fire you."

I'll never forget all the salesmen saying later, "Golly, Richard beats the hell out of him and they take him to lunch, and if we talk about it we are fired." At lunch Mike devised a plan of action. He said first of all, "Why wouldn't you tell me this guy is messing with you so I could fire him?"

I said, "Mike, I'm a big boy. I can take care of things myself."

"Yes, but you're not a teenager anymore and in the real world, there are laws and consequences for your actions. So here's what's going to have to happen. You are going to pay this guy's medical bills and after his treatment, I am going to have him sign a general release, releasing you and this company from the liability of this incident."

I told him, "Mike, I don't like having to pay his bills when he is the one that started the fight."

Mike said, "This is not an option, this was not a company-sponsored event, and I cannot have the company liable for your actions." Basically, if I did not agree to it, I would have to leave the company. I agreed to it, and after about a month and $700 in medical bills, the company and I obtained the release of liability from Cecil. About a month later, after the dust settled and the ink dried, they fired him.

Dan, the used-car manager, was intent on making the used-car department classier. He continuously hired guys who were good-looking and had a good appearance—whether or not they could sell was another matter. One of them was Rudy a tall Hispanic, semi–good-looking young man who thought he was the Julio Iglesias of car sales. He had a sidekick from Mexico named Ernesto who, if it had not been for the fact that he had a family, you would have sworn was gay. In fact, if he was not gay he missed one heck of an opportunity to be one. He became the runner for Rudy. He would go and get the customers and bring them to Rudy and together they would make sales. I used to tell them that the pair of them together wouldn't make a freckle on my ass.

I said, "If you both try and work real hard, you can aspire to become a freckle on my ass." I welcomed the competition because I always thought competition made me perform better.

As a top salesman I was constantly invited to lunch by Dan and Mike the General Sales manager. They would use me for a sounding board as to why I thought business was slow. This often confused me because business for me was never slow, however, often I was the only one selling cars. In fact, if I ever did have a slow spell, my wife was a great motivator for me. She would ask, "Is it slow for everybody or just you?" This would make me think well so-and-so sold one yesterday and so-and-so sold one today, and this made me think that if anyone was going to sell a car, it would be me, and oftentimes that was the case.

There was a tall blonde salesman named Clay that Dan had hired. Clay even bragged about doing modeling jobs on the side. Well, on one of those very slow days when we were all waiting for a customer to show up, a car drove up with an elderly couple in it and Clay ran up to meet them. He opened up the driver's door for the gentleman to step out. As Clay stood courteously behind the driver's door, I stepped up and greeted them and shook the man's hand. I greeted the couple and immediately made them feel welcome as I began showing them some cars. I could tell this was a buyer and I was determined to make this a sale, or die trying.

When I went into Dan's office to get keys to show them cars, Clay followed me in and started screaming, "What do you think I'm here for? Do you think I'm your door man?"

I said, "You would be lucky to be my door man, and I don't know what the hell you're here for." Dan's face was flushed with red but he couldn't help but laugh.

The next time I went back in for keys, he actually threatened me. My philosophy has always been: If you are going to do something, do it. I don't give warnings and I don't need a warning. I looked him back in the eye and said, "Who do you think has more to lose, Pretty Boy? Me or you? My face has been through many battles while you still look like a virgin." I made the sale, and it was the only sale that was made that day. Later on after I left to go home, he went into Dan's office and threw his demo keys on the table and quit.

The company's philosophy was that the more salesmen they had, the more cars they would sell, so they were constantly hiring more salesmen. Since I had a knack for getting rid of them, this became my thing. As they would hire them, I would get rid of them. I often passed by Mike's office in the morning and he would stop me and say, "Here's two sets of keys. Your latest victims came in and quit. They are quitting in pairs now."

Of course I would get a big laugh out of this and say, "What did they tell you?"

He'd say, "Oh the usual: I can't stand him, I can't out sell him, and I don't think I can kick his ass, so I'm leaving."

I couldn't believe how easy this was. When we often had twelve salesmen, I could quickly reduce them to eight or nine and make the odds better in my favor. Rudy and his sidekick Ernesto kept selling cars however, so I began to work on getting the sissy out of there to break up the team. I used to imitate the way he walked and talked and make other salesman laugh at his expense. One day I made him so mad he said, "I'm going to hit you," and I laughed so hard I almost cried, and all the other salesmen did as well. He started dancing around flicking jabs at me like he was trying to hit me.

I tried to reason with him and said, "Look, you can brag that you were beaten up by Richard, but I'm going to be accused of beating up a retard."

He persisted in his attempt to hit me, but I decided I was not going to hit this boy so I pulled his sport coat over his head and pushed him in a corner and left him there, wrestling with his coat. When he recovered, he went right off to find Rudy. Several hours later when I was out on the porch Rudy came up yelling at me saying, "If you have anything to say to me, say it to my face!"

This confused me and I told him, "I always tell you to your face." I've never been one to mince words, but I learned that he had just used this as an opening line to start swinging at me. He stood considerably taller than me at about 6'2" but he telegraphed his punches so I could see them coming from a mile away. In fact he took three swings at me and I ducked every single one, I was pleading with him to stop. I didn't want any more trouble at work. About that time he reared back to throw another punch and I reached up and grabbed him by the hair and pulled him down to my level. I stuck his head between the two pillars of the used-car porch and pushed him down until he was on one knee. I pulled his head out from the pillars by his hair with my left hand while I began hitting him with my right. I only hit him three or four times, but it was enough. Then I pushed him off the porch which was about a four foot drop, and he sprawled across the pavement like "road kill." Dan was on the new car side and was screaming over the intercom to stop. He immediately sent us both home and said we would deal with it the next day because Mike had been out of town.

The next day when Mike arrived, he called us into his office one at a time. The sissy guy Ernesto was fired immediately mostly because he was useless. Then I was called in and Mike asked me about my most recent fisticuffs and said he was sorry he'd missed it. He said, "So what do you have to say for yourself?"

I said, "Mike, I pleaded with him not to fight with me. I even gave him three swings at me. I don't think I'd even give my wife three swings, and I know she would put up a better fight." When he stopped laughing, he told me to get the hell out of there and go sell a car.

CHAPTER 9
MY WORLD OF USED CARS

Anybody at the dealership during the time of 1984 to halfway through 1986 would tell you that the used-car department was my world and they were just lucky to be a part of it. I dominated the sales, I made the rules regardless of what the managers thought, and when I didn't like someone, I simply ran them off. I often was by myself in my own office when some offices had two or three salesmen because Dan knew if he put someone in my office, it was a sure thing they wouldn't last long.

But Dan often tried. A retired Major from the Army comes to mind. I don't recall his name, but I called him Major Harris. He was a short, burly white-haired man who looked like he was used to giving orders. I couldn't see that he had any sales ability. He was good at getting people to follow him around but the problem was, he didn't know where he was going.

One day I had letters sprawled all over the desk that I was sending out to previous customers. I stepped out for a moment and he walked in with a set of customers and pushed all my stuff to the side. This infuriated me because all the other offices were empty, yet he went and moved all my stuff over just to have a conversation, not even trying to sell a car.

I went in to retrieve my paperwork and put it in an orderly place when the customers were still sitting there. I told him, "By the way, the cars are still outside. They are not sitting in here." His face blushed red and I knew this had pissed him off.

A short time later after the customers had left he came out to the porch and started complaining about me to the other salesmen. He was like "Can't we all just get along? After all we are all in this together."

I said, "Oh, yeah? Well I didn't fucking invite you!" Then I stole a line from what my dad used to tell me and I told him, "Why don't you teach me a lesson and run away from home?"

Soon there was a chorus of laughter from all the other salesmen and I went off to lunch. When I came back from lunch, Jonny an older salesmen came up to me and asked what I had said to him. I said, "Nothing, why?" He told me Major Harris had already been in there crying to Dan and turned in his demo keys. He had a fresh box from the parts department and was inside packing his shit.

I was shocked at how easy it was. I mean this guy was a career solider used to giving it out and taking abuse. I'd been around many retired military guys who had said, "Man, I wish I'd had you when I was in the military!"

I used to tell them, "I know why, because shit runs downhill and you figured if you out-rank me, you can dog me, but we are here in the real world, and you have to command respect, not demand it." In other words, you have to respect the man, not his position.

Even though I worked really hard, I still partied even harder. We were constantly going to Bennigan's Tavern with friends and I often came into work hung over but I still came into work. I believed if you do the crime you do the time. I remember when they were having the grand opening for Bennigan's, it was a rare moment for me and I didn't have any money. My wife had called me and expressed that she would like to go. Just about that time a wholesale buyer named "Coach" walked in. It was probably not his real name but we all called him that because he used to play for the Cowboys. He was a mammoth of a man. He walked around with a huge wad of tobacco in his mouth and he loved to gamble. He would walk up to any salesman and throw a quarter on the floor and say, "Call it for ten or twenty!" So I counted out the fifteen dollars I had in my pocket and said, "Call it for fifteen, Coach!" and he threw the quarter and I won. Then he said, "Call it for twenty!" and I won again. This kept on and I kept winning. He continued to walk around with a wad of bills in his pocket so I knew I couldn't break him and it was just a matter of time before I would start losing. When I lost two in a row I quit. I ran behind the building to count my money and I had $165, more than enough to go to Bennigan's. That's the way my luck ran—it was usually always good. Years later when I needed to lose weight I went to a professional outfit where they analyzed the way you eat. I was told I was a "celebrator" and that was what motivated me to eat. It was to celebrate by eating or drinking—that was how I appreciated our good fortune.

One thing I always did, I wore cowboy boots for years. As time wore on I realized my feet were taking quite a beating from the asphalt lot. It didn't help that I would jump off the porch to be the first one to approach a customer. During this time I started developing aches and pains in my feet. Dan my used-car manager referred me to a podiatrist who went over the issues I had with my feet. He was recommending surgery on both feet to correct my hammer toes. I was trying to find the right time to do it but there is never a right time for this.

At the dealership a man named George retired from being general manager and Mike was promoted to the position. An older gentlemen named Tony became used-car manager. He could tell some great jokes but he was pretty much clueless about how to run a used-car department, so I usually went around him to Dan or Mike whenever I needed something.

We had old age units and one of them was a piece of shit, an Audi 5000 that I had sold. I sold it to an army lieutenant who was a fan of the product. He immediately began having problems with the vehicle, so I had him talk to Tony. Tony told him that he bought the car "as is" and would do nothing for him. I normally wouldn't care, except I knew this guy being a lieutenant would make trouble for us. Sure enough this guy went to "JAG" the military attorneys and they began saying that if the car was not fixed, they would tell the credit union not to honor the payment of the contract. I had received a $500 bonus on this sale and I didn't want to lose it. I told Tony again but he persisted he would not do anything, mostly because Audi's were expensive to repair. They soon had the car towed to the dealership and did not honor the contract.

At this time I had planned to go ahead with the surgery on my feet. It was already June of '86. I only missed a couple days of work but I was forced to wear some flat shoes with no heal or arch support, and I had wrapping around my feet. When I arrived to work after my surgery, Mike was in the used-car department as the acting manager and he had fired Tony. This didn't shock me because of the Audi fiasco, but what did surprise me was that all the other salesmen were saying that I was going to be the next used-car sales manager.

Mike took me to lunch and told me he wanted to see my magic one more time and that he was going to work hand in hand with me for one month as used-car manager, and he wanted to see me earn the top salesman award. I said, "Mike, I don't know if you realize this but I just had both feet operated on, and I am wearing these stinking platform shoes."

He said, "Oh, is that the way it's going to be? You're going to be the guy that looks for excuses? Oh, the weather's bad, the sun is in my eyes, etc. Or are you going to be the guy that can deliver on a deadline and ignore the pain and deliver like he is supposed to?"

I used to think selling cars was easy until I had to walk around in those stupid platform shoes. I still worked just as hard but I could no longer jump off the porch. When I got home at night I had to soak my feet in a tub with hot water. However, I got to see firsthand how Mike ran the used-car department—everything from dealing with vendors, to wholesale buyers, to how he treated the other salesmen. He was optimally very patient with the other salesmen, nudging them along and motivating them and trying to make them better than they really were. This worked up to a certain point until it got to where we weren't selling enough, or any cars.

Then Mike would have what he liked to call a "Come to Jesus meeting." At this point he would demand accountability for every customer that the salesmen talked to or prospects that they had. The rule in the car business is, if you ever walk a customer or let them leave without reporting the situation to the manager or even introducing them to the manager, "You walk along with them." So in this "Come to Jesus meeting," Mike would say, "The next salesman that walks a customer without reporting to me walks with him."

This usually pumped me up because I knew all the other salesmen would be afraid to wait on a customer. It's like a batter in baseball being afraid to go to bat because he got hit with the last pitch. Of course with me, all I wanted was more opportunities. And this is what it gave me. I would have one customer in the office, one in the waiting room and another on a test drive and I would still answer the phones. So whenever he did this I had a week where I would sell eight to ten cars because all the other guys were afraid of getting fired if they didn't report to him. Mike asked me later why I was the only one waiting on customers, and I told him all the others were afraid of getting fired. He asked me why I was not afraid. I told him, "If I don't sell enough cars, you will fire me anyway, so what do I have to lose? I may as well go down swinging. The way I see it, there are only two things you could do to me: fire me or kick my ass, and I don't think you can kick my ass."

The goal for the dealership was to always sell one hundred cars a month. I believe that month we sold 105, and twenty-eight of those were mine. As the month was coming to a close, Mike knew I was going to win like he had challenged me to do so. He invited my wife and me to go out to a nice dinner with him and his wife where he would offer me the position of used-car manager. My wife was so enjoyable and charming that I knew they would love her and they did. That and the fact that he offered me the used-car manager's job were two of the only three things I remember from that night. The other thing I remember was when they brought our salads, Mike attempted to stab his cherry tomato with a fork, and it somehow flew across his plate and across the whole restaurant. For some reason this cracked me up and I couldn't stop laughing. His wife kept looking at me with a look that said *don't laugh at him* but I couldn't stop.

Soon I was to take the used-car manager job and I wasn't even sure if I wanted it. It was just that way with Mike. He was my mentor and whatever carrot he dangled in front of me, I wanted.

My life was about to change completely. I would suddenly have to care about things I never cared about before like other salesmen, company policies, company politics and a perceived gentlemanly manner to which I was unaccustomed. Just the thought of it was exhausting to me. It was like I was carrying the weight of the whole department on my shoulders.

That first month Mike worked with me hand in hand to show me how he wanted the work done, my own form of on-the-job-training. It seemed as though the first ninety days I spent being chastised for one thing or another. The service advisor came to me with a large stack of tickets. For an example, a $300 bill that I would change to $200. I constantly changed the prices because I figured they were charging too much for the repairs. This would prompt the service advisor to go to his manager and cry the blues. Then the service manager would go to Mike, who would call me in for a meeting. This was a daily routine for me. If it wasn't them, it would be the other vendors like the painters and tire vendors saying that I made them cut their prices too low. I was trying to keep expenses down and the profits up since I was responsible for the bottom line. Mike understood this but he knew it was the way I was approaching things—it was my rough manner that was rubbing people the wrong way.

Then I had the salesmen to deal with: the ones that I had berated and belittled now had to look up to me and seek me for guidance. One thing I knew how to do was to sell a car, and I told them if they wanted to survive and make a good living, they should get me involved in every sale, even if it meant me taking over the sale and putting the customer in the right car where we could make the most profit. The smart ones did this and used me in a manner that I was accustomed too. Of course there were the usual slow, lazy pathetic whiners who wouldn't do what they were supposed to and I would have to end up firing them. This wasn't easy for me. Before I would run them off and make them quit. Now I was forced to work with them patiently, nurture them and put them on probation before I would fire them.

There was one kid named Gary from East Texas. He would come in like a ball of fire and he worked great with me. He made a lot of money for the first four months. Then he started to go bad, drinking a lot, not showing up to work and not selling any cars. Mike told me that I should probably get rid of him. I said, "No. He may come around. Remember he sold twenty cars last time." Mike said that was three months ago and now he's only selling six or seven cars a month.

This was a real dilemma for me because I knew the guy could be good if he got back to the level he was at before. Mike said, "If you have a problem with it, I'll make it easy for you. It's either you or him to go, but I'll help you along and show you how it's done." Mike got on the PA system and paged Gary to the general manager's office. When Gary came in Mike stood up, shook his hand and closed the door. The three of us where in there for a meeting.

I had never seen anything like it. Mike complimented the young man, told him how bright he was, and what a bright future he had in store for him but unfortunately we would have to part company. I mean he really made the kid feel good. He told him how I was conflicted in terminating him, because I could only remember how well he had done before and I could only see the good in him. Mike even told him about this blind spot that I had that had almost cost me my job. He told him how this was not an end to anything, but a new beginning for him how this was not an end to that potential, but a fresh start somewhere else. While terminating him Mike motivated him and made him feel all the pressure off of him so that he could relax and fulfill his future at another dealership. The guy must have shaken our hands three or four times each and smiled at the possibility of a bright future at another dealership. Gary even asked if he could hang around and drink some coffee and chat with the other salesmen before he left. Most people can't wait to get out the door when they are fired let alone want to hang around; and he was walking about ten feet high at the possibilities of his own bright future.

Although I was not to be involved with the antics of the salesmen anymore, I could not help it, because, after all, it was me who had instilled the tradition. When salesmen were close to the point of being fired, I made them try out an old coat and tie which had been left on the coat rack. We called it *the graduation gown*. We made them try it on and walk down the steps while we all hummed the graduation song, and they had better do it and they always did. I never had anybody refuse or it would be worse for them.

One day as I was walking from the new car side to my office on the used-car side, the used-car salesmen all had a guy named Jose wearing the coat and tie, walking down the steps. The idiot was laughing about it. I couldn't help but be embarrassed for him. He was good at telling jokes but nothing more. In the middle of his graduation ceremony he stopped to tell me a joke. And after we all laughed, I looked at him and shook my head and said, "Boy, we are going to miss you!" His face became serious and he followed me into my office and asked if that was it. I said, "Yes" as I took out the paperwork to fire him. It was the easiest termination I had ever done because he had already given up on himself so it was only natural for him when I gave up on him as well.

Appraising cars was an art in itself because you had to ride a fine line between taking the car in cheap enough to where you made a profit on it, and giving enough for it to where you could actually obtain the car. If you gave too much, there goes your profit; if you give too little, they accuse you of trying to steal the trade. One of the worst things you could do is what they called *stepping on your dick*, which means you gave way too much for a car which virtually means a guarantee of no profit and a possible loss. I did this my second day on the job. I looked at a Ford Bronco as though it was a four wheel drive and it was not, and that was over a $3,000 mistake. When Mike found out, he said he would show me how to get rid of it. We did a quick detail and service job on it. Then we put it on our special ramp where we put our Special of the Day, for only an $800 profit. Someone made us an offer and we broke even on it, but it taught me a valuable lesson: if you identify a problem and attack it early enough, you can get out of anything. Mike used to have a saying about a mouse caught in a trap—while lying there with its little head caught in a trap the mouse would say, "I don't really want the cheese. I just want to get out of the trap."

Like Dan before him, Mike's goal was to make a gentleman out of me. As a manager, it was easy for him; he was tall and a white man from North Carolina, a southern gentleman by nature. I remember when he talked to some of the lessor employees like the janitor for example, and he would address him as Mr. Rosales. He didn't have to work at having a gentle nature like I did. So

Mike became my complaint department. Anybody that had a problem with me would go complain to him, this included salesman, other managers, vendors and office personnel. This was exhausting, and if it was exhausting for me, it was probably for Mike as well. This took away from my strength which was selling cars for maximum profit.

The biggest thing he wanted me to have was empathy for the customer when they came back with a problem. When I told them they bought it "as is," they would immediately go complain to Mike. One time when he was chewing me out, he said, "You wouldn't treat a dog that way," and then he asked me if I had a dog. He asked, "Do you ever feel bad for her?"

I said, "Mike, I was walking her the other day and she got stickers in her foot, so I sat on the curb and put her on my lap and pulled all the stickers out and rubbed her little foot so it would feel better."

He jumped up immediately so I jumped up as well. He said, "What the hell are you standing up for?"

I said, "I thought you were going to start swinging and I wanted to be ready. I don't win all those fights by being ill prepared."

He got a big laugh out of it, but he said, "Now that's how I want you to treat your customer, by caring for them and helping them, nurture them like you did your dog."

Soon after this meeting I got a chance to prove his theory. I really didn't want him to know about it, but a car we sold had major problems, and the parts would take two to three weeks to arrive. We tried not to give loaner cars and these people were grateful that I was helping them. But when they came to explain their situation to me as to why they needed a loaner car, they brought their baby who was deformed. He was a tiny infant whose body was twisted like a pretzel.

For the first time I knew what Mike meant about having empathy. I immediately called for a salesman to loan them his company demo. They explained that they would be driving back and forth to Las Cruces, NM three or four times a week for the baby's treatments.

About three weeks later when the company was conducting a demo inspection, the salesman explained to the auditor that his demo was on loan for an extended amount of time. He was forced to call the customers in so that the vehicle could be inspected. Mike saw that they had put over 1,500 miles on the demo and immediately called me into his office. He said, "Explain this to me. Why would you loan a car out for three weeks and 1,500 miles?" So I explained to him the car we sold needed work and we were waiting for parts; and the final thing I told him was that they had a baby that was all twisted. He said, "Let me get this straight. You actually felt bad for the customer?"

I said, "Yes. They had a baby that needed help and needed constant treatment and he need medical attention every day." He jumped up again, and so did I, but this time it was to shake my hand. He was ecstatic that I had finally found an opportunity to show empathy for a customer, and that I had used my authority to help them.

Mike was my general manager and my mentor and in many ways I tried to emulate him. The most difficult way to do that was his way of giving sales meetings. Mike was a dynamic speaker with a buoyant personality. He had been a keynote speaker for meetings at Chrysler-sponsored events. Even though I had been to Bible College and studied public speaking and how to preach, he was a tough act to follow. Even still, that was exactly what he wanted me to do—because he knew that Dan, the general sales manager didn't have the ability, nor did any of the other car managers there. He would say to me, "This is what I want you to do, motivate them, teach them, inspire them," in our three sales meetings a week.

Our meetings were a forum where the managers had time to say what was on their minds and what things they wanted to prioritize in their departments. It got to the point that when I called on Mike, he would have nothing to say because he wanted me to say it. I figured, if I'm going to speak I'm going to speak on the things that fuel me like books, music, movies and jokes and I hoped the things that motivated me would motivate them as well.

I remember giving one of my best speeches which was on a movie called "The Color of Money." In the film Paul Newman is teaching Tom Cruise the ropes about being a professional pool player and he explains to him that you have to be a "student of human moves to know and feel how the other person is going to feel and react to what you do." This was never truer than in the car business where you constantly had to react to a customer's objections or reactions in the process of a sale. I thought it was brilliant and had made me a fortune while selling cars so I thought it would work for them. The managers all loved it and even the guests we had from Chrysler loved the examples.

The message reached everybody except the targeted audience which was the salesmen. It went over the heads of about 85 percent of them except for that exceptional few. It turns out that you cannot teach pride to a person and you cannot instill in them a pride in their work. It's amazing to me how mechanics, carpenters or construction workers can all have pride in their work, but not a salesman. When I first got in this business and several of us would go to a bar to meet girls, they would say, "Hey, don't tell them we sell cars. Tell them we work for the city or something else." Having no success in the business made them have no pride in it, and they didn't realize success was just inches away if they would only give the effort.

I remember having to let go of one of my wife's good friends named Hector. He worked for me for about a year and a half and was average at best. To me there was no excuse for being average because I would be involved in every sale. All they had to do was make the effort to wait on the customer, bring them to me and get me involved, and I would find a way to make the sale happen. I believed that if a salesman didn't make it under my tutelage, it was because he was lazy and weak and I told them so.

I remember Hector crying when I let him go and I said, "I didn't do this to you, you did—you fired yourself basically for not making the effort." I didn't leave him there however, I told him he still had potential to make a good living in sales, I followed Mike's example of how to let a salesman go and still left him feeling good about himself. Hector was in the Naval Reserve and went once a month to serve and the guys used to kid him and call him "Pela Papas" which meant "potato peeler." As it turned out he went back to the Navy full-time and became a Naval Recruiter. He later won awards for being one of the top naval recruiters in his area.

Chapter 10
Used-Car Manager,
a Full-Time Job

Being a manager for one of the largest dealerships in the city gave me access and attention, wanted or not, throughout many venues. I remember when I was a salesman, I could actually be off and not worry about what I did, but as a manager that was not the case. I went to bed thinking about problems I had and I woke up with them as well. As a salesman I never showed fear of failing at the job, but as a manager I worried constantly about the salesmen not being aware and motivated to do their jobs. There was a time when I acquired four really good salesmen and that really helped. One was Gary a tall blonde salesman who was ex-military. He was a good-looking kid who followed instructions really well, also hardworking and that was all I could really ask for. Another was Efrian, a tiny older Hispanic salesman who stood at about 4'10". His initials were ET, and this was at the time, the movie came out, and everyone on the intercom would say, "ET phone home." He was also very hardworking and polished as a salesman. My favorite thing to tell him was, "What do you get when you cross a hooker with a leprechaun?" The answer was "A little fucker like that," and I held my hand about three feet high.

The other two were Bob and Terry. They were affectionately known by Efrian as the *winos*. They would sell a lot of cars but sometimes they wouldn't come to work. A couple of times they even slept in their demos in the parking lot after getting drunk at night after closing. Bob was very intelligent and polished and later he became the new-car manager. I also had a tall blonde salesman named Clay who was more of a lady's man than a salesman. He had some great stories about his escapades at night when he went on the prowl looking for a woman. Mike asked me about him one time saying he thought Clay had the chance to really become a good salesman and he wanted to know what I thought. I said, "Mike, he might be management material—he's tall, blonde and he can't sell cars. Hell, he might be the next general manager." It was no coincidence that his appearance closely resembled Mike himself. And Mike replied, "Fuck you!"

One day in a sales meeting I gave what I thought was my best motivational speech. As it turns out we had visitors from Chrysler in the room, I spoke about my favorite movie *One Flew Over the Coo Coo's Nest*. When Jack Nicholson spoke about picking up the water fountain and throwing it through the window so he could go watch the World Series, all the other patients said he couldn't do it and they started betting against him. Of course he took all their action and started betting on himself. When he got down to try and started huffing and puffing, they all started to laugh. He said to them, "Oh, I was just warming up!" Then he really got serious about it. This time he had veins popping out of his neck and was trying with all his might and was turning all colors. He finally stopped and said, "At least I tried, goddammit, at least I did that." I used this as an example to the salesman who had either given up on themselves, the business or both. The men from Chrysler Motors were so impressed they encouraged me to get a letter of recommendation from Dick Poe to enter into the Dealer Minority Program to acquire a dealership of my own.

This opened up a whole new can of worms for me. Soon I received the letter of recommendation from Dick Poe and gave it to them, but I didn't realize how involved it would be. It turned out to be great conversation across the dealership that Richard was going to get his own dealership but it was not meant to be. It seems that the Chrysler program was quite involved. You had to have $80,000 in escrow and attend dealer school for nine months to learn every facet of the workings of a dealership. I asked, "Who's going to pay my bills while I do this?" and the gentleman from Chrysler said I would have to allow for this. Of course I didn't find this out right away which kept the mystic going for about 90 days as to whether or not I would get my own dealership. It did make for a lot of flattery and interesting conversation while it lasted. People I knew told me that had I been with the Ford Dealership, the process would be a lot easier, and I kept this in the back of my mind.

One day after our sales meeting Mike called for a meeting of the entire department heads. This included service managers, parts managers, office managers, and new-car managers. I had some drinks the night before and was really hung over. I was not in the mood as it turned out for this ass chewing: We all sucked and were way behind on our sales for the month.

After he chewed on some other people, he got on to me and said, "What's on your mind? You always have something to say."

I asked what he meant and he said, "Just tell me what you are thinking."

So I said, "Remember the movie *The Exorcist* when the girl is sitting there growling and the psychiatrist is attempting to hypnotize her? She starts by holding her hand in front of her face suspended in air. Soon he walks up and says, 'If Regan is hypnotized, then the person inside her must be hypnotized as well.' He says this while standing in front of her, and at that moment, she reaches out with her hand and grabs him by the nuts, crushing them with all her might. She sends him to the floor screaming and begging for mercy."

Of course I said this in a room full of people including women from the office who were trying their best not to laugh in front of Mike. Mike turned to me and yelled, "What the fuck does that have to do with anything?"

I said, "It's just what I was thinking about."

He said, "You've got serious issues," and dismissed the meeting.

One time when I was at the New Car desk covering for the new-car manager, Mike came from a meeting with the company attorneys. It was a super windy day in the spring. He ran up the steps to the building and tripped on the last one, sending all his papers and him flying all over the floor. I immediately came down from the podium to help him but I couldn't help laughing. I tried not to look at him so he wouldn't see me laughing but I couldn't stop shaking. He finally caught me and said, "You son of a bitch, you are laughing at me!"

I said, "I can't help it, Mike! I love slap stick." It reminded me of the three stooges.

It turned out Mike was going to the attorneys to see if it was legal to hire Jerry back, who had been away for a few years. He had been involved in a scam to steal people's social security checks, and the company was checking to see if they would be liable if they hired him back. Mike warned me what it would be like working with Jerry as a salesman. I had worked with him before but never over him as a manager. Mike said he was not to be trusted and that I couldn't believe anything he said, not even the year of the car he was representing on an appraisal. I asked the same thing everybody else was asking and that was "Why bring him back?" Mike said he offered instant profits to the store on whichever he sold new or used, and also it was a challenge to keep us all on our toes to do business the right way.

One day Jerry sold a Plymouth Colt to a soldier in the Army. It had no air conditioning and the guy came back a month and a half later when it started to get warm and complained that there was no air. Jerry immediately offered to trade the man into a better vehicle but he would need $4,000 down. The man said he only had $3,000, and, of course, the bank wouldn't approve it. So Jerry did the next best thing. He took the man's $3,000, had an air conditioner installed and upgraded the radio—all at the total cost of $1,000 and, of course, he kept the difference.

Much of my practice as a manager was from memory on how other managers worked and what not do to. Many managers I had worked with were oblivious to what was going on around them, how salesman were acting and reacting to the business, and how they were working deals. Some managers yelled and screamed and fired people every other day like old Wendell. When I worked at the Pontiac dealer under Louis, I actually considered him to be a pretty good manager. He had a habit of reading all the other dealership advertisements every Friday morning at our meetings. This was counterproductive and rather depressing because our dealer (before Dick Poe bought the store) would buy a tiny, little six inch advertisement. The Chevy and Lincoln dealerships across the street from us would have huge, full page ads in color, and Louis would read every line to us. One time as he was reading the Lincoln advertisement word for word, the room grew silent because we were all wishing we were somewhere else. He finally came to the end and read the last words on the page, "All these savings will be yours at the sign of the cat." And this guy named Frank sitting across from me imitated the sound of a cat hissing, like in the commercials.

I laughed so hard I almost fell out of my chair. I've been told all my life that my laugh is contagious, and all the other salesman were trying not to laugh but they couldn't help it. By now Louis's face was flushed with red and he kept telling me, "Shut up, goddammit!" Just like growing up with my dad when he would tell me to shut up, this always made me laugh harder. He finally told me to get out of the meeting, but to my knowledge he never read another advertisement again. We had cured him.

My style was to be involved with every facet of a sale, consequently I spent a lot of time in every department of the dealership, especially the new car department. I had to cover for the new car managers when they were gone or take my inventory to them when I was gone or needed to leave early. It took some time to get used to working a new car deal because I had never sold very many new cars. The reality of it was that with new cars you could lose money on paper and still make money for the dealership by retaining *hold back money and dealer cash*. I personally was not in the habit of losing money on used-car sales.

During my six years as used-car manager for Dick Poe I must have worked with at least seven or eight different new-car managers, including my old sparring buddy Rudy. He had a brief tenure as new-car manager. He tried to look the part but he couldn't perform and he was scared to death of Mike. The thing that always worked for me whether selling or managing was that I was not afraid. I was not afraid of the general manager, or to lose, or even the consequences of failure. I believe this lack of fear and my positive attitude are keys to success in business.

I was not naive but I always believed the good in people whether it be a customer or sales manager. For example, many salesman do what is called "curb qualifying" when a customer pulls into a lot. They analyze them and say that he is "buried" if he's driving a late model car or if he's driving an old car, they would say that guy can't buy anything. When I was selling, I loved having these guys around because while they would hesitate, I would approach the customers and get as many customers as I wanted, while they were still analyzing them. But as a manager, these guys were poison because they create negativity for the other salesman who was trying to approach the customer. I went out of my way to try and prove the naysayers wrong and I helped the salesman who had the guts to approach the customer—I helped him prove them wrong and make the sale.

Having spent more time in the New Car Department, I got to know some of the salesman better. One of them was an older Hispanic named Joe. In his younger days he had been what was called a "Charro," a type of a Mexican rodeo cowboy. He walked like he spent half his life on a horse, bow-legged and he wore his cowboy boots all the time. He possessed a quick wit and was one of the funniest people I've ever been around. He had an on-going feud with the title clerk named Blanca. She was attractive but a little over weight and he picked on her constantly. For example, he would say, "Do you know Blanca is in mourning?" We'd ask why and he'd say, "Because she just killed three burritos and a diet coke and she's wearing a black dress!"

She had a thing for dating cops and almost every date she went on was with a cop, so Joe made up a flyer called "Blanca's Emergency List." It said, "In case of emergency dial 911 ext. 248 Beto, 219 Carlos, 262 Pepe, etc." He made a bunch of copies, passed them around the dealership and put them up in offices. At least twice a day she would come from the back offices screaming, "Where's that goddamn Joe?"

Once when she was taking the place of the switchboard operator, Blanca leaned over to get a customer's license plate. Just then Joe turned the corner and—I wouldn't believe it if I hadn't seen it—reached out and grabbed a hand full of her ass and said, "Putting a little weight on, huh?" She started screaming and even cursing him in front of the customers who were shocked. These days you would be sued for that, but everyone got a big laugh about it then.

Once a black soldier approached Joe on the showroom floor and said, "I'm looking for the cheapest ride you've got."

Joe thought about it for a moment and then walked him over to the corner of the showroom where they had a mechanical horse for kids and said, "Here, this will only cost you a dime."

One of the new-car managers for Suzuki was Tony the "Italian Stallion from Back East." He worked out a lot and many of the guys were afraid of him. Of course, I was not. As a manager we were all awarded an afternoon off. You only had to work until noon and then take the rest of the day off. His afternoon off was usually on a Wednesday, but on Fridays he had visitation with his daughter, so he often had an additional afternoon off when his ex-wife dropped off his daughter at the dealership.

An additional afternoon off was created for him on Fridays which I thought was very convenient for him—how does this guy rate two afternoons a week off? One Friday I had the operator write a note to Tony saying, "See me about your extra afternoon a week off," signed Mike. As it turned out Mike was in meetings all afternoon with factory reps from Chrysler and this kept Tony pacing around the showroom with his daughter until 5:00 p.m. About 6:00 p.m. Mike drove by my used-car building and said, "You son of a Bitch! How could you do that to that poor guy? Making him hang around all day with his daughter?"

I denied it and said, "What did I do? I didn't do anything."

He said, "Tony was so mad that he was shaking and stuttering. I don't know if you believe in karma but you're going to get it someday."

I said, "It serves him right! Who the hell does he think he is taking two afternoons off?"

Another manager we had was Paul. He was close to retirement age and was actually Dick Poe's brother in law. His claim to fame was that he had played pro football back in the '50s. We all joked that it must have been before they had face masks because he was dumber than a sack of rocks. He had also been a failed home builder and he used to brag that he made his wife a millionaire but one of the guys would say, "Yes, but she started with ten million!" Once a month we had a managers meeting when we all went to dinner and had drinks afterward.

One night there was just a handful of us left including Mr. Poe, Mike, Paul, myself and a few others. Paul kept going on and on about being on the road when he was playing ball and staying in hotel rooms. He said the sound a vacuum cleaner would get him erect because he had so many flings with the maids at different hotels.

Mr. Poe didn't like that kind of talk and kept telling him to be quiet, but then he started going on and on about how he wished he could still get it up like he used to when he was young. He kept saying, "All I wish I had anymore was a hard dick."

After he said this like three or four times I finally said, "Okay, Paul, where do you want it?" His reaction tickled the hell out of me. He got so upset and furious that I couldn't stop laughing.

Even Mr. Poe told me, "It's not that funny, Richard."

But Mike said, "Yes, it sure is."

Paul was the closest thing to "Mr. Magoo" that I had ever seen. I would not have believed it if I hadn't seen it with my own eyes. I once saw him using the touch-tone phone instead of the calculator, saying, "This damn thing doesn't work." His salesman were always coming to me to do the math for them on deals because his calculator was not working. I hope he's retired by now.

There was a New Car Salesman named Manny. He lived across the border in Mexico and was a "wannabe" matador. He even showed the cars that way. He would slide the door open and say, "Ole! This is the Chrysler New Yorker!"

as he stomped his foot for effect. He wanted so much to be a matador that he even went and trained with them, with the little babies called "Beceros." When he arrived at work afterward, he was limping and acting like he had been gored. Everyone laughed at him and humiliated him.

One Saturday when we were all eating lunch in the back conference room, he was hesitant to eat his food, as if he was uncomfortable. I said, "Manny can't eat without his little match box."

He said, "What do you mean?"

I said, "The little match box you carry with roaches and flies in it so you can let them out, and they run around the table just like if you were at home."

Another time when the salesmen were putting balloons out on the cars, Manny walked by and a salesman reached out planning to "goose" him as he passed by. But instead of walking on by, Manny stopped and the salesman's hand went halfway up his ass instead. Manny turned around furious and started cursing but everyone else was cracking up laughing. I said, "What's the matter, Manny? Did he catch you with your mouth open?"

Carl, the redneck from Tennessee said in his country way, "At least we know he isn't a queer because he didn't like that worth a shit."

There was an older Spanish Salesman named Gus and you name it and he did it all. He was an ex-matador, ex-Olympian and ex-boxer. None of this was true of course. We used to say he was a legend in his own mind. Whenever he was challenged, especially about the matador part, he would swear that he had been gored and that he could prove it. He would reach down low between his legs and grab his genitals and say, "Touch it right there and you can feel the hole where the bull got me with his horn."

We all laughed and one of the guys said, "You picked a great spot. No one is going to make you prove that."

I don't know why but it seemed as time went on, I drank more, whether it was from the stress of the job or other pressures that were involved. I spent at least a couple of nights a week at Sioux Street, the restaurant-bar just behind the Dealership. During this time my wife and I had started to look at newer houses in the Upper Valley part of El Paso. This seemed to be a natural progression since I was doing well as a manager and she was doing well in her job. We settled on a really nice Southwestern style two-story. It sat on a half-acre lot, was beautiful Santa Fe style decor, and it was more money with a higher payment then I ever dreamed of affording. We bought it and made the transition and it seemed like my stress mounted.

One day during the rainy season in El Paso, as I was closing the dealership, the rain came pouring down on us. I went next door to Sioux Street to dry off a little before going home. Some friends were there and we started drinking Tequila shots. I thought I had enough and started on my way home, but since I was now living in a different area with new surroundings, I got lost in the storm. I wound up on a back road in the Upper Valley and unfortunately I ended up in a field with my Lincoln stuck in the mud. Drunk as I was, I remembered what I had seen in a movie so I took off my shirt and stuck it under the tire thinking it would help the car spin out of the mud. All it did was suck my shirt in and left me shirtless out there in the rain.

I walked a ways down to some houses and started knocking on doors—here was this drunk, shirtless man knocking on your door at eleven o'clock at night. Somebody was bound to call the cops. When the police arrived I was nowhere near my car. So they asked me if I had been drinking and I said, "Yes." Then they asked if I was driving and I said, "Not anymore."

One cop told the other, "We can get him for a DWI."

I said, "I mean no disrespect, but how the hell are you going to give me a DWI with no car as evidence."

One cop was determined to find the car, even at the risk of getting himself stuck in the mud as well, but the more sensible cop said, "Look, let's just take him home."

He asked me, "Do you remember your address?"

I told them the address, and they took me home and explained to my wife what had happened. I went inside and tracked mud all through my brand new home, and in the morning I called the tow truck company and had them find the car and take it to the dealership. I got a little bit of an "ass chewing" from Mike and he insisted that I had to pay for the wrecker out of my own pocket. It took two wreckers, two hours, and cost me $250. I should have taken this as a warning sign, but as it turns out I'm hard headed and even that didn't do the trick.

CHAPTER 11
ADayThatWillLiveinInfamy

It was now the fall of 1990 and there was a shortage of used cars, so Mike said he was going to show me how to go to the auction in Phoenix, Arizona and buy used cars. He said this was a fast-paced auction with six lanes going at once, and I would have to prepare for it a couple weeks before we left. In the process of preparing for the auction I had to register and inform them as to my credentials so that I could be authorized as a purchaser for the Dealership. I began speaking to a woman at the auction who sounded really sexy on the phone. We began a flirting thing going back and forth and started calling each other about the sale information. I've always been good on the phone with both my voice and my charm, so she could not wait to meet me. As the time approached for our trip to the auction, Mike suggested we go have some drinks the night before. I thought this was not the best idea of all, but what the heck, he was the boss.

The Wednesday we were leaving, I was sitting in a Southwest Airlines plane at 7:30 in the morning, way hung over and not looking forward to going to Phoenix which is usually over 100 degrees every day. I believe I was at the point of being hung over or still drunk from the night before. At any rate the flight attendant spoke on the intercom and started going over the safety procedures. Then he said something I've never heard before or since, "In the event of an anticipated crash landing, you should lean forward as far as we can, place your head as forward as you can on our lap and between your legs."

Before he could finish I yelled out, "And kiss your ass goodbye!"

Mike and everyone on the plane broke out laughing. The attendant was so embarrassed that a female attendant had to take over for him and continue the safety procedures. Mike looked over at me and said, "I can't take you anywhere."

When we arrived in Phoenix and the auction, I met the woman I'd been dealing with and flirting with—not that I'd planned on cheating, but I thought she would be at least attractive which was not the case. I thought of my dad when he had his business and he'd be getting ready to go to the Market in Dallas. He'd flirt with the entire staff of women he talked to on the phone. The one time I went with him to Market he couldn't find a "hot one" in the whole bunch and they were all following him around saying, "Freddy, Freddy where are we going tonight?"

I guess we both had the same gift of gab, but as far as the auction went, Mike made sure that I did it the right way. This meant putting your hands on every car you were interested in and checking it, inside and out before it went on the line so that when it was in line, this was not the first time you saw it. Easy for him to say, when I was the one out there in 100 degrees making notes on a notepad for the cars I was interested in.

The auction started at ten o'clock and we were successful in buying many of the cars we targeted, but I learned something else. Most of the men buying were middle age and older, and so by noon, "fatigue had made cowards of them all," a famous quote from Vince Lombardi. So from noon until about 2:00, I made most of my best buys of the day because there was scarcely anyone else there to bid against me. Mike had joined most of the "older guys looking for shade and a cold drink."

Later that afternoon some bad weather came in and our return flight was canceled and we had to fly out the next morning. The woman I had met at the auction got wind of this, and she began paging me at least six times hoping this was our chance to get together. When Mike and I went out to eat dinner that night, he kept asking me, "What the heck is going on with you and this girl? I hope you're not planning on doing anything with her because Dora is a lot prettier than she is."

I said, "She just took serious what I poked at her in fun." That was my dad's favorite line to say whenever he saw a pregnant woman, "She just took serious what someone poked at her in fun."

A couple of weeks after I returned from the auction, the Dealership began to get ready for the new car showing. The Dealership had been in existence for over 70 years and this was a big deal for them. They sent out invitations to all their previous customers. On the designated day I had to move the entire used-car inventory to the back parking lot to allow for the customer parking for this all day affair. When evening came and the sun went down, the Dealership had catered appetizers including wine and cheese, and music by a local band. This lasted till about eight o'clock in the night, and the date was October 2 of 1990. I had been at work since seven a.m. and I had also been dieting, so my resistance was low when the alcohol hit me. As the day progressed into night and the dealership was closing, all the employees naturally gravitated to Sioux Street, the restaurant-bar around the corner.

As usual my custom was to be one of the last ones to leave. I asked the bartender for another drink and he said, "I'll give you one, if you give me your keys," which I did. He was a good guy and I had known him for a while so I ordered another one "for the road" and he didn't care because he was going to call a cab for me anyway.

I said, "Oh, before you call the cab, let me go get my briefcase out of the car."

He said, "Where is it and I will go get it for you?"

Being a car salesman I somehow tricked him and managed to get him to give me the keys. In my mind I really planned on going back for my briefcase and just waiting for the cab to come, but once I got in the car, I soon found myself behind the wheel and driving out of the parking lot. My car naturally went out and took a left on Montana Avenue going to where I used to live heading east bound, even though I had recently bought a house on the Westside of town in the opposite direction. As I drove east on Montana, the streets became darker and I soon realized I was heading in the wrong direction so I turned around. Now I was going the proper direction but fatigue and the booze had done their tricks and I found myself dozing off.

I found myself quickly approaching a red light with a car sitting there waiting for it to change, and if I had not swerved to the right to avoid it, I would have plowed into the back of it. As it turned out I wiped out about 200 yards of fence and a telephone pole, and the car had flipped a couple of times—funny they are not meant to be driven on the roof. The next thing I remember was a cop holding me by the front of my shirt yelling at me saying, "Do you realize what you did?"

My natural reaction was to punch him in the face, but when I tried to raise my right arm to hit him, it didn't work. He realized this and said, "You wanted to hit me didn't you?" and I said, "Damn right!"

The other cop yelled at him, "Can't you see the guy is injured? Just wait for the ambulance, and don't move him." Soon the ambulance picked me up and took me to the hospital. It was not so much the pain, but I felt like a shot of electricity had gone from my upper right side of the neck and down my right arm. The end result was that I had nerve damage but it would take over a year to find this out and begin the proper treatment for it. The hospital representatives called my wife and asked her to come to the hospital and just like before she said, "No, I'll just see him in the morning." I was forced to endure my pain and my humiliation all by myself.

When my wife came to get me out of the hospital, she took me to purchase a new pair of glasses since my other ones had been shattered in the accident. She was not happy and her silence was deafening.

We had always had a custom of spending my money and saving hers, so she had a nice nest egg saved up for our "future use." I had spoken to Mike on the phone and, of course, he knew about the car and the damage I had caused to the city property by the airport. I knew I was possibly facing termination for what I had done and my future was at stake. To top it off, my wife had calmly told me that evening that she would be using her nest egg to purchase a brand new Jaguar for herself. She said, "I don't go out and get drunk and wreck cars and wind up in the hospital." I just filed this in the back of mind along with everything else that was on my plate.

The next day I made calls to any doctors who could see me and possibly help with my arm. I had to make appointments because nobody could see me right away. Basically I sat at home horrified and thought about my future, and my past. Just about then Mike called me and asked what I was doing and if I was going to see doctors that day or not. Then he asked, "Can you walk? I know you can talk, but can you walk?" I said, "Yes," then he said, "Get your ass in here and get to work."

I asked, "Mike, do I still have a job to go to?"

He said, "As far as I am concerned you do. You just need to come in and face the music about what you did. You need to let everyone fuck with you and make fun of you just like you did to them."

I said, "Mike, I feel like shit."

He said, "I don't care what you feel like or even if you just sit on my couch and face the music and let everybody harass you about what you did."

On the third day after my accident, my wife took me to work, and we met with Mike and Mr. Poe. We told them how sorry we were and my wife natural-ly apologized for me. She is a saint and as always, a classy lady. She walked in there with me to face the owner and the general manager and even walked to the back lot with them to see the damage I had done to the car. I consider this above the call of duty for a wife. She left me there and I stayed at work to try to do my job. No one told me to pack my stuff but Mike told me I would have to drive a cheaper car because the one I totaled was valued at over $20,000. In the coming days, I slowly got back in the groove of making deals and selling cars and seeing some of the doctors who had little hope of helping me with my arm. I was feeling better about my situation even though I had huge challenges ahead of me. The car was not insured and Mike had not yet told me how we were going to handle paying for it.

I was worried that with the money we had, my wife would spend it on her new Jaguar—I had not forgotten that she said that. I told her I wouldn't drink anymore and she said, "Yeah, I've heard that before." We got along okay, but it was mostly with me walking on eggshells afraid to say too much. I mostly bit my tongue and waited for her to bring up buying a new car again.

The next time she brought up me wrecking cars and her buying a new car with her money, I let her have it. I said, "The next time you throw that in my face again about my wreck and about you buying a new car, I will file for divorce. We can split the money and sell your beautiful new house, and you can go on your way. I have enough challenges with my job and my medical condition without you having to throw it in my face every day. I am drawing a line in the sand like they did at the Alamo and you have to pick a side—you are either for me or against me." She began to cry and I knew I had hurt her feelings, but it needed to be said. I have always felt that a woman is like a shark that senses blood in the water when they sense fear in a man; they will go for the kill if left unchecked.

I was not proud of the way I handled the situation with my wife but I knew she could be a worthy ally or adversary, and I wanted her on my side. I knew I had hurt her feelings but she never brought up the accident again.

Sometime later Mike sat me down and told me he had worked out a fi-nancial proposition for the car I had wrecked. He had a Mexican wholesaler who would buy the car for $10,000 even though it was not worth that much, and we would, in turn, give him a lot of business for his body shop. The com-pany would write off $7,000 as a loss, and I would be charged $4,500 to the tune of $450 for 10 months. To help me cover my portion, Mike gave me a raise of $500 a month on my pay plan—that along with more responsibility to justify it. I would have to oversee the Honda lots down the street to keep them clean and make them more profitable. This was just in case the comptroller and Mr. Poe were wondering why I wrecked a car and got a raise.

Business went on as usual for a while, with me still looking desperately for someone who could help me with my arm. I went to numerous doctors, orthopedics and chiropractors until I went through the $6,000 allowed by the company on my accidental disability insurance. It would be almost two years until I found someone who could help me with my nerve damage.

One day I walked by Mike's office and saw him packing stuff in boxes as though he was leaving. He said that Mr. Poe had a fit when he found out Mike had written off the $7,000. Mr. Poe thought I should have paid for the whole amount. Mike told me, "If he felt that way, he should have told you so that day when you came in and apologized for the accident, and said you would do anything you could to make it right."

Mike went on to say, "Mr. Poe said that he was leaving it up to me, and that's what I decided. He was the one who put me in the position to decide the financial outcome of the accident." He said, "I'm not going to let him come in after the fact and say he doesn't like the decision I made, so I'll just resign."

I said, "Mike, you can't do that for me. I'm not worth it. Just go ahead and fire me or charge me the whole amount."

He said, "This is a matter of principle, that I am in the position to decide company policy, and I made a decision. This is not about you. It's between me and Mr. Poe."

They must have patched things up because they were pretty much back to normal, except that every time a representative for Chrysler came to see Mike, the rep would suggest that he fire me. I had cost the company a lot of money with the city property I had destroyed, such as the fence and telephone pole I wrecked. Mike suggested a couple of times that I might need to buy my own car and insurance to protect the company. I assured him, just as I told my wife, that I would never drink again, and if I was ever to be in a wreck again, it would not be my fault. That was good enough for him. Somehow as time went on, I got better and better at my job, and our used-car lot was more profitable than ever.

The result of this success meant several trips to Las Vegas as a reward.

These trips also included our wives, of course. Mike was such a high roller that he had his own account at Cesar's Palace and they would even fly us there in a private jet. We were wined and dined with the best that Cesar's Palace had to offer and that included the shows. While I did gamble a little, I was never tempted to drink again. Knowing what it had done to me, I couldn't even stand the smell of it anymore.

A funny thing happened to me on the way to my sobriety. I had been allowed into a diversion plan to dismiss the DWI from my record. This included many hours of classroom on how not to be a drunk. I guess they call it community service now. I was shown films and given testimonials by people who drank and had recovered from alcoholism. I had discovered a very important fact, and that was that I was an alcoholic. I had never known what made a person an alcoholic. I had heard all the myths: if you drink before noon or if you only drink hard liquor, or if you can't go a day without it, etc. I realized that all these were myths and excuses made up by alcoholics. The real truth was the control factor; it a physiological effect. For example, you suddenly realize you are in a field of mud soaked with rain as I had been and wondered how you got there, or found yourself going the wrong way out of town, or driving in the wrong direction as I did—these were all control issues; the failure to be in control of one's faculties. The average person who can calmly call a cab or have someone else drive is probably not an alcoholic. The lack of control is what they used to call "being a black out drunk." That's when people ask, "Did I do anything dumb or did I say anything dumb at the party?" This was a very pragmatic approach for me, and I'm nothing if not an intelligent person. Had I known these things before, or had I taken these classes before, I never would have drunk and been in this situation. It turns out October 2, 1990 was the last day I ever touched alcohol.

CHAPTER 12
THE ROAD TO RECOVERY

The road to recovery was hardly a straight one. As I mentioned, I looked around for two years before I found a doctor who could help me with my nerve damage. It was after I saw my third orthopedic surgeon, and he had the decency to refer me to a real neurologist. His name was Dr. Monsivais. I did some research on him and discovered he had been a war combat surgeon in the first Gulf War and had acquired fame for reattaching limbs that had been blown off by explosions. Not only had he reattached the limbs but they were full functioning, complete with nerves, tendons and all. There was a lengthy news article about how he had reattached a boy's leg. The boy had been run over by a drunk driver and lost his leg. The good doctor not only reattached the leg but the boy was able to play sports again following his recovery. I made an appointment to see him and was shocked when he told me he could help me.

He explained to me how he would perform the surgery. He was going to transfer a nerve from my left leg to what they call my upper right trunk, the place between my right shoulder and neck. I looked at him as if he was explaining some revolutionary experimental process, and I asked, "Have you ever done this before?" He said, "Only about 50 or 60 times not including laboratory animals." We set a date for the surgery and I was confident that I would get the desired results.

In the meantime the new car department at the Dealership had suffered the loss of another new car manager and a new one would soon be hired. It was to be Bob, one of my own used-car salesman. He was bright, aggressive and very intelligent, but he was also nick named as one of the "winos" and that would, one day, become a factor. As I mentioned he was very aggressive and the new car department flourished because of it. He worked long hours and the new car salesmen really believed in him and his ability to make deals. Because of his experience in used cars, he felt that he knew the value of a used car, and he tried to maximize the value of the trade on every deal. This would translate into more profits for the new car department. This was fine with everybody because we all got paid on profits from new and used cars. Until this time most of the dealership's profits and sales had come from only the used-car department, and now we were making money on both ends, new and used. But this would come with a price: When you over value a trade-in, you immediately lose profits on the used-car side because you have to allow for reconditioning costs, expenses and the most important thing, time.

The longer a used car sits in inventory, the less value it has since a used car depreciates in value monthly. When Mike the general manager, and Dan the general sales manager, were glowing about Bob their "New Fair Haired Boy," and all the profits he was making for new cars, I cautioned them about the potential problems I was seeing on the horizon for the used-car department. However, they cashed their checks and said, "Oh, don't worry! It will all work out." But as the next three or four months came around, I saw our overaged list on used cars growing and these represented little or no profit and even potential losses for the company. This was partly brought about because Bob was appraising many of the trades himself when I wasn't there. The new car salesmen were waiting for me to go to lunch or to be off early so that Bob could appraise a majority of their trade-ins. Meanwhile, the time for my surgery was fast approaching and I dreaded being off for any length of time, for fear of what Bob would do to my used-car inventory.

The day of the surgery approached and it took twelve hours of intense micro surgery. The doctor cut a jagged line from my knee to my ankle to remove the nerve and transplant it in my upper right trunk from the neck to the shoulder. Much like you would slice an electrical wire to make the current pass. I was even given an epidural to help me endure the pain like woman receive when they are having a child because of the length of the surgery. With that and the morphine they gave me post-surgery, I was feeling a totally nice buzz that I hadn't felt for a while, like I did when I drank. In the recovery room I remember being surrounded by my wife and our immediate family members while the doctor was trying to explain the surgical process to them. I woke up and immediately told a few jokes feeling no pain, but I was very weak and ready for more rest. The only question I had was for the doctor. I asked him, "Doctor, did you meet my wife?"

When he replied "Yes," I asked, "Isn't she pretty?" I began to pass out, but before I did, I remember the whole room saying, "AWWW!"

And the doctor said, "Yes, and you're very lucky."

The next morning I woke in ICU and I felt trapped in my bed. The rails were up to keep me from getting out and I had to go to the bathroom bad. I buzzed for the nurse and a Filipino woman brought me a bottle and a bed pan, depending on which one I would need. I began telling her, "I don't think you understood me, I need to GO to the bathroom."

She said, "This is what you get. You are in ICU and cannot be out of your bed at all."

I waited for her to leave the room and then I started to climb over the rail. This was tedious and exhausting but I did it. I was so proud of my accomplishment—like I had somehow beaten the system, dragging my IV and all the attachments with me. Afterward I was exhausted and didn't attempt to get back in bed but merely sat in the chair next to the bed. When she came to check on me and saw that I was out of the bed, she asked how I did it. She said, "You are a strong one and very stubborn, but you must be feeling better." She brought me a TV and allowed me to sit in the chair for the rest of the day. I was told I could not receive a regular room until my doctor had seen me. He later released me from ICU after I had waited and waited until he finally arrived at eight o'clock that night. As much as I admired him, I balled him out for waiting so damn long to get to me.

I finally had a room that night to rest in but I woke up the next morning at five o'clock. I was bed ridden and tired of sleeping. I began to get ready as if I was leaving that day. I started getting dressed and the nurse came in and asked, "What are you doing?"

I said, "I plan on leaving as soon as the doctor sees me today." They all thought I was crazy but I was determined to leave that day. I was fully dressed and they even brought me coffee and a newspaper so I could look the part. Both my left leg and right shoulder were bandaged heavily but I covered them with my clothes.

When the doctor arrived I told him, "I want to go home."

He said, "If you're sure and if you can rest at home, I will release you. But I hope you don't plan on going to work anytime soon."

I said, "Probably not till the day after tomorrow at least." He recommended three to four days of bed rest at home, and I agreed to take two.

I wound up missing only a total of four days' work for a massive surgery that took over 12 hours and over $100,000 in cost. Because my wife worked for RJ Reynolds Tobacco, I was medically insured through her company and my expenses were minimal, maybe $2,000 total. This was mainly for miscellaneous expenses not covered by the insurance company.

After my two day's rest I went back to the Dealership and looked at all the trade-in vehicles that I had acquired while I was out and I was shocked. One of the secrets of the used-car industry is how to manipulate "the book value" of a car. Every car is to be looked at for far less than the book value because you have to allow for reconditioning and the perceived amount of time it can remain in your inventory. What Bob was doing was valuing all the cars at book value which included cars that should never be anywhere near book value such as an Audi or a Peugeot. There was an old saying amongst salesman, particularly when you go out for drinks, that when you see a woman, "She is at least a dime back of book value, even if she thinks she is a 10." She is really just a "four" who says "Yes" on the first date. In my single days, when I'd meet a girl at a club, and she did something she hadn't planned on doing, she would say, "I've never done this before, not on a first date." I would say, "This wasn't even a first date; I just met you in the club." On the subject of some women who over value themselves, I like to say, "I would like to buy them for what they are worth and sell them for what they think they are worth." The same could be said for our used-car inventory since much of it had been over valued at the time it was appraised.

I saw trouble on the horizon and I warned Mike and Dan about it. Much like our economy when faced with a crisis, it's because of overreaching and overspending, and it is unsustainable in any economy, and in a dealership.

I never plotted to get rid of Bob but I knew I wouldn't have to, that some things just take care of themselves. I heard Sean Connery say in a movie once, "If you sit by the river long enough, you will soon see the body of your enemy come floating down." Bob's sales in his new car department had started to drop dramatically and he began to drink heavily, just like he used to when he worked for me. One week he got drunk for four days straight and didn't show up for work. In fact the day he did finally show up, it was only as a passenger in a car with his wife coming to pick up his check. Mike went out to talk to him in the car and he came back in shaking his head saying, "He's still drunk."

Mike took over the new car department for the remainder of the year, and as the year ended we had our own "Come to Jesus meeting" regarding the used-car department and its current state. Mike armed himself with his ledgers and his books, and he and Dan approached me asking where I wanted to go to lunch. I suggested Smuggler's Inn, the place where I had first met my wife, and had my infamous fight. It was only fitting that if this was to be my "waterloo," that it should be there.

At lunch I ordered a big steak and was having a good time, no alcohol of course. I noticed Dan had hardly eaten. His stomach must have been turning flips because our used-car department was a reflection on him.

Mike began telling us how basically "fucked up" our used-car department was. I approached it pretty much the way I do everything with no fear. I calmly told them I had been warning them for months that Bob's actions were "way over the top" while he was trying to sell new cars. I didn't even notice that Mike had asked me the question, "Why should I keep you as used-car manager?" In fact, I had not even noticed much of what he had said at all. I was kicking back, enjoying my lunch and listening to a song playing in the background.

He finally asked me, "What you are thinking about now, big guy?"

I said, "I really like that song," and he and Dan turned all colors at the audacity of my statement.

Mike said, "Is that all you have to say for yourself?"

I said, "Listen, Mike, I've said all I've had to say for months. If this is to be my last meal on the company dime, I'm going to enjoy it and have dessert as well. My only comment is to ask who you think is going to get you out of this? Do you think you can find somebody who sells more cars than I do? Good luck with that. If we didn't know what it was like to be so successful, it would not hurt so badly when we are not."

I had been around Mike for years, and I knew that his whole objective was to make someone squirm and beg for their job, and I refused to do that. My health was better and my state of mind was better than I had been since the accident and I was confident that if I had to leave, I could make it somewhere else.

They waited patiently for me to finish my dessert, just like I said I would have it, and I kicked back and listened to the music playing in the back ground, and the rest of the meeting was pretty much silent. When we arrived back at the Dealership Mike left me in front of the used-car building. I said, "I only have one question. Should I pack my shit or go back to work?"

He said, "What do you think? Get back to work." My fearless attitude and confidence were the things that always attracted him, and he knew I could thrive in the business, so naturally he didn't want to part with that.

This was at the start of the year 1992 and in the coming months we not only survived but we thrived in the used-car department. I began gaining a reputation in town. I had one before but it was as a salesman, now as a used-car manager and head of the department, things were different. I even began receiving calls from other dealerships as to what it would take to hire me. These were more exploratory inquires such as a wholesale buyer letting me know that a dealer was asking about me. I didn't take these very serious since you get all types of crank calls in the car business. There was even a woman who began calling the Dealership talking to certain salesman wanting to engage in phone sex. One new car salesman had the bright idea to transfer her to me to see how I would handle her. Since I've never been shy or one to mince words, I let her have it and started telling her I was going to tie her upside down and spank her and do all these crazy things to her, and she was loving it. I put her on speaker phone and all the guys stood around and listened to her carrying on. She began calling and asking for me and always wanted to talk. One day she called and I was super busy and I didn't really have time for her. She began telling me, "I am so wet. Tell me why I'm wet?"

I said, "You just got out of the shower." I slammed the phone down and she never called back again.

I told that story later at dinner with a couple of friends of ours. When I got to the part where the woman asked, "Why am I wet?" my friend's wife Laura slammed her drink on the table and was not very happy. I didn't think about this very much since my wife knew about the story and wasn't bothered by it because she knew about life in the car business. This couple was married because of us. My wife had met the woman at a club in the restroom and brought her over to the table to meet Dave. They began dating and got married and they were married for over 30 years.

CHAPTER 13
TEMPTATION EYES

I mentioned before that I was a late bloomer, a shy kid in high school who didn't date. I didn't come out of my shell until I started to work at McDonalds after high school. The McDonalds I worked at was on Airway Boulevard and I took the bus to get there. The bus stopped a block away from Dick Poe Chrysler and I walked by the front of the Dealership every day on the way to work—the same dealership where I would work for a total of 10 years and manage for seven. You could call it poetic justice, I guess.

When I finally did start dating, I never thought of myself as the handsome, dashing type but I was never at a loss for female company. Even when I went to college, I was never afraid to approach the prettiest girl in the room. I was confident and I had even been told I was handsome but it had more to do with my study of human nature; my feeling is that the prettiest girls are not approached that often because guys are afraid of being shut down. Consequently, this leads to many gorgeous women being unaccompanied due to all the men around being cowards, as most men are. In college I met many women, including some at United Parcel Service where I used to work who were very attractive, and even though I didn't have the money to take them out, some would offer to take me out.

There was a very attractive young woman named Maria who worked in my area at UPS. At that time you had to arrive at work about an hour and a half early to find parking, and even then it was six to seven blocks away from the facility. This was the largest hub in the United States and it was located at 3000 East Washington Boulevard in Los Angeles. It seemed she liked my company so much that she would wait for me every day so that I could walk her to work. Even though countless guys waited for and wanted to accompany her, she would wait for me. We liked a lot of the same books and literature and she was bright and intelligent and had a good sense of values which I admired very much. One day I suggested we should get together on the weekend. It was a Saturday and we planned to go to the beach. She came from a very strict family and I could not pick her up at her house, so we were going to meet at our designated parking space for work and take my car from there.

On the Friday night before our date, we were talking on the phone and as we were speaking, I asked her where she was in her house, and she said in a bed in her room. I asked her, "Do you mean when we hang up, you are going to go to sleep?"

She said, "Yes. From here my head hits the pillow and I'm out till tomorrow morning."

The thought of her being in bed and the anticipation of seeing her in a bathing suit the next day got the best of me and I told her, If only I was your pillow."

She said, "You're crazy!" And we hung up and I wrote the following words:

YOUR PILLOW

"If only I were a pillow while nightly caressing your cheek,
I'd listen to your gentle whispers, I myself without a word to speak.
I'd be embarrassed of my attire with you in silk and lace,
And me in all simplicity, a plain old pillowcase.
With the daylight hours so dark and dreary,
I'd wait in constant despair until the time your return,
I'd feel your warm embrace and the tenderness of your hair.
Night after night as I watched you sleep
Though odd as it might seem,
I'd like to flee from that pillowcase and find you in a dream."

That's the poem I wrote for her. I made it as neat as I could and gave it to her the next day. This both flattered and confused her but we still had a great time. I can't remember when I spent a more enjoyable day with a girl and at no point did we become intimate or romantic, but I knew I had a gift of writing, especially poetry for women, and I'd use this for years to come. That was the only date we went on as the thought of getting serious with her scared me to death. I later invited her to the Junior Senior Banquet at our school, but I cancelled for fear of getting too attached to her. I shared this story later on with my wife and she said, "Oh, you should have gone with her."

I replied, "I would not have met you. I would have settled down with the girl and had three kids and never come back to Texas." I was always careful not to bare my soul. It was as if I knew my destiny lay elsewhere, somewhere else down the line.

All through my time in college, even though I dated attractive women, I made it a point to never become attached. It was as though something was driving me to stay available and keep my options open. The school I went to was Life Bible College, and many people jokingly called it "Life Bridal College" because so many people admittedly went there looking for a mate. I did understand the psychology of this and I felt bad for many of the girls. Imagine the pressure that must have been on them from their families saying, "You've been going there for two years and you still haven't found a husband!" Many of the females that I dated wound up with friends of mine, becoming serious and getting married. This was fine with me because that was not what I was looking for.

One in particular was named Gloria. When it was announced that she was engaged, I met her in the hall at school and I said, "Congratulations!" She glared at me and said, "Well, you quit calling me." I felt bad for the poor fiancé who probably felt like the runner up.

I don't know why but all through school it seemed as though every woman I dated wanted to marry me. I don't know what it is—maybe it's the towering 5'8" that I present or the charm that I possess that sneaks up on them. I am not bragging when I say almost every woman that I dated in college would have married me. My wife even jokes that in college she only dated "tall blonde guys," then she looks at me and says, "Look who I wound up with!"

I stated all that to state the obvious: When it came to attractive women, I could be tempted. Temptation came one day on a bright sunny afternoon when I was used-car manager. She stood about 5'7", part Spanish and part Filipino, thin with long shapely legs and a beautiful face. Her name was Kathy and she was about twenty years old and she was selling advertising for a local shopping guide. I invited her into my office to visit for a while as she explained her advertising campaign, I was mesmerized by her and I couldn't keep my eyes off her. My wife is also very attractive and I had her "glamour shots" on my desk. The woman complimented me on my wife and how attractive she was. Of course I was hypnotized by her and I was not even thinking about the words she was speaking. I asked how much the ad would cost and when she told me, I immediately ran to Mike. I said, "Mike, I need to advertise with this shopping company."

He said, "You're nuts. We aren't doing that."

I begged him and said, "Please. You've got to come meet her yourself." He came to my office and met her and allowed me to run the ad for a month on a trial basis.

The more I saw her, the more I wanted her, or at least I thought I did. I started caring more about my appearance and losing weight. It was at this time that karaoke became a big deal and I started singing to her as well. It would just be a matter of time until I would write her a poem. Things were not the same with my wife and me since the accident; it seemed to have driven a wedge between us and we were not as intimate anymore. It was a natural excuse for me to find attention wherever I could like most men do. I put myself out there by flirting with her but I had little faith that she would respond. I thought, what would she would want with a short, chubby used-car manager? But after I did the initial flirting, I could not get rid of her. She came around for lunch a couple of times a week. I never went out with her at night for fear of what might happen. She got to know some of my salesman and asked them about my schedule and when I was closing. Almost every night at eight o'clock when I closed, without fail she would show up and say, "What are you doing now?"

I would tell her, "I'm going home."

And she would say, "Don't go home to your wife. Go somewhere with me instead." She was beautiful and beguiling, just like the serpent in the Garden of Eden. I was flattered but determined not to have an affair even though I had initiated the involvement.

For some men it was easy, the whole idea of cheating. My friend Steve was one who seldom turned down an opportunity. We went to lunch one day and the hot looking hostess seemed very friendly and receptive to his flirting with her. She had mentioned that her family was from Durango, Mexico, where there were many ranches, and how she loved to go horseback riding. Steve said, "You must know how to mount really well."

I remember her response was, "Oh baby!" From there all he had to do was reel her in. She was getting off from work soon, so he paid the tab and decided to wait for her and I went on my own way. He told me later how he never even asked for it; he just assumed she wanted it. They went to the store in his car and he asked her what kind of wine she preferred. Then he drove straight to a hotel to get a room; he then had sex with her all afternoon, never once asking if it was okay. In sales this technique is called, "assuming the sale," in this case he was "assuming the pussy."

I only had one opportunity to ever prove this theory myself. It was shortly after I first started with Dick Poe Chrysler, I came out of a meeting and saw an attractive Asian woman waiting for her car by the service area. I walked by her and said hello as I stopped do get a cup of coffee from the machine. I introduced myself and she told me her name was "Dawn." She was very thin and petite, with fair skin and deep blue eyes. I would find out later that she was bi-racial and well educated.

It was in the early spring and very windy, I have stated before that when the wind is blowing hard in El Paso it can be very slow for business, and that was the case on this day. I came back to the service area after an hour or so, and we began an in-depth conversation, I saw that she was enjoying my company, and found me funny and charming. It was also very apparent that her car had serious problems and would be there for quite a while. As the noon hour approached she still did not have an estimate for her car, so I invited her to lunch with me.

I took her to a breakfast type of restaurant, which of course had a hotel attached to it, just in case I got lucky. As luck would have it, she was really attracted to me, we began to talk about sex and she told me she was very inexperienced at it, and had only done it a couple of times with her boyfriend. He was also a novice and apparently had caused her a lot of pain during their love making attempts.

Perhaps it was the topic of our conversation, but she began to get very nervous and said "You are married, what if someone sees us together?"

I asked if she would feel better if we found a more "private" setting. She said yes, so the next thing we knew we were by ourselves in a room. Whatever shyness she exhibited before was gone, she sat on my lap and we made out in earnest. I took off her top and began to fondle and kiss her breasts, but that was it. I touched her through her pants and she did the same with me, after about an hour I left her there. I had obtained a loaner car for her so she had her own transportation.

Later that evening she called me at work, she began to tell me how good I had made her feel, and that I had left her so wet, she was sure sex with me would not hurt her. I said thanks for the compliments and by now I had customers and was focused on selling a car and I had basically moved on. The next morning, when I walked by the service area I saw her. She waived me over and began showing me pictures from her vacation. They were of her and her sister in skimpy swim suits, very revealing indeed.

I said "Why are you showing me these now?"

She said "I want to go back to the hotel and get naked with you. I think you will make me feel good, and I even brought protection with me."

I said "Let me think about it and get back to you. Ok?"

Every part of me wanted to go do this right, except for my moral compass. It was one thing to go with her earlier when I knew nothing would happen, but now to premeditate it and knowingly go to bang her, I just couldn't do. I had not been married that long and loved my wife. I had proved my point while remaining faithful to her, oh well! No regrets!

One day my wife went out of town for business for one night and it just so happened that Kathy called me that afternoon to see if I could do something that night. We agreed to go to dinner and at dinner I explained to her that my wife was out of town and I was all alone. She pulled out all the stops and initiated "a full court press" to try and have me to do something I had not planned on doing. We went from making out in the car to finding ourselves at a hotel room. At the hotel she became nervous and started having second thoughts, and this initiated my own doubts. After half an hour we both went our separate ways.

I didn't hear much from her until a couple of years later when I moved to Houston. She found out where I worked from some of the other salesman that had worked with me in El Paso. She began calling and telling me she wanted to visit me, and that we should make up for lost time by having nonstop sex. By that time I had moved on with my life and was pretty much over her, even though I had initially written her a poem and flirted with her.

Realizing that I would not cooperate with her and put her up to come visit me, she did the next best thing that some women do: she decided to tell on me. One day when I was working late, she called my wife at home and told her the whole story, or at least her version of it. I didn't find this out till a month or so later when my wife found an opportune time to tell me.

Most women will excuse an affair as just being a physical attraction, but the thing they hate the most is if you get emotionally attached, like writing a poem or becoming romantically involved. I worked with a woman for many years whose husband was a truck driver and she said she didn't care what he did on the road, as long as he didn't catch a disease or fall in love.

At dinner one night my wife said, "I spoke to your friend Kathy from back home and I know the whole story about you and her." I almost choked on my food at the horror of this new found knowledge of hers. Yet I felt confident in knowing that I had not committed the ultimate act of betrayal.

I asked her, "So what did she say that we did?"

My wife said, "You wrote her a poem and you went to a hotel room with her."

I said, "That's right and nothing else happened and even though I was tempted, I didn't cheat."

My wife became emotional and said, "So why didn't you?"

I said, "Because I'm married and that means something to me, even though I acted like a fool."

She said, "But you could have done it."

I said, "I could even have done it 100 times. Every time she came to the Dealership when I was closing, she wanted me to go with her instead of going home." I said that I didn't want to be the guy twenty years later crying in his beer saying he lost the best thing he ever had, which was the case with most guys in my business.

I learned the hard way that when you flirt a little with someone, they might receive it and say "Yes" and create a world of trouble for you. I didn't keep many tabs on her over the years, mostly because she had planned on ruining my marriage, but I was sad to find out she had passed away as a result of injuries from a car accident.

CHAPTER 14
HEAD HUNTING

I had heard over the years about businesses involved in scouting talent and acquiring them for dealers but I had never encountered them. Then one day I met Al. Al had worked for a company previously called Pat Ryan and Associates. It was a nationwide company involved in training and hiring talented people in the automobile industry.

This came at a time when I felt somewhat unappreciated at the Dealership. I had paid back my portion from the wreck and had even hired an attorney to try and receive re-imbursement for the dealers' portion. My responsibilities had grown dramatically, yet I had only received a small raise to help buffer my portion of the payment for the accident. Every time I asked Mike for a raise, he went down a list of the things I needed to improve on. Mike was an amazing individual. When you were expounding on your attributes, he could change things around to a list of your faults, and he'd leave you walking away saying, "Boy, I must really suck at my job. I am lucky to have one." I'm glad I wasn't the only one because every manager who worked there felt the same way when they were asking for a raise.

Naturally I was very interested when Al began calling on me confidentially and asking me how happy I was at my present dealership. We spoke on the phone two or three times and finally agreed to meet for lunch. He even asked me to being some copies of our financial statements showing the profits of our used-car department. I didn't provide him with copies, but I was happy to show him the glowing numbers of our dealer's profits particularly the ones for used cars. These meetings were very "cloak and dagger" like CIA type. We met on the other side of town away from dealers in my area and this was not an overnight courtship. The process took a month and half total.

On about our third lunch meeting he explained to me that he was actually the general sales manager at Casa Ford. He had previously worked for Pat Ryan and Associates and that's why he was so familiar with their way of doing business. He was a tall Cuban fellow, intelligent and very articulate, and I had no reason to doubt him when he made me a job offer. He brought me copies of their financial statements and asked me how I could better their used-car department. I said I could dramatically improve it and bring them back to the status they enjoyed during the '80s when they were one of the best used-car departments in the state. He explained to me, and showed me the numbers, and said if I did what I thought I could, I would likely double my salary with the pay plan he had in mind. I told him I needed some time to think it over and I would get back with him.

I approached Mike and told him that I had an offer somewhere else but I would gladly stay if he gave me some incentive to my present day plan.

As I mentioned I had hired an attorney to possibly recover the money the Dealership had written off during my accident. This in itself was a brilliant plan, if I do say so myself. My sister worked for a law firm and they gave me the lowest lawyer on the totem pole and his name wasn't even on the letterhead. I explained to him what I was trying to do to retrieve the money back. I was going to sue my wife's insurance company for the liability portion. He asked what legal precedence I had for doing this. I explained that when she bought the insurance, they asked for my name and driver's license even though I was not on the policy. In my mind this was implying coverage—otherwise, why would they ask for my information? The attorney told me that he would work on a contingency basis, but if it didn't work, I would have to pay him $500. I told him that was fair but when he wrote the letter, he had better go after enough for his attorney's fees and not to come after me for more if I retrieve my money. He wrote the letter asking for the $7,000 that my company had written off, the $4,500 I had paid, plus his attorney's fees. I was determined to settle my accounts with Dick Poe before I ever left the company. I put off the job offer for at least a month, so that I could settle all my accounts with Dick Poe.

The attorney notified me immediately that the insurance company had sent its letter of rejection. I went to his office and stood over him and made him type exactly what I said. I couldn't believe what a numbskull of an attorney this man was. I explained to him that this was a case of liable and my name and reputation were at stake. I reminded him that because the insurance company had asked for my name and license number when my wife bought the coverage, that this was implied coverage. I told him to request the same amount of money and now interest would be compounded daily, and they had only ten days to respond to this letter.

I knew we had them by the throat when they responded back quickly and said they would repay me the $4,500 that I was personally out of pocket plus his attorney's fees. So I stood over him again and told him what to type and again request Dick Poe's money, and if they dragged it any farther, we would also include the damages that Chrysler had to pay for the city property.

During this process I told Mike what I was doing and he laughed at me and said, "I'll kiss your ass on the showroom floor if you ever get a dime."

About a week later my attorney told me they had responded and we would be receiving the full amount. The knucklehead even told me, "I should have asked for more in attorney's fees." I don't think he's practicing law anymore.

I went by Mike's office and made sure there were people around and said, "Pucker up, baby! I'm going to get our money." He couldn't believe it and was proud of what I had accomplished.

As the month went on, we went into more serious talks about the possibility of me leaving, and I told him again I'd be happy to stay if he gave me some kind of incentive as far as a raise. I hinted with him about the kind of money they were talking about paying me. He told me, "Richard, I'm going to tell you something you may not know: Not all the people in this industry will always tell you the truth. You have had the luxury of being in a place where people are always honest with you and above board with their dealings with you, and that's not always the case in this industry." Truer words were never spoken, but never the less, I gave my two weeks' notice. I was at the point in my career where I believed I was worth more than $100,000 a year and I was determined to prove it.

As much as I tried to keep it quiet, the word soon got around to some of the salesman that I was leaving. I had met again with Al from Casa Ford to reaffirm the new pay plan I would be receiving and felt confident that it would be worthwhile for me to make the move. Some of the salesman, particularly Efren, began bringing me customers as a challenge to see if I still had the ability to make deals. Fort Bliss Army base in El Paso often had soldiers from other countries, particularly from Iran training there. Iranian soldiers were notorious "tire kickers" and hardly ever bought anything. Every once in a blue moon you found one who was actually looking to buy a car.

This was the case that particular day and we had a super clean five-year-old Honda. We owned the car for $3,000 but the salesman didn't know what we owned the car for, so he brought the Iranian to me, and he offered $5,000 for the car. I took one look at the guy and thought, *Holy cow, did this guy just get off the banana boat or what?* I knew the guy didn't speak much English, but I knew there was an International language he would understand. At this time I was at the sales podium on the new car side, so I looked down on him and I told him, "This car is tight like pussy." At first he didn't know what I was saying and I thought, maybe he's never had any tight pussy, so I asked him, "Have you ever had any tight pussy?"

He said, "Yes," and I said, "That's what this car is." He immediately went up to $6,000. I leaned over again and asked him, "Do you like pussy, or do you like boys?"

He said, "Yes, I like it!"

I said, "Which one?"

Then he said, "$6,500."

I leaned over again and told him, "If you ever want to have tight pussy again in your life, you need to give me $7,000 for the car."

He agreed, and we made the deal. The story became legendary not only because an Iranian had paid a $4,000 profit on a car, but that I had used pussy to close the deal, even though I was not fully convinced that he didn't actually favor men.

A few days later the same salesman brought me another customer. This man was Hispanic but he wanted something nearly impossible; he wanted a small automatic pickup truck for under $200 a month payment. When he first brought the customer to me all he said was, "This man wants to buy this truck for a payment of under $200 a month."

I said, "Tell me, do you have 7, 8, or $9,000 to put down?"

The man responded and said he only had $1,500 to put down.

As I started calculating the numbers, I started singing, "To dream the impossible dream." As I was singing, the man said, "Okay, $220."

Then I sang, "To fight though your arms are so weary," and he said, "Okay, $240."

I kept on singing, and he said, "$250. That's my best offer."

We were actually getting close, but I wanted more profit for the company. I told the man I would need another $1,500 down, and he said he could get a $1,000 but he would need a couple of weeks. That was no problem because I told him I could take his check and hold it for two weeks. By the time he left, he had financed for a payment of $275 a month with a total of $2,500 down. The increase in down payment, as well as a higher monthly payment, represented more in profit and a higher commission for the salesman. After the deal was over Efren, my salesman, told me what we used to tell everyone else, "Boy am I going to miss you!"

It was at this time I also had to clean up all my old account receivables because as a manager, I could allow people to hold off on their down payments, or even payments for repairs on used-car purchases. Knowing that I was planning to leave, I had very few left.

One was for a young lady who purchased a car for her boyfriend from Mexico. She gave us a check for $5,000, and he was supposed to pay her the money, but he never did. The car was purchased in the woman's name and she had actually come in and picked up the title from the company not knowing the check was invalid.

Of course she gave the title to her boyfriend who immediately broke up with her and took the car and the title with him back to Mexico. Realizing this was now my dilemma, I began calling the young lady who not only didn't have the money but she didn't even have a job. I did some investigating and found out that her mother had a business in downtown El Paso. I called her mother at her business and I acted like a concerned citizen. I explained to her that I had passed by the comptroller's office and heard him explaining to two detectives about her daughter's situation and that she would soon be arrested for fraud and theft of the automobile.

I told her it was not my place to do anything about it but that I was just concerned that she would want to know. She said, "Sir, you have to help me. I can't let my daughter go to jail." I asked her if she had the money and she said she had half and she could give $2,500 now and the rest in a week.

I said, "Let me check with the office and see when they are going to arrest her and I will call you back." After speaking with Mike we devised a plan that we could hold her accountable for. We would redo all the paperwork putting the car in her name, which was the only way to hold her liable for the balance.

I called her back and explained to her that we would be putting the car in her name and she said, "What car?"

I said, "The car your daughter helped her boyfriend steal."

When she agreed, we redid the paperwork and I had a salesman go to her house and pick up both checks, one good now and one good in a week. Mike was amazed how I was able to solve the problem and retrieve the $5,000.

The last case on my ledger would be the most difficult. I had actually been chasing this guy for months. I called him morning, noon and night. When I was home on the weekends or at a restaurant and I had his number with me, I called him. When I woke up at six in the morning to get ready for work, I called him. This went on for about three months. I was determined to clear the account before I left. He owed $3,200 and this was not even my problem but I had inherited it. His name was Louie and he had owned a failing used-car lot on Alameda. A customer had traded in a car that had a balance on it of $3,200 to release the lien on the title. At this time he closed his car lot, so he took the $3,200 and ran, never even giving us the title to the car. Consequently the dealership was forced to rescind the transaction to the customer who had traded the car in, but we were still out the $3,200 we had paid to the dealer.

I had even complained to Mike asking, "How is this my problem? This man closed his lot and I had nothing to do with it." Mike explained to me that if it had anything to do with a used car, it became my problem. Not only that but Mike had a unique way of management style which was if you answer the phone, it became your problem. When I first became a manager things would pop up and I would say that's not my job, or that's not my problem, and he would explain to me that if I answered the phone or fielded the complaint, it became my problem.

I knew there was no getting out of this deal until I got the money. One day just about a week before I was scheduled to leave, as I was coming back from lunch, I saw Mike running across the parking lot toward me. He said, "You know this guy Louie that you've been bugging for that $3,200 he owes us? He came and paid right now while you were at lunch, in cash! He came and laid the money on my desk in my office and said, "Now tell that motherfucker to quit calling me!"'

Mike was not in awe of many things and it took a lot to impress him. But this impressed him because we had nothing over on this man. We had no promissory note or even a returned check—it was just me hounding the shit out of him. I later found out that this man had a terrible demise. He had become involved with the Mexican Mafia and he had been tortured and killed.

The time soon approached when I would be having my final meeting at Dick Poe Chrysler and Mike decided to give me a "roast." He talked about everything, my success as a salesman, and my many fights on the way to becoming a manager. He went over the success I had as a manager, and the dramatic profits that I had brought to the company. He spoke about my accident and even having the insurance company repay the Dealership, and that it had cost them $0 to back me up. He spoke of many of my success stories, and even talked about the little girlfriend that I had. I felt so sentimental about the meeting that I almost didn't want to leave, and somehow I knew my life would never be the same.

CHAPTER 15
A NEW BEGINNING

It was January of 1993 when I started at Casa Ford. I was to be the complete used car director over the location on Montana Avenue and also oversee the bargain lot on Paisano. I had little to do with the consignment lot which was run by the dealer's idiot son-in-law. I worked directly under Al, who was the general sales manager, and Clay, who was the general manager and the dealer's son. Their system was made up of four team leaders instead of a traditional new-car manager like I was used to. These "team leaders" had six to seven salesman under each one of them and were responsible for their salesman's production. My responsibilities were mainly to control the used-car inventory and make sure that the cars we owned where in a position where we could be profitable. The total dealership's profit for used cars up to that point had been about $75,000 to $80,000 a month. This was pathetic and about half of the number I was used to. I made an immediate difference and we started making dramatic profit on our used-car sales. I had also established myself with a reputation as a "deal closer" and many of the salesmen knew this. They could not wait to get me involved in their deals because they knew I would maximize the profit and help them make the sale.

This immediately rubbed the team leaders the wrong way because I was stealing their thunder and because they thought they should be the "closers" for their team. But as it had been in most cases, talentwise, they didn't make a freckle on my ass. They would even try to trap me by claiming that I was appraising the cars too low in order to maximize the used-car profit. And this was the profit they got paid on so I didn't understand their point. Nevertheless, they had me talk to a customer about their trade-in, even if they were buying a new car. They would say to the customer, "It's just to explain the low evaluation on your trade-in." Consequently, I wound up closing the sale because the trade was actually incidental to the real issue which might have been the payment or the interest rate. By getting involved I got to the heart of the matter and closed the sale. I didn't realize this at the time but the "team leaders" had formed a constant "conga line" outside Al's office complaining about me. They were constantly bringing me situations that were seemingly impossible, and somehow I would make it possible.

One situation was on a busy Saturday. A man had bought a used van about a year before and it was sitting in the service department with a blown engine. The man was upset and making a scene on the showroom floor. Al came to me and explained the situation and that it really wasn't my problem because he had bought the van a year before. But having worked with Mike I knew that everything involving the sale of a used car was my problem, so I immediately took over the situation.

The van was several years old and it was a conversion van which was still in excellent shape except for the engine. The man had paid $10,000 for it and I knew that I could get at least $3,000 for it at wholesale value, even with a blown engine. The dealership had some new vans that were over a year old in the inventory and they carried a $4,000 incentive so I asked the man what if I could give him the $10,000 that he had paid for the van which included incentives, discounts, and the whole sale value of his van. The man was ecstatic and looked at me like I was Santa Claus delivering his Christmas presents. Not only had I solved the problem, but I had sold a van that was over a year old and had actually made a profit off of it.

When Al asked me how I made the deals I made, I always explained to him the course that I had taken and he was constantly amazed. At the end of my first month my gross pay was over $13,000 and the used-car profits had been close to $145,000—nearly double what they had been prior, and I was very pleased. Over all Al and the general manager were very pleased with my efforts but there was something sinister churning in the waters.

I was unaware of it when I started there but Al had a propensity for the devious side of people, for example two of his favorite books were "Management skills of Attila the Hun" and "Things they didn't teach you at Harvard Business School." His managers, or in this case "team leaders" prided themselves in stabbing each other in the back and gossiping about each other. One of them seemed to be a decent guy. His name was Alfred. He was the only Hispanic in the bunch and I got along with him pretty well. We went to lunch every once in a while and one time I told him about the movie *Scent of a Woman*, which had recently come out at this time. The overall situation at Casa Ford reminded me of what Al Pacino said in the movie, "You're building a rat ship here, a vessel of seagoing snitches," which is what I felt was going on at the Dealership. Words or gossip never bothered me because I had long since grown a hard turtle shell but it was the culmination of these things as they got to Al and the general manager which made them think and start to doubt me.

I did my job and used-car profits were better than they had been in years so no one could really say anything about me; however, I did my job so effortlessly that I think they started to think anybody could do it. The team leaders were "desking" most of the deals, that is conducting or handling the business mechanics of the transactions—not the sales action and they began to feel responsible for the profits instead of me. The way I managed the department was what enabled them to make a profit. Anybody who knows the business will tell you that having a good, clean inventory is the best guarantee of profitability. Whenever possible they would "throw me under the bus," so to speak, and give me an impossible situation to try to go close a sale for them.

But nine out of ten times I would close the deal and this really pissed them off. I became a hero to the salesmen because instead of having to split the commission with another salesman, I would close their customers for free and maximize the profit as well. One of the team leaders was a guy named Ken, a black guy. He was the biggest ass kisser to Al and became the biggest threat to me. He would actually become visibly angry when he sent me to talk to one of his customers and I closed the deal. He would smile and try to act like it didn't bother him, but it reminded me of that song, "The Backstabber": "They smile in your face all the time, trying to take your place, those backstabbers."

I thought I knew how to compete on any level but I found it hard to compete with that. I was brought in to improve on the situation and I had done that, in spite of all the occurrence of negativity.

Mike called to see if I was happy with my move. He sensed my frustration and decided he would try to cheer me up. And one day he invited me to lunch with him and Joe, who was one of the older salesmen from Dick Poe and was one of the funniest guys I had ever known.

Naturally Joe started talking about Blanca, the girl from the back office that he always made fun of. He said I walked by Blanca's desk the other day and said, "Hey I sure wish I had a little pussy," and she said, "Me too." Then he told about her going out with one of her cop boyfriends for lunch, and as the story went, the cop had made a bet with all the buddies at the station saying that he would nail her during lunch. The cops at the station asked how he could prove it and he said, "I'll leave the police radio on so you can hear what is being said and done in the car."

He figured he would actually have something to eat before the "nookie break" so he brought a couple of sandwiches with him. It was lunch time and he drove her to a secluded park and they started to eat their sandwiches. When he started eating his sandwich, it accidentally fell on the floor. He picked it up, dusted it off and started to bite into it when Blanca said, "You're not going to eat that dirty thing are you?"

The cop said, "Sandwich. Please say 'sandwich.'" Then Joe said, no kidding, that Blanca's boyfriend told her he wanted to fill her pussy with ice cream and eat it all up. He said she actually became depressed and when he asked what was wrong, she replied, "Nobody can eat that much ice cream!"

They succeeded in cheering me up but I still had problems when I got back—I still had to work at the Dealership. After our lunch Mike called me and told me he wanted me to apply to be the general sales manager of Dick Poe because Dan had left to go to another dealership. I said, "Mike, I appreciate it but is it going to include a pay plan? You know I'm making really good money here." Mike said it would be more than I was making before at Dick Poe, but not as much as I was making now. I thanked him for the offer, and told him I would think about it. I had been offered a second chance at redemption but I was on target to hit $100 thousand that year and I felt that was what I was worth, and I didn't want to go backward.

One day Alfred and I were talking and we decided to go out to dinner with our wives on a Saturday night. We made reservations at the Dome Grill at the Westin downtown. Somehow Al the sales manager got wind of it and figured out a way to invite himself. Our four-some became a six-some and it was very uncomfortable with Al and his "milk toast" wife. She was very pale, Al was Cuban while the rest of us were Hispanic, and needless to say, she stood out in a crowd. I have nothing against white people, but in my vast experience as a Latino, I think a Latino man who marries a white woman is seeking acceptance, from the "white" world. Therefore, it is not uncommon that most of the time, they regret their selection. After dinner and drinks we wound up at the bar where the dancing became lively. My wife and I loved to dance and Alfred and his wife liked to dance as well. This left Al and his wife sitting there, just watching the action.

After a while Al started dancing with my wife, and if I didn't know any better, I would say he was hitting on her. My wife is very attractive and very friendly, but she knows how to keep people in their place, and somehow she let Al know that this was just a friendly gesture and there was nothing else implied, it was just dancing. Alfred told me later, while back at work, that he walked into my office several times only to catch Al staring at the pictures of my wife.

After that evening and during the next week I seemed to sense more tension with Al. He started to "write me up" for different things as a reprimand. I thought this was comical because I had written up salesmen from time to time for not doing their job, but I was doing my job and we were making a ton of money in used cars. I all but laughed in his face when he told me I was not to change the appraisal value or increase it so we could make the deal. I said, "I don't understand. You'd rather walk the customer, then have me make a deal by putting more money in the car?"

I tried to explain to him in abstract terms that the value of a car is subjective, and therefore subject to change just as someone changes opinion, and opinions are like assholes, everybody has one.

I looked at a car for what it would retail for, what I knew in my mind I could own it for. And on that basis, I could increase the value of the appraisal.

I explained to him that this was a creation in my mind because I knew the used-car market, and I could, therefore, adjust the appraisal on the fly.

And because of all this that I was explaining to him, what he was asking me to do was ridiculous, and I was not going to do it. To change the way I was doing business would be to deny everything I knew about the car business and it wasn't the kind of business where you could "take a measuring cup and follow a recipe." The car business involved imagination and creativity.

When I had finished, he looked at me and said, "Who are you, David Koresh?" Koresh, of course, claiming to be a prophet, had made news at that time as the former leader of the "Branch Davidians."

I said, "I guess when it comes to used cars I am, because you have to have imagination and creativity to create the kind of profits I have."

After six months of getting paid handsomely for my job and my efforts, I was about to have a rude awakening: Al was going to change my pay plan and my income would go from $13,000/ $14,000 a month to $6,000/$7,000 if I was lucky. I explained that there was little justification for this because our profits were better than ever. He said that his managers were generating the profits and I had little to do with it except for managing the inventory.

Anybody in the business will tell you that managing the inventory is everything, and it's what puts you in the position to make a profit. This bastard had recruited me and moved me from a dealer where I had spent almost ten years, only to pull the rug out from under me. There was no changing his mind because, little did I know, his managers had been sneaking into the back office to find out just how much I was making. The theme of the sinking rat ship continued.

I had to sign this new pay plan, otherwise I wouldn't get paid at all. Fortunately, the month of July we had a contest where we had teams and I was placed with Alfred and another manager against the other two managers and the finance director. The winning team would gain about a $4,500 bonus so I still managed to squeak out $11,000 for that month. Had it not been for the pay cut, I would have made easily about $16,000.

I could see the writing on the wall. Once a month we were given a 3-day weekend off so I decided to use my time to look for a better position in the industry. My wife and I had visited our friend in Houston several times and I loved the layout of the city. I longed for the challenge of a big city arena to display my talent. I began buying the Houston newspaper and looking through it when I was off. It was filled with huge dealerships spending millions of dollars on advertising. I began compiling a list of prospective dealers to talk to and calling and inquiring as to who was their general manager. Whenever I had off time, I made phone calls to the general managers to set up interviews during my next 3-day weekend off. I always figured I could sell cars anywhere and my wife, bless her heart, was willing to relocate as well with her company RJ Reynolds.

I had two strong leads for my next three-day weekend, one was with Charlie Thomas Motors and a man named Mr. Rose, and the other was with Interstate Ford and a man who went by the first name Ray. The time came for our 3-day weekend and we flew out early that Friday morning. I was scheduled to meet with Ray from Interstate Ford that afternoon. We didn't know the area so well, and this was at a time before GPS, so we got lost several times and I was late for my interview. It was supposed to take place at "Steak and Ale" on I-45 North.

There was a terrible rain storm, and there were three "Steak and Ale's" on I-45. After going to the first two, I finally made it to the third one about an hour after lunch. My hair and suit were soaked and even though I was late, Ray and his other managers stayed to interview me. I could tell I impressed them but Ray wasn't prepared to make me an offer yet until he made a few phone calls. He was familiar with Pat Ryan and Associates, the company Al used to work for and in fact, he even knew Al. I asked him please not to talk to anyone at Pat Ryan because it could somehow get back to Al and he would know that I was looking for a job elsewhere. He said any inquires he made would be discreet and strictly confidential, yeah right! That was my Friday meeting.

Saturday went really well with my meeting with Mr. Rose for Charlie Thomas, and this dealership was on I-45 South. If you are familiar with Houston, this highway is humongous and this dealership is near Clear Lake on the way to Galveston. Mr. Rose took my wife and me out to eat lunch on Saturday at a high rise hotel overlooking Clear Lake. It had beautiful views. He not only offered me the job but he wanted me to start as early as September 1 as used-car manager. I told him that I would probably take the job, but I would let him know as far as a starting date, and he said that was fine, to just keep in touch.

This was about the middle of August and if it was possible, things became worse at the Casa Ford dealership. Al had started a promotion where we did silent auctions for used cars that were available for wholesale. These were supposed to be sealed bids. We would park our cars on a vacant lot. Prospective buyers would mark their bid and seal it in an envelope and place it on the car with the name of the dealer on it.

I thought this was the stupidest thing I had ever heard of, and I told Al so. When he asked why, I told him it's subjective just like I told him the appraisals are, and these guys would ideally want to buy it for one price, but they could be persuaded into another price. I explained to him if you took the highest bid at face value, you'd lose your ass on most of these cars.

He asked what I suggested he do and I suggested we take the high bid and start negotiating from there—that way we could maximize our profit or minimize the loss, depending on the situation. Even then, I was giving him sound advice and managing the situation while protecting the company's assets.

As the month of August came to an end so did my career at Casa Ford. Al who had sought me out and hired me for the position didn't even have the balls to terminate me. As it turned out, word got back to him from the dealer that was going to remain confidential that I had been looking for jobs in Houston. It was at the end of August when Clay, the general manager, called me in and said we would be parting company at that point. Along with my termination notice, he gave me a $6,000 severance check.

With that I had made $114,000 for the year and it was only September. Needless to say, I contacted Mr. Rose in Houston and told him I could start by the middle of September—that I just needed a couple of weeks to get my move planned and my house in order in El Paso.

We had a realtor friend who found a renter for our home. It was a godsend. They would be moving in as we were moving out. My wife found a moving company who would move our essentials and store our remaining belongings until we purchased our new home in Houston. Everything was happening extremely fast. Even though I was getting calls from other dealers in El Paso who wanted to employee me, I was frustrated here and longed for the big city atmosphere. I thought of myself like the explorers from the early days who wanted to go out and conquer the new world. I thought what else can I do? I could go work for some of the dealers in town who were being run by salesmen that used to work for me—and they weren't even very good. Or go back to Mike with my tail between my legs and wait for a manager's job to open. Mike actually came to the house to visit with me before the move to make sure that was what I really wanted to do.

I wanted to go somewhere new. To become a big fish in a big pond, to make a name for myself where nobody knew me, and I was convinced that I could do it. I had the faith and conviction that somehow it would all work out. Call it blind faith or being naive, either way we were set to move and there would be no turning back.

CHAPTER 16
THE BIG CITY MOVE

When the day came for our move, the movers came and cleared out our house and we spent our last night there with blankets on the floor and our three cats. The house was empty and void of furniture and all at once I was filled with fear and anxiety. We drove my wife's car to Houston with our luggage in the trunk and our cats moving around freely throughout the car. We had never traveled with our animals before and obviously, we didn't know about pet carriers. Our world was going to change completely but we were still young and excited about the possibilities. After the long drive to Houston my wife found a rental agency that would help us find a suitable apartment in Clear Lake near the dealership I where I would be working.

We were going from a 3,400 square foot home sitting on an acre lot in the country to a two bedroom apartment in the city. As I settled in at work, my wife began consulting a real estate agent for a house to purchase.

The apartment sat on a nice piece of property, but unfortunately we rented a space up front and close to the street. The street was El Dorado Boulevard and I'll never forget it because at 5:00 every morning, we could hear the traffic rolling down the street. So with me being a night owl and going to bed about 1:00 in the morning, I was averaging four to five hours of sleep a night which added to my anxiety plus the cats were also nervous and could not sleep. They walked around "meowing" at night because they had lost their acre of land to roam on.

During this time my wife found a property she wanted to buy and we made an offer on it. We had wanted a corner lot but they were hard to find so we got the next best thing. We found a home in a nice quiet neighborhood in Clear Lake that was at the end of the block and next to a large community walking trail and park. We would only have one neighbor and plenty of room for our cats to roam.

Within a couple of weeks, my wife got word from her mother that her father had a heart attack. She was not working yet although she was scheduled to start soon with RJ Reynolds in the Houston area so I sent her home to be with her folks.

My life was filled with stress. I had the new job that wasn't going so well, the move, the two bedroom apartment and no wife to come home to. We also had the home we were going to purchase that we would be closing on soon.

I found out that Mr. Rose, the man who hired me, was on his last leg with the Dealership and he had hired me to provide a big splash to help him keep his job. This was not good news because I was caught like a deer in the headlights: a "small town" guy in his first month in a big city. Mr. Rose was constantly talking to me asking me what we could do to improve our business. He would say, "I hired you because you were a creative bright idea man, so let's see those ideas."

He was so desperate to improve on his own situation that he was putting more pressure on me, as if I didn't have enough. When I was off work and I had time on my hands, I thought about my predicament. I had everything I wanted. I had big city life and anonymity where nobody knew me, and I had the chance to create a reputation and make a name for myself. I also appreciated how lucky I was to have such a supporting wife who was willing to go across country with me and allow me to follow my dreams.

I guess I missed her, so I decided to write her a poem, one of many.

TO MY WIFE

"My life's foremost accomplishment, my greatest feat to date,
was meeting you and winning you and choosing you for my mate.
Some men dream of great wealth and power, any measure of success,
all with the hope that somehow this may lead to their happiness.
But I found in you the ultimate power
and I'm blessed with a wealth beyond measure,
for I found in you my love's lone ambition,
and my heart's unlimited treasure."

I have probably written my wife one hundred poems and sung her at least a one hundred songs and out of all the women I ever dated, she has been the least impressed. I asked her once why my poems and songs didn't send her to the moon and make her swoon, cry and melt in my arms like every other woman. She said, "Because it's part of who you are. You are the salesman trying to close the deal."

My wife's dad recovered and she was soon back with me in Houston. What didn't get better was the situation at work and at the end of a month Mr. Rose, myself and everyone associated with him were terminated.

We were set to close on our purchased home in two weeks and I was now out of a job. I wasn't worried about a job because in the car business, it's not a job—it's just an opportunity. I always said the lot boys and porters have a job. In sales we just have the opportunity to make money.

The one good thing that Al had done at Casa Ford was provide me with lists of the top used-car dealers in the state. I had a list compiled for the whole year and the two top used-car dealers were in Houston. They were Lone Star Ford and Landmark Chevrolet. Both of them were on I-45 North. This was clear across town because I lived off I-45 South. I decided to interview at both places and see which one I liked best.

One day I set out to do my interviews with my briefcase, my resumes and my entire manager's experience in tow. I was hoping to obtain a management position but I knew it probably wouldn't happen. I went to the Ford dealer first and I was told what almost every dealer had said to me before: They wanted to see me in action as a salesman first before they would even consider me as management material. Apparently there were a lot of smooth-talkers going around trying to get manager positions, but by now I was perfectly content to be a salesman and not have all the pressure and headaches that go along with being manager.

What I didn't like about the Ford Dealership was that all the bonuses were tied to selling at least three to five new cars a month. I detest new cars and I've always said the best thing about a new car is that it becomes a used car as soon as you put the plates on it. A used car is unique. There is not another car like it. The mileage and wear and tear make each one individual.

After they agreed to hire me at the Ford dealer, I said I would consider it, and I went off to interview at Landmark Chevrolet. These dealerships were huge. Landmark Chevrolet alone covered almost two block exits on the interstate, and the used-car department was bigger than the whole dealership of Dick Poe where I used to work.

The thing I liked most about Landmark was the advertising. You could pick up the newspaper on any given day and see over a 100 advertisements, and that was just one source. They also had TV, radio, mailers and flyers. They were constantly inundating the public with their advertising. I walked into the used-car building and asked who was in charge. I was introduced to an Iranian man named Jay. I had never meet an Iranian man on that side of the table. Usually they were the customers, not the head guy in charge. Landmark Chevrolet was the Number One Chevrolet dealer in the country. They sold between 500 and 600 used cars a month. I was speaking to the man who turned the wheel for that production and he liked me. I told him that I was deciding between him and Lone Star Ford.

Now, I had been a "T.O. Man" in the business—that is the closer, the one who goes in and closes the deal when someone else can't. And a T.O. Man was about to do it to me!

I leaned over and shook Jay's hand and told him I was going to consider his offer. I stood up and was starting to leave when a young man named Marco (an assistant manager) suddenly appeared in the office to talk to me as Jay stepped out.

He started expounding on the merits of the company: the bonuses and the amount of customers they had, which by now, I could see for myself were many. Before I knew it, I was filling out the paperwork to work there. I explained to Jay that I hadn't owned a car for twelve years. He said I would need to buy one but that I could borrow one for now. He told me later that when they ran my license through a search, as was company policy, the office told him not to hire me because of my DWI, which had been dismissed but was still on record. He ignored them of course, and hired me in spite of their fears and doubts, and I was glad he did.

I was informed there would be meetings every day at nine o'clock and if I missed three in a month's time, I would not participate in any bonus plan. I lived clear across town and I had to give myself an hour and a half to get there because I still was not familiar with the city and the freeway system. My morning commute consisted of traveling up I-45 from the south to the north side, through downtown with all the traffic and proceeding on I-45 North near the Intercontinental Airport.

I was basically numb every day as I drove thinking about what the day's prospects would bring. All my life I had never been afraid, whether it be a fight or the sales business or even going to college in California. I had faced it all without fear but for the first time in my life, I felt fear. It was the fear of failure and the pressure that comes with it. Pressure does different things to different people and I had always used it as fuel to motivate me. I had given countless sales meetings to motivate the salesmen to do better and become better, and now I had to do it for myself.

Most of my commute I spent talking to myself trying to inspire myself to get off my ass and do what I had to do. I spoke earlier about the faith that it takes to do this business: faith in yourself and faith in this career you have chosen. And for me there was no turning back. I could not fail.

And even though hundreds of customers came in daily, it wasn't until the fifth day that I sold my first car. I didn't know it then but this was the ultimate bait and switch house: one car is advertised for bait but the plan is to sell the customer another car. Back in El Paso when the company advertised a car, there it was for all to see with the miles and color that was advertised and everything else it had but not here.

The sales desk at Landmark Chevrolet had four to five people answering the phones constantly, and when a new man was hired, such as me, they would try to help me by giving out my name. Some of those customers drove three hours to get there looking for the nice little car that was advertised; they were pissed when I didn't even know what car they were talking about. A guy once even wanted to kick my ass, as if I needed more aggravation. I remember a big cowboy pacing around the showroom waiting for me so he could tell me he drove two hours to get there and how frustrated he was looking all over the lot for the "mythical" car in the ad and he still hadn't seen it. I was actually with another customer at the time so I asked the manager Jay to let someone else help him, so naturally they did and they sold him something else, and every time he saw me, he would glare at me like I was an asshole.

It began to dawn on me that I was putting too much thought into this. I looked around the building and saw that the guys who were selling the most cars were the seemingly the dumbest ones. They just let the customers' complaints roll off like water on a duck's back and showed them something else. It reminded me of what my dad used to say: Sometimes to get ahead "You have to look dumb and act stupid." I have already told you his favorite joke about the Mexicans with big shoulders and flat foreheads—when the teacher asks a question, they shrug their shoulders to show they don't know and when they hear the answer, they slap their foreheads as if they should have known.

Before I sold my first car, I remember my wife and me praying every night that it would get better for me. She made sure I walked around with a couple of hundred dollars in my pocket as well as credit cards so that I could eat and buy what I needed during the day. But I didn't spend any money. Somehow I believed that by depriving myself, I would keep my fear up and work better. My clothes were hanging off me because I was losing weight but I was still determined to make it work.

My wife scolded me and reminded me that although we had $25,000 in our checking account, I was walking around eating peanuts from a machine. I told her, "I deprive myself because I want to feel good about what I am doing and I will not enjoy a meal or a lunch during the day until I do."

One day it was as if the light went on for me and I decided not to think things through on a deal. In El Paso they had rules about financing the car; it had to be less than five years old and have less than 80,000 miles on it in order to finance it. None of those rules applied here at Landmark because this dealer gave GMAC so much business that they would finance anything, even a ten-year-old car with 150,000 miles, as long as the customer was credit worthy. I had put too much thought into it because of my past manager's experience and I was abiding by a set of rules that didn't exist here.

The first vehicle I sold was an older Mazda pickup with over 130,000 miles. It had been in inventory for a long time and it carried a minimum $500 commission or 75 percent of the profit, whichever was greater. I would have been happy with just the $500 and I would have sold the car for no profit except Jay, who worked the deal with me, was intent on making a profit. Before I realized it, we had made a large profit and I had made a $2,500 commission.

I quickly made up for the four or five days I'd gone without selling a car. The best thing of all was I was learning the system and things weren't what they appeared to be. When I first started I remember their talk in the sales meeting about our full page advertisement. We had late model Toyota's for $9,995. As I researched, I found out that we owned them for $11,000. I would think to myself, *Why are these guys excited about selling a car for below cost?* The reason was, of course, because nobody sold one for that price—it was just to get the people in the door. This may be hard to swallow for the average consumer and will probably make people detest the average car salesman, but these were merely ploys to excite the customers and make them take action—then we could put them in the system and do our business. There is a saying that goes "When you have a man by the balls, his heart and mind will soon follow."

CHAPTER 17
LAND SHARK

This became a common term for Landmark Chevrolet around town because of their reputation from the bait and switch tactics. It took a while for their tactics to become second nature to me, but the less thought I put into it, the easier it got. It was a method of undressing the customer. By that I mean if a person intended on buying a car, we would immediately register them into the system, getting their full address and social security number. They either complied with this or wandered aimlessly around the used-car lot. At any given time we had between 50 and 60 used-car salesman. We had blacks, Native Americans, Spanish, cowboys and Middle Eastern (mostly Iranians) and we were well represented like our own UN of used-car sales. Among the better salesmen were Kelly, a tall, good-looking baseball player, Tommy a typical redneck, and Emerson who was a black preacher. He actually had his own congregation complete with a long line of drug dealers who were constantly buying cars. At that time I met my *Compadre* Norbert. He was "middle of the road" as far as sales went but he was a great guy who welcomed me into his office and helped me get my feet wet. Office space was critical because there were guys who had none and worked out of their briefcase. After talking to Norbert, I learned the right way to commute by using the 610 Freeway which cut my commute time down to 45 minutes or an hour, at the most.

The term "compadre" is often misunderstood, it is actually an affectionate term for two couples linked together by baptism. My wife and I became "compadres" with Norbert and his wife Blanca, when we agreed to baptize their daughter Lindsey, and we became her "God parents" as well.

Shortly after I started working at Landmark we signed the papers for our new house. I felt much better about my situation. I began to have success selling cars and some of the fear dissipated. I knew I would make it but I wanted to make it big. It may sound silly but when I was encouraging myself, I thought of the words of the song by BJ Thomas, "Rain drops keep falling on my head." In particular, I was inspired by the part where he says, "But there's one thing I know, the blues they sent to greet me won't defeat me. It won't be long till happiness steps up to greet me."

My buddy Norbert, for never being educated in the United States, was very creative. He actually learned how to forge check stubs for proof of income which was often required on car deals. He was very careful of who he did this for. He had a typewriter and skills like I'd never seen before. Forging documents is a very serious matter and on any given day, he made two of three hundred dollars on the side by providing salesmen with this service on their deals. Salesmen came to the office and pitched to him what they wanted done. He then said, "Okay. $100 up front." Then they said something like, "No, I'll pay you when I get paid," and he said, "Get the hell out of here! *Next!*"

They used to call Norbert "wrinkle free" because he was always freshly pressed, complete with tie and button-down collar. He had been the head waiter at a fine restaurant and he definitely looked the part.

As I became more comfortable at the Dealership, I started to let my personality show through. One day when I was parking a trade-in the back lot, I saw an old man out there looking through the land where we parked all the cash cars. He was looking for a specific car from our ad in the newspaper—of course it was one that didn't exist. He stopped me and asked for my help, so I started asking him questions like, "What are you looking for? What is the most you want to spend or could you possibly finance?"

He said listen, "I'm looking for this specific car right here."

I said, "If it's still available, it's probably around here, but most likely it's been sold because all our cash cars are right here."

He said, "What the hell do you know? You look like you should be washing them instead of selling them."

I said, "Look who's talking! You look like you just got out of the mental hospital with your wrinkled up shirt and pocket protector."

He screamed, "I'm going to report you! What's your name?"

I said, "Pancho, of course."

When I returned to the main building, I saw him complaining to Jay, *the used-car director*. I snuck by and tried to listen, but all he was saying was that

Pancho said he looked like he was from a mental hospital. Jay was screaming, "Who's Pancho?" By then all the salesmen near Jay's desk were laughing. Finally Jay said, "You probably did come out of the mental hospital," and he walked away. Somehow the salesmen all knew it was me.

On another occasion I was by the import lot. Our import area represented Nissan, Toyota and Honda. There was a large cowboy out there with his family. He had a newspaper and was looking for a specific import car that he had seen in the paper. He stopped me and said he was told the car he was looking for was there but he could not find it. I started to qualify him and asked him if he was going to pay cash or finance because I had better cars than that. He looked me in the eye, pointed his finger at me and said, "Look chief! I'm looking for this car."

I pointed my finger right back in his face and said, "I am not your fucking chief!"

His wife said, "Oh, he didn't mean it."

And I said, "Yes he did." I knew he was going to complain because there were only two kinds of people there: those who buy cars and those who complain. I knew he wasn't buying shit. He had probably just taken his family there to prove that the car didn't exist so he didn't have to spend any money.

I followed him inside as he went up the desk to complain to Jay. Before he could open his mouth, I shouted out to Jay and said, "Jay, this man called me Chief, and he will be lucky if I don't sue his ass for using racial slurs."

Jay stood up and immediately knew what I knew: that this guy wasn't buying anything, but rather, he was just there to complain. Jay shouted at him, "You called my salesman a 'chief'? Don't you realize you could get sued for that?" With Jay and me shouting at him, the man could barely get a word out, and he was quickly looking for the exit. Once again I had the whole room laughing at my antics.

There was a huge man we called "Hammer" who was responsible for billing and he would process twenty-five to thirty deals a day for used cars. He was a mountain of a man. He stood about 6'6" and easily weighed 400 lbs, and he loved me because I always had deals to bill.

At this Dealership there were scavengers, salesmen looking to weasel in and get half a deal by making some small contribution on a pending deal with Hammer. I never looked for such opportunities, but on occasion, when the

132

need arose and someone was on thin ice and close to being terminated, Hammer would have me correct small issues with a deal and give me half of the credit.

He would never let anyone climb on my deals. This was very significant, especially during "close out," which was the last day of the month when it was not uncommon to be at the Dealership until 3:00 in the morning. The close out was not only to include that day's sales, but also any deals that were pending and needed a final touch before going to the back office.

One time a big red neck did a slight adjustment on one of my deals at about four in the morning during "close out," and he was going to get half of an $800 commission. I immediately sought Hammer out the next day and had him sign a form that would reverse that transaction. When the salesman went and complained to Hammer, not only did he blow him out, he fired him on the spot for trying such a stunt with me. Needless to say, I had a great relationship with Hammer and he was a good guy to have in your corner.

One day while I was sitting in my office completing some paperwork, a woman walked by and poked her head in my door and she asked me if I could help her find a cash car for three or four thousand. I stood up and pointed at the direction where those cars were and I even offered her a pen and paper so she could write down the ones she liked. She started to walk away but then she came back and I noticed she was stacked, I mean she was built. She was wearing short shorts and a super tight blouse with no bra. It seemed she was trying to hide her bulging breasts so I thought, *well I'll give her like five minutes of my time and walk out there with her*. I figured she might buy something and she wasn't terrible to look at.

As we walked outside she pointed to this tall Hispanic man walking around with his little girl. She pointed at him again and said, "You see that big retard out there? That's my husband." She said, "He hasn't touched me in six months, I mean look at me." I took a good look at her and she said she was about to leave him and was looking for a car for her and her little girl to get around in after she left him.

I suggested a little Mazda for her. It was a clean car and we owned it very cheap. It was a stick shift and I asked her if she knew how to drive one. She said she used to and could learn it again. I drove first and I drove to a park in a little secluded area so she could try to drive it. Instead of switching places so she could try to drive the car, she lifted up her top to show me her breasts.

I said, "Very nice but do you want to drive the car?" Then she started grabbing me and touching me and said that she needed some action. Well, I immediately thought this was a big waste of my time. I said, "Do you want to buy the car or not?"

She said, "Yes, I'm going to take it. Let's go back to the dealership." We went to my office and I filled out the paperwork selling her the car for $3,495.00 and she turned to her husband and said, "Go ahead and pay him."

The big dummy, her husband, said, "I didn't bring the money." She yelled at him and called him names and told him to go get the money and take his daughter with him so she could stay there by herself.

As we waited the sun began to go down, and whenever we walked outside, I kept thinking *good thing there are no cameras around here.* She used the occasion to grab me or put her chest on me but I had a plan: I wanted her to save all that emotion she had built up for "a special friend of mine," and I would get Hammer to do her paperwork. When the husband came back with the money, I told her she would have to wait in line for my friend Hammer, who sometimes signed people up on their contracts, as was the case on that day. As he was preparing to take her in to sign the paperwork, I described her to him, and I told him he better close the blinds of his office before she came in. Then I told her this was a special friend of mine and that it was his birthday. I told her that Hammer ran the whole store and she was supposed to give him a present, a showing of her luscious breasts. It took him like forty minutes to sign her up for the cash deal that should take no more than five minutes. I never knew what happened in there nor did I care. His face was flushed red when he finally opened the door and as far as I know they dated for a while. I made a $700.00 commission on a cheap car and everybody was happy.

During this time my wife, the cats, and I had settled into our new home. One of our cats was deaf, a little white kitty named Grubby. We found out he was deaf when we installed an alarm system. The system acted up and sounded off when he was asleep right underneath it but it didn't wake up. All three of our cats were male and had all been neutered, but Grubby was pound for pound the meanest cat I had ever seen. There wasn't a neighborhood cat that he hadn't beaten up in El Paso or Houston as well as his own brothers.

We tied a bell around his neck so we could hear where he was when we couldn't find him, and it was not uncommon, when I called my wife to say I was coming home, for her to say, "Your cat is still out there." Often when I arrived home at eleven o'clock at night I would pace back and forth outside hoping he would smell me and come home. Then I would hear the little bling, bling, bling three or four houses away down the street. Next I would hear the screaming of cats fighting as he got closer to our house.

There was a mean dog that lived across the street from us. He barked and chased us if we rode our bicycles. He was a medium sized mixed mutt that thought he owned the neighborhood. One night I arrived home at about midnight. As I was coming down the street and I saw a white object sitting in my driveway. It was Grubby, our little white kitty, having a "stare down" with the dog across the street, with neither of them backing up an inch.

At the Dealership financing was incredible. There was virtually nobody who could not get approved. We had our financing mostly through GMAC, as we generated millions of dollars a month with them through our finance income. Then there was *special finance*. The funny thing about special finance was if you just showed them an application, they would fill out a little form called a "greeny" that looked like a check. They then paid you ten dollars on the spot just for letting them see the application. Some guys actually made a living off of this by making forty to fifty dollars a day instead of selling cars, just before they would be fired. I seldom fooled with special finance deals because they were too time consuming and had too many rules and fees for me to get involved. It was much easier for me to find a good credit customer and go through GMAC. In the event that GMAC and special finance could not help them, there was another way to finance—there was a broker on the premises.

Using the broker was easier for me then special finance because you would turn over the whole file, the customer and everything to his people. You did none of the work, but if they were able to make the deal, they would pay you one hundred on the spot and the company would pay you the minimum commission.

There were many ways to get paid at the Dealership, but the bad thing was that some of the salesmen created problems with our relationship with GMAC. For example, the preacher Amerson sold many self-employed individuals—more than likely drug dealers. They would find one family member with good credit and put five or six cars in that name. Banks weren't as strict as they are now about such things, and the buyer would put so much money down that the computer would approve it. But when GMAC ran an audit, they would discover that the "grandma" for example was paying $8,000 a month in car payments on a $3,500 a month income.

One salesman, Tommy even sold a car to a dead person. A widow came in a couple weeks after her husband died and realized she had no credit. When she provided her husband's information, they found that he had excellent credit. His death had not yet been reported to the credit bureau so they used his credit to co-sign for her to get the car financing approved. Of course they printed the paperwork for her to take home to have her husband sign, which she did herself.

The best thing of all was the insurance program. There was a large insurance agent named Lloyd who looked like Hammer's twin brother. Together he and Hammer were responsible for protecting the company's liability insurance. By that I mean we often sold cars to customers late at night but they had no insurance. Our first time buyers were immediately funneled to Lloyd's insurance company. Before they left the lot we called Lloyd and give him all the customer's information along with the make and model of the purchased vehicle. He told us how much the down payment was and how much the monthly payment would be. Then it would be up to the customer to go to Lloyd's office the next day and sign the insurance papers. The beauty of it was that Lloyd billed the company for the down payment and it was taken off the gross profit of the deal. For example, if I had a $3,500 profit, they may charge $250 of that for the down payment of the insurance which cost me about $80 out of my pocket. Then any down payment I could get out of the customer that day or the next was mine to keep. The actual down payment had already been paid for by our company.

Lloyd often heard me on the phone with a customer telling them how much more they had to bring me on the next pay day. He would always laugh and tell me, "You are the worst! Nobody gets more money out of them then you do." This was fun. On a Saturday I could make $500–$600 on the side just in insurance down payments.

Another common practice in the company was to pay you 25 percent commission on cars less than thirty days old and 30 percent on cars over thirty days old. Would you believe I never sold a car less than thirty days old? By that I mean after the sales manager completed his part of the deal and signed off on the cover sheet saying the car was nine days old, as if by magic a three would appear in front of the nine making it thirty-nine days old. The company was so big and did so much business that nobody was going to back check a deal that a manager already signed his name on.

I mentioned before there were sales meetings at nine o'clock every morning and by missing three, you would forfeit your monthly sales bonus. Our meeting took place in the upstairs conference room and if you failed to attend, they would put an X next to your name. Three Xs meant no bonus. If I ever had two Xs, I sneaked up to the meeting room and used Wite-Out to wipe them out. I even asked my buddy Norbert if he wanted me to wipe his out. I figured this store was like the Old West and you just did what you had to do. I even found a way to put gas in my own car instead of the customers; I would never put gas in a car for a customer. At this dealership, my idea of getting a car ready for delivery was getting the trash out of the back seat, and any newspapers or other trash that was there. I would then point the car head first to the driveway so they could "go over the curb" as soon as possible. I never bothered to put in gas or wash it.

One time we had a big sale as we did every Saturday. Saturday was a zoo and we would have four or five radio remotes going on at one time. There were country guys out on one side with country music blaring. There would be Spanish guys inside the showroom yelling in Spanish for people to come in. There would be black guys on the side porch with soul music playing, and then we would have rock and rollers on the other side. We even had scantily clad Budweiser and Pepsi girls riding around giving people drinks. We often had live bands playing at the same time. All this often put the customers in a frenzy and made them think that if they didn't buy a car, someone else would buy them all.

After one of those days when I was leaving about ten o'clock on a Saturday night, a man and his two kids stopped me so I could help them buy a car. I told him I was leaving and he asked me to please give him a few minutes because he needed a car for a new job which he was starting on Monday. I brought him to the office and said, "Let me get your information to see if you qualify."

He said, "Please don't make me do that. I've already been through the ringer today. Can't you just show me a car before I give you my information?"

I felt some sympathy for the man since his kids were with him, so I went out and showed him a nice Toyota. I said, "Okay, now let's go in and get your information." His credit was so bad nothing could help him. Not the special finance and not even the broker.

I asked him how much he had down and he said $3,000. I said, "Good, 'cause you're approved for cash, which means a $3,000 car." I explained to him that if he couldn't get financed here, he couldn't get financed anywhere, so he might as well settle down and buy a car for cash. I went to my sales manager and had him pick out three cars for me that we could sell for $3,000 and still make a good profit.

I was still holding his driver's license as security when I went and laid the three keys in front of him and told him to go pick from the three cars. He started saying, "Well, what if I don't like it and what is the price?"

I said, "They are all $3,000 and you better like one of them because this is your last stop and everyone else is closed."

As he and his kids went to look at the cars, I went and put my briefcase and lunchbox in my car. I returned to my office and he was sitting there with one key in front of him. He said, "I kind of like this one." I did his paperwork and collected his money and got the hell out of there.

Another Saturday we had people pre-registered with our used-car secretary—they had provided her with all their credit information. We had a party company blowing up balloons for the customer's kids, but we had our own agenda. One of the sales managers was screening the credit applications, so if the customer had good credit, they were given green balloons. If they had mediocre credit but were still finance worthy, they were given yellow balloons, but if their credit was just awful, they were given red balloons. Naturally everyone flocked to the green balloons leaving all the ones with the red balloons yelling, "I can't get anybody to help me!" Man that was some funny shit!

Houston is a melting pot of different races and many of them are Asian. The Asian persuasion, you could say. The funny thing was nobody at the Chevy Dealership wanted to deal with them. They called them "too high" because every price was too high. One day I ran across a group of four very indignant Vietnamese gentlemen who begged me to wait on them. I said, "If we are going to do this, it is going to be my way. We need to pull your credit and see if you qualify."

They said, "No, we need prices."

And I said, "No you don't need prices if you don't qualify," so we went to my office to see who qualified. One by one they gave me their driver's license so I could pull their information. It wasn't until the fourth one that when I pulled his information, I found one that could actually buy a car. Since I didn't have any other security such as a deposit, I kept his driver's license in my front pocket to keep control of him.

I found a van they liked and put them in the system with my manager so they could be quoted a price and payment. We soon agreed on everything and I started filling out the paperwork. All the while the Vietnamese man kept asking me where his license was and could he have it back. I said, "Sure. As soon as you give me the down payment, you can have your license back."

He said, "No, not until I see the paperwork and the final payment."

And I said, "Fine. Then I will keep the license." I took them over to the finance manager Gary. He didn't even want to talk to them since they hadn't given me the down payment yet. I asked him to do it as a personal favor for me and he did.

He soon signed them up and they agreed on everything, and I then went in to collect the down payment. The Vietnamese man told me in his broken English, "Okay. I signed the papers and I gave the down payment. Now give me my goddamn license!"

My manager Jay even got a kick out of it and he went and congratulated the man for his purchase calling him "Mr. Dang Foo," short for dang fool. I became even more of a hero for the locals because I had just made a $4,500 profit on somebody from the Asian persuasion.

One night at about nine o'clock a big cowboy walked in and said he needed a truck right away. I was almost out the door going home so I said, "Come on, let's make this quick," and I took him to the office to obtain his credit information. I asked how much down he had because we were short on time. He said he had $500 and an old car to trade in. I took all his information to the manager Kelly who was the ex-baseball player. Kelly said, "The only way you are going to make any money is if you put him in one of those 'cab and chassis' pickup trucks that we just took in." By definition cab and chassis means the truck has no bed or rear end. It is meant to have a trailer attached to it.

I asked Kelly how much I could make on a deal like that and he said at least four pounds, which means a $4,000 profit. In other words, a $1,200 commission for me. I got excited and got two sets of keys to show the man and yelled out in front of everybody "Let's go show you the four pounder!" All the salesman and Kelly heard me and were laughing and snickering as we walked out the door.

The cowboy asked me, "Why do you call it a four pounder?"

I explained to him, "It's like going fishing when you catch a nice four pound fish. That's how nice these trucks are." I handed him both sets of keys and said to pick the one he liked and pull it up to the front of the building while I got his paperwork ready. About five minutes later he pulled up in a blue one. Soon he was back in the showroom and he shouted out, "I got the four pounder!" The salesmen were all cracking up laughing. He didn't know why. He thought they all were just really happy for him.

On another occasion I had a Spanish customer from Mexico. I didn't know this but he thought he was really slick. He had been waited on by some of the salesman there and had actually gotten close to making a deal, but then he somehow weaseled out of it. The man had good credit and the means to buy but he was just real shady. Shady like you would call a car salesman, but this was a customer. I didn't know all this at the time so I just continued on with the deal.

He was trading in a van that didn't have a starter so of course, he didn't have it with him. He also didn't have the title to it. The van itself would need to be towed in. Thinking nothing of it, I told the man to send his son home to get the title. He called his wife and told her to have the title ready, and I went into the office and called a tow truck to bring the van into the Dealership. By the time he came out of the finance office, both the title and the trade were there so he had no way out—he had actually bought a car this time.

The man was in his late '50s and very distinguished-looking, so I thought it strange when two days later he showed up with purple hair. He was complaining about the payments and the high interest rate they gave him. All I could do was look at his hair and say, "What the hell happened to your hair?"

He became embarrassed and said, "It's because I dye it."

And I said, "Man, they really fucked up." He went on and on about the payments and I said, "I'm not even allowed in there with you because its privileged information between you and the finance department, so I don't even know what you signed."

He kept screaming, "This is a robbery," and I told him to quit saying that or else they were going to call security on him thinking he was going to rob the place. The other salesmen who had dealt with him before got a big kick out of it because he had finally met his match and could not get out of the deal.

I had been with the company for about six months now and had purchased a little Buick Skylark for $4,000, it was a clean car and I only had a $140 a month payment, but I was ready for an upgrade. I kept my eye out for a nice little SUV and one came in it was a 1991 Chevy Blazer with low mileage, I could buy it for $8,500 so I kept the keys and told my boss Jay, that I would buy it the next day. At Landmark Chevrolet the keys ruled, if you were selling or buying a vehicle you did not turn the keys over to anybody that is how you kept control of the sale of the vehicle. The next day I did the paperwork for the Blazer, and I decided the Buick Skylark would be on the market. At Landmark Chevrolet everybody sold their own car, that's just the way it was; there were so many customers there that nobody could tell what was coming or going. A few days later I had a doctor as a customer, and he was looking for a new car for his son. He explained to me that his son was a forty-year-old "low life and a drunk," but he still needed an upgrade on a vehicle. He was looking to spend $5,000–6,000; after talking to the doctor for a few minutes I could tell that he was clueless about cars, so I took him to look at a few cars that were real "Junkers" and told him those were the cars selling in his price range.

He claimed he had been looking at cars in the ads and I explained to him that the ad cars are never available; it's just part of the program, to get customers in the door. He said that he could pay a little more if it was for a better quality vehicle. I then told him about my Buick Skylark that I had just advertised for $7,900, and he said the most he could pay was $7,500 and I agreed to that. Then the doctor told me, "Now what about my son's trade-in?" and I told him, "I'm not a dealer! I don't take trade-ins."

He said, "Come on, you're in the business what am I going to do with it?"

The car was an old Dodge Lancer. I asked him if he had it with him, and he said yes, we walked over to his car, and I told him to start it and then the engine made a loud knocking noise.

I told him, "You do realize that the engine is out in this car right and that's the engine knocking you hear, it is like knocking on a door. I really don't want it but I'll give you $200 for it just to help you out."

He then signed over the title to me, and he told me to follow him back to his office where he gave me a cashier's check to pay for the Buick. I had made a nice profit on the Buick, so now I had to sell this doctor's trade-in, and hope that I could get something for it. I showed it to one of the mechanics at the dealership and he said he could "sweeten it" by putting in some additives and clean the spark plugs, which would take away the engine noise; that and a detail would only cost me $100 total.

The car cleaned up really well, and without the engine noise, I thought this might be a $3,000 car after all; I parked the car in the back and waited for the right opportunity. One day a black man came in looking for a car for his daughter and he wanted to spend between $2,500 and $3,000. The art of the "setup" is doing it just right, like I had done with the doctor. I showed him some real "shit boxes" and told him those were around $2,500–3,000. I mean stuff that was barely running, or you had to use jumper cables to start them, he finally said, "Don't you have anything else?"

I told him, "Well, I do have this doctor's car that I'm trying to sell for him it's out in the back." When he saw the car and compared it with the crap he had been looking at he could not believe it, he said, "You mean this car is the same price?"

I said, "Yes, but there's only one catch: it is sold completely as is. I do not represent the car, and the company does not represent the car. It is between you and the doctor and I cannot give you his information, you get the title that has his name and that is all."

The man said, "Tell the doctor I'll pay $2,800 for it."

I asked, "Do you have it in cash, and do you have it with you?" I excused myself and said I was going to call the doctor and get the title from my office. I told him to start counting the money and to have it ready by the time I came back. I even took the keys with me so that he couldn't rev up the engine and have it make that knocking noise again. When I came back he was sitting in the car with the money in his lap, he handed it over to me as I handed him the title.

I said, "This sale is as is, and I never want to hear from you again, and that doctor doesn't want to hear from you either, do you understand?"

He agreed and drove off into the sunset, never to be heard from again.

Our pay period at Landmark was biweekly, to be paid on deals that were processed during that pay period. I prided myself on making between $4,000–5,000 during the two week time period. Nobody knew what you were making, but they could look up your sales gross profits by using your employee number, so the guys that were close to me always knew what I was doing and how I was doing it, but I preferred to keep a low profile. One day Jay, the used-car director, called me out in a sales meeting in front of all fifty used-car salesman.

He said, "Do you know what this guy is making? You see how he walks around all quiet and unassuming."

We had just been paid that day so Jay asked me in front of everybody and said, "What was the amount of your pay check today?" I asked him, "Do you want the take home or gross?" He said, "Take home," to which I answered, "$4,300," as he marveled at that, he began scolding the other salesmen. He said, "Do you see the amount of money you could make here?" "You guys are making bread money and can barely pay your rent, and this guy is taking home over $4,000 for just two weeks."

One weekend we had a "Vegas weekend" where it was tied into selling old age inventory, the older the car you sold, the more rolls of the dice you would get. I sold one of the oldest cars in stock which meant I would be paid at 100 to 1. It also meant I rolled against the house, so if I rolled a 9 it would equal to a $900 bonus. The key was you had to beat the house which would be my manager Jay, on the following Monday in our big sales meeting. Everybody who was eligible got to roll at this meeting. This would be conducted in front of all managers so there would be no cheating and the cash would be paid on the spot. When my turn came, Jay asked me if I wanted to go first and I said no you go first to give me something to shoot at, he rolled double 5s, which is a 10, and he looked at me and said, "I'm sorry, Papa." I rolled double 6s, and he couldn't believe it, and he was so happy for me as I collected my $1,200. I was really proud of that moment, but my biggest source of pride came at the beginning of every month when we would have a big breakfast meeting with the entire sales force, and all the managers at a huge dining hall at a Hotel.

There they would go over the figures for the month and every individual sale person's production was recorded on a huge bar graph chart. They seldom went passed the first page bragging about the salesmen, but I was always on the first page. In fact I was usually in the top five and seldom did anybody in the store have more gross profit per sale then me. This was the number one Chevy dealer in the country, and the number one used-car department in the country and I was kicking butt. One of the general managers named Charlie would always brag about me, and he couldn't even say my name properly, he would pronounce it "Ochowa," and he would say look at this Ochowa and how much profit he generates for the store.

Pretty soon it had been a year that had gone by since I had been there and I discovered that an old nemesis of mine had come into town. Al the man who had hired me at Casa Ford, and then turned on me, had come into town and opened a Ford dealership in Baytown. He had brought several of the people with him from El Paso to work there, by coincidence he knew Gary one of the finance managers at Landmark and found out that I worked there. One day he contacted me and told me he wanted me to come see the dealership at Baytown Ford, so I went and it just so happened I had been paid that day. It was almost a year to the date that I had been let go at Casa Ford in El Paso. After showing me around his dealership he sat me down and asked me if I wanted to come and work for him. I was amazed at the nerve of this guy, after he had screwed me out of my money at Casa Ford and now he was asking me to work for him.

I asked him, "What would I be making if I come to work for you?"

He said, "You will be making comparable money to what you used to make at Casa Ford." At that point, I pulled out my pay stub from Landmark Chevrolet and showed him that I had already made $115,000 and it was only September. He looked at me in wonderment and said, "I had no idea you were making that kind of dough here." I just looked at him and said, "I don't need you now, and I never needed you to make that kind of money," and with that said I walked out. Some people would call that "poetic justice," I would have to agree.

CHAPTER 18
LIFE IN THE BIG CITY

We had read up a lot about Houston before we ever moved there, and had visited several times and were anxious to explore the big city and all it had to offer. As I was struggling with my first job and still living in our two bedroom apartment, my wife had signed us up for season tickets to the Opera. Being that I worked six days a week the only times for us to go were Sunday afternoons for the matinee. I had been a lifelong Dallas Cowboys fan and they were coming off their Championship season, and I was giving up a lot to attend the Opera on a Sunday afternoon. At first I thought this isn't going to work the only experience I had watching Opera was watching the movie "Moonstruck," which revolved around the Opera "La Boehme." Our first Opera was going to be "Madame Butterfly;" and the weather was awful we were in the midst of a tropical storm, and it took us over an hour just to get to the Opera. In Houston, the Opera takes place at the Wortham Center in the theatre district of Downtown Houston. There are huge sculptures and beautiful art designs everywhere, it was a lavish area filled with an array of artistic beauty. My wife had been told it was an event and to dress accordingly, so she was in a black dress and I was in a suit, as we entered from the ground level and went up the escalator. We were in awe at the sight of some impressive, massive displays of sculptures of cellos and violins that lined both sides of the escalators.

As we arrived to the second level and we were told that we could go in the line and order a drink which would be served during the intermission. In theory when you came out for the intermission, your drinks were already waiting for you, with your name next to it. They also had an assortment of specialty coffee, wines, mixed drinks, etc. We were people watching as we gazed upon those who were also enlightened enough to appreciate the Opera, with soothing piano music playing in the background. As we approached the entrance to the hall a tuxedoed man approached the entrance playing a handheld instrument that resembled a xylophone, this was to announce the beginning of the event which was like "first call." You may think I'm goofy, but I was very impressed with this "touch of class." When we were directed to our seats I was amazed at how close we were, we were in the eighth row in the center of the orchestra section. My wife had spared no expense in order for us to gain our appreciation for the arts, and she told me these would be our seats for the next six shows.

As the show began I could only think of one thing; one of the people I admired most was Jim Valvano who was the ex-basketball coach of North Carolina State and the founder of the V foundation for cancer research. In his famous speech he said, "If you could laugh, cry, and feel emotion all in one day and do that every day, then you would live a full life indeed." That in essence is what the Opera was to me; the story overwhelms you, and overpowers you and forces you to feel, act and react to it. The opera itself was a pageantry of elaborate costumes, outstanding music and storytelling. It was an epic unforgettable tale that left us emotionally drained. When the show ended we had made plans to go to Kim Son a famous Vietnamese restaurant also in the Downtown area on Jefferson St. It had rave reviews and was voted one of Houston's top ten restaurants, and it lived up to its reputation. The vegetables were crisp and fresh, the sauces were spicy and flavorful an overall incredible experience to couple with the Opera we had just seen. This began our Houston experience; from then on anytime we had time off we would take in a new restaurant or a concert. We wanted to take advantage of, and appreciate all we could in this vast city that we had now become a part of.

I'd make it a point to get out early on Saturday nights so we could enjoy all the flavor of the city, one local radio station had what they called a "disco Saturday night" and would play retro disco songs from our era, songs that we used to love to dance to. We would ride around in the car through the Galleria area looking for new sites to see, new restaurants, or clubs to attend all the while rocking out to our old disco music in the car. My wife even started carrying an old boom box with us in the car to make recordings of the stations music. We stumbled on to our first ever Barnes and Noble Store, and we had never seen anything like it. We spent three to four hours there exploring all the books and endless possibilities like music and videos that they offered. I was driving down the street to what they called the "Flower District" on Fanning

St.; some fog had rolled in and made the street cloudy, and spooky looking, when we saw there were twenty-to-thirty-foot-tall topiaries, which we were seeing for the first time. These were large plant sculptures of giraffes or dinosaurs, and the street was lined with them, all different types of animals, including deer and cows. Our mouths were agape as we got out of the car and walked around them, as if we had discovered a new life form, from another planet.

Another of our favorite restaurants to go to was America's; it was a fine dining restaurant on Post Oak near the Galleria area. This was voted one of the top ten restaurants in the United States and featured Central American food such as black beans, plantains as well as steaks and seafood. It offered an exquisite atmosphere coupled with excellent service. From there we could often go to Elvia's Cantina which featured live Latin music, and Salsa. Being from El Paso we had only been associated with people of Mexican descent, but now we were exposed to Latinos of all types, they were from Honduras, Cuba, Ecuador and Nicaragua. They were all very friendly with us since we were also Latinos, and they exposed us to different types of dances, some that we had never experienced before.

When we didn't feel like driving across town, there was plenty to do in our own neighborhood of Clear Lake. Kemah was a city close by to us and was famous for their waterfront boardwalk, and there was an array of seafood restaurants lined up and down the boardwalk, with a gorgeous view heading out toward Galveston Bay. It seemed like every other week they had a different type of boat festival and the boats lined up and trolled through their waters going to Galveston and back. We often went to Galveston as well, to visit the beach and the fine restaurants they had there, one of our favorites was Landry's Restaurant, which sat at the very tip between the bay and the actual gulf itself. Before the sun would set on a Sunday afternoon, we sat out there and would watch the boats come in, with the sea gulls trailing as they were hoping for scraps of fish. I would constantly think of the Otis Redding Song, "Sitting on the dock of the Bay." At that point I was determined to get a boat, now that I felt comfortable about my own job situation.

At Landmark Chevrolet it became a regular thing to hang out with the few guys that I associated with, and they would come around and ask me what I did on the weekend. One guy in particular was Ted, a large Russian man who spoke with a thick Russian accent. He was constantly in awe of all the things I could manage to do on a Sunday. I would tell him "you live in the same city, why don't you explore it for yourself?" Even my compadre Norbert and his wife Lily, had to be carried and taken to restaurants by us to show them the appreciation for the city they had lived in their whole lives.

One day I made a decision to actually visit a boat shop in Clear Lake, I told them I was looking for something fifteen to sixteen feet long and in the price range of $7,000–$8,000 like a repo that I could get for a good price. I left them my pager number and told them to call me when they got one, within a week they called me that they had acquired Sea Ray that was in excellent condition. I purchased it with a loan at the bank. Of course my neighborhood would not allow a boat in your driveway, so I had to acquire a storage unit for it. The whole investment would only cost me a couple of hundred dollars a month; this of course did not include maintenance on the boat which was unpredictable at best. There is a saying, "The happiest two days of your life are the day you buy a boat, and the day you sell your boat." As for myself I was pleased with my purchase, and I felt like a Houston native, now I was happy. We began by taking it out on Clear Lake and Kemah, some of the more peaceful waterways, but when we would try to take it out of the gulf we would be thrown around by the more aggressive waves.

About this time my wife had gone back to work with RJ Reynolds Tobacco and she was feeling the stress from her job after not having worked for about six months. One day on a Monday we took a sick day and took the boat out with hardly anybody on the water, we spent a peaceful romantic day out on the water hearing songs by Anita Baker on my boat's cassette player. To this day when I hear Anita Baker I often think of that day out on the water with my wife. At the end of the day when we took the boat back to storage, we ended up at the Kemah Cantina on the water front watching Monday night football, a fitting end to a fine day.

Soon after that our friends from England came to visit, they are Mark and Dale, and after showing them the sites of the city we decided to take them out on the boat on the lake. We had toys that we would drag behind the boat like an inner tube, which you could ride on and hop around with while in the water. Usually I was the one driving the boat, while Dora and her friends were hopping around the back on the toys. I would closely monitor their progress and be looking back constantly to make sure they were all right. After a couple of hours of this, my wife Dora said, "Why don't we switch, I'll drive while you ride the tube in the back?" I agreed, like a fool I was wearing my glasses thinking that she would monitor me like I did them, but instead she drove with one hand on the wheel. She talked aimlessly with her guests while I was twisting in the wind and water, trying not to drown after losing my glasses. I was screaming and yelling and cursing in the wind and nobody could hear me, until finally Mark noticed me and said, "Dora you better stop." When they pulled me to the boat I was so pissed I had lost my glasses, my pride and my nerve. Understand I was usually the one laughing at others not being the object of their laughter. After we put the boat away and went to the mall to buy me a new pair of glasses, all Mark could say in his English accent was, "you shouldn't have worn your glasses, Richard." After about the third or fourth time he said it, I finally told him to shut the fuck up. Something about the way I talk or my accent would crack up my English friends, I could be making fun of them, or at that time saying, "Shut the fuck up," and they would still laugh. Even though I was not in a laughing mood it still made the whole day easier to swallow. It reminded me of another day when I was the object of intense humiliation.

It was when I was in high school in El Paso and my best friend Alex and I decided to go horseback riding, my mom had drove us out to the stables in far east El Paso. There we rented the horse for an hourly rate, and being stable horses they had a mind of their own, and would not let you take them out beyond a certain point. They wanted to stay close to their food and water, Alex had been raised on a Ranch in Fabens Texas so he immediately knew what to do. He jumped off his horse and grabbed a stick; I watched him hold onto the reins as he did this and saw him get back nimbly onto the horse. He didn't have to strike the horse with the stick, he would merely show it to him, and with that he had the horse do whatever he wanted. Myself being a city boy and having no experience with horses I did the next best thing, and I said, "Mom give me a stick so I can do like Alex." My mom went to grab a stick and hand it to me and as she got close to me with the stick, the horse looked at her and took off "like a bat out of hell" so I couldn't get the stick; and he was bucking me like a rodeo Bronco trying to get me off. When he finally stopped I was hanging off the side of the horse holding on for dear life with Alex cracking up laughing. I said, "Mom, you can't do it like that, you have to sneak up behind him and toss it to me so he can't see you." As my mom approached the back of the horse with the stick, just as she got close he turned back and saw her and took off again "like a bat out of hell" bucking me and trying to throw me again. Alex was practically pissing on himself at this point he was laughing so hard. We tried every which way to get me the stick; tossing it to me, or handing it to me. We spent the whole hour with my poor mother trying to give me a stick; and the horse just kept tossing me back and worth. I really believe the horse knew exactly what he was doing, because when he would finish bucking me, he would turn around and take a long look at me. Alex and the horse had the last laugh, because I never got the stick, but I heard about it for years to come whenever Alex wanted to humiliate me by telling the story of our horseback riding experience.

This was now in the fall of '94, and even though I had surgery to correct the nerve damage from my accident I was told upon a visit to El Paso from my doctor that I would need another major surgery to further enhance the mobility of my right arm. This meant that I would need to sock away some money to prepare to be off for six to eight weeks post-surgery. At this time my manager Jay had begun speaking to me about getting promoted to finance manager since I was doing so well with my job. This would be a huge feather in my cap to be at the largest Chevrolet Dealership in the country and become a finance manager; those guys were making $20,000–$25,000 a month. One finance manager was Gary, who I saw his production on our companies computer, he had generated $330,000 by himself in a month. With his percentages and bonus plan he easily made between $40,000–$50,000 income for himself during that month. Most stores in El Paso would be happy with a $120,000–130,000 in finance income in a whole month and here Gary had generated over $300,000 in a month, by himself.

I explained to Jay that I had scheduled my surgery for the day after Thanksgiving and I would probably need to be off for four to eight weeks for my recovery time. I was hoping to do both, have the surgery and get the promotion, but I would just have to wait and see how things would work out. I set a personal goal to have $12,000–$15,000 in the bank during the course of my surgery and recovery for security, and to help pay bills while I was off. This did not include my wife's income which I never included; her income was for vacations and putting away for our future. I began work in earnest and took no prisoners, before that I would walk around haphazardly and stumble into a customer every now and then, because there were so many of them you could be trying to leave and you would run into one. I began to aggressively go after customers and follow up with them, which I hadn't done for so long because customers were so plentiful, but now I wanted to take advantage and close more sales. I had tremendous sales closing skills that were not being utilized at this store, and the reason for it was because the system closed the customers.

The dealership employed what they called a "Four Square System," the clear description of it would be to acquire the customer's credit information first exposing them and leaving them naked, as far as their credit goes.

Then one would employ what is called a four square sheet, describing the vehicle they are looking at and the stock number of the vehicle. The manager then would pencil in a price and a payment. The price was usually five to six thousand over cost, and the payment was extremely high in comparison to the price of vehicle. At first I feared it, because the price and the payments were so high; and me being from a small town like El Paso, I feared the customer's making a run for it. Then I realized that most customers here were used to it, and they just fell in line, like training a dog to do new tricks. The way it works is that it's sort of a slight of hand, like a magician, while you're worried about how he pulled the rabbit out the hat; he's busy taking your wallet or your watch. The same concept applies here, if the customers complain about the price you focus on the down payment, or the monthly payment, and get their mind off the main thing which is the price. More times than not, the price became irrelevant because you would focus on the down payment and bringing down the monthly installments. The manager usually recommended a down payment equal to one fourth of the cost of the vehicle; this gave you lots wiggle room to manipulate the customer. If they complained too much about the payment, I then would say, "How much more down payment can you give to help you get to a lower payment?"

I learned to present this in a "masterful and unthreatening" manor, one that when I would walk into the office, often with the sheet faced down, I would explain what I was going to do before even showing them. I would tell them that this was the companies' preferred way to buy the car. It may not be their way, but it was the companies' "preferred" way, and I was obligated to present it. I would empower the customer by telling them that they would have the right to tell me "their preferred way" to counter offer the Dealer. As I presented the figures for example, if the paper said $5,000 down the customer may say, "I can do $2,500 down," and regarding the payment they would tell me what the maximum payment which they could afford. For example, if the form said payment of $550 they might say they wanted a payment not to exceed $400. On most occasions I was allowed to maximize the gross profit using this system, even though they agreed to a $400 payment with me, they would come out of the finance office with a $450-$475 payment.

I absolved myself with the customer by always telling them that what they did in the finance office was privileged information like going to confession with a priest, that I would never know what payment they agreed upon and that it didn't matter to me, I just represented the company and the vehicle. Armed with new found dedication, and in order to save some money, I pulled together some of my best month's I've ever had in the business. At any given point one could access your months production by entering your employee number into the computer, that month of October, I put together a near perfect month I had sold 28 cars for $48,000 gross profit. With bonuses I figured I made about $16,500 that month. In years to come I would make that again on several occasions but at this moment that was a high water mark for me. This brought about more bragging from my managers about me, not helping my desire to keep a low profile, all it took was about a 15 percent more effort on my part to make that much more money. As for my scheduled surgery, my wife had planned to fly her parent's back home with us to help me with my recovery; in other words I would be eating real well while recovering.

My wife is an only child so I always bonded with her parents and treated them like family as they did me. As the time approached for my scheduled surgery I took the time off that I had requested and still hoped for the opportunity to get into the finance department. We flew back to El Paso a couple days before Thanksgiving and the surgery actually took place the Wednesday before Thanksgiving, my goal was to have the surgery Wednesday and be home by Thanksgiving to watch the football games. As it turned out the surgery was quite extensive, they took a muscle from the right part of my chest and placed it into the bicep of my right arm. Then they took ligaments and tendons, from my left leg to place in various parts of my right shoulder, I was even given an epidural like a pregnant woman to help absorb the pain, as well as a morphine drip with a button that I could press every half hour to shoot more into my system. I hadn't had a drink for years now but I have to say that morphine was a nice buzz; I can see why it's illegal. My wife and I spent a memorable Thanksgiving Day in the hospital watching the Cowboys and other football games. My arm was placed in a brace held up in an upward position, as if I was telling someone to stop and I would have to wear that brace for at least six weeks.

The only drawback with my surgery was that in the part of my chest where they had removed my muscle, it had caused a drip of blood and other bodily fluids so there was a bag attached to a hose to drain the excess fluid. At this point I was just hoping to make my flight on Sunday back home to Houston, on Sunday my doctor came in and discharged me, and an orderly came in to remove my drain and the hose that was still attached to my chest draining the fluid. The orderly changed my bandages, removed the hospital band and then almost as an afterthought, he reached down and grabbed the hose and yanked it. It must have been about six-eight inches inside my body and was probably the worst pain I have felt in my whole life. Though I was still in pain I swung at him with my left hand barely missing his jaw, I'm convinced I would have broken his jaw had I made contact. My wife cried out "Richard!" with my face turning white from the pain. I was going through all this commotion and we still had a flight to catch. My wife had even bought an extra ticket for me since my arm would be imposing on someone who had the misfortune of sitting next to me.

Dora's parents and I had a unique bonding experience upon our arrival to Houston, with Dora's mom there we ate like Kings, we had Chile relleno, enchiladas, and all the best Mexican food you can imagine. To avoid gaining weight, her dad and I would go for walks on the walking trail next to our house, we had customized the house so that the main living room was on the other side of our master bedroom. This worked out great for me so that I could watch movies at all hours of the night and not disturb my wife who had to get up early for work every day. I've always been an insomniac and this was even worse because I was so uncomfortable, I found the best way to sleep was sitting up in a recliner with a pillow underneath my brace and the T.V. on low. My arm was developing a rash were my arm sat on the brace and my mother-in-law would cure it with alcohol and various oils. She had become the head chef of the kitchen which included feeding our cats, I mentioned before that I had a little white cat that was deaf and she began to use sign language to communicate with the cat.

My mother-in-law speaks no English, which worked out well because the cat spoke nothing and heard nothing, but I'd walk in and catch her waving her arms around as if trying to communicate with him. This worked out well because I think he spoke the international language of food, and she would feed him constantly with little pieces of chicken, or beef. My mother-in-law tolerated the cats but she was deathly afraid of them, she was scared to death that they would come into her room at night and sleep with her, and she believed that old wives tale that they would steal your breath away and make you die. Naturally my wife would make fun of her constantly and put a cat on her lap and say, "Go to Grandma." Needless to say, she didn't want to touch them, or be touched by them.

One day when she was busy putting the lotion on my arm and her hands were occupied, the little deaf kitty came up to her and began rubbing his ass on her leg and she started screaming, "No, go away!" she said, but of course he couldn't hear her. He was just showing affection to her since she would feed him all the time, but she was going nuts with anxiety. My father-in-law and I were howling with laughter, it's one of those moments you wish you had on video. During this time we explored many new restaurants since my wife's hours were not like mine and she had weekends off. One of them was "Bonnie's" on I-45 South, which is where we discovered the "Blue Dog" paintings. It seems Bonnie was a collector of the famous Blue Dog paintings by George Rodrigue. At first I was sad when we began going there for dinner, because it reminded me of my little miniature Collie which had recently passed away. But then by reading the story about how the artist had also lost his little dog and used these paintings as a way of bringing her back to life, I became less saddened by the art work, and instead looked forward to a time when I could collect my own pieces.

We also discovered a place on I-45 South called Pinches. If you know anything about the Spanish language, you would know this is a bad word, yet upon entering the restaurant, they had a plaque displaying their definition of a pinche as a kitchen boy. I didn't care what they said. I knew what it really meant, so I called a young man over who worked there and asked him if he was a pinche. Dora and her parents were trying to hold back their laughter as he responded that no he's not but his friends say he must be one since he works there. My wife said, "Leave him alone it's not his fault they named the place like that," but when the waiter came to take the order I went into a tirade, how about some "pinches tacos," or some "pinches enchiladas," or the "pinches house special." Needless to say we had a great time; the food was so average that the restaurant didn't last too long probably because people couldn't get over the stigma of their name.

As the holidays approached we discovered a new area to visit, the area was by Rice University it was an art district filled with art deco style buildings that were black and white. It had elaborate restaurants one of them being Blue Mesa Grill, which featured Northern New Mexico Style cuisine made famous by chefs like Bobby Flay. You could go crazy just sampling some of the twenty different salsas they offered. Upon entering we saw a large Christmas tree made out of Chile Peppers, my wife asked the Maître D' were it came from, and he said oh, "I make them myself in my spare time." I'm not judging him, but he was the gay "artsy fartsy" type. My wife asked him how much he would charge to make us one he said, "Give me a week and about $450, and I'll make one for you." To this day we still have it in our home, it is decorated with lights and we turn it one for special occasions and holidays. For Christmas week we went to the Kemah Boardwalk to watch the Christmas boat parade. As Christmas and New Year's approached I became more and more impatient and wanted to go back to work, until I received the call, it was my boss Jay the used-car director at Landmark Chevrolet. He called to inform me that I was being offered a position in the finance department. It was the position I had worked so hard for and had waited for, yet my arm was still in a brace and I was not healthy enough to take it.

Soon after the New Year we all flew back to El Paso because it was time to see the doctor and have him remove the brace. The next step in my recovery would be to put my arm in some kind of sling that rested on a pillow and on my side. With that I would be able to go back to work which at this point was in mid-January. When I did finally go back to work I realized that they gave my finance position to another Iranian salesman he was nowhere near as good me, but he thought he was "big stuff" in finance. He was a close friend of Jay who is also Iranian, so one could see the connection, but in Jay's defense he did offer me the job first. It did take me some time to get back to work and in work mode because I had been home resting and watching movies and I was now back in the fast paced atmosphere surrounded by customers. I used to tell my wife that driving clear across town to work there was like walking a tight rope without a net, and I often dreamed about it at night. I also would dream about being in a crowd of nameless faces that represented the many customers that I would see all day long.

One weird thing happened about the third day I was back at work, it was the return of a customer, one of the first customers I had sold to there, he was a young man in his midtwenties and as were many he had been a "first time buyer," when I sold him the first car. I had told him he had the option in about a year or so to come back and trade in the car in for something that he liked better, once his credit was established. I didn't realize but he had been there two or three times before while I was out, and he was now working with my friend Norbert who I shared an office with. When he saw me he became unglued and came up to me and said, "You lied to me."

I said, "What you are talking about?"

He said, "You said I could trade the car in, and they said I can't."

I asked Norbert what the problem was, and he said he needed $3,000–4,000 down just to trade out of his car I said, "There you go, you just need to put the money up, and then you can trade out of it." The guy literally came after me wanting to kick my ass, Norbert and a couple of other guys held him back and he was screaming at me that he wanted to beat me up. Me with an arm in a sling and a pillow at my side I told him, "I'm not psychic. I didn't know what the bank was going to tell you when I sold the car to you a year ago." Jay came up and instructed me to stay away from the guy so he wouldn't cause a scene to where they would need to call the police.

About a week later my friend Norbert got arrested and I received a call from his wife in the middle of the night, asking me to go bail him out of jail. Norbert is a calm and peaceful man with a wife and baby and is very responsible, having just bought a home for his family. I was shocked that he had been in any trouble at all. It turns out that one of his old roommates, when he was single and had several roommates, had gotten traffic tickets, while using Norbert's license. He had never bothered to tell my friend about it, and they were now several years old. By this time they had incurred the penalties and interest to the tune of about $1,000. I had no idea where I was going to get the money in the middle of the night, but as it turned out my wife had it, while working for Reynolds Tobacco she kept a certain amount of petty cash, for buying cigarettes from wholesale accounts. I would have to replace this first thing in the morning, because she could not be without this money less her company think that she stole it or something worse.

Now I was going to have to determine how to navigate through Downtown Houston with the entire criminal element there by the jail, and me with my sling and pillow. I thought that's all I need is to look defenseless and have someone come up and rob me of the money. I took off my brace; it was the first time in over two months that my arm was free without any type of brace or support. It was about three weeks early of when I was supposed to remove it, but I felt the situation warranted it. When I paid the fine and got Norbert out, he was shocked to see me without the brace, and I told him why I removed it, that I didn't want to look vulnerable to the criminal element there. Overall my arm felt better, and I decided from that point on to go without the brace and let my arm heal and recover naturally as I allowed my arm to function normally.

Something strange was happening with my wife and her company; she was doing really well with her job, and we thought that a promotion might be on the horizon for her. The other strange thing that started happening was she started having what her doctor referred to as panic attacks brought on by stress. In those days, she had a cell phone, and I had a pager, and often she would page me to call her back in the middle of the day; she would be stopped on the side of the road in her company van, where she would just be crying for no reason. My wife is one tough cookie, and I often thought if she were a man, she would have kicked my ass many times over for the things I had done, so it was unusual to see her that way, and my heart was breaking as well. Yet I knew somehow she would toughen up and get on with her business and that a promotion would likely involve relocation for us. Previously she had been the top sales rep in El Paso, Texas, for her company, but nobody got promoted in El Paso; they just patted you on the back and said good job. The Houston metro area was a different story altogether; if you did the job well there, it was noticed, and you would be promoted. It was just a matter of time.

CHAPTER 19
THE BIG EASY CALLING

As the spring went on, she was soon notified that she had an offer to become a sales manager with her company and it would be in the New Orleans area. This was very exciting as not only would she be receiving a nice raise, but her company would pay all our moving expenses, and even pay the closing cost on a new home purchase. Not only that, but we were given two months to try to sell our house as we made arrangements for the move, but if our home didn't sell the company said they would buy it for fair market price. We had visited New Orleans on two or three occasions including taking Dora's parents; one time by ourselves we actually went to look at houses and visualized ourselves living there, which was a foreshadowing of things to come. About a month before our scheduled move we took a visit to New Orleans to look for a house to purchase. We were assigned a real estate agent by the company. The company also had their own relocation service which would include people to help me find a new job, create a resume for me, and provide me with a list of prospective employment opportunities. They offered to set up interviews for me, but I preferred to arrange my own. Dora had made a few phone calls with a couple of the other managers before we went there and they suggested we look on the North Shore.

This area was across Lake Pontchartrain, which was only forty-five minutes from New Orleans. It was more affluent and safer with less crime, and a much a healthier lifestyle than New Orleans. However, our real estate agent was determined to show us everything from Downtown New Orleans to across the river which is known as the West Bank. Having done some reading and studying of the city we also determined that the North Shore would be the best place for us because I would have to be working until late at night and I didn't want my wife to have to worry about the criminal elements of the city. The North Shore consisted of three major cities: Slidell, Covington and Mandeville. We soon ruled out Slidell, because it was very close to New Orleans and had more of the criminal element that we were trying to avoid. We settled on Covington because we found that they had much larger lots just like our old home in El Paso, they consisted of half acre to acre lots with tons of trees. Our price range was from $150,000–$200,000, and we don't know what list this lady was thinking, but everything she showed us was somehow not acceptable. My wife was becoming impatient because we only had a couple more days left to find a suitable home to purchase.

One day as we were on Highway 21 in Covington, and we took a right turn as the realtor drove up the street looking for one of the houses on her list. We passed a beautiful Southern home with red brick and white columns in the front of it. You could tell it was not finished yet, but I could see my wife looking at the home, and her jaw dropped in amazement. As the agent stumbled up the street trying to find the houses on her list, my wife kept asking about the other one which was not on her list. As it turned out, our agent knew another agent that lived up the street, and she stopped to ask her about the home. Her name was Blanche, and she was a more local agent that represented the Covington area. When my wife described the home to her she said, "Oh, I know that home and the builder. I can put you in contact with the builder of the home and the agent that represents the home." The home builders name was Haley, and the reason the home was unfinished was because he had been building the home originally for his family, but he was now getting divorced. It was among the nicer homes that he had ever built because it was for himself, and he usually built homes on the lesser price range, more like in the $130s. With the remaining days we had left, we negotiated the purchase of that home and even got to pick out the tiles, counter tops and other amenities that would go in it. We were assured by the builder and the real estate agent that the home would be completed by the time of our move which was thirty days away. My wife and Blanche became good friends as she asked her to keep tabs on the home and update us on its progress, our purchase price would be $175,000 and it was well worth it. The home had four bedrooms that included an office for my wife, and it sat on a one acre tree lined lot, with an abundance of full grown pine trees.

Before we would make the move and close on the new house we would have to take care of unfinished business in Houston such as closing on our house there. I mentioned before that we had sixty days to sell our home, or

Dora's company would purchase it for fair market price. I know this is crazy but the one thing that would bother me was the damn front door, Dora had spent $3,500 on that front door alone through our remodeling process of the home. It was a deep cherry wood with fancy beveled glass and I spent a lot of time looking at it mostly wondering how this damn door could cost $3,500. I used to tell my wife, "When I die put that door on my coffin and bury it with me, so I can appreciate it throughout the life hereafter." I remember we used to look out sometimes when we would hear little hoof noises and see the wild deer parading around our lawn in the front since we lived next to a walking trail.

As our time approached for the move, maybe out of protest I told Dora that I would not be going with her for at least the first couple of weeks until I tied up my loose ends at Landmark Chevrolet. It must have been out of protest but I wanted to hang out with my buddy Norbert and do some things I thought that I could only do in Texas for instance to have some huge Texas sized steaks, and visit some topless joints where they actually give you a real "lap dance," what I call good clean fun. The reason I called topless joints good clean fun is because it's a total fantasy, the girl has no intention of going anywhere with you, and if you're smart you know this and you are both just pretending. She is pretending to be working her way through college to be a doctor or lawyer or who knows what, and you're pretending to give a shit as you look at her cleavage and have her dance on your lap. The only time I ever saw one of those girls outside of the club was back in El Paso when I was used-car manager at Dick Poe.

I had a bunch of cars I needed to sell at the auction the next day and a wholesale buyer named David took me out to a topless joint. David started talking to this red head and told her how much I needed to sell these cars at the auction the next day, and could we hire her for the day to help us represent the cars. To my surprise she arrived at the auction the next day with David and he told her to dress professionally. You could imagine what she wore, a tight blouse, short skirt, panty hose and of course no underwear. The skirt was short enough, but it had a slit up the front that left nothing to the imagination. I got David aside and told him, "I'm not paying her," and he said, "Don't worry, I've got it." What he had told her to do was that when my cars came through the line to; model them like those models do on the game shows on T.V. this included getting in and out of them, and of course bending over to look under the hood. Most of the buyers are all men so this sent off quite frenzy, as they were whooping and hollering like they were at a topless bar themselves. Except to the auctioneer this hooting and hollering meant bids. I'm sure at least half a dozen cars were sold unintentionally, but I was able to sell most of my cars and walk away pretty content. The girl was another story she kept calling me or David to see if she could come help us again.

As the time approached for me to make my move, I had told Dora two weeks and my time was finally up, it was with great sadness that I would be leaving Landmark Chevrolet and spending my last day there; because I knew there was no other dealership like that in the world. It was truly a "big pond" and I had been a big fish and excelled there. As years would pass some of my friends would have contact with the dealership and ask if they remembered me, and without exception every manager they asked spoke highly of me. I remember driving up with my boat and tow behind my blazer as I received my last check and cleaned out my office. All the guys I knew were all lined up outside to say goodbye to me, including the used-car managers Jay and Kelly. I began the six hour drive from Houston to Covington Louisiana. Upon my arrival in Covington I was pressed with the task of arranging the house in order, as Dora had left everything in boxes since she started her new job. My days would be spent with unloading boxes and arranging furniture while looking at the information given to me by her company as to what potential work places there were available for me. The relocation company had typed out a resume for me with references and a complete guide of every dealership within a 50 mile radius of me. Some of the prospects looked promising but they were across the river which meant crossing the greater New Orleans Bridge after crossing Lake Pontchartrain.

I determined that crossing the lake would be enough and that was as far as I would go. This would limit my search to either Metairie or New Orleans. After going for a few interviews in the New Orleans area I determined that I didn't want to work in the hood. There were some dealerships close in proximity to me in Covington, Mandeville or Hammond Louisiana but these were all "sleepy" little towns. The dealership in Covington was averaging thirty to thirty-five used cars a month; I told them I did that by myself at Landmark. In Hammond they were doing a little better, selling fifty to sixty used cars a month, and they offered me a manager position that paid $5,000 a month plus bonuses. This was a nice offer considering they didn't know me, but they had checked out my references with Landmark and Dick Poe. I thanked them for the offer and told them I thought I could do better selling cars on my own.

Don't ask me why but I settled in on a dealership called Julian Graham Dodge on Veterans Boulevard in Metairie. The used-car director was a guy about my age named Doug, he rode motorcycles and liked rock 'n' roll music and he fancied himself as a band leader, which I thought was pretty cool. He also offered me a position as a team leader that paid $300 a week plus commission and bonuses. He also said that he would set me up with a Spanish radio station and do live remotes to encourage Spanish customers to come in, and since I was the only salesman who spoke Spanish that was a plus. He and most of the other salesman are what I considered true "Coonasses" or true Cajuns.

I'll never forget when I meet the general manager for the first time, he was a short "baby faced" Napoleon type named Troy he looked like he was barely 30 years old, if that. When he met me he put out his hand to shake mine and asked if I spoke Mexican. I looked down on him and said, "The correct term is Spanish, little man." I must have struck a nerve, because he got mad and yelled "don't call me a little man," I said don't call me a Mexican, I was born here. After that, we got along just fine, and I would be associated with him for many years to come. It took some getting used to, this new cast of Motley characters at this place. Some of them were Bob who drank like a fish day in and day out, my buddy Joe, the Italian Stallion, and Ricky who was Doug's son-in-law. There was Bipolar Lester who was the big burly strong man. There was a guy named Jeff who we called the "crime dog," because he looked like the dog in the crime dog commercials. There was also Shannon who was a "reformed" alcoholic, or an alcoholic depending on how close it was to payday. Many of these guys were racists and they wouldn't even hide it. Not so much with me but mostly with blacks because they just didn't want to deal with them. I would get more and more opportunities this way, with a TO which is what they call when you turn a customer over to another salesman. It wasn't because they were difficult customers but these guys just had no common ground with them, and didn't know what to say to them. We had nowhere near the abundance of customers we had at Landmark, but I kept myself busy taking their customers and mine and staying busy on the phone.

One day Jeff handed me a folder and asked me to help some black customers for him and I told him, "What's the catch?" I looked at their credit report and it was good, and the vehicle they picked out which was a nice Dodge truck. I asked him again, "What's the problem?" and he said, "They are "Ragoonas" which was not an endearing term for black people. Whether telling a story, or selling a car the art of setting it up is everything, and how well you set it up will determine how well it works. I went to talk to the people and told them I could not achieve the price they wanted to pay for the truck, but I had made special arrangements with the lender to provide them with a comfortable payment. I sold the truck for $2,000 more and stretched out their payment for 72 months so that they could afford it and in the end everybody wins. I figured if I had to split the commission with Jeff, I needed more profit. Many customers would try to shorten the term and say they didn't want to pay for a vehicle that long, and I would refer to one of my favorite jokes as I say, "A man goes to a doctor and they only give him six months to live, but he can't pay the bill, so they gave him another six months."

One day when I was bored I was looking through the phonebook and stumbled on to a gay and lesbian recreation center in New Orleans. My friend Joe the "Italian Stallion" was very homophobic. I knew this because every time he would bend down, I would goose him and he would pitch a fit screaming "I'm not a homo what's the matter with you?" I called the number to the gay and lesbian center and a sweet young boy answered, I told him how much I would like to go and visit their facility but I had not "come out" yet, that my name was Joe, and I was Italian and my family wouldn't understand. He was very sympathetic and understanding, and told me I could call him anytime so I did. I called him at least on two other occasions and told him how difficult life was for me still being in the closet. To me, that is the art of the "setup." Everybody had pagers in those days, so one day I paged Joe with that number to call back. The next thing I knew, Joe was going around screaming, "Who the hell called this place?" I went to the main office were we could all listen and he vented telling the whole story about this gay and lesbian recreation center. He said, "This guy knew my name and that I was Italian and I had not come out yet." I looked at him with an incredible look on my face, as did everyone else, acting as if I could barely believe the story, until finally I couldn't keep a straight face anymore and started laughing. He started screaming "you mother fucker you did this didn't you!" Joe was also a team captain so we were on equal footing, but he was pissed for days.

Sometime after celebrating my first month there we had a party about a half mile away at a place called the Spot Light that had karaoke and a live band, and Doug actually got to play with the band. There were some female groupies hanging around and being bored, and being that I was out with the guys, I started talking to one of them. Doug even came by and said, "Your wife's on the phone." The tall brunette I was talking to said, "It's okay with me if you are married," and I realized it was time to leave. The next day Joe showed up to work about three hours late, and when Doug started blasting him for being late he started bragging about this brunette he took home from the party that night.

Doug said, "You mean the one Richard left there so he could go home to his wife."

Everybody started laughing, because he had taken someone's leftovers and thought it was a big deal, Joe looked at me and said, "Was she really with you first?"

I said, "She could have been, but I left and went home. I don't want to say anything to harsh but they did name a city after her."

He said, "Yeah, which one?"

And I said, "The Big Easy."

CHAPTER 20
LIFE IN LOUISIANA

Having settled in on our jobs and our home, we started to settle in on life in Louisiana and explore the best restaurants and clubs which ended up being in New Orleans. This was mostly on weekends because it was almost an hour drive into the city from our home in Covington. Some of our favorite places included: K-Paul's, Chef Paul Prudhomme's place. This place always had a line outside of people waiting for a table, but I became friends with the head bartender who gave me a card that had No Pass Line written on it and that meant we didn't wait in line, we could just come straight to the front and be seated immediately. This worked out great especially when we were out with another couple, or if we had people visiting us to just wave a card and go past everyone in line. The food was outstanding and they would greet you with a basket of warm bread of all kinds: raisin bread, molasses and jalapeno corn bread just to name a few. The portions were outstanding and huge, and we always left with food to go, but if you finished your plate they would put a star on your cheek because you ate all your food. All the shrimp dishes were "to die for" and simply delightful. Another favorite place to go was Café Giovanni owned by the famous Chef Duke who lives in Mandeville, a city close to our home. Their dishes were quite exquisite as well, but what they are really known for was their Opera singers, on weekends and special occasions they had a male and female singer with a piano player that would perform famous Opera tunes, such as Phantom of the Opera. The ambiance was so unique and romantic it makes it a favorite place for birthdays, anniversaries or holidays. A rowdy place to go to was on Bourbon Street called The Cat's Meow, it was a very popular college joint where they would sing karaoke live and where Dora and her friends from work liked to go. It almost got me in a fight on one or more occasion and I don't even drink anymore.

One of the most important things in Louisiana is leisure time, by that I mean in the Big City like Houston people live to work, in Louisiana people work to live. We lived near several water ways like the Tchefuncte River and Lake Pontchartrain where we could visit restaurants or take our boat out on the lake. There were Seafood festivals, Crawfish festivals, and the Wooden Boat Festival that was just in the area where we lived. If you crossed the lake into New Orleans, there was Mardi Gras, the French Quarter festival, Strawberry Festival, and if you're into it, the Gay Decadence festival. One of my wife's favorite things to do during Mardi Gras is to go to the Gay costume parade on Saint Ann street in the French Quarter, not everybody that goes is gay of course but people from all over the country come in costume such as: Mayan, Aztec, Egyptian and roman soldiers. It is hosted annually by two transvestites who are local stand-up comedians and are very funny. It takes place in front of a gay bar called OZ with loud music blaring through speakers outside the bar. My wife often liked to go to Oz with her friends when it wasn't Mardi Gras, just to watch the hunky guys doing table dances for one another. I myself was not threatened by the gay community, but the only thing that bothered me was standing at the rail of the bar during the parade and having everyone rub up behind you saying excuse me. Even when there was room to pass, they would find a way to rub up against me. I once told my wife if we don't leave here soon I'm going to switch teams.

Even though we loved the leisure lifestyle my wife's job was very demanding, and was taking a toll on her physically. We always said that the Tobacco industry was easy as long as they had never lost a lawsuit, well guess what? It was the spring of 1995 and they lost their first lawsuit. As with anything shit rolls downhill and her job became increasingly more difficult, where she could spend 12 hours a day working and still not be caught up. She had exhibited early signs of depression in Houston which they called panic attacks, but by this time it was becoming more prevalent. I've learned that depression is brought about by stress and that depression is most often self-induced. My wife has always been a perfectionist and is extremely hard on herself when things do not go as she planned. This was one of the things I admired most about her, but it was also somehow a curse. I could always focus on the next day, and the next opportunity that would come my way and believed in the positive aspect that somehow good things would come to me, and I believed the same thing for her. My wife is a beautiful woman inside and out, she has no ill will toward anybody and no malice in her heart. To her a bad dream would be a dog suffering or cat being mistreated, instead of thinking of murder or violence toward anybody.

I remember being a young boy growing up in Texas with my aunts and my and how they were beautiful Spanish women. I remember thinking to myself, "I want one of those." To my delight I found one and she had beauty, brains and everything a man could want. She was an only child and even had car insurance. I used to joke all the time with her friends that she was a "miracle child" she was an only child from a Hispanic family with a college education, and automobile insurance, a rare find indeed. That's why it was so sad for me to see her suffering and up all night worrying about her job and all that she had to do. She suffered from her own fears of failure, and with the guilt that it was her job that had moved us to Louisiana and she didn't want to disappoint me. All I wanted was for her to be happy and enjoy the leisure life we had there. We were doing quite well financially and could afford to do anything we wanted to do, it was just finding the hours in the day to do it, during this time we went on exotic vacations to places like Bora Bora, Egypt and Tahiti. No matter how far we went or how exotic the trip, I could feel her anxiety building as the last couple days of vacation came to a close and the anticipation of her work load piled up.

My own business was doing very well, I had started with Julian Graham Dodge in April of '95 and in May of '95 I experienced my first Louisiana catastrophe. It was early May and I remember the guys at work told there was a tropical storm brewing in the Gulf of Mexico, I told them, "What the hell does that mean it's going to rain? "Big deal!" I remember them telling me to be careful going home over the causeway bridge because it could affect your visibility. I thought "yeah sure" and when I got on the bridge traffic was moving at twenty miles an hour because you couldn't see with the sheets of rain that were coming down. The next day many of the roads were closed, and the bridge itself was closed until after four o'clock in the afternoon, so many people did not go to work. The next day afterward I was hearing the news about many places experiencing flooding, I had no idea what this would mean in the community.

The day after when I finally did go back to work, we were bombarded with customers and phone calls of people needing cars after they lost theirs in the flood, so I began to realize that local catastrophes could be great for business. A friend of my wife's even had her garage flooded and her cat had kittens and they thought one of them was dead, a little black and white kitty. Her husband had thrown the cat into the trash. The wife had taken the kitty out and used a hair dryer to revive it, she offered this miracle cat to my wife and we named her Tiki. We brought her home and we still have her to this day, I always tell people she is a flood victim who survived the may flood of '95. I didn't realize the traumatic affect it would have on the car business, but even the dealership itself had lost about fifty to sixty new cars to the flood and possibly thirty used cars as well. I don't want to say that anyone did anything illegal but it was suspected that Troy, the general manager, pulled a lot of strings with the insurance company to net the store some big profits. In other words, the store received insurance payments on vehicles that were damaged, and then the dealership refurbished them, and sold them to the public of course with a disclaimer that they had been damaged in the flood. We had a very successful rest of the year and somehow during the process Troy obtained enough money to buy his own dealership which became Toyota of New Orleans at the beginning of '96.

In his defense he may have been saving up for it for a while. I'll never forget when I met his daddy Corbin; I didn't even know who he was and one day on a Saturday when it was very busy I had two customers at once. One was in the office finishing up a deal, while I had the other customers on a test drive by themselves. He stopped Doug the manager at the door and asked him who those customers were that were "riding by themselves." I heard him and I got up and explained that they were with me. He started to yell and raise his voice and say that if I wasn't with them in the car, then the car was not insured. I told him, "They had full coverage insurance and I had a copy of it as well as their licenses and who the hell had appointed him the referee." The man started yelling and screaming and Doug had to take him out and around the corner, so the customers wouldn't hear him while he pitched a fit. Doug told me later that I couldn't talk to him like that, and I said it would help if I had known who he was, and not just that he's Troy's dad. I asked, "Does he have a paid position here? Is he in charge of anything? Because he sure doesn't know shit about me!"

He said that he held a certain measure of respect because of his experience and of course being Troy's dad. I told him that respect from me had to be earned, I did not just give it freely, and if he talked to me like an asshole that I would treat him the same way.

Doug was always getting on my case about some of the privileges I took like coming in late, leaving early or not locking the cars at night. I explained to him that fairness did not matter because life was not fair, there are those who lock the cars and those that sell the cars, and I was among those that sell the cars. He would say that I would have to lead by example; I would explain to him that I was leading by example, I was showing them how to sell cars and make money. I explained to him that this would have to suffice until he decided to leave so I could have his job, and show them the proper way to run a used-car department.

I remember when people were scrambling for cars after the flood, it was closing time and I had received a phone call from a man that needed to replace his taxi cab that had been lost in the flood. I didn't normally do this, but I had the man coming in at closing time which was about a quarter to nine. I had a car that was so nice I knew that if we waited it would not be there the following day. He had said on the phone that he had $5,000 to spend, and I had a really clean Grand Marquis that would make a perfect taxi for him (and I only owned it for $2,000) With everybody watching on the front porch waiting to go home, I put on a show. I pulled the Grand Marquis up front and I opened the hood, the trunk and all doors to show that it was not water damaged. This was a very large black man with a skull cap on and he stood at about 6'4" and he asked me the magic words, "Is this car flood damaged?"

I said, "Man, if a car is flood damaged, you have to look for a sign."

He said, "What do you mean a sign?"

I looked up at the sky and said, "Lawd Lawd shows me a sign!" I thought he might get pissed but I took a chance, he liked the car so much that he started laughing and started counting the money out right there. He also paid me six thousand for the car.

On another occasion I took what you call a TO where a salesman turns a customer over to me with the managers consent because the other salesman couldn't get anywhere with them. This was a rather large couple, they were huge, and they had picked out a minivan, we had pulled their credit which was very good, but they just needed to be convinced of it. The weather outside was hot and steamy and it was midafternoon when I began to speak with them, I asked them if they liked the vehicle and if they were somewhat satisfied with the price and payments. They said yes to everything and I said, "What's keeping you from doing business now?" They responded as usual, "We just want to look around some more and want to see more vehicles." I said, "Great, I have at least five more vans you could test drive if you'd like." I remember the wife telling me, "I'm very picky" and I took one look at her and the husband and said, "Oh, I can see that."

They said we actually thought of going to another dealership, and I said, "Do you really want to start this process over again, in all this heat and humidity?" I had noticed that they were already sweating. They finally broke down and told me the real truth, they wanted to go get something to eat and talk about the deal.

I said, "Why didn't you say so? We have pizza already coming."

They said, "Oh really?"

I said, "Yeah, and if you tell me what you want on it, I can call them and get one just for you." I slipped the salesman some money and told him to go order the pizza the way they wanted it. When the pizza came I told them that they would have privacy in the office and be able to discuss the deal while they enjoyed their pizza. When it came time to walk them across the lot to the finance office, I suggested getting a big bag of chips to drop and leave a trail for them to follow, but it wasn't necessary they left full, fat and happy in their new van while the other salesman and I split a $1,200 commission. As that year came to an end I had had a pretty successful year, I was salesman of the month for six out of the eight months I was there, and had made $80,000 that year, not counting my time at Landmark Chevrolet.

Before the year came to an end, the dealership began to remodel the used-car building which was already small and was now about one third of its size. As the construction began they hired a new salesman that they called, "Little John," he was at least 6'8" and 350 lbs of nothing, but dead weight. The guy was totally useless and he took up a lot of space, every time I was trying to work a deal he was in the office taking up space and talking about nonsense. One day after my customer left I went back into the office and I screamed "what's with this huge pile of shit?" I said, "I'm from Texas, and I didn't know they stacked it that high." Everybody laughed, and the guy became indignant and started trying to push me around. Then I walked out of the office and he started to follow me, he came up from behind me and grabbed me into a bear hug, a huge mistake, because I reached back and grabbed his nuts with my left hand and crushed them for all they were worth. It was hilarious, he started screaming in a high pitch voice for me to let go, I said, "Sure, you let

170

go of me and I'll let go of you," but he wouldn't turn me loose. So he began to crumble like a 6'8" cookie taking me down with him, but I still wouldn't let go. First he went down on one knee, then he was on his back; the whole time he was holding on to me, and me crushing his nuts. The managers and other salesmen came out laughing and screaming at him to let me go so I could let him go. When I finally let him go, he charged at me, and tried to pounce on top of me while I was still on the floor. I put up both feet on his chest and pushed with all my might shoving him backward into the sheetrock. I swear he made an indentation on it that looked like a cartoon of his huge frame. Everybody separated us, and by then he was really upset and embarrassed. To nobody's surprise he quit a couple of days later; they may have him pulling a wagon in New Orleans for some touring company, I believe.

CHAPTER 21
ThingstoLoveaboutLouisiana

In my neighborhood in Covington we were less than ten minutes from the river; we were from the desert of El Paso Texas and had briefly been exposed to the water ways of Houston, now we could have our boat in the water less than half an hour from our house. We actually knew our neighbors, we had several couples that lived in close vicinity and we became friends with them not like in Houston where we didn't know any of our neighbors. We would sometimes take boat rides down the river and go to a restaurant called Friends that sat right on the river. The views on the river we saw at Friends were spectacular and the food was decent but the views are what made the difference, watching the river with all the trees lined with the Spanish moss. Jack and Kathy were our next door neighbors and we were closest with them. Jack was a hunter, and he hunted everything, quail, duck, deer, and squirrels. He and his hunting buddies would freeze all that they would kill, and then throw a big feast, a BBQ to consume it all, at least they would eat what they killed. I used to make fun of Jack saying that I wish I was a duck flying above them as they were sitting with their asses freezing, at 5 in the morning with their duck call going quack, quack. He would say you better be glad you weren't a duck because then you would be on that plate there. As the spring of '96 rolled around, everyone was preparing for Mardi Gras.

Jack invited me to ride with him in the Orpheus Parade in Mandeville. So I accepted and we had all kinds of meetings and planning for the parade, including purchasing our throws. This Orpheus parade is actually one of the oldest in the area; Harry Connick Jr. actually copied it to create his own parade in New Orleans. Speaking of Harry Connick he may be okay on records, but we saw him in concert one time in New Orleans, and it was so bad people were leaving in droves. Part of his mass appeal was to appeal to an older generation by trying to sound like Frank Sinatra, but as we walked out about half an hour into the show an older couple walked passed us, and the old man turned to me and said, "Let's hurry up before he sings another fucking song."

My first ride with Orpheus was a blast, my in laws had come in to visit and my compadre Norbert from Houston and his wife Lily also came. The ride actually takes place with you on a float with two or three other participants, each with his own section for their throws. Even though Jack had showed me how to set mine up in an orderly manner, it took some getting used to. At first I found myself looking down a lot and gathering the throws making me miss part of the show, this included all the people lined up to receive the throws and women flashing their large American breasts. Jack's family had a motor home parked on the route where our friends and Dora's parents could use the facilities. It was pretty successful for my first Mardi Gras ride; we then took Norbert and Lily to the French Quarter for the New Orleans parades.

The hardest thing to do when you go to a parade in New Orleans is to go to the bathroom, because all the restaurants and bars have signs posted that say, "For Patrons Only." Not that we haven't broken the rules and gone and used one anyway, but it's the hardest thing to do and that's why you see a lot of people peeing in the streets. We had finished watching one parade on Canal Street as another was preparing to start. We tried to cross the street to get to the side where our car was and go home. Just then the cops put up barricades and said no one could cross, these parades can take up to two hours. Dora pleaded with the cop to let us through but he said, "No, no one else can pass." It had recently rained as it usually does in New Orleans, so a lot of beads on the ground were filthy and soaking wet. During Mardi Gras beads are flying everywhere as they are being thrown from the floats, and some people in the crowds that don't like the beads will throw them back. My buddy Norbert and I were off to one side and my wife and Lily were off to another. Two black guys walked by us and one of them said, "Did you see what that chick did?" I said, "Which one?" and he pointed at Dora, and he said, "She pulled up a stack of wet beads from the ground and threw them right at the cops head." As I turned to look all I saw was the cop looking around and doing a 360 to see who had thrown it at him, he looked like he wanted to pull his gun. That night ended with us going to Bourbon Street to see all the action and the kinky costumes, one of the more memorable ones was 3 people wearing nothing but fig leaves and pasties on their boobs. They were painted green and had signs and called themselves Adam, Eve and Steve.

When we came back from our trip my in laws had been babysitting our friend's daughter Lizette, we came home to find her all scratched up from the cat. We had told her to play with Andy, who was a gentle older kitty, but she insisted on playing with Grubby, the little deaf cat who loved to fight, and he took it out on her. We felt so bad, she had scratches on her face, upper and lower arms and my in laws said they told her to leave him alone but she kept following him around and insisting to play with him. A couple of days later after they had returned to Houston, it was our turn to take my in laws to experience New Orleans, we bought them purple, green and gold shirts and little hats to wear as well. We went during the daytime, which we thought was safer, because all the crazy shit happens at night. As we walked down Bourbon Street taking in all the sights I just remember Dora's mom carrying a 16 ounce glass of beer and as she'd see something to right or left she would swing that way spilling her beer on everyone. People liked her, they were yelling "get down Grandma!" and all similar comments to that effect, she knows how to party I figure that's where my wife gets it from. The only gross part was when we took them to a restaurant late in the afternoon and a guy just two tables down lost his cookies all over the floor, needless to say we left and I discovered a new place to go. It is in an area called the "West End," it is the parallel to what Mandeville is on the North Shore; but still on the South Shore in the New Orleans area on the lake front. We discovered a Joe's crab shack were you could sit out and enjoy the water and we enjoyed the rest of our day.

As time went on we became more associated with people from Dora's work as well and were invited to a crab boil, this is a famous Louisiana past time going to a crawfish boil or crab boil. This usually takes place at what they call a "camp site" which is usually just a shack on a water way held up by wood pillars. This is a getaway for many people to escape the mundane life and go fishing for a weekend. Usually you take a boat and ride up to your camp and park you boat there, which is what we did. Even though my wife liked seafood she did not like the process of putting animals alive into boiling water; the first time we went she asked the host if she could save one of the crabs, and throw it back into the water. He said okay but just one, so she promptly took a little crab out to the cooler and let it go free. Of course after a few drinks and when he wasn't looking she grabbed four or five more and started throwing them back into the water. After a while he said hey, "I said one, because those things are expensive."

Besides the crab they usually serve shrimp or crawfish with a spicy Cajun mix along with corn, potatoes, and Jambalaya rice. I'll never forget the first time we went to such a feast, and the way it is served on a huge sheet of newspaper in the middle of a table with no plates I found it disgusting. Believe it or not even though I'm Hispanic, I'm used to eating with a fork and plate. The first time we went to a crab boil, Dora asked for plates and everyone was laughing at us, as we sat in the corner with our plates eating mostly jambalaya, corn and potatoes. We began to love the lifestyle so much that when my wife's office moved, she kept a poster that hung there, and we still have it to this day in our home, and it states,

You know you're at home in New Orleans when . . .

You drink "Dixie," not sing it.

You not only say Tchoupitoulas, but you can say it without laughing.

You begin to believe that purple, green, and gold look good together and will even eat things these colors.

You know exactly what you are going to eat next Monday. And the Monday after that. And after that.

You are no longer shocked when someone advises you to "suck the heads and eat tails."

You are not afraid when someone wants to "axe" you a question.

You consider it an honor, on certain occasions, to have cabbages or coconuts thrown at you.

You describe items of a certain hue as being "K & B purple."

You get on a bus marked "Cemeteries" without a second thought.

You have discovered that those four-inch-long cockroaches can fly, but have decided to retain your sanity anyway.

You do not think about spinach when you see the word "Popeye's"

You know that living anywhere else in the world would be very sad.

Jean Patterson-Terrell

As the year progressed at the Dodge dealership a lot had changed with Troy the GM leaving to start his own company at Toyota New Orleans. Even one of the managers that worked at our clearance center lot Steve, I called him the Viking because he was a huge guy with red hair and a red beard. Steve saw the writing on the wall and took a manager position at Benson Toyota; Tom Benson was the owner of the New Orleans Saints and owned five dealerships in town, this being one of them. He soon called me and told me that he had put my name in for a management position I was hoping it was used cars but it was new cars and I had never done that before.

My wife Dora and I on one of our many Vegas trips
as a used car manager for Dick Poe.

My mother Maria Elena Ochoa at Christmas time.

My brother, Freddy, while in Viietnam, he never made it back alive RIP.

Me striking a pose after one of my many salesman of the month victories.

My rival at Dick Poe Chrysler, "Jerry the great!"

Me in a very fancy "glamor" shot picture.

A copy of the newspaper article of my first ever salesman of the month award. I carried this around in my walet to show girls I would meet at the clubs, including my wife on the night we met.

My wife, Dora, stikes a pose at our home in Louisiana.

My wife Dora and I attend a wedding in Houston for our "compadres" Norbert and Blanca Solis.

On vacation in Mexico with my "compadre" Norbert Solis.

My wife and I with her parents, Mr. and Mrs. Guzman.

My wife, Dora, looking sexy while on vacation in Mexico.

Another salesman of the month victory, posing with my manager, Dan Carter.

Another victory lap for the "good guys." I won sales man of the month again.

My wife, Dora, celebrating Mardi Gras at the annual "pooch parade" with our dog, Tiffany.

These victory pics just keep on coming, right?

A third place finish for Tiffany at the "pooch parade."

My mom and dad, Fred and Nena Ochoa, while on vacation.

My car lot kitty "Spooky." I used to call her "Spooky Carlotta," she is the only cat with her own chapter in the book.

Myself on vacation in Cabo san Lucas, Mexico.

My wife, Dora, on vacation in Cuba, where we met out friends from England, Mark and Dale Crane, still friends to this day.

My best friend since grade school, Alex Garcia, and his wife, Liz Garcia, at our 25th wedding anniversary party.

My lovely wife, Dora, in Havana, Cuba.

Dora and I at our 25th anniversary party. A great time!

Dora and I dancing and enjoying our anniversary party.

My wife Dora and I renewing our vows on our anniversary,
with uncle Mando, aunt Irma, and our pastor, the late rev Paul Mckeachern.

CHAPTER 22
IMAGINEME, ANEW-CARMANAGER

I was soon contacted by Joe C who was the general manager of Benson Toyota for an interview; he said I came highly recommended after checking my references in El Paso and at Landmark Chevrolet in Houston. Joe C was a tall no nonsense, Italian man with a goatee and deep dark eyes. One could have almost mistaken him for a mafia boss, which there is plenty of in New Orleans. Joe C told me that my position would primarily be in the new car department, but he had bigger plans for me within the next sixty days. What I found out was the big promotion coming was that I was going to head the Kia department. That was a new line of cars coming out of which the dealership would have a franchise and I would be its head man. I left the Dodge store and took a position as an assistant manager at Benson Toyota, my primary function was to track the sales and close deals. I've always hated that aspect of the business which is new cars; I always said that "the only thing good about new cars is that they eventually become used cars." Even the customers were different; this was at the time that the internet was exploding with sites that would inform the customer what the dealership was paying for a car so of course they didn't want to pay a profit.

I had many skills in the car business, and I knew there was more than one way to skin a cat, I could talk about trade-in and hold-back profit on their trade or speak about financing and how we could make that more appealing for them; anything but the obvious that they were paying too much for a car. When it came down to it they would point back and ask me just how much profit we need to make on this car? I would say well our average is $1,800 but for you I will do it for $1,500 over cost. It happened quite often when they'd bitch moan and complain, I'd say, "Why are you afraid of the dealer making a profit?" "Do you not want us to be here to service your car, if we don't make a profit we can't stay in business?" Then I'd say, "Do you go to Sears and complain about how much a washing machine costs to build in Taiwan, and that you pay $300 for it? "Or do you complain that the jeans you are buying are sewn in Costa Rica in sweat shops, yet they are charging you $29.99 for them?" Then they'd say what to me, was the ultimate kicker, "Joe Schmoe down the street will sell it to me for this amount." I would advert to my ultimate attorney position causing reasonable doubt, and I would say, "How do you know they will sell it for that, did they tell you that, did you see it in writing, did a manager sign off on it, or did a salesman on the phone tell you they might do that?" 9 times out of 10 they had just made a phone call to a salesman and asked what where the chances that you could sell the car for that price. It was a job that I didn't particularly enjoy, but I did it for the paycheck and for the new opportunity that was coming.

People were skeptical about the Kia product because it was a Korean car, even though Hyundai had already been around for a few years. Nevertheless we planned a big grand opening, and I met the manufacturer's representative and my own factory sales rep. I was allowed to hire my own sales force, must of them were rejects, that weren't hired by the different department's new cars or used cars at Benson Toyota. One was a female named Diva; she was an attractive girl from Columbia who had no sales experience whatsoever. Another was Alfred, a former service advisor, and then there was Harold who was a former telemarketer, he had a wild and crazy personality and would talk your ear off. The best of the bunch was Sean a tall black man who had a lot of sales experience but he was such a con artist that I had to watch him closely. They would be my sales force going forward, three African American men and one Hispanic woman as we pioneered a new product and all the doubts and fears that it represented. Had I seen how difficult a task it was, I would not have taken the job though it paid well, it took the majority of my time. Had it not for the incentive plan I might have quit right on the spot.

My factory sales representative said he had a special plan for me; this was an incentive plan that would escalate depending on how many cars we sold in a ninety-day period. I was getting paid between $10,000 and $11,000 a month from the dealer, but this plan would be totally separate from that. This would be a check given to me by Kia manufacturing company themselves and totally independent from the dealership. Needless to say, this perked up my interest and got my attention. The first thirty cars would pay me seventy-five a car then it would go to $150 for the next twenty then as long as I went over the seventy-five cars in a ninety-day period, the last remaining would be at $225 a car. So I put my heart into it, and I usually worked nine to nine every day with very little days off or time off as I tried to close every sale. Many of our sales were "just get me done" customers who were just happy to get approved and be driving. I remember when Harold had a whole family of black people and none of them qualified, until finally we asked the grandpa to run his credit and finally he had a decent score. When I told him "You're the winner," his face lit up, and his whole family started celebrating as if they had won the lottery. I was determined to be successful at this position if nothing else for those ninety days to get my money; I had fully intended to go back to selling used cars after that.

Not being one to always play by the rules, I did my own thing since my building was in between the new Toyota building and the used-car building, I had signs painted on the windshields of my Kia cars facing both sides. I would put "low ball" payments on them, since my cars were so much cheaper than Toyota's, I would put like $169 a month or I would have them write "compare with a Toyota and save" with big dollar signs. I'd even put some on the used cars side and say, "Why buy junk, when you could have a six year warranty?" This pissed off both sides of the department managers, but I didn't care, "all's fair in love and war." This was the kind of situation where they would always tell me to watch my back because the other managers would be gunning for me. I didn't care, because I would watch my own back, I was there longer than them and I worked longer hours than them and Joe C the general manager knew it. I didn't need anyone to watch my back; I had a stronger work ethic than them. I had constant battles with the Finance Director named John; he would constantly tell me that the banks didn't believe enough in the product yet, even if it was a new car. Even when we had a good credit customer, the banks didn't want to loan enough to cover the deal. But what would really piss him off was when I would take the deal to Joe C and have him call the lender and ask why they wouldn't finance the deal, when it was a new car and they had guidelines for financing new cars regardless of their personal feelings. After several occurrences like this, John was not happy with me, because Joe C. was getting the deals approved and not him. I've never been one to be politically correct; I care more about getting the job done than someone's personal feelings, or their opinion of me. As the 90 day period came close to an end I talked to Steve my friend who was the manager in used cars as I prepared for my position to go there and sell after my 90 day period was up. When the 90 days was over the factory rep from Kia came to visit me, and he gave me a check for almost $15,000 for the ninety days' worth of sales bonus money from Kia.

This was totally independent from the dealership and I would not be taxed on it. After I went to the bank and cashed it I took my little filing cabinet over to the used-car building to begin selling used cars there. I went over and spoke to Joe C and told him of my plans, in retrospect I should have done it differently, because he was a good man and deserved better than that. He had entrusted me in a job and I had fulfilled my part, and he was disappointed that I was leaving a position he had brought me there for. My career selling used cars at Toyota would be short lived, since I had pissed off so many people at Toyota while I was managing Kia; but I would have a good four or five months there.

The Toyota used-car department was the ultimate TO house, they would turn a customer over two or three times if necessary to try and make a deal. This was good for me because I was always the closer riding the advantage of others peoples leftovers to finalize the deal and receive half the commission. One day while on the lot an older black gentleman approached, I greeted him and started to show him some vehicles and he held up his hands and said, "No offense, but could you get me an African American salesman."

I couldn't believe it. I said, "What! I went to school in LA and worked at UPS with hundreds of black guys, played basketball and you want me to get a black salesman!" I was in shock. I told the customer "but I even speak Jive," if you are familiar with the movie Airplane at all; there's two black men talking and nobody could understand them except for one white lady who spoke "Jive" and she could interpret for them. When I told the customer this he got even more pissed, and said, "All the more reason that I need a black salesman." I went and told the manager and turned him over to a black salesman, as the sale progressed the salesman could not close the deal, so the manager called me to take my turn with the customer. I approached the office and I walked inside and greeted him and I said, "Remember me?" and he said, "Yeah, you're the one that speaks Jive." As we progressed I made the deal and he was very cordial and happy with me, and he made the purchase. I guess nobody wants to say they bought a car from an asshole even if it was true.

There was a huge black salesman named Sheldon who was a former player for the New Orleans Saints, but he had gained more weight and every afternoon after lunch he could be counted on to take at least an hour and half nap. This in itself wasn't news except for this one guy, Ronald from Honduras, who would go mess with him while he took his nap. Sheldon was such a sound sleeper that Ronald would measure his nose from the width and from top to bottom, and began saying things like "this is how early man was before the Neanderthals and Cro-Magnon stage." He would be talking about the width and size of his hands and feet and describe him as "early man at the dawn of civilization." Anyway, it was a funny bit, and the rest of us would be trying not to laugh too loud so as to wake Sheldon. Sheldon would wake up and start chasing Ronald around the used-car building and all the way outside. Sheldon was a good guy, and we would often buy him lunch just to watch him eat it, he could put away a po' boy in seconds.

I only saw him get really pissed at Ronald one time; that time Sheldon had fallen into a deep hibernated sleep and Ronald got some light green and yellow markers and painted his face like an Aborigine, and when Sheldon woke he was fit to be tied, Ronald had to actually go home early for fear of retaliation. During this time I had heard that the old Dodge store had turned over completely of all the people, and my old buddy Doug the used-car director, was running the Hyundai lot across from Toyota. He came by several times to see me at Toyota and invited me to go work with him over at the Hyundai dealership. Hyundai was owned by the Price brothers, who also owed Lexus of New Orleans which was part of the same facility and franchise. It was if he had as is if it were the best of both worlds one of the least expensive car franchises, with one of the world's most premier franchises. I told him I would keep it in mind; and when I had my first run in with John the finance manager, I packed up my little filing cabinet into my Blazer and drove across the street to join Doug at the Hyundai dealership. All my old friends from the Dodge store were there with Doug, this included; his son-in-law Ricky, my Buddy Joe, the Italian Stallion, and Bob the alcoholic.

I let Doug know that my time there would be somewhat part-time, because I had started a new venture on my own, that of buying cars form Sherriff's auctions in Baton Rouge. I had obtained a line of credit from the bank and was going to buy and sell cars by putting them through an advertisement in the paper. I let him know that I could sell my fair share of cars at the dealership but that I would be strictly on the "C" shift as in "if you see me I'm here." He didn't like the idea at first but he got used to it, especially when I would come in for three or four hours and still sells cars and close the deals where other people couldn't.

Part of the process in buying the cars was finding them, by that I mean the Sherriff's office would come out with a list, but they weren't at the same location, so you had to physically find them to be able to see what you were buying, or do it blind, which I refused to do since I was using my own money. This process was time consuming in itself, but then when I actually bought cars I would have to take a porter back when he was off to pick up the cars to drive them back to the dealership and sometimes it took two or three trips. Since my friend Doug was running the Hyundai dealership he didn't mind that I had two or three cars on the premises that I was selling. Of course when the salesman couldn't find anything on the lot that interested the customer they would ask what I had to sell and how much they could make off of it. After a while Doug started saying, "Hey where's my cut?" so then he insisted on buying the cars through the dealership so they could make more income by financing the car through the dealer. Then he had the gall to complain that I was making money on him by selling the car to the dealership. I would say Doug "I made three trips to Baton Rouge to get this car as well as using my own money on my credit line that I'm paying interest on, if I can't make at least $1,000 on my money it's not worth it to me."

The buying process in itself was rather comical; because it was only me and one other guy that knew what the hell we were doing when buying these cars. There were a few other regulars that were bidding on the cars but they seldom bought any because they were afraid of making a mistake. This one poor guy always bid on them, and then he would ask me" is that a good car?" because he hadn't seen them. I'd say sure and actually let him buy a couple that he paid way too much money for. One of the best buys I made was a Kia Sportage that had a stick shift and four wheel drive. I paid $3,500 for it; I had to spend a couple of hundred dollars on cosmetic issues, but when I put it in the paper it sold for $7,800. Another good buy I made was on a three-year-old Toyota Camry that had some body damage and no keys; but since the car only had forty-seven thousand miles I knew the car still had manufacturing warranty up to sixty thousand miles. I knew if I had engine or transmission, trouble it was covered on the power train warranty. So I just rolled the dice and hoped that the air conditioner and power windows all worked.

It turned out I was lucky everything worked in the car; I spent $1,000 on the body work and made $4,800 on it when I sold it. Those were some of the best buys I made but the wells started to dry up because the banks representatives started going to represent the cars and bump up the price. For example if the bank loan on the car was for $11,000 and they sold it for $8,000 they would lose $3,000 in addition to the percentage they would have lost on financing income. Once I almost bought a Chevy Tahoe that was worth $24,000 and I had bid as high as $21,000 when the bank rep from GMAC arrived and pushed the bid up to $24,000, so I walked away from it. The scariest thing for me during this process was that vehicles I purchased didn't have insurance on them, since I paid cash for them. At one point I had $38,000 worth of cars out there, and that's why my goal was to sell them as fast as possible. I wound up staying at the dealership more and more because the buying process was drying up in Baton Rouge.

As I mentioned the dealer that owned our store also owned the Lexus building next door so we had certain privileges, on occasion to go to their building especially for the gourmet coffee and Danish. Instead of second class citizens, we were more like third or fourth class citizens, compared to their store; so naturally they looked down on us but we didn't care. Some of our people were going over there and spying every day to see what promotion they were having like finger sandwiches in the afternoon for their service customers or a buffet lunch for new customers. No matter what promotion they had, we knew well in advance and would take advantage of it, and pounce all over them. I especially liked the gourmet coffee and fresh muffins which were meant for their service customers. Doug was under a lot of pressure to sell more and more cars and to make the store perform well, as a former used-car manager I could see the writing on the wall; when someone is buying cars, and I can see they are paying way too much for them. I know that someone may be lining their pockets a little bit, and getting ready to make a move. It was soon winter and with the cold weather business got slower and slower.

One day on a Saturday when it was cold and raining, and there were no customers, we were watching the NFL playoffs hollering and cheering. Doug came out of the office fuming that we were having such a good time, while he was suffering with our lack of business, so he walked over and turned the TV off and he said, "You better not turn it back on." I waited a respectable amount of time, about half an hour before I walked over and turned it on again. This time he came out really pissed and said, "Who turned it on?" and I said, "I did it, turning it off is not going to make customers appear." Then he turned it off again and said, "Anyone that turns it on again I'm going to fire them, and I don't care who it is," and he turned and looked at me. After he went back to his office, I pulled out all the stops, and started to act out one of my favorite movie scenes from "One Flew over the Coo Coo's Nest." In the film Jack Nicolson is deprived of watching the World Series while he is in a mental hospital, so he stares at the blank TV and starts acting out what he sees in his mind, "it's a base hit" or "a home run" with all the crazies yelling and screaming as if they were really watching the game. I did likewise, the Cowboys were playing so I said Aikman's under center he's got the ball he's throwing deep and it's a TOUCHDOWN!

Pretty soon I had a group around me looking at the blank TV. Watching me act out what I thought could be happening during the game. I had them yelling and cheering about my antics while looking at the blank screen, after a while Doug came out, red faced and fuming; ready to fire somebody, and then he saw that the TV was off and he said, "What the fuck are you doing?" I said, "I'm using something that you don't have, I'm using my imagination, and you can't stop me from appreciating the moment, even if I can't see it I can still enjoy it. You should try putting your mind someplace else to help you cope with your troubles." He saw that I had a crowd around me supporting me, so he went ahead and turned the TV back on, anyway the Cowboys lost.

About a month later when I made one of my trips to Baton Rouge I came back to find a ghost town at the Dealership, Doug and all my close friends had been fired. There was a note on my desk telling me to go see one the Leblanc brothers next door at the Lexus dealership. They gave me a lengthy presentation about me running the dealership, and why I should do it and that they needed my help. I asked them to let me think about it and I went back to my office to start packing my stuff. Not knowing what else to do I called Troy, who now had his own dealership and was the former GM of Julian Graham Dodge, he now owned Toyota New Orleans on the Eastside of town in New Orleans. As soon as I called him, he already knew about Doug and everyone else being fired from the Hyundai store. I asked him if he had anything for me, and right away he said yes sure I'll make you assistant used-car manager, I will give you a salary and you can even sell, come on down. That was the answer I was waiting for, so after I packed all my stuff I went back to Lexus to talk with the Leblanc brothers again. I told them here's my answer NO! You pay like shit, you treat people like shit, and besides you just fired all my friends.

CHAPTER 23

SELLING CARS IN THE HOOD

Upon my arrival at Toyota New Orleans Troy gave me the Royal Tour and it was not pretty, the dealership was on Chef Menteur Highway in the hood, it was such a rough neighborhood that unlike other dealerships that would close at nine, we would have to close by seven because after that bullets would start flying, and if you kept the managers late like 7:30, they would literally get scared and say, "Hurry up, I have to go." Nevertheless, I always thought that if anyone could do it, I could do it; Troy agreed to pay me $500 a week salary, as well as I would earn commission off of what I sold. Plus I received manager's bonuses as well as salesman bonuses. I had to close two nights a week. 85 percent to 90 percent of the dealership was black, this in itself wasn't bad, and except they would always ask me what part of Mexico I was from, so I'd ask them what part of the Congo they were from. After some dialogue like that we got along pretty good, there was one guy named Mark who was white and was a personal friend of Troy's. I don't think we had drug testing back then, because this guy certainly would not have passed. The guy would literally be flying around one minute, and then be crumbled up asleep at his desk the next. One day when he was in "accelerated mode" I heard someone named Mark being paged to the Service department, so I said Mark they want you in Service and he went running. Sam, the other manager, and I started cracking up laughing. We knew they weren't calling him, but they were calling a porter named Mark. Then he came back about half an hour later after chasing his tail around the dealership, and he said, "What the fuck is wrong with you?" I said, "I heard them call Mark and I thought it was for you," and he began screaming that he was going to tell Troy. I just laughed in his face, and I said that if he didn't like it he could go ahead and kick my ass.

They say that Jesus could not have been from Mexico, because he could never have found three wise men and a virgin; it was equally as hard there to find a good credit customer it was like looking for a needle in a hay stack. The best you could hope for was a cash buyer, or if they had a third of the money down and could prove their income. I relegated myself to do some advertising for the cars on the lot. I would take fine vehicles like Toyota Avalon's or High line Camry and put low payments on the windshield with these peel off neon numbers, this would immediately induce conversation with the customers. I told the salesman how to respond when asked how to achieve that payment the correct answer is, "with a third down and your good credit." This would automatically trigger a response like "my credit is not that good," or "I don't have a third of the money to give down," either way it got them not to talk about price, but it enabled us to see what they qualified for and maximize our profit. All things being equal the dealership did have some talent, one of the finance managers, and the new car manager did go on to acquire their own dealerships some years later. After going through the second used-car manager, I knew the time would come when Troy would want me to run the used-car department. I really didn't want to; because I knew I would be taking a pay cut. I was easily making $8,000–$10,000 a month, and I knew as a manager I wouldn't make that much. Plus if I was the manager I would have to deal with Troy's daddy which was no picnic, we used to say, "He would squeal on a flat tire."

One of the best deals I've ever made there was when I had waited on an older black man who was there with his family, and as he was looking at the cars he asked about how to get the payment on the window and I gave him the line about with your good credit and a third down, he said, "Oh, I've got that" and I said which one "the down payment, or the good credit?" and he said, "Both." When it was all said and done I had made about a $2,500 commission.

The strangest deal I ever did there was when the bus literally stopped in front of the dealership's used-car lot one day. An older black man got off the bus carrying a duffel bag, and he walked right up to me. It was a rainy night at about six o'clock during the winter and he had overalls, long hair, a scraggly beard and a fishing hat. He looked straight out of a horror movie, a black man's version of "I know what you did last summer." It was almost as if when I would ask him a question and lightening would flash, the thunder would roar, and then he would answer. We picked out a car that we thought was in his price range and began the paperwork, it seemed everything I asked him for was in his duffel bag, proof of income, proof of residence even his birth certificate, you name it. Then I asked him for the down payment, and he took out "five stacks," which in the hood means five grand. I took everything to the finance manager and he suggested that for us to make any real money we would need another two thousand down. Naturally I went back and asked the man for another three thousand down, and he said, "I'll give you two and that's it." As he reached in his bag to get the money I thought I saw the glimpse of a pistol, so I said, "What else you got in there?" and he pulled out his "Glock pistol" to show me. He said, "I know this is the hood and I came prepared." I'm not sure, but I think the lightning and thunder struck again when he said that.

I was selling cars and doing my job as an assistant, I was making good money at least $8,000–$10,000 a month but I knew tough times were coming because I dreaded the fact that the used-car managers would not stay with the company. I knew that Troy would want to offer me the job, and it was not something I wanted or coveted. Soon enough the manager Sam, who was there when I was hired, had left, and Larry was next in line, and I feared I would be next after him. The used-car manager's job carried more responsibility, less pay, and I did not care for that. Another reason to not want the job was you had to answer to Troy's dad, Troy was the owner and his dad was a pain in the ass. I had run in's with Troy's dad before, his name was Corbin, that's when Troy was general manager of the Dodge dealership. At that time his dad had no job title, but now he had a vested interest in the company seeing how his son owned it. Troy and his family had undergone a revival and become born again Christians, for most people this is a good thing for having this change in their life makes them happier and more pleasant to be around. I was well familiar with this myself having going to Bible College and being a Christian myself.

In their case it made them more judgmental, less tolerant, and exhibiting less patience with others. I used to tell Troy instead of throwing around the "fire and brimstone," he should be showing more of the joy of the Lord, that is if he had any. Troy would carry his thick Bible around with him and I would say, "Hey, little man, you might want to know what that thing says instead of just carrying it around." I would quote things from the Bible that I knew, and he didn't even know where they were. He would just stand there with his mouth open and then say, "Hey don't you ever call me little man again!" His dad was the worst though, we used to say he would squeal on a flat tire, and he would look around the lot for trash or any reason to complain of things not being right. Plus he was a designated buyer for the used cars and he had no clue what a car was worth, and would pay too much for them. The most disturbing thing to me was that this cantankerous old man would go around to local churches sharing his testimony on how the Lord had changed him, and made him a better person. One could only imagine what he was like before. He would even sometimes carry huge black and white posters of himself that he would post at the churches where he would speak. One day he left a dozen or so of his pictures in the used-car building, and I don't know who; but somebody painted mustaches beards and horns on all of them, and he was so mad, he was fit to be tied. In some ways he reminded me of my dad who was the same way after he became a Christian. I remember one time telling my dad that it's a good think he wasn't there when Jesus said, "Let he who is without sin throw the first stone," because he would have sent a stone flying like a projectile to hit the man. To this my mom cracked up so hard saying, "Isn't that the truth." My dad started screaming, "Shut up, goddamn, it's not that funny!"

Larry's tenure as used-car manager only lasted a few months, and soon it would be my job by default, to be the used-car manager. By then I had brought my friend Bob, the alcoholic, who I knew from other dealerships to be my assistant; as long as he kept his nose clean, and he didn't drink too much. I also assigned Bob to be the liaison to Troy's dad, so that I wouldn't have to deal with him. The job was as I expected more demanding, and more anxiety for less pay, it's a good thing I only lasted about five months. I had been talking to my old buddy Doug who used to run the Hyundai dealership and was now the used-car director at a very profitable Chevy dealership in Kenner. He kept calling me and telling me that I should go join him there, and go back to selling cars. As it turned out one day at one of Troy's manager meetings, he always had a way of putting pressure on you about how you had to step up, he would say, "You had to step up or step out." Myself being fed up with the situation, I said, "Well, I guess I'm stepping out." In my short time as the manager, there were two things that really bothered Troy. One that I sold a peach colored Hyundai to the dealership, my last purchase that I had bought in my car buying days in Baton Rouge, it took forever to find a black person to buy that car. The other thing that bothered him was when I bought a car myself, by trading in my old Blazer that had a ton of miles on it, he claims that I over appraised it, which I did, because it was my right and my position to do so, and I bought the other car at cost. I even had the finance director get me a preferred rate on the car loan. I remember him being pissed about that for about a month, but we sold my Blazer, and made money on it anyway. I even remember him commenting when I was loading up my truck with my personal belongings to leave, how I had "stolen" that vehicle.

CHAPTER 24
TOUGH TIMES AHEAD

The tough times had nothing to do with me going to sell cars at Best Chevrolet; the store was very successful, and the used-car department was in good hands with my friend Doug. The store was secretly owned by Tom Benson the owner of the New Orleans Saints, and it was one of the last of the dealerships that he kept, that and the Mercedes dealership. The tough times we faced were when my wife had slid into full blown depression from the stress of her new job. At first she was just being treated for it with therapy and medication, but it got so difficult that it made her unable to work. At first they put her on a ten week program, where she would continue to get paid while treating her illness and just to focus on getting well. My wife is not the kind of person who can sit around the house and do nothing so we joined a health club and she began to work out constantly. One day she ran into a friend of hers who owned a daycare not far from our house, it was called Apple Tree. She asked Dora if she would like to go there and volunteer to see what it's like, and to help with the kids. Soon Dora decided to take a job at the Apple tree on a volunteer basis and was an assistant teacher; this was good for her because it gave her purpose, and a daily routine to count on.

As usual my wife does not do anything half ass and soon she became the assistant manager and would open the place up at five thirty in the morning, to greet the parents that would bring their kids in early. Her friend was taking note of all the hours she was putting in and told her she fully planned on paying her at some point. Dora explained to her that if she received any compensation that this would violate and jeopardize her job with R. J. Reynolds, so this had to be on a strictly volunteer basis. This became a source of conflict with the owner's accountants and her wanting to pay Dora for her time, I remember her getting up extra early one day crying and saying that she didn't want to leave the job because it made her feel appreciated and wanted by the kids, and the parents that she dealt with. This might seem strange to a lot of people because we didn't have kids, but this was nurturing to her state of mind and her personal wellbeing. I went with my wife to see the owner of the day care to explain to her that by no means would we ever go back to her for payment of my wife's services, that my wife's work was strictly on a volunteer basis. I even told the owner that if she wanted to give Dora a gift like a computer or something we wouldn't be opposed it, but as far as compensation she didn't have to do it. Sometime after that I received a call from the owner of the daycare while I was at work saying that Dora had had an accident, and she was in the hospital. It seems her doctor had changed her medication, and she had a reaction to it. The changes made her have a seizure, and a fall, she also hit her head leading to a concussion. So she was forced to stay a couple days in the hospital and this dramatically cut back on her volunteering days. It also changed her position with her R. J. Reynolds's job, because of the seizure and concussion; she was now on semi-permanent disability and needed to be evaluated every six months.

In my heart I knew she was getting better because she would actually laugh now, and was getting to be more pleasant and she hadn't done that in a while, I remember taking her to see the movie, "As Good As It Gets" with Jack Nicolson. I remember her laughing extra hard at the author Jack Nicolson played and his OCD antics. When someone you love is going through depression you look for a glimmer of hope, or any sign of them coming back to the person they were, just to hear her laugh or see her smile would make my day. I think one of the biggest things she felt was guilt, that if she failed her job, I would be disappointed, because it was her job that took us to Louisiana in the first place. I would reassure that it was fine, that it was a beautiful place to live and I was doing fine with my work which I could do anywhere, and it didn't matter where we were as long as we were happy together.

Meanwhile back at the Chevrolet dealer I was kicking butt as usual. Doug had tried to get them to pay me a salary but all he could manage was a $400 car allowance and 30 percent commission across the board. This dealership had some of the best talent that I had ever been around. Peter B. was the general manager, Joey was the general sales manager, Sean was the finance Director and his buddy Craig was also a finance manager along with Ricky, Doug's son-in-law, and of course my friend Doug was the used-car director. Before I really got in rhythm at the new dealership I had to deal with my old boss Troy, the owner of Toyota of New Orleans. We had a disagreement regarding my vacation pay, he had admitted to me that he owed me my vacation pay, but once I left, he refused to pay it. So I refused to return my company car. He even had Bob, my old assistant call me every day, to please bring it back. His dad even called me once, and I laughed, and hung up on him. Finally, Troy called me from his office, on a speaker phone, and said he had the sheriff, and his deputies were there with him. I acted dumb and said, "Did you do something wrong?" The sheriff laughed, and asked if I still had the company car. I said, "Yes, and does he still have my money?" He told me they were only obligated to retrieve the company vehicle at this time. I said, "Go ahead and retrieve it, what are you waiting for?" He asked if the car was in my possession, and I told them where the car could be recovered. It had been a full two weeks since I had left Troy's employment; I knew he wasn't going to pay me, so I thought I would just aggravate him a little while.

It didn't take me long to find favor with all the various managers; for example on a slow day I could even go through the dead deal file in the finance office. They had a box of dead deals that for some reason didn't go through, they didn't get to sign, or they needed more paperwork and I would work them. I've always read my share of detective novels and I prided myself like a "cold case" detective artist and would go through files even six months old and make something out of them. I remember one in particular, an African American lady who wanted to buy a Corvette; she had a decent credit score and not much down. After five months I got her back in and sold her a used corvette. I made a $4,000 profit having assured her if she paid on it for a few years we could put her in a new Corvette. I developed a reputation like a hired gun; they would call me to close deals either new or used, it didn't matter as long as it was a workable deal, one that I could profit from. One thing I liked about the dealership is that they had constant promotions and sales and we would get a nice group of customers there. I was the master at qualifying people quickly and finding out if they would buy, if they could buy, and if someone was just being ridiculous I would say, "You must be looking for a good buy" and when they would say yes, I would say, "Goodbye." If there was any reasonable doubt, I would run their credit and leave them exposed knowing that I knew all about their credit history. I would equate it to like being on a second date with a girl, and you already got her top off on the first date, so there's not that much left to be imagined after you've gotten that far, and you both know it. Selling cars is like a seduction when you get down to it.

One day we had a big sale like event and I had a lady with her daughter looking for a small pickup, she wanted a really inexpensive truck with a low payment. I said, "Lady, there are no inexpensive pickups unless you are willing to buy a stick shift with a lot of miles on it." She said, "Oh no my daughter needs an automatic, and it's got to be good on gas." I said, "Well, you must have $4,000 or $5,000 to put down then," and she said, "Oh no, I only have $1,000." I said, "Well then, you must have an ideal credit score like from 700 to 750 right?" She said, "Oh no, my credit is not that good." I said well let's go inside and see what you qualify for," she said, "Oh no, I don't want to run my credit until I see something I want to buy." She went on to say, "Well, what can you do for me?" I said, "Well, based on everything you've said, you are dismissed." I said, "I can't help you, but maybe someone else can, I've only been doing this for twenty-five years." Somehow she wandered into the New Car Building and ran into Joey and Sean the finance directors to complain about me. They both came over to used cars to look for me, and by now I had a new customer, one could actually buy a car, and I was working with them.

Joey called me aside and said, "You told this lady she was dismissed," and I said, "Hell yes, I did, I said based on what she told me she is dismissed." He said yeah "well I've got a new car salesman working with her and you watch we are going to make that deal." So I gave Joey the line that Mike gave me a long time ago and I said, "You make that deal and I'll say I'm sorry and kiss your ass on the showroom floor in front of everybody, otherwise she's dismissed." Sometime later after I took my other customer to finance, I ran into Joey and Sean again and I asked, "Well, what happened to that lady?"

He said, "Oh, we couldn't do anything with her," and I said, "I was right then, she was dismissed," and I laughed in their faces. I sold so many cars and made so much money that I ruled the roost again, as was my custom, very seldom was I challenged or put in my place.

One Saturday a big old heavy set man, with his heavy set son came in looking for a truck. He wanted the cheapest truck he could find with an extended cab so I pointed him to a work truck with a stick shift; it was clean with good miles. We started the truck and looked around and it was certainly clean enough but the man was strictly a payment buyer, and he was determined for me to go for a drive with his son. I suspected that he wanted to go next door and price a new similar truck, and I didn't want to give him the satisfaction. So I told him, "Why don't we go inside and run your credit and see how low of a payment we can get for you? And then you can see if the truck works and if you want to buy it." He was determined that his son had to drive it, and that I had to go with him, I knew better but I obliged him. I'm not one of these people that think the customer is always right, on the contrary I think most of them are assholes, and in this case I was right. No sooner than I got back with his son did I pull up and see him at the new cars sales desk inquiring about the new ones. When the son came back and parked the truck, I switched places with him and peeled the tires as I drove it to the back lot to take it far away from the dad, the man even screamed at me as I drove away and I ignored him. This time I went straight to my office sat down and threw the keys on the desk, and I said, "I don't want to talk about it. What do you want? I thought you wanted to buy a new one?" My peeling the tires had prompted another meeting with Joey and Sean talking to me about my treatment of the customer. They were outside my office and called me over, and I told them I knew he was going to go shop for a new one as soon as I drove away in the used one, as I discussed this with Joey and I was not whispering, I was certainly saying it loud enough for the customer to hear. Joey told me to lower my voice, and I told him I didn't care, I said, "Trust me, Joey, he's not buying anything, he's not buying the used one or the new one." I told him, "Go let someone else deal with him, that I just want him out of my office and out of my face." So naturally Joey got him another salesman and was apologetic and saying let's see what we can do, and just as I was right before, I was right again, the man's credit was no good and he didn't buy anything. I had made a living in the trenches and prided myself in being a student of human moves; that means knowing what a person will do before they even did it, it's called anticipation. I had made over six figures quite often by using my cunning and wits, and knowing what people would do before they even did it. As in the book, "The Art of War," "the battle is won or lost before it is ever fought."

There was quite a cast of characters at the used-car department of this dealership as well, Dan was one of them, he was an ex-Vietnam veteran who had quite a temper and would fly off the handle for no reason. When I think about him I think about people with Bipolar Disorder. He would come to me and ask me about the scriptures, and then the next minute I would piss him off and he'd want to fight. Whenever I got bored, just for kicks, I would go push his buttons and watch him go crazy. I was once talking about a friend from Texas who was a Vietnam vet as well, no kidding, this guy Arturo would be in the middle of telling a story and would jerk his head while yelling a loud "whoa!" and we would all yell "Mambo!" Like as if he was singing with a band. I was telling Dan about the story one time, about Arturo the guy from Texas, and he said, "What do you think was wrong with him?" I said, "I think he suffered from too much Agent Orange in Vietnam." Dan got super pissed and said, "You fucking idiot Agent Orange is a chemical that causes lung and skin damage" and that he had suffered it himself. Instead of correcting myself I said, "Do you think maybe you'll start yelling Mambo like that too?" Dan got so pissed he wanted to fight, but we were near the managers desk and the manager told him instead to go home. He picked up his briefcase and left, and the next day at work he acted like nothing was wrong.

Another salesman there was a good friend of mine named Harris, Harris had black skin but he was a Latino from Honduras. He turned out to be my office partner and a good buddy of mine. Harris got a kick out of every day when I would aggravate Dan and make him mad. There was a little short guy named Stevie who wasn't very productive but had been there a long time. Doug, the used-car director had got it in his head to hire a man just specifically to answer the telephone. He did this every now and then when I would work with him at various places, because he thought it was in the company's best interest to hire a quote "phone professional." The problem was most of them were two bit losers and I could run circles around them on the phone or anywhere else, and all they were doing was taking away opportunities for me to answer the phone. I have conducted whole transactions over the phone, run credit reports and gotten people approved. This latest phone professional was named Bob but they nick named him Thumper, he was a skinny older white guy with a beard like Santa Claus. He only got paid if a customer purchased a car after proving he spoke to them, logged and documented them as his prospect. The problem was that his deal to get the customers in was he would lie to them, and promise them anything just to get them in, when it was not even necessary to do so. Everybody hated getting a customer that he brought in because he had lied about the color, the miles and the equipment just about everything to get them in. I would tell Doug how useless he was, and how much better off we would do when he was off, or out sick. I became so aggravated with him that when Christmas time came around I wrote a poem for him. I cut out a cardboard picture of a skinny Santa Claus, and on the side of it, I wrote to the tune of "comfort and joy":

God rest he merry gentlemen

that nothing you dismay,

remember Thumper Bob will send you

flakes today; to save him all the trouble

while they holler and complain;

In his office he'll remain

while basking in his comfort and joy;

while basking in his comfort and joy.

Of course I made multiple copies of it, and spread them around the dealership. That was Christmas time, and by the end of the year he was gone, probably I shamed him into leaving.

At the first of the year Doug hired another phone professional, also named Bob, and this one was as fat as a hippopotamus and mean spirited as well. He started at the first of the year and he did not stay long enough to see Groundhog's day. This guy was so fat that he would hardly get off his fat ass and get out of his office at all, he would yell across the showroom to thank customers for coming in and he was just a fat lazy pig. One day when I was on the phone with a customer taking credit information he was yelling across the showroom at someone, and there was a loud echo, I put my customer on hold and went over and told him to shut the fuck up and get off his lazy ass, and go speak to them in person instead of yelling. What happened next really surprised me; about 20 minutes later he came into my office with an umbrella and was waving it around like he wanted to club me with it. He slammed it on the desk two or three times, I was surprisingly calm as I sat there and looked at his red face; that was the most I'd seen him exercise since he'd been there. I calmly told him, "Bob, if you don't get the fuck out of my office I'm going to stick that umbrella up your ass and open it." I started laughing and the other salesman did as well. I said, "Could you imagine Bob squawking up and down Veterans Boulevard trying to pull that umbrella out of his ass?" Harris and Dan and the entire sales crew were dying laughing, while Bob was humiliated. Fortunately Doug was off that day having gone to the auction, so Bob went home early since he was angry.

The next day when I arrived at work Bob had already quit and was gone, Doug had called me into his office and asked, "What the fuck did you do to

Bob?"

I told Doug, "I did you a favor. In fact, I did all of us a favor by getting rid of him."

Doug said, "Well, I have no designated phone person now, so you're it."

And I said, "I'm not going to stop selling cars because of it."

He said, "You'll do it in addition to selling cars," so I just had to monitor and log the sales calls. I have excellent phone skills and was a master at getting people in over the phone. One day an old man called and asked about a car we had in the ad and said he wanted a detailed description of the car, so I took the mobile phone outside and gave him a complete description of the car. The man said, "I don't know if I should come in or not, it's often a waste of time because of what they tell you the car is, compared to what it really is when I go see it."

I said, "Sir, I've been doing this a long time and I have a great reputation, the car is exactly what I said it was so if that interests you, you should come in and see it, now do you have a trade-in?"

He said, "Yes, I do."

And I said, "Okay, describe your car to me."

I asked him what he thought it was worth, and he was pretty realistic about it, and I said, "We will need to see your car as well."

He said, "I don't know, I just don't want to waste my time."

I said, "Look, sir, I'll make you a deal, I'll go take the phone out by my car and start it so you can hear it run, and you go do the same. You take the phone out to your car and let me hear it run, that way we both hear each other's cars. What do you say to that?"

He said, "That sounds pretty lame. I probably should just come over instead."

I said, "That's what I've been trying to tell you." And when he came in, it took me less than half an hour to make the deal.

One day I had a family of midgets come in the tallest one was about 4'6", and they were looking for a minivan; there was two kids, a mom and a dad and I didn't know if he could reach the pedals or not, but he could. They had come from about an hour away, and everything about the deal I made them was perfect, the vehicle, the price, the payment and everything was satisfactory to them. Except for the fact that they said they wanted to think about it, I asked, "What is there left to think about?" They said they wanted to go pray about it. Their plan was to go all the way home and pray about it and then come back if they got a good response. I said, "I don't know about you, but I know God is everywhere, so what if you had a private office where nobody would bother you and you could pray there, and wait for your answer." They all nodded like a bunch of Santa's elves, and they said that would work for them, so I walked over to Doug's office and asked him to clear out because they needed the space. He had a long couch in the office, and they all knelt by the couch and before I closed the door I said, "I'm also going to pray."

A few minutes later, I peeked in through the blinds, and they waved for me to come in. When I opened the door I said, "God told me yes," and they all yelled in unison "he told us yes too!" They practically ran next door to the finance department to do their paperwork.

I was having a blast at work, but eventually I would have to come home where my wife was dealing with her depression, she had good days but mostly they were bad. We'd pray every night and I would always pray that God would take it from her and give it to me, because I felt I was strong enough to take it. Eventually she had more good days then bad, and she decided to learn all about the spa business. This came after receiving more or less, ultimatums from her company R. J. Reynolds telling her to pick a date when she could go back to work. Since she had no intention of going back to her job because of the high stress it caused; I told her to ask them for alternatives and tell them or what? Finally the time came when they offered her a "buy out." They offered, and then gave her a lump sum of cash to leave the job behind. We accepted this, which freed her to go to massage school and learn about the spa industry, so that she could start her own business. It was her belief that while helping others, just as she had done at the daycare, would give her the gratification she needed that would fulfill her in business. Unlike the tobacco industry that was brutal and cold, the spa business would be nurturing in giving of oneself to others to enhance their lifestyle. I knew when she was feeling better when I started coming home and she would be playing romantic music, and then we'd make love like we did when we were on our honeymoon. I must say with that, and the fact that she felt better, I felt like the luckiest man in the world, and I still do.

CHAPTER 25
THEBESTOFBESTCHEVROLET

I was at Best Chevrolet for a total two years from 1998 to 1999 and was salesman of the year for both of those years, as I mentioned before there was some serious talent there from Sean the Finance Director and Joey the general manager. Joey was Italian and had the capacity to be a real con artist; we used to say he had more moves then ex-lax. Everyone used to say that he had his way of getting his fingers sticky, but nobody had a way to prove it, because there was so many cars being sold and so much money being made at the dealership. Sean, the finance director, was a clean cut good looking guy and one of my customers even thought he was Troy Aikman, because he had that athletic look about him. One day I had a rough and rugged looking black customer that kept bragging about how he had just got out of prison, but he couldn't buy anything because his credit was so bad. We had to put the vehicle in his mom's name. It was a late model Suburban, and he was happy and tickled pink just to be driving it. However, a few days later he called to complain that the payment was too high, the interest was too high, etc. etc. and that he was going to come and kick the finance guy's ass if he didn't change the paperwork. I was standing outside of Sean's office telling him about the guys call, and Sean told me that there was nothing wrong with that deal, it was a clean deal and the contract had already gone to the bank. As we were talking the man called me again on my cell phone, and Sean could hear him yelling from where he was sitting and asked, "Is that him?" Sean said, "Let me have the phone," so I passed him my cell phone, and Sean yelled back at him, "What's your problem?" The man started bragging about how he had just got out of prison, and Sean said, "You think you're bad because you just got out of prison? Well I just got out myself, so bring your black ass over here and let's get it on!" The man had mistaken Sean's clean cut look for weakness, which was a big mistake and it wouldn't be the first time or the last. That man never called back, or came in again.

Sometime after that, there was a deal that had nothing to do with me, believe it or not. There was a black couple in Sean's office complaining about a contract they had signed. These people were yelling and cursing really loud and Peter the general manager came from his back office to try to calm things down. Now Peter was whiter than white, and he wore thick wire rimmed glasses. Soon when the woman got out of hand, she yelled at him and told him he had nothing to do with it; Peter told her to shut up and the man stood up and popped Peter right between the glasses, breaking them on his face. Sean got up and tackled the large black man, and Craig, the other finance manager, came out of his office as well and jumped in. Pretty soon it was a melee, with Craig and Sean beating the hell out of this man and his girlfriend. Not only that, but they dragged them down the hall, and carried them into the showroom floor with Craig stomping the man on the head. There was blood and broken glass everywhere, and it looked like a bar room brawl. Not only that, but this guy was out on parole, so when the cops came this guy went back to prison. No charges were filed against our people, but we established a reputation, don't mess with Best Chevrolet.

Craig himself had the same kind of look, a real clean look, but I knew he wasn't a sissy either because the first time I ever dealt with him, we got into it as well. He was complaining about a deal that I had taken him when he first started, he was complaining how he could never get to the payment the customer wanted and I muttered under my breath, "well if you're too much of a fag to deal with it, then I'll just wait for Sean." He gave me a cold stare and said, "If you ever say something like that to me again, we're going to take this outside." I said, "Fine with me, but I think you'll regret it more than I will." He eventually calmed down and made the deal, and afterward we made our peace. Still I figured he was not to be taken lightly, as this was well before the fight, but I knew not to piss him off, because I knew what he was made of.

There was a tall blond salesman named Gary, he wore a light beard and reminded me of Shaggy from the old Scooby Doo cartoons. He was from Mississippi and had a very peculiar illness. He suffered from Tourette's syndrome, this is a neurological disorder; with symptoms of violent twitches often accompanied by shouting a string of obscenities. He was very active and aggressive, and a very good salesman, as he walked the lot with customers he would often kick his leg out; simultaneously waving an arm, and cursing. This was with him taking medication to lessen the effects of his illness, imagine if he didn't take the medication? Soon after he started having success in his sales, he started mixing some hard drugs along with his medication. I saw him once taking an application with some customers, and he threw a hard and violent kick at the man across from him, under the table. He quickly said, "I am sorry, but I may do it again, because I can't control it." Soon Joey used the company's influence, and funding to check him into a drug rehab center, no one ever knew what became of him after that.

One day as I was near the front of the used-car lot facing Veterans Blvd, and it was about five or six in the evening when the weather was warm; I heard some people screaming, like road rage going down the road, soon they stopped right in front of the used-car lot and some guys got out of the car brandishing guns. Within seconds one car had two guys jump out of it, the guys with the guns, the next thing I knew they had three guys lying on the grass in front of me, and were handcuffing them already. It turns out they had waved their gun at the wrong guy, because he was an undercover cop. The whole thing lasted about half an hour, but man it scared the piss out of me.

Another day Dan, the Vietnam vet, was arguing with a black salesman over some car keys, as he was stocking in cars that had come in from the auction that Doug had just attended. The little black salesman was saying, "I just need this one key here for ten minutes to show the car," and Dan wouldn't let him have it because he was still putting tags on them. I was in my office and next to mine was a salesman working with a little skinny white guy who was slight, and unassuming. Their argument proceeded to get loud, and the black salesman suddenly grabbed the key and ran away with it. So Dan ran after the kid and grabbed him by the shoulder and spun him around. Using the force that Dan spun him with, the salesman threw a right hook and hit Dan right on the jaw, he got him good. Not only that, but within seconds the little skinny white guy that was in the office trying to buy a car, was in between them. When Dan protested, the skinny white guy had both his arms pinned behind his back, like he was ready to cuff him. It turns out he was an undercover cop as well. This was shocking to me, because the guy was so quiet and unassuming that you wouldn't think he could manhandle Dan like that, who was twice his size. By now he was screaming at Dan and telling him if he wanted to calm down, or go to jail, because he was a cop. Dan eventually calmed down, and needless to say he went home early again.

After that, armed with fresh ammunition, I started making fun of Dan, calling him "glass jaw," as tough as he tried to act all the time, and he probably was. Yet I had witnessed him get practically knocked out on his feet by a shy little black kid. It was so funny that he would get mad at me, and ask me if I wanted to try taking him on. He even tried throwing "your mama line jokes" at me to get me to fight, thinking that because I was Spanish, I would have to get mad. I threw so many "your mama jokes" at him, and jokes about his family in general, being from the backwoods of Tennessee, saying that they had to use corn cob for toilet tissue. I soon had him so pissed that he had to leave early again because he was fuming, and even my friend Harris would tell me to leave that poor man alone. They wanted it to be like the mercy rule in a little league game, where when one team is beating the other so bad, that they call the game off, making them quit.

It must have been about Memorial day, in fact it was Memorial Day, when on the way to work I heard a radio broadcast that was a replay of Ronald Regan speaking to a group of veterans. These were veterans of the D-Day invasion at Normandy. It was so moving that it almost brought me to tears, how he spoke to them about how they could give so much of themselves hanging on inch by inch to get to the enemy, with machine gun fire flying all around them, risking every inch of their being for the salvation of our country. Coincidentally that day I was dealing with a man that I suspected was a Veteran, the man was trying to trade in a Chevy Cavalier that he owed way too much money on. He wanted to buy a Chevy pickup and he could only do so by putting $3,000 down because of what he owed on the Cavalier. For some reason we started talking about the war in Vietnam, and about how my brother had died there, and my dad served in World War II and won a bronze star medal. Then I told him about the radio broadcast I had heard on the way to work that day, and what Ronald Regan had said. For some reason I had been looking down at the paperwork as I told the story and when I looked up I saw that his eyes were full of tears. This was so moving that I actually shed a few of my own, and then he spoke, he said, "I don't know why I am doing this, but I want to do business with you. If they can get me approved on the truck without trading the Cavalier I'll do it." I genuinely liked the guy, and I didn't want to hurt him financially, so I asked if he was sure he could handle both payments. He said that by the time the first truck payment would be due, he would find somebody in his family to take over the payments of the Cavalier. I learned a valuable lesson then, sometimes you just have to be real with somebody and meet them on their level without an ulterior motive. I shared a little bit about myself without the intent of getting anything in return, and in return I received the sale that I needed, and probably made a friend.

CHAPTER 26
ALONG CAME SPOOKY

Best Chevrolet was in close proximity to the BMW dealership; in fact it was next door to us. There was a salesman named Charlie there that was a pretty nice guy, and he would walk over to visit with us on our front porch. One day when he was visiting he was telling us about his favorite cat that was a little grey and white kitty, and was one of the four or five they had that were staying under their building. Their building was raised up about five feet above ground, which made the underside of it a haven for stray cats. As he was talking about her suddenly she appeared on our porch, she had followed him over from the BMW dealership. She was grey and white and had little markings on her face as if she wore a mask almost like a raccoon; she also had short stubby legs, and a little crank of a tail like four or five inches long. We immediately took a liking to her, and I named her Spooky, since it was close to Halloween. She would soon become our mascot, and I got Dan to go half and half with me to get her shots and get her spayed, because we didn't want her having any kittens, we also wanted proof that she had papers and was legit in case Joey or anybody else complained and didn't want her hanging around. She soon would find her way inside the building when we would open the doors to air it out from moving cars in and out of the used-car showroom floor. She especially liked coming inside when it was rainy or windy, or when she could smell that I had Popeye's chicken.

One day Harris and I had a late lunch didn't start eating lunch till about three in the afternoon when she came in sniffing the air, I remember telling Harris because I had already finished mine. I said to him, "Come on, give her some chicken," and he did so even though he didn't like cats. One night Stevie one of the salesman, was making a car deal and he had his customers standing watching the cat sleep on the chair that they could have been sitting on. As

Stevie filled out the paperwork, I told him, "Stevie, kick her out so she can come with me," and he said, "No, I can't, she's asleep." These were people with excellent credit buying an expensive vehicle, yet there they stood watching the cat on their potential chairs. One day I bought a little Koala teddy bear from the dollar store and brought it to work as a little toy for her; I tied a noose around its neck and hung it from the front porch rail so she could whack at it. This did not go over very well with the managers when they saw it, and I had no idea why. It turned out the dealership had gotten a lot of media play in the newspaper and even on television about a black guy and white guy in the service department who had been playing jokes on each other. The white guy put a noose around the neck of a little black doll and tied it to the garage door; so that when you opened the garage door, you could see the black doll was swinging from the noose. I knew nothing about this; but it was so bad that the black guy was suspended, and the white guy was terminated. It's a damn shame that in this world of political correctness, two grown men who were obviously friends should have to go through that, so the rest of the world can try to understand it.

Needless to say I had to keep Spooky's little bear in the drawer until she was ready to play with it. Spooky had become quite a source of conversation at the dealership, Joey and Sean would even come over a few times suggesting that we get rid of her, or leave her outside. Dan would quickly pull the paperwork showing that she had had her shots and had been spayed. I began to think that it would be best that someone take her home, but we had three cats at home already and I didn't want another one. I began to ask around, I asked Charlie at the BMW store, and I asked Stevie if he could take her home, Stevie would have been perfect he had a ten-year-old boy that loved to play with her but he had asthma and couldn't take it. Stevie lived close by and on Sunday's would bring his son to come and play with her. As time went on Joey became the general manager after Peter left, soon after the fight and Sean became general sales manager, or second in command. As such, Sean become more involved in the sales aspect, instead of just finance and started coming around more often to the used-car building. I think he was mostly checking on Doug the used-car director and with good reason. I started having the old funny feeling when I would see how much Doug was paying for cars, lining his pockets a little and getting ready to make a move.

I would not confront him on this, but I would always ask him why he was paying so much for cars all of a sudden. My old boss Mike had taught me, and

I learned from experience, that the money was actually made when you bought the car, because how much you pay for a car directly effects how much you can sell it for, after you cover the reconditioning cost. Just as when cars are bought at too high a price you know that there is no money to be made on them, but that somebody made the money somewhere else. I was right again, soon after that Doug opened his own place called Dealing Doug's, he would later flood the market with corny infomercials about his car lot, and even had one riding his motorcycle and going to get a haircut. They brought some nitwit in to be the used-car director that I wouldn't give two cents for, I don't even remember his name, but I remember telling Sean that he fit the profile, he was tall and white and could not sell cars to save his life, or as Dan would say, "He couldn't sell pussy on a Troop train."

One day I came in after my day off and all the guys came into my office, Dan, Stevie and Harris as if they wanted to tell something. They were hesitant at first but they finally told me, it seems that the new-car manager had been in the building the day before; he was a skinny, country, "trailer park type" named Jesse. He thought he was a lot tougher then he really was, the idiot even had a Superman tattoo on his chest that he would show off sometimes and open up his shirt. While visiting the used-car building he had seen Spooky inside, and with her being used to being around people she was not afraid. The bastard had reared back and kicked her as hard as he could. He had gone off laughing and bragging about how he had actually kicked our little mascot. Fortunately for him I had been off that day, but I had a plan. I casually walked over to the New Car side after saying Hello to Sean and after stopping by the finance office. Soon I went over to the new car desk; Jesse was pretty much alone so I started asking Jesse about a new truck promotion that they had. Then I casually mentioned that I heard he was by the used-car building the day before, the idiot started laughing and bragging about how he had kicked the cat the day before, not knowing that I had been one of her sponsors. At this point I leaned in close to him as if I was trying to hear the story better, but I was really trying to brace myself. I took both hands and shoved him hard against his skinny little superman chest throwing him against the wall. I screamed at him and said, "Why don't you come across the parking lot with me and show me how it's done, show me how you did it." He yelled "what do you mean?" and I said I mean "I'll kick your ass up and down Veteran's Blvd that's what I mean." I didn't know this but Sean had been close by waiting for something like this to happen, all of a sudden he was standing between us and putting an arm around me walking me to the used-car building.

I was suddenly embarrassed by my actions and told Sean I was only kidding, and he said" no you weren't I could tell by the look in your eye that you meant business, he said didn't you?" I finally admitted it and said, "Yeah, I would have kicked his ass." I remember him asking me why I would risk all the money I'm making over a cat, and I said, "Better yet, why would you have a piece of shit asshole like that working for you as a New Car manager, one who would do that to a defenseless animal?"

I said, "Besides, Sean, and I want you to keep this in mind, I can do this anywhere, the dealership did not make me what I am, I do this everywhere I go, and I can do it again." Whenever we would go home to visit El Paso we would visit my uncle George who was instrumental in helping me get into the business, and he would always ask how I was doing. When he would hear how well I was doing wherever I went, he would apply a saying in Spanish, "Un gallo donde quiera canta" (a rooster crows no matter where he is, because he knows he's a rooster).

It soon became more apparent to me that someone was going to have to find Spooky a home and it was probably going to be me, and I think Spooky knew about it and suspected it. She knew that I was going to be taking her home, either that or somebody told her that I defended her honor and from that point on she followed me everywhere I went. I would often be talking to customers by the front row on Veteran's Boulevard, and they would say, "Oh, is that your cat?" and she would appear behind me listening to the conversation. She even started following me to my car at night when I was leaving to go home, I even told my wife Dora; that she would speak to me telepathically saying," you have other kitties at home you could take me home." It was like a comic strip or carton with a little bubble coming up from her saying, "Take me home, you have other cats at home." I kept dealing with this and the idea that I had to do something to salvage her, when all of a sudden a cold front hit, it was going to be raining and wet and the temperatures were going to drop down into the teens. I was going to be off the next day and I couldn't sleep worrying about Spooky so at three in the morning, I woke up my wife and told her I was going to go get the cat. I grabbed a little pet carrier and drove the 45 minutes to work, I brought her home that night and we kept her for the rest of her days, her full name was Spooky Carlota, because she was from the car lot.

The dealership wasn't quite the same without Doug there because that other used-car director had no clue as to what he was doing, it was not to the point that I would be looking for another opportunity but I would welcome one if it ever came along. It was getting toward the end of 1999 and everybody was worried about Y2K, would the world end, would the stock markets crash and how just would the computers handle it? Our own resident nutcase Dan, had even bought property up in Tennessee in the mountains with other family members, and had built a fortress with food and guns. He would describe it in great detail with how many guns they had, and how much ammo they had, I would ask him one thing, if he had a decent place to take a shit, or if he would just go out to the outhouse like he did growing up, I'd ask him just to listen to him scream.

The only thing I did to prepare was I drafted $10,000 from my credit line to have cash in case the banks went down for a little while, and when nothing happened, I paid it back. What did happen before the year ended though was I was given a proposition by Sean in deep secret in fact "double secret." It seemed Sean had been offered a job with a local dealer named Ronny Lamarque, he would be the new owner of the dealer which was "formerly" Julian Graham Dodge, it would now be Lamarque Dodge and Sean would be the second in command. As such Sean would be able to pull strings like he would be doing with me; he invited me to lunch at Ruth Chris Steakhouse where he would go over his plan for me. He said, "Richard I could bring anybody I want from the dealership but I'm only bringing you and this is my plan;" I would be selling used cars at 35 percent commission instead of 30 percent plus 8 percent on finance income, instead of 5 percent or 6 percent per cent which was common. I would also have a $1,500 salary per month plus a $500 car allowance, which were both unheard of. I kept Sean's plan a secret but before I knew it there were other people coming like Craig the other finance manager, who had helped Sean beat up the black people on the showroom floor, and Ricky, Doug's son-in-law. No other salesman were invited though, by the end of the year word had gotten out, and even Joey had taken to drinking heavily because he knew that all his best talent was leaving.

The year ended, Y2k came and ended without a hitch, and soon we all started at the Dodge store, as typical just to make a splash I asked for a $1,500 advance just to see what they would say, Ray the general manager handed me the check the day I walked through the door to show me his good faith. There's quite a lot of pressure when somebody tells everybody how good you are, and how you are going to blow everybody away, and you have to go in and do it. I've always taken the approach of being humble and not bragging about myself I let other people say it, I don't say, "I'm going to do this, or that" I just quietly go about and do it. I tried to take the approach that Jesus taught in the parable where he said, "If you are invited to a banquet, don't go and try to take the seat of honor, lest they tell you to move to a lesser position; instead take the lesser position of humility and let the Lord of the manor say come and take the seat of honor and elevate you to a higher position." "For whoever humbles himself shall be exalted and he who exalts himself shall be humbled."

CHAPTER 27
THE NEW DODGE STORE

The Lamarque family of dealerships were very cliquish to say the least, most of them hailed from St. Bernard Parish, to them it was affectionately known as just "the Parish" to me not being Louisiana born I called it the Land of the Inbreeds. This didn't sit so well with many of the salesman there, but it was true, and they had a reputation for it. Some of the cast of characters were Mark the used-car director, Wayne his assistant, salesmen Steve and Pepito, Mike the obnoxious Yankee from New York, and Frank who had been the former "top gun" before I got there. There was also Charlie who was a rugged mess, he had long scraggly hair and a beard that looked like a mountain man, and he smelled like one to. I used to say his forte was "he never met a meal he didn't like." No kidding, he even walked around with a picture of a pork chop in his wallet and would whip it out and show it like it was one of his kids, saying, "Have you ever seen a prettier pork chop than that?" I used to comment, "Oh yeah, they are so cute at that age." Pepito used to sit there and quiz him about the food he had eaten for example he would say, "Have you ever eaten, raccoon, squirrel or possum?" As it turns out there was nothing that the man had not eaten, except I don't think he had eaten dog or admitted to it. He often broke out the grill and started cooking stuff out there as if anyone would eat it; I remember getting on the PA system singing, "salmonella, salmonella," symbolizing the poison we could get.

The finance director was named Mike, and he had a large aquarium in his office with a baby alligator in it. This had to be the most useless alligator in the world because Mike would throw baby mice in there and he could not catch them. One day someone threw a pretty white mouse in there and I wanted to rescue it, but I had to wait for the cover of darkness. When the evening came about I took a deal to finance for delivery and I snuck in there with an empty paper cup. The alligator was no threat, because he was on the other side of the aquarium looking blankly out the glass window, so I reached into the other side and grabbed the mouse by the tail and put it in the cup. No one was in the office at the time so there was no threat except for the damn mouse. The mouse should have been the alligator, the damn thing bit me five or six times on my hand on the way to the used-car building. By now they had started paging me to come to finance because they knew what I had done, but it was too late. I had gotten to the used-car building and let him go by the Dumpster. One Saturday, when we all got to work we had seen that the useless alligator had passed away, so some of the salesman decided, and I won't say who, to tie a bunch of balloons to him with a string and launched him into orbit. When Mike, the finance manager, came in he was sorely pissed and he wanted to blame me, but I knew nothing about it. One of the service people soon brought him what was left of the alligator, after it had come crashing down by the service department.

Shortly after I started at the Dodge dealership we were informed that they were going to begin remodeling, funny thing about remodeling is they say it's going to look really nice in the end, but for the mean time you are working out of trailers. The end result will be a state or art facility but for the next six months you are going to be working out of a shitty mobile home. I had left a state of the art facility at Best Chevrolet to take this job, but with the pay plan that Sean had given me here I would make the best of it, so I couldn't really complain. The draw back to working in a trailer is that there is no privacy, it was an open space and everybody could see you in action, and see how I would work. That means my usual working possibly two to three customers at one time, having a customer on the phone with me while one is in front of me and one is outside waiting for me. Mark was the manager and he was a tall guy and a true Cajun "a coonass," Mark would ask me if I needed what was called a "turn over customer." In essence to have another salesman help me with a customer, I would say, "No, I've got it," and they were all amazed that I could handle two or three customers at one time. As usual whenever we had down time I would tell them jokes, this salesman Steve wore a funny looking toupee, and at this time the movie Gladiator came out. They had an announcer at the arena where they had the battle scenes, and he looked just like Steve with his toupee. I would tell everybody that Steve must have come out in that movie wearing his Toga.

One day Steve helped Frank close a deal with a guy, who was a commercial fisherman, and he was buying a Dodge truck, this guy had a funnier looking wig then Steve did, and I would say he looked like Bozo the Clown. I would say they were going to have a dance off but instead with their wigs, with Steve announcing like the guy in the Gladiator movie, and the other guy dancing around like Bozo the clown. At one point the guy was underneath the truck adjusting the trailer hitch, and Steve came up to me and said, "Did you see that guys wig?" I said, "Stop it. You've got no room to talk." Steve's sons went to Catholic school and he was always selling raffle tickets for one promotion or another. One day when we were all on the front porch, Steve said he was going to go down to Gambino's Bakery and he said, "I know the owner so I'm going to try and sell some tickets." We had an affectionate name for Steve, among others one of them was "Moss Head," because he looked like he had a bunch of Spanish moss on his head. We watched and waited for his car to pull into the bakery, and then I ran inside to call them. A young black girl answered and I quickly went into panic voice, and I said, "There is a man in there and you have to call him to the phone quickly, but he's hard of hearing, and you have got to say this really loud."

She said, "Okay, what's his name?"

I said, "Moss head."

And she repeated, "Moss head?"

I said, "Yes, and you have to scream it really loud."

She said it, but I said to her, "You have to yell louder." She had a lisp, so instead of Moss head, she was yelling "Moth Head," and no matter how loud she did it she kept screaming "Moth head" and I kept yelling "louder, louder!" As we all laughed, I told the other guys "nobody say anything when he comes back." When Steve came back he had a perturbed or confused look on his face like he couldn't understand what had just happened to him. I waited about 15 minutes and then I asked him if anything had happened when he went to the bakery. His eyes rolled back in his head and he said, "You mother fucker that was you that did that!" He said, "All these ladies were in there buying bread looking around, looking at me because I was the only one that fit the description, since I had the moss head." He had walked out embarrassed and didn't even talk to the owner about the tickets. On days when it was windy or raining, Steve wore a baseball cap, we started calling him "the man with two hats."

One day Frank, who had been the top salesman before I got there, had talked to a customer on the phone but as usual being the lazy man that most salesman are, he did not ask for their contact information. I knew this because later on when the customer had called again I looked at the logs and Frank had not put anything on there. So in the log book, I logged the husbands name and phone number and that I had an appointment with him at four o'clock that afternoon. Naturally when the customers arrived they asked for me, because I had spoken to the husband a couple of times and given him the information he wanted about a car they were interested in. When Frank saw that I was working a customer and what car it was he said, "I am going to be on that deal, because I talked to them on the phone," and he went crying to Mark the manager and Mark said well you don't have it on the log and he said, "Oh well, I'm going to log it in real soon." What he did was wait for me to actually make the deal and give a copy of it to Mark, and when Mark was not in the office he took the paper and went and logged it on the sheet. When I took the people next door to the finance office, which was 100 yards away into the new car building; I snuck around through service and came in the back of the used-car building and I saw what he had done by taking my copy and reproducing it on the log sheet. With nobody in the office, I took the whole log sheet and went and flushed it down the toilet. Then I went back the same way I came in, and I went back through service to New Cars to wait for my people at the finance office. As they finished their paperwork, by now the shit had really hit the fan, and Frank was going nuts that someone had ruined the used-car log sheet, and ruined his chance of getting half of my deal.

Sean called me over and asked me what was going on and I acted all innocent, and said, "I don't know what you are talking about; I'm waiting over here for my people in finance." Sean smiled to himself and looked at me and he said, "I know you better than that Richard you did something."

I said, "Well, if I did go ahead and tell him to reproduce it, if he has their information on file he should be able to go and reproduce it on a new log sheet." As I finished my deal Sean met with Mark in the used-car building and they determined that since Frank could not produce any of the customer's information that he would have no part of my deal. It was a nice commission I made a little over $1,000 on it and since we were in a trailer and the space was open, Steve asked me about the deal, and I told him about it with Frank listening in the corner office. After about half an hour Frank looked at me and said, "You are a piece of shit Richard." I looked at him and smiled and said, "Thank you Frank, coming from you that's a real compliment." The next day when I got to work he actually gave me a little "clip on" for my key chain and it said, "Genuine snake," of course he meant it as an insult but I wore it as a badge of honor and I said, "Look what Frank gave me, isn't it nice?" For about a week I would stop anybody like the new car salesmen, and show them my key chain and say, "Look what Frank gave me, isn't he nice?" This would piss him off even more, because what he gave me as an insult, I took as a compliment, and wore it like a trophy.

Sometime after that when we were actually getting along better, he reached out with a folder and wacked me in the nuts as I walked by, it was a real light tap, but it was enough to cause pain. An hour later Mark called us over for a meeting and as we were all standing there, I had a rolled up newspaper in my hand and Frank was standing across from me, so I swung at Franks nuts with the paper fully excepting him to move away, so I did it a little harder than normal. I would normally be trying to catch him as he moved away from the blow, but the only problem was he didn't move. Either he didn't see me, or just didn't move fast enough so it hit him with blunt force, he buckled over and went down on one knee. As Mark was laughing he looked at us and said, "Well, you might want to start wearing a cup to work."

On another occasion they called me to deal with a customer that spoke only Spanish, it was a guy from Central America looking for a car for his wife, and he wanted something small and economical so I showed him some Dodge Neon's that fit in his price range. In my experience in the business I've been on thousands of test drives but never one like that, this was fucking insane. He thought he was Mario Andretti in a fucking Dodge Neon, he would speed in front of cars, pulled in front of three lanes of traffic turning left, and these cars don't have the pick up to do what he was doing or attempting to do, he was taking risks with my life as well as his wife's. When we pulled onto a back street behind the dealership at a stop sign, I reached over and turned off the ignition, threw it in park and I said, "Get out." I got out of the passenger side and slammed the door with all my might and I made him move, he was hollering and complaining about what I had done and I just told him to "shut the fuck up." I drove back to the dealership. I parked the car and started walking inside, as he was complaining he tried to stop me by standing in front of me, and I almost bowled him over to get passed him and go inside. Mark, the manager, asked me what happened and I told him, "This guy is a total psycho and I don't want anything to do with him," and I went into my office and sat down. That knuckle head still came to my office and tried to talk to me, and I told him, "Get the fuck away from me or I will deck you."

Now this was Frank's chance to be the hero, and give me a pay back at the same time, as it turns out this guy did speak English. All Frank could do was tell Mark all the bad things the customer was saying about me, and I said, "Go ahead and make the deal, teach me a lesson." The guy couldn't buy anything, and didn't know anyone who could co-sign for him and help him buy a car. I'm not going to say I'm always right when I it comes to judging a customer's intentions or ability to buy, but I usually bat about 90 percent. I had mentioned a salesman named Mike before; he was the Yankee form New York, he had a son and his wife was pretty well off, she actually was the owner of a court reporting school. Mike was a pretty good salesman who averaged 15 to 16 cars a month which was pretty good by most standards, he only had one problem, and he was a closet pervert and stalker. On one or more occasions, when he sold to a female customer a car he would haunt them at their place of business, or work place to check up on them. One was a family owned restaurant and the father of the girl that bought the car came in to talk to Mark and told him that this guy was coming in three or four times a day to talk to the daughter, pretending to buy coffee or tea just to talk to the daughter. On top of that Mike wore these shitty old black shoes that were worn out and funky looking. I would have make-believe conversations like I was his wife calling him saying, "Who are you stalking now? They recognized your shoes." I made up a story that he was outside a woman's house peeking through her window and when she caught him he ran away so fast he left his shoes behind as evidence, because he was the only one that would be seen in public with those shoes.

One day it was discovered that he did indeed have a checkered past and had actually appeared in porn movies, one of the salesman had found the tape or DVD and made a copy of it. One day a bunch of guys climbed into a conversion van that had a TV in it and decided to watch his movie. They wanted me to watch it with them, but I thought "this sounds really gay, a bunch of guys watching a porn movie together in a van of a guy we work with," so I refused. It seems it was gay porn after all, and the image that was told to me was of three guys in a shower together that duplicated the look of those "steel collision balls," the kind you see in a psychologist office of one crashing into the other making them all move simultaneously by kinetic energy. Mike was the middle man, catching and receiving. He had a stage movie name that was like "Tony Montana from Scarface." I felt really bad for the guy because the whole dealership knew about it, and in fact the whole town knew about it. I always had a reputation of not being the friendliest guy in the automobile business, but when this happened and no one would hang out with him again, I soon became his only friend and I never mentioned it to him.

One day as further proof of our shitty environment, a big rat ran into the used-car office, I was walking back after taking a customer to finance and saw it run through the building. One of the guys had a customer inside, and when they saw it they went running out of the building as well. The next thing is they closed the door, and Mike and Frank got brooms and went after the rat, it seemed like a cartoon as all you could hear was furniture flying around as tables, desks and chairs were being moved as they were trying to trap and kill it. Soon they came walking out carrying a garbage bag with the rat in it, proudly displaying that they had killed the rat. I said in front of Mark and everybody "you think it's over now, it's not over you are going to have its whole family to deal with now."

Mike asked, "Why is that?"

I said, "Haven't you seen in the movies where the guy says, 'You dirty rat, and you killed my brother'?"

I mentioned before that Mark the manager, and most of the salesmen, were true Cajun and nothing was more evident than watching them eat crawfish. Crawfish is an acquired taste and one thing that I never acquired, every now and then a vender would bring a big bucket of crawfish and the guys would stand around with lightning speed peeling them, eating them and throwing the shells in the trash. But Mark had a bad habit of going around the building and leaving a trail of farts wherever he would go. He was tall about 6'2" with a huge head on him, one of the guys would even tell him that he had a head like a Down syndrome kid. One day I was eating lunch and he left a huge fart behind him when he turned and walked away, and I was determined to get him back. One evening, a few days later, I was searching the metal box behind his desk for a key to a trade-in. I heard him on the phone and I could tell he was talking to the owner of the dealership, and he was kissing some ass saying, "Yes, Ronny this, and yes, Ronny that." Knowing that he couldn't retaliate, I leaned my backside on the back of his chair and let him have it, with a huge double barreled fart. I could tell by his face that he didn't know quite how to retaliate. His first instinct was to push me away, but then he grabbed me and pulled me toward him and that was a big mistake, because when he pulled me toward him I let out a really big one. In his anguish he dropped the phone and was stumbling around for it saying, "Oh, sorry, Ronny. Ronny, are you there?"

He was so pissed I actually had to stay away from him the rest of the night for fear he might actually take a swing at me.

Then there was an old guy named Julio that used to work with me at the Chevy store and I recruited him for the Dodge store, Julio was a great guy he was in his midseventies and didn't give a shit about anything. He was quirky and he would mumble when asked direct questions about a deal or why he was late, and then just walk away. He always wore a tie that he wouldn't quite tie all the way, it just hung near the top half untied, and it was his token trademark. But his favorite thing to do was to go to the racetrack and watch the horse races. When the racing season was on every Friday and Saturday, he would disappear for four or five hours and not tell anybody where he was going, even though we all knew. One day Mark was going nuts looking for him and it was a Friday afternoon around one and he was asking everyone, "Do you know where Julio is?" "Do you know where Julio is?" I said, "I don't know," and then I made a noise sounding like the snorting of a horse, then I pretended like I was stomping my hooves, and Mark said, "He better not be at the track." When Julio finally showed up Mark had me go in the office with him as a witness because Julio mostly spoke Spanish, even though he understood English. Mark said, "You knew you had something pending on that deal that you needed to take care of." Then I informed Mark that I had taken care of it for Julio so he wouldn't get in trouble. Then Mark, not knowing what else to do, told Julio, "Do you realize I could fire you for this?" Then Julio in his "Don't give a shit" voice mumbling said, "Don't you realize I've been fired from nicer joints then this?" Then I asked Mark if I could talk to him in private and I said, "Look, you know what he is going to do, he's seventy-four years old, and he's not going to change what he is doing, let me take care of the things when he is missing, he is a good man and it's not worth firing him over something like this."

But the year was coming to end and as Christmas was coming, I decided to express my own Christmas sentiments, so I wrote a poem for Charlie, the big overweight guy that had a beard like Grizzly Adams, and stunk like sweat and cigarettes. He's the one that never met a meal he didn't like and always carried the picture of the pork chop with him. I wrote this:

FOR CHARLIE AT CHRISTMAS

"'Twas the night before Christmas
and all through the house,
not a crumb in the cupboard,
that goddamn mouse;
Charlie's clothes stood by
themselves close by,
near his bed,
while visions of pork chops danced in his head;
suddenly he arose with a noise and a clatter,
his stomach was growling that's what was the matter;
he relaxed as he thought of the munchies
the next day would bring,
it made him feel glad it made his heart sing;
for most Christmas is a time of joy and peaceful tranquil,
for Charlie it's a big smorgasbord and a belly that's filled;
I could swear that I heard him later that night as he belched,
and farted and laid on his side,
Merry Christmas to all and
to all a Good night!"

I made about one hundred copies of it and hung them all over the dealership, Mark liked it so much that he read it aloud to everyone at the Christmas Party, even the office ladies, and everyone couldn't stop laughing. Charlie was so mad he was following me around saying I need to talk to you, and I just kept avoiding him telling him I had a customer, thinking that he really wanted to deck me.

Then there were the guys who I call the "munchkin brothers," they were all short and it ran in their family, Brain was the tallest standing at 5'2," Craig at 5" and Kerry was 4'10". Brain and Craig were managers and had the short man's complex. Brain used to get so mad when I would make the short man's jokes and say, "I'm going to punch you in the nose," and I would say yeah, "and who's going to put you up to it?" Kerry was the most humble one, and he actually joked about his shortness, which was funny because he looked every bit like a troll. There was a local advertising magazine called "Steals and Deals," and as Christmas approached they produced one with three elves on the cover ice skating. I took the picture of the magazine, embellishing it with their names. I wrote "join us at Lamarque Dodge for the huge Christmas extravaganza and watch the Munchkin Brothers perform on ice." I put their names by each elf stating "featuring Brian, introducing Craig, and starring Kerry." Of course I made multiple copies of this as well, but it didn't end there. Our store comptroller, who knew everybody in town, made copies and faxed them to all the other dealerships so everybody that knew the brothers where calling and laughing. Brain was fit to be tied, he being the oldest and proudest of the bunch. If it would have been like the old days, I think he would challenge me to a duel, instead I told him, "Why don't we just have an ass kicking contest, and I'll go first."

As the year came to end we were set to receive our Christmas bonuses, this is derived by the dealership taking out $15 for every car you sell, and then matching it at the end of the year. I remember Ray the general manager bringing my check over personally to the used-car building saying that it was the largest bonus check that he had ever handed out. At years end I had made $138,000, my best year to date so far in the car business, but it came with a price. My friend Sean that had brought me to the dealership had a falling out with Ray the general manager and Ronny the Dealer and would soon be leaving.

CHAPTER 28
TAKE THIS SHOW ON THE ROAD

I started the new year and I was still at the Dodge store, and still doing well, but after a couple of months I received a call from Sean and he wanted to meet with me and Craig, the former finance manager from Best Chevrolet, to tell me what they were doing now. At our meeting they told me they were working for a company called GMA and were doing promotions on the road. The dealers in small, out of the way cities, would spend a ton of money promoting their repo sale, and Sean and Craig being a team would receive a large percentage of the four day event. They in turn where going to branch out and open their own company and have several teams of which I would be a part of. In order to get to that point I would have to start as a salesman and go on the road with them as part of their team, this prospect had pros and cons. Cons were you had to pay your own expenses, the hotels, airfare, meals and all. The pros were you would receive a tax free check for all the money you made from the dealer within three or four days of the sale plus you would only work four days, allowing half a day of travel time instead of the normal six days a week that come with long hours at a normal dealership. Plus the schedule would be three weeks on and one week off, so in theory you would make great money and only work three weeks out of the month. Another plus for me was that they would use the four square system that I had learned at Landmark Chevrolet and it should be easy for me. Within two weeks they would be going to Enid, Oklahoma and they wanted me to go with them. My whole goal was just to try it out and see how I liked it, so I asked Mark for a week off. In hindsight, I shouldn't have told Mark what I was going to do with my week off, but I told him where I was going and this immediately put him on the defense. It wasn't so much that he didn't want me to benefit, but he didn't want to knowingly be put at odds between Sean and Craig vs Ray and Ronny. In other words, if he allowed me to go he would be allowing me to consort with the enemy.

Nevertheless I bought my ticket and intended on going, the day before I was to leave I was packing my stuff together to go and Mark came to my office and said, "Are you planning on going?"

I said, "Yes, I already paid for my ticket."

He said, "Don't go because if you do I will have to terminate you."

I explained to him that I planned on going and I wanted to try it out and that he should give me a week off, I sold enough cars and made enough money that I was entitled to a week off. As the next day came I took the trip to Oklahoma with Sean and Craig and helped them prepare and arrange for the sale. I believe we flew into Oklahoma City and the people from the dealership picked us up and we drove about an hour to the city in the middle of nowhere. As the sale began I could not believe the people that were coming in, it was like lambs to the slaughter. The deals were fast and furious, and before I knew it the week was over and the deals were over, and I had made $6,800. It was a nice gig and easy money but I was not thoroughly convinced, that is until I went to the dealership and saw that Mark had Steve started to pack my belongings. They informed me that I had been terminated because I went without permission. I'm convinced that this was all done in order for him to save face with the dealer Ronny, I always figured that Mark's loyalty came with a price to the highest bidder.

My decision was made basically for me, so I planned for my future sales to go with Sean and Craig. Sean's brother Mike also joined the team, one would be the finance manager, the other would be the closer, and Sean as the team leader. They had a crew of other salesman that they had incorporated from other sales in Indiana, there were three of them, and they asked me to recruit someone to be my traveling buddy. I called on my old friend Harris from Best Chevrolet and he joined us. He would become my traveling, companion and roommate and close friend on the road and this would be important because what I learned was that many salesmen that went on the road did drugs, and used this as an outlet to do drugs. But not Harris and I, we took it as a job that we were going there to make money for our families.

We had such confidence in each other that he had my credit card number and I had his, and whoever found the best deal on airfare would charge it and then we would split the expenses. We set sail for such exotic cities as Bloomington, Indiana, Broken arrow, Oklahoma and Joplin, Missouri. A favorite of mine was right near Nebraska, Council Bluffs, Iowa. These places were little pockets of the country that harbored innocent trusting people with good credit and an eagerness to buy cars under the guise of a sales promotion like ours. We had a sales pitch that we used; that we were representing local banks that were looking to dispose of these repossessions at scarified prices. In reality we were representing the dealers and selling the cars at prices that maximized their profit. Many of the guys referred to the sales as clubbing baby seals. I didn't care, I was making anywhere between $5,000 and $7,000 a trip, and I didn't care what they called it, as long as I was making money. All the while I kept a close track of my expenses for tax purposes, which would have huge write offs.

The fact remains it was a lot of pressure, I've always dealt with a lot of pressure in this business, pressure to be the best or to be the best that I could be. This was different, this was actually spending $1,500 before the trip and not knowing exactly what you are going to get before you got there. Some of the environments that we went to were not very friendly toward us, because they were not receptive to us going there into their dealership and making money. Oftentimes they tried to block us out from getting customers, some of the guys like my friend Harris were often intimidated by this, and of course I was not, and soon they realized that there was no stopping me, and this would loosen things up for guys on my crew as well. My goal was to cover my expenses on the first day, and to try and make $1,500-$2,000 on the first day so that the rest would be gravy. This was not always easy and sometimes the sales were slow and I was trying to pull it out and make something positive out of the trip and make some money by at least the third day. Most of the time the math worked, I could spend $1,500 and make $5,000, but there were a few times were I spent $1,500 and was lucky to make $3,000, and that did not work out. One such trip was in Walla Walla, WA this was a beautiful area were they grow the Vidalia onions and many other crops and there were many Hispanics there and people willing to buy cars. The problem was the dealership, they didn't supply us with enough cars and they cheated us, they cooked the books. They added about $1,000-$1,500 to the cost on each car to ensure they made a lot of money, while we made no money. I was so mad that I left on the third day and considered the trip a wash and a waste of my time. I caught hell from Sean and Craig, the owners of the company and my friends, and I told them I am a contract employee and I didn't see the validity of that contract.

They planned a huge sale at a convention center in Joplin, MO where it was to be a six day sale with three dealers participating. It was to be a huge sale with lots of cars and tons of advertising. I didn't know this at the time but this was to be an audition for me, and some of the other guys to see who would be the "closer" for a future team. At this sale I would be a closer, and not a salesmen, this means that someone else sets up the deal, and I would go in and close it, to maximize the profit. My job was to work closely with Craig who was the former Finance manager at Best Chevrolet and one of the co-owners now, years later he would brag on how I would close 34 deals for him in one day. For the six day sale I closed almost 100 deals and made $8,500. Another time we went to another dealership in Missouri and some of the salesmen that went with us were black, and from New Orleans; and the owner of the dealership came up to them and said, "What are you doing here Nigger? We don't have Niggers at our store!" He made them go home. The black salesman looked at him and at first and thought he was joking, and he said I'm not joking you need to get your black ass back to Louisiana." I guess he didn't have any problems with Mexicans, because he didn't tell me anything. I remember telling Sean and Craig that if they had any "back bone," they should have pulled out of the deal on principal. But they had committed so much money and time to the sale that they couldn't do it financially and they said, "We are all a bunch of horses and as long as we are getting paid you have to do what is necessary." I thought to myself it was more like being "a bunch of whores."

One day it was in the fall of 2001, and Harris and I would have our routine down where one time one would purchase the airline tickets, one would buy the hotel, and we would split the costs evenly. We had trusted each other enough to do that. As I was on my way to pick him up at an off-site parking garage near the airport, and I was leaving my house when I saw the news that a plane had just hit one of the twin towers in New York. I got in the car and turned the radio on to keep hearing the news all the while unaware of how this would affect our future travel plans. By the time I picked him up at the parking lot we had heard that all flights had been canceled so there was no sense in taking in our luggage or pursuing anything. We received a call from Joey the former general manager of Best Chevrolet, who was heading up the team. He asked us all to go to his house in Mandeville for a meeting to see how we would get to our sale in Missouri. By the time we arrived at his house it was determined that we would be driving Joey's suburban with all five of us to head out to our sale. Like the rest of the country we were in shock to find out why; and how it happened, along with all the details about the attack and especially the most devastating, to discover that the towers had since collapsed. We pondered this all the while as we were making our 12 hour drive to Jefferson City, Missouri. It was a bizarre and eerie feeling to look up in the sky and not see anything that even resembled a plane inflight. Add to this the constant news on the radio and it just gave you a bizarre and tragic feeling. The sale itself progressed very well but I found myself at times brooding, while away from everybody, and perhaps shedding a tear at the thought of America being under attack in my lifetime.

I guess it was naive on my part thinking that the possibility of it could never happen in my lifetime. I've always seen America as this beacon of hope reaching its arms out to everyone wanting to come in and make a better life for themselves. My own father having battled in World War II and become a hero, had never finished high school, yet ran a successful business for many years, showing that the American dream was there for everybody. As the week progressed we were dealing with information of our following sale that would be in Minnesota, it was supposed to be very huge and profitable; and we all were concerned with our ability to travel there with all the airports closed. We found out as the week progressed that the airports would be open, but they would be under heightened security, however we could still make our trip.

A funny thing happened on the way to Minnesota, we got to the airport and it was Harris and Rambo, another salesman from New Orleans, and myself. The plane itself was a huge passenger jet with a total passenger count of 18 including us three. As we took our seats the flight attendants told us we could sit wherever we wanted, so we each got an aisle seat with a row to ourselves so we could lie down. We were busy passing sports magazines back and forth, and of course Harris was talking to me in Spanish. After they had shut the door and the plane was backing away from the gateway the pilot announced, "we are going to have to return to the gate, sorry for the inconvenience." In all my years of travel I have never heard of that, especially after the door was closed. When the plane went back they called each of us by name and asked us to declare our citizenship and where we were from. Now Harris is Black, but he is Hispanic with a thick accent and they didn't know what to make of him, and I remember he shouted out, "Oh if there is an Arab on this plane I am not flying!" I told him to shut the fuck up and let me do the talking. I've been told I look Hawaiian, Hispanic and Middle Eastern but the one thing I have is a good command of the English Language. I offered to show them all my frequent flyer miles cards from all our previous business trips, and I explained to them the reason for our trip. The other fellow in our group was Rambo, who was a light skinned black man, and he could easily pass for Middle Eastern; he had a thin black mustache and short nappy hair. But when he opened his mouth to speak you could tell that he was 100 percent Southern Creole.

The airline people immediately apologized and offered to sit us in first class with food and everything. On the trip many of the flight attendants came to talk to us and told us about the horrors of the flight attendants during the attacks. They told us how many of the flight attendants had been cut by the box cutters of the terrorists. I remember telling them what one flight's passengers did when they took over and fought back, and that action should be the norm not the exception. I told my wife for years that's what I would do if that ever happened, there's no way I would just let someone sit there and take over the plane. I told them if the flight attendants only knew what they had as a secret weapon (that drink cart), it could knock the shit out of anyone. The Minnesota trip was monumental in my mind, as far as my travel sales experience went, not only because it was the week after 9/11 but because it was so huge and profitable. The dealers name was Danny Hecker he owned 16 dealerships, the sale was conducted at a Stadium were they had a semi-pro football team. Rain was in the forecast and upon arrival we were all issued bright yellow rain gear that said Danny Hecker Automotive Group, which I still have to this day. Upon my arrival as well on this trip, I was a salesman not a closer, we were all issued a sheet that had a list of bonus cars, these cars when sold regardless of the price, and the salesman was issued his bonus on the spot. The bounty or bonus money ranged from $1,000–$2,500 per car sold from the list.

The bonus money was paid in addition to any commission earned, although many of these cars lost money on the actual sale. The dealer, Danny Hecker himself, walked around with a pair of overalls and briefcase full of cash handcuffed to his wrist. Of course not all the vehicles for sale were bonus vehicles, but there were enough of them out there to keep you interested every day. There must have been sixty to seventy salesman there, all of them wearing yellow slickers and it would be funny when you would talk to a customer and they said, "I just talked to a guy in a yellow jacket." My first day I made about $3,000 in cash bonuses, that's a wad of money; "3 stacks" in my pocket, and Harris made about $2,000. We celebrated by going to Rick's Cabaret which was right around the block from our hotel. The women were gorgeous there, until they opened their mouth, all they said was "yep" and "nope." It reminded me of the butler from the movie "Arthur" with Dudley Moore; where his butler would tell the hooker, "you have such an economy with words I await your next syllable with great eagerness." At the end of each night of the five day sale they had a huge giveaway of a large screen TV; this was done at about eight o'clock with the sale closing at nine.

By the second day the dealer, Danny Hecker himself, would start negotiating with the salesman when we were selling a bonus unit that we better raise the price by at least $500 on the sale, or he would not give us the full amount in bonus. That's when I meet Marty who was a Mid-Westerner from Wisconsin, he was a big guy about 6'4," and he had also been on many sales with other teams, but this was the first time I had met him. I happened to be working a deal in close proximity to Marty who was selling a bonus car when I heard Danny Hecker tell him that if he didn't raise that car by another $1,000 that he would only pay him $1,500 instead of $2,500. Marty turned to him and said, "I'll raise the price by another $1,000 if you guarantee that they win the TV tonight." I remember Danny Hecker turned to him and said, "Son, do you think I'm stupid?" Marty said to him, "I don't know if you are or not, but if you are, I sure don't want to miss you. What the fuck do you care who wins? Somebody has to win—either way, all you have to do is make sure that whoever draws the names draws their name."

The dealer had probably never had anyone talk to him like that before, so he agreed. Marty raised their car's price by $1,000 got his $2,500 and the customers went home with a new TV.

It turned out Marty was really talented, and I would come to work with him quite a bit. He was the life of the party and could tell everyone jokes for hours. Like most of these guys that worked on the road, they could not wait for the opportunity to cheat on their wives when they were out of town. Not that I'm so innocent, but I found myself missing my wife when I went on these trips. As the sale went on and ended on Saturday, we all went to a bar where they had an "oldies night." There were tons of women my age, and the guys were going crazy especially Harris; at one point Harris came looking for me and found me in the corner of the bar on the phone with my wife. He said, "Man, are you talking to your wife?" I said, "Yeah, they are playing our music and I miss her." That week I went home with over $10,000 in cash even after spending some of the money there, and I received another $4,000 in a check for my remaining commission for a total of over $14,000 on a six day sale, my best ever.

As time passed more and more people from the New Orleans area started to work with us, including two of the munchkin brothers Brian and Kerry. Brian the older one took himself much more serious than the others, and he always failed to see the humor in his shortness. I used to tell him "you need to learn to laugh at yourself because everybody else does." As things worked out I wound up being on a team with Brain and Marty, the big guy from Wisconsin.

In conducting these sales one of the most difficult things was becoming acclimated with the environment in each city, for example one would have to act a certain way in the South and the Midwest in order to communicate properly with the customers and be able to reach them at their level. This was mostly done on the fly, because we would have only one day to prepare for the sale and actually four days to conduct the sale. We went on such a sale to New Jersey, Brain, Marty and myself. I don't know if it was the neighborhood we were in, or if all the people from New Jersey were like that. They had a certain "in your face style" that demanded a response, and if you didn't talk to them correctly they would lose all respect for you, and disregard you. At this particular sale Brian was the finance manager, Marty was the desk manager and I was the closer. Brain, on occasion, would take his wife on the sale with him. I don't know if it was because he missed her, or she would help him or a little of both. She would help him keep organized, and pull the customer's credit reports. On the second day Marty and a loud mouthed customer get into a heated debate, with neither one of them backing down an inch. Consequently they made the deal, and afterward they were like best friends, shaking hands and laughing about it. Everyone was happy except for Brian's wife, she chose to stick her nose square in Marty's business, and told Marty "I think it was very unprofessional of you to yell and scream at the customer like that, and treat him that way."

Marty was just doing what had to be done, because that's the kind of customers we had, I myself had to do the same with a few customers but she just didn't understand that. After she spoke her mind Marty turned to her in front of everyone and said, "Who the fuck asked you, you stupid cunt!" Marty was huge by anyone's standards 6'4"–6'5" and about 260 lbs, and Brain was tiny by most people's standards, I turned to Brian, because Marty had done this in front of everyone, including the salesman from that dealership. I told Brian, "You have to do something Brian, go kick him in the knee or something you can't let him get away with that." I was so mad I almost challenged Marty on his behalf but I knew it was not my place, but I knew that Brian had to do something to retain the respect from our troops as well as the dealership. I kept telling him "sneak up behind him and jump and hit him in the back of the head or something, or get on a chair and jump on his shoulders, anything!" He thought I was just fucking with him and he kept telling me to shut up because everybody could hear my comments and what I was suggesting for him to do, and laughing at it. Finally he called Marty aside, and they went outside to talk in private seeming to resolve the situation. But I knew better, because as the day went on Marty kept joking about how he had shut down Brian's wife right in front of him, and how Brain didn't do anything about it. For some reason my friend Harris didn't make the trip and I ended up rooming with Marty, which was a chore in itself, because he was usually up drinking and partying all night. When he finally did show up to the room he started laughing and joking again about how he had insulted Brain's wife. I guess it's something to do with being a big guy and having the big guy complex that makes him think he can get away with things like that, so I turned to him and told him, "If you ever say anything about my wife and she's not even here, I'll kill you in your sleep." He started laughing like he thought I was joking and I said, "I'm serious, and if you think I'm joking go ahead and say something about her now, and see what happens, you're liable to wake up and roll over with a knife up your ass." He grew real quiet and went to bed and he never said anything about it around me ever again.

As time progressed it became more and more difficult for me to go on these trips, Harris my traveling buddy had quit, and that's what made the trips fun, we were both-likeminded we treated it like a job and were there for one purpose and that was to make money. We would work all day and grab something to eat at night, or workout at the hotel gym, and prepare for the next day just like we would if we were home. We had mutual trust and respect for each other, we had also been out as couples with our wives when we worked at the Chevrolet dealer together so we knew each other's families, there was a trust and bond there. Even though Brain and Kerry were decent fellows it wasn't the same, and I was not often paired with them to go on these trips. Many of the other guys were just total scum, most of them worked the road trips because there was no drug testing and they could run around all night and cheat on their wives and party until dawn. One of these was my old boss Joey who had been the general manager at Best Chevrolet; they had formed a team with him, another guy named Mark and myself to travel together.

Joey is very talented and has a flamboyant presence, which is shocking in itself, because on our trips knowing that I had been to Bible college; he would sit beside me and carry his Bible and ask me all about the scriptures and the purpose God has for him. Then as soon as we would land he would turn to Mark and say, "Hey, where do you think we can score some weed, or maybe cocaine?" Then he would brag to me how he would never cheat on his wife, and then on the side he would be talking to Mark about where they could score some whores on the trip. Many of our trips were to Wilmington, Delaware at a Toyota dealership. They were so familiar with us that I guess Joey thought he could party even harder while he was there, he oftentimes didn't get home from partying until four or five in the morning, and we had to be at work at 8:30. I'm not the person that's the worrying type, but I was ready for work every day, and I depended on them as a team to do their part but I couldn't even count on them to keep their eyes open.

This was one of the many reasons that I preferred to be a salesman and not a manager because I knew I could depend on myself, and not on other people. It got so bad that we had to send Joey to the hotel one day to sleep for four or five hours, then of course I was hearing it from Sean and Craig asking why the sale is not going well. Then I would have to be the one to put the finger and say it's because these guys are sleepy, and hung over, because they only sleep for two hours since they are partying all night. It got so bad that I actually thought I was getting an ulcer, I even had to go to the doctor because one of my testicles had swollen up, I don't think it had to do with the ulcer but the doctor had to give me medicine for it, and he said it was stress related. I'm a pragmatic person when it comes to business and I don't think I should be spending $1,500–$1,800 a trip when I'm only making $4,500, the numbers just don't add up, and when I'm away from my wife and home and have to put up with all this aggravation.

The real kicker came in early 2002 when my dad had been suffering from renal failure and I went to El Paso to visit him, and spend time with him. I remember telling him joke after joke to make him laugh, he laughed so hard that he was in pain. Every day I would call him to ask him what he wanted to eat and he would send me to pick up exotic things like green chicken enchiladas or menudo from various "hole in the wall" places in town. Years before I had offered him a kidney when he needed one, and he had to have one removed after suffering from prostate cancer. I told him I would gladly take the test to see if I was a candidate to offer him one of mine but of course, he refused. I remember my wife telling me "why would you offer him one of your kidneys when he doesn't even like you?" I remember telling her "he's my dad; I'd give him both of them because he's my dad." That turned out to be our last visit together and a good time as far as our memories together goes.

Around mid-January I was on a sale at a hole in the wall place in Richmond, Virginia and it did not look promising. I was working with a tall blond guy named Ray that thought he was God's gift to the car business; he used to be a Finance Director at Lamarque Ford in Louisiana. I was receiving calls from my sister that dad was really bad off, and that I should return home as soon as possible. It was the second day of the sale and I felt no qualms about leaving early since I had gone as a salesman and the sale itself had stunk. I had one of the porters from the dealership take me to the hotel and I packed my stuff and went home to Louisiana and prepared to go home if he passed away. I had told one of the managers at the sale, Scott who was one of the owner's brothers that I had to leave because my dad was sick, and he was supposed to communicate that to Ray. As I was flying back, and when I had my phone off on the plane, Ray had left a nasty message that he didn't believe my dad was sick and that I was just a chicken, that I was running away because it was a bad sale. It was such a nasty, unsympathetic and immature message that I saved it for a few years, and I would listen to it to fuel me for the moment we would meet again, I swore to myself, that if I ever saw him again I would beat the shit out of him, but I never did get the chance.

Soon after my return I received word that my dad passed away and my wife and I began to make travel plans to go back to El Paso, it was only months since 9/11 and security was still heightened at the airports. When we arrived at the New Orleans airport I was referred to a manager at American Airlines that was giving me a special rate, which was a bereavement rate, this gives you a discount when you are traveling for a funeral. She was very helpful and assisted us in every way, and then we went on to go through security. For as long as I can remember I've used my money clip to hold my money and this was a gold filled one, and I put it in the basket to be scanned along with my keys and wallet and incidentals. There was a rude Hispanic man doing the screening and he said, "Oh, you can't take this, this can't travel with you, it has to be confiscated," He took the clip off of my money, and kept it. I said, "What's the matter with you it's a money clip, don't you have any money haven't you ever used a clip?" Upon me raising my voice a Sherriff appeared there and said, "Oh no, you can't travel with that," and he bent the money clip opening it exposing one of the long pieces and put it between his knuckles making a fist showing how it could be used as a weapon, do you see this?" he said. So I reached up and grabbed his pen out of his pocket and put it between my knuckles like he did and said, "What about this you can make a weapon out of anything?" I said, "Steven Segal could probably take a napkin and kill twenty people with it." The Hispanic security man, with the attitude, said, "There is only one thing left I can do with this," and he threw it in the trash.

I was so upset with that, along with being that my dad had just passed away, and then having to go through this I said, "What a fucking asshole!" My wife had already gone through security and she was stuck there waiting for me, as two armed National Guards men with rifles came up and said that they would escort me back, because I called the security guy a fucking asshole and I could not fly anymore. Fortunately for me, they took me back to the nice supervisor from American Airlines who had already helped me, and she was shocked to see me walking back with two guardsmen. I explained to her what happened, and she told the guard's men "I will take care of it from here," and she immediately walked me back to the security area to face the Hispanic officer that said I couldn't fly. She told him, "This man is flying, he is going to his dad's funeral, and I have already screened him and made all the arrangements for his flight." The Hispanic officer said, "But he called me an asshole." I apologized and he let me through. I couldn't resist as I met up with my wife on the other side, the man kept staring at me and I mouthed the words "asshole," and he started yelling to the lady again, and said, "You see he called me asshole again." When she looked over toward me, I just shook my head like I didn't know what he was talking about. After the funeral my days were soon numbered working on these sales trips, I figured I could do just as much at a dealership and not have to spend all that money, not to mention the days away from my wife.

CHAPTER 29
BACK TO DODGE

Lamarque Dodge on Veterans Blvd in Metairie, Louisiana, was still a well-run and popular dealership. There had been a few changes since I was there last; Mark who used to be the used-car director was now the car buyer for this store and Lamarque Ford. Wayne who used to be the assistant to Mark was now the Director and my old buddy Steve, with the wig on his head, was now the assistant manager. There were a few new characters in used-car sales, one was Kenny a good-looking young Black guy and his claim to fame was he had been a lead drummer in the drum line of his high school St. Augustine, and it gave him popularity in the black community, especially with the women. He was well dressed and well-spoken, and my go to guy whenever I needed help with a black customer. Kenny had what they call "game" when it came to dealing with women; they would follow him around like a stray puppy. On the other hand there was Joe, who was Wayne the manager's nephew, who had no game; this boy could not get laid with a hundred-dollar-bill taped to his forehead in a whore house. He also couldn't sell cars either; we would say, "He couldn't sell pussy on a troop train."

He once had a female customer practically throwing herself at him and he didn't know what to do. He was running around as if saying, "How do I get out of this trap, how can I get out?" I would revert to my Howard Cosell voice and use sexual metaphors like, "You gotta put the biscuit in the basket, you gotta take it to the hole" or my favorite "If you only knew what you were doing, you could go all the way." There was also a young man a named Derek whose claim to fame was that his dad had been a manager with the Lamarque Company and he rode his dad's reputation to get a job there. Since Hollywood had started making a lot of movies in the Louisiana area, he had been cast as an extra in a lot of films, and he thought of himself as a wannabe actor. At this time, they were filming *Dracula 2000*, and I think he received a "bit part" in that movie. That means they probably bit him and killed him real quick just to get rid of him. He was constantly using his wannabe acting auditions to miss work, or leave early and I would make fun of him, and ridicule him in front of everybody and I would say, "You don't have to audition to be a lamp post, or a bird feeder." I even made a song about him to the tune of, "Mack the knife," it went like this:

"At that car lot, at the car lot you must stay till nine o'clock. Don't be sneaking out the back now and say I forgot. Well Saturday morning well Saturday morning don't you know? Don't you be calling in sick because you can't hold your liquor because you know that excuse just won't stick?"

This dealership was run by Timmy Lamarque, one of the famous Lamarque brothers in the area. His second in command was Roberto a Hispanic from Nicaragua. On the surface you would think he was a good guy, being that he was a Latino, but in reality he was a major "wannabe." The pay plan I had was decent, but it was nowhere near what I had before, when my friend Sean had taken me to the store. The one thing they had going for us was, if you were salesman of the month you got paid 40 percent commission for the following month and 10 percent on finance income, my normal pay was 30 percent commission across the board and 6 percent on finance. Once I started again in March I quickly became salesman of the month, and this I did for three months straight because I wanted that 40 percent which was equivalent to the pay plan I used to have. Using this to my advantage for those three months I made between $13,000–$16,000 each month. These are traditionally the best months of the year for selling cars, because people are getting back their income tax. At the end of the third month was when I made my largest check, since my return, I made $16,000 and everyone got paid except for me. Since I didn't get my check and I asked Wayne, the manager, "where's my check?" and he said, "Roberto has it." I mentioned before that Roberto was the General sales manager and I thought "ok cool, maybe he wants to congratulate me or something personally." I went to the new car building to find Roberto and I said, "Do you have my check?" and he said, "Yes, come on in." He called me in his office and closed the door, and he said, "I want to talk to you about this and I said, "Okay."

He said, "I didn't realize you were making all this money," and I said, "What you mean? I'm selling the cars to make the money."

He said, "Yeah, but I'm talking about this 40 percent deal that's not happening anymore, because you made more money than I did."

I said, "Well you are obviously better than me, why don't you join the sales force and beat me, since you are more talented than I am and you deserve to make more money?"

I immediately got pissed, and had a full head of steam, and I said, "Where were you when I was here at nine o'clock at night, at home in your jammies?" "Or when I'm on the car lot sweating in the heat and humidity while you are taking a two hour lunch, I think I worked a hell of a lot harder than you did and I earned that money." He said, "I'm not trying to discredit anything you did, but from now on the salesman of the month will get a $300 bonus and the second place will get $200 instead of this 40 percent business." I said, "Well, you can take that $300 and wipe your ass with it, I won't try to win anymore I'll just sell the cars I sell for more profit, and I can easily make more than $300 like that." I said, "In the meantime, give me the check that I earned," and he kept stalling me. I think he really wanted to go back into the office and change it, and I think he would have if he could have. The more he stalled me the madder I got and I said, "Look you skinny little prick, give me my check or I'm going to kick your ass!" He became all defensive and said, "Look, you don't have to threaten me," I said, "Look this is not a threat if you don't give it to me I will kick your ass, and if it's not the right amount, I will really kick your ass." He reluctantly reached in the drawer and handed me the check and I just walked away. Later, Timmy the general manager stopped me and said, "It's nothing personal, we just decided to make this change," and that he and Roberto were offering to take me to lunch on Friday to make peace, because he heard I had gotten upset with Roberto.

Timmy was a good guy and I wound up talking to him more and ignoring Roberto and enjoying a nice steak on the company dime since the 40 percent was over. Many of the other salesman who had been salesman of the month before I came back, were amazed at how much I made, it's like everything else a sales job is just an opportunity and it's up to you to maximize that opportunity and make the most you can. That's what I did, as one of the trainers I used to listen to Jackie Cooper said, "You have to believe in what you are doing, understand what you are doing and practice what you are doing." Because everybody calls you lucky when they see how much money you make but true L.U.C.K. is a metaphor for "laboring under correct knowledge," and I always used every opportunity as a learning experience whether it was a no sale or a sale. Losing, whether it is a sale or a game, is often a great teacher. Whenever I would lose a deal I would sit down and analyze how I lost it. Most salesmen I know would go home and cry about it to their families, and look for someone to blame like the customer or manager. With me I always looked at the things I had done, and I looked for ways to change them. The next thing I would do was go out and immediately try to make a better sale than the one I lost, if I had lost a $700 commission I would try to make a $1,000 commission and say, "Somebody is going to pay for this." Losing a sale is the equivalent to hitting a home run and forgetting to touch the first base. In theory it looks good, but in reality it sucks.

There are variables in every sale that can cause it to go south, for example the customer doesn't have the title to their trade-in, and you tell them to bring it back the next day, where as I've learned you have to get it now follow them home to get it so you leave nothing undone, everything needs to be done the day of the sale. Many customers say I'll sign all the papers right now and then come back and get the car with my husband later on. In Louisiana non delivery of a vehicle can make the deal void by law, so they have to take the car when they buy it. I witnessed one such a deal with one of the finance managers, a thirty-year-old woman and a single mom had purchased a car and they made a pretty nice profit off of it, but she didn't take delivery of the car because she wanted to bring her boyfriend back to see it. When she returned with her boyfriend he had coached her that she had paid too much for the car, and needed to back out of the deal and that because she had not taken delivery she had the right to back out, and he knew this. The finance manager began to act all high and mighty saying that she had signed the papers and the deal was already off to the bank. He mentioned the contract so much that she said, "Where's my copy of it? Am I not supposed to get a copy of the contract?" She said, "I don't have any copies of anything I signed, so I think you know it's not valid."

The finance manager said, "We were just waiting for you to come back for the car, and I have your copies in a folder waiting for you."

She said, "Forget my copies, I want to see the original you keep saying that you have, I want to see that." So the finance manager, still thinking he was in a position of power, went back to his office and got the originals and showed them to her. When he handed the originals to her, guess what she did, she asked, "Is this original?" he said, "Yes," and she ripped it into pieces. She outsmarted him, and she said, "What do you have now?" So I made it a point to learn from others people's bad experiences. As for me, it was not enough to learn from my own mistakes but from everybody else's as well, and there are many such examples in the car business.

My old buddy Steve was now the assistant manager or as we would call him "The Man with Two Hats" because he used to wear a baseball cap on top of his wig. He used to have a signal for me when we were selling together, when he was having trouble with a customer he would tap his left wrist like they would do in baseball calling for the left handed pitcher; as long as I was in the building he had told the other guys to just tap their left hand so I could go rescue them and we could salvage the deal. So my boy Kenny, who used to be the drummer in high school, would do this constantly and we split many deals this way and likewise I would use Kenny for black customers when I was having trouble them, and losing control of the sale. I would always introduce him as Mr. Kenny because he was always well dressed, and well spoken. In the South using the term Mr. along with someone's first name is a term of respect. Even my wife at her spa, or other businesses would instruct their employees to address them as such; this made even an older person feel younger while still being respected. I always got along very well with black people ever since I played basketball in college in California, and on playgrounds, and I worked with many of them even before Louisiana. But in Louisiana they are a very curious bunch, and in some ways comical yet predictable. For example on Martin Luther King Day you would see a family come in dressed in their Sunday best and you knew that if there was any way they could buy a car, they would buy one, just to celebrate Martin Luther King Day.

On such a day I was working with a well-dressed black family, they were looking at high line SUV's like Expeditions and Tahoe's, but I couldn't get them to test drive anything. They were very polite but stand offish. So I said, "Let me get my Supervisor Mr. Kenny" and he immediately went out there with his slick look and his handkerchief in his coat pocket. I said, "This is the man in charge Mr. Kenny" and they were immediately impressed that a young well-dressed black man was in charge of the used-car department, or so I said anyway. I stepped away from them and assumed the position of humility and awaited instructions. After talking to them for a few minutes Kenny called me over and said, "Get me the keys to these three vehicles," and I said, "Yes, sir." They had only driven two of the three with Kenny before they had selected one of them. Then he instructed me to take the one they had chosen to the back to get it washed and cleaned for them and he would do the paperwork. As per his instruction I brought them coffee and even snacks as he filled out the paperwork. They were so pleased, and happy with their overall experience that the result was a $7,000 profit and a $1,000 each commission for us. Kenny was one of my favorite black salesmen that I had ever worked with, he not only had "game" with the customers, but he also had tons of girls coming in running after him. He was kinky too, he told me one of his favorite things to do when he went out with a girl was to use his finger on them, and then make them suck it afterward. He told me "if you ever see me out on a date don't go shaking my hand because you know where it's been."

Many people think they are enlightened, but to me it's someone who understands the world around them, and sees things for how they really are, if you can see through the bullshit like Kenny did with the other black guys telling their war stories. When you get three or four black guys telling stories there is only two ways it can end; they either beat the shit out of someone, or they took the girl home and fucked her. That's why Kenny would tell them "don't talk about me, I know I don't want to get beat up by you and I sure don't want to fuck you." One black guy used to brag about how he played football for LSU for a while, someone did research on it and it turned out he used to be a flag bearer, and they even had pictures from the yearbook as proof. So when he started bragging about playing football I would tell him yeah Brian, "you're a legend in your own mind." He would say, "Look at my physique, and look at my build," and I would say, "Oh yeah, I think I've seen you in a magazine before or in a book." He immediately became proud and said, "Oh yeah, where did you see it?" I said, "In one of those history books where it talks about the early stages of man going from Neanderthal to Cro-Magnon."

It was not unusual for me to walk up to three or four black guys on Martin Luther King Day and say, "Happy Martin Luther King Day" and say, "Let's all celebrate and get a bucket of chicken and some watermelon, I'll even pitch in." Some would get all indignant and say that I was racist; I would say, "What do you mean? I'm willing to pitch in, are you saying you don't like chicken? I'm going to put you in the Guinness book of world records as the only black man to not like chicken." Some of the black guys refused to laugh when I made fun of them and would try to make Mexican jokes but I would fill in the blanks and supply them with even more jokes because I knew more Mexican jokes then they did. I believe that being a true person of the world, or worldly wise, is seeing the humor in all races. We even had some Vietnamese guys working with us, and when we would see a cat run across the road and I would say, "Oh look, dinner!" We had this Vietnamese guy named Tommy and he wanted to go with some of us to the Chinese buffet and I would say, "They don't serve your kind of food there; they don't serve dog or cat." He started cursing me under his breath in Vietnamese so I did the same to him in Spanish. I used to tell him, "what do Vietnamese say when dinner is over? Dog gone!" I actually got along pretty well with him and used him when we had Asian customers, which we often did. I was making a sale to a Vietnamese customer who was a fisherman he had very little credit history, but good credit and was putting $4,000 down on a $10,000 car. The deal sat in finance for about a week and the bank still would not approve it, so the finance manager took it upon himself to address the bank, he drew a little diagram it was a man in a boat on the water. It said, Mr. Chang fishing on the water, then he drew an arrow to a little pile of money that said $4,000 down, then from there he drew an arrow to a little minivan which was what he was buying and said van. So it was "Mr. Chang, fish, down payment, and van do you approve?" and faxed it to the bank. The banker got such a kick out of it, and laughed so hard that he approved the deal.

There was another Vietnamese guy named Bill who was a locksmith, so we would call him a couple times a week to make keys to replace those we had lost, and this guy would actually travel with his dog with him that was a little poodle. I used to call him "Mr. Yankee" and he would ask me why I called him that and I would say because all the time you "Yankee my wankee" like in the movie *16 Candles*. I used to tell him he should be in the Guinness book of world records because he was the only Vietnamese person I had ever seen that had a pet, and he didn't eat it. His little poodle was his constant companion until one day he was not with him, I had told him many times about the joke of what they say after dinner, he would say, "Don't tell me dog gone!" He wouldn't tell me, but he told Steve that the dog had passed away, and I didn't want to rub it in too hard so I just said, "Was the dog good?" I had everybody laughing at that except Bill, who was upset with me and didn't talk to me for about a week.

Another thing I found comical around my black salesman is how much they like going to church, especially with how much they party, drink and go chasing after women. One guy told me that it was because of all the women that he would even bother to go to church. He said any self-respecting black woman that hoped to get a man, would get all dressed up and go to church on Sundays. It was a meeting place for both sexes where they could say they met a respectable person, because they met them at church, when all the while they were just waiting to do the nasty. We had a real thin attractive black girl who was the operator at the dealership, she was really involved with her church, she might laugh at an off color joke of a sexual nature, but make no mistake she was a good church going girl, or at least I thought so. Until one day a tall black ex basketball player named Jake was talking to her on the phone, I didn't know who he was talking to but he was talking all shady like setting up a date with someone and using the phone in my office.

So I asked him, "Who was that?"

He said, "Oh, man, that's your girl," because he knew she and I were friends.

I said, "Who?"

He said, "The operator."

I said, "Oh, you are going to go out with her?"

He said, "Man, go out with her. I don't have to go out with her. I just go in with her." He said he took her for drinks one night, and she took him back to her apartment and came out in her underwear and rocked his world. So after that he didn't even need to take her out she would just say, "Meet me at the apartment at six o'clock when I get off from work."

As far as I knew she still stayed really involved with her church, but during the week she stayed real satisfied. You don't have to blame the church or society, but ever since the Cosmopolitan magazine came out, women were taught to satisfy their own sexual urges. I knew from my experience and from going to Bible college that things were not always like they seem, but I never heard of people meeting in church for sexual encounters until after talking to a few of these black salesman. Several times when I was in college at what we would call "chapel," some of the preachers would stand up and say that we had to be wary of sexual sins and I always thought this was very scandalous because everyone would be looking around the room to see someone crying and say, "Yep, you know she's doing it." As the scripture says there are only three things that will bring you down, "The Lust of the Flesh, the Lust of the Eyes and the Pride of Life." In reality all forms of sin boil down to these three things.

One of the things I loved to do when there was a slow spell in the dealership was to make a really good deal to demoralize the others. I always figured anybody can sell when it's busy but if you can pound out a nice deal when it's slow you have really accomplished something. On such a day I arrived to work on a Friday morning missing the ass chewing meeting that everyone else was getting for not selling any cars that week. When I arrived and pulled up to the dealership I saw a man looking at trucks with his son, after I approached them I found out that they were both looking for trucks; and both of them had brought in their trade-ins. It didn't take long until they each found a truck they had liked. I had put the deals together and pulled their credit, with both of them having over 700 for a credit score. To make sure that nothing could go wrong I got about $2,000 from each of them plus their trade-ins to make sure the deals went through. The finance department had been struggling at this time to get deals approved, so I made sure to cover all my bases. The other salesmen were pissed because while they were all in a meeting getting their ass chewed I was putting these nice deals together. When it was all said and done I had made about a $4,000 profit on each deal and about a $3,500 commission for myself on both deals, I know real estate agents that don't make that good of a commission for selling a house.

I remember taking the deals to the finance manager who was one of my favorite munchkin brothers Brian, as I laid it on the desk I said, "Here, even you can't fuck this up." Brian in his own right could talk tough even though he let Marty run all over him when we worked on the road together, but his brother Craig was another matter. Craig had become the new car manager and they once asked him to speak at a meeting to all the troops. As usual, I was in the back and I couldn't help myself and I said, "Stand up!" as he paced back and forth trying to figure out what to say, and soon all the other salesmen were yelling "stand up, stand up!" and he turned so red he couldn't get a word out. The whole room was laughing as this was a highly embarrassing moment for him. It's hard to earn the men's respect when you are so tiny and you literally don't stand up for yourself.

One fine day I approached some customers, it was an older lady with a younger couple. As soon as the lady opened her mouth to speak I could tell she was hearing impaired because of the way she spoke. The couple was her nephew and his wife, the ladies name was Stella and she began to tell me she was looking for a late model pickup with low miles. She kept saying, "I want a low payment, I want a low payment." I found her a Dodge Truck with 3,000 miles on it, and after we test drove it we went back to my office, and she was satisfied with the truck, but again she began telling me "I want a low payment." I said well I have got to see your credit to see how low it will be. I saw that she did possess a very high credit score so I went back to talk to her and said, "Just how low a payment do you want?" and she said, "I want it at about $200," and I said, "A week?" She flipped me off, and I started laughing then I said, "Seriously, what you are going to do put half down like $6,000-$7,000." Then she told me that $2,000 was all she could put down. At that time they were offering, for a short period of time, used-car leases for cars with low miles such as this one. So I asked her to give me a few minutes and I took the paper work to the finance manager to see if they would give her a lease. As it turned out she did qualify for a used-car lease and we could make a $7,000 profit with her payment at about $270 a month. So I came back and told her I could give her the car with $2,000 down and the payment at about $275 and she said as long as you keep my payment under $300 I think I'll be fine. That profit paid me about a $2,300 commission and all the other salesmen would look up at the sky, as if lightening was going to hit me when we were on the porch, because of how much I had made off that poor deaf lady.

Not only that, but a couple days later when I came in at noon she was there with the truck saying that it was not running right, the manager Wayne had taken it to service and said that it was running to standard and properly. I asked the lady "what's wrong?" and she put my hand on the wheel and said, "Feel it, it shakes, and it doesn't run right." To which I said, "It's running, and if you turn it off it won't shake like that." She said, "I know my rights, I've got thirty days," and I said, "What are you talking about?" and she said, "I've got thirty days to bring the car back." Of course she didn't have that, but someone must have told her so, so to this I said, "Well, it's only been two days, so come back in 28 days." I turned my back and started laughing at her, she ran to the front of me and said, "It's not funny, it's not funny!" All the salesmen were trying not to laugh loud because they were all on the porch listening and she kept saying, "It's not funny." They all kept looking up at the sky waiting for lightening to strike me, as if God was going to punish me, soon the lady left with her car, because what else she could do? I would often ask my wife if she felt bad about how much I would make off a customer, and she said, "No, if not you, someone else would do it."

One day my friend Steve, he with the funky toupee, decided to go on a diet. This would involve him eating potted meat, cheese, and crackers during his lunch break, Steve was a manager now and he thought that entitled him to a certain amount of respect. The first time I saw him serve up his version of his new "diet lunch," I let out a loud "Meow!" This was, of course, to imply that he was eating cat food. Everyone in the building cracked up laughing, the salesmen, the vendors, and the other managers. I could hear Steve cursing to himself, at his desk, but he decided to come over to "reason" with me instead. He told me how he looked out for me when I wasn't there, and he reminded me how he saw to it that I received all my bonuses on time. In the end, he wanted me to know that I owed him this courtesy, to not fuck with him while he ate his lunch. I nodded at him in a humbling manner as if agreeing with him, and I waited for him to go back to his desk. As soon as he lifted his fork to his mouth with another bite of his potted meat; I "Meowed" again, even louder than the first time; and everyone laughed even more than before. This process went on for about an hour, and at the end of it, he was so mad that he went out to eat instead. A week later I sold a car to a friend of his who had been on an African safari; he said they offered some potted meat to the Africans that carried their luggage. The men refused to eat any of it.

It wasn't always easy for me, just like everyone else I would suffer through slow spells where I would go two or three days without selling a car, even though I had multiple opportunities. One of the things that worked for me was what people call "affirmation," where you confirm things to yourself that you believe to be true about yourself, that you know you can prevail and given the right circumstances, you know that everything will work out for you, I never doubted that. Some people call it "positive reinforcement," when I was young I saw Mohamed Ali fight. In his corner they would tell him, "all men fear you; all women adore you, because you are the greatest." Even while I was growing up in my world, and I was told by my father that I was stupid and I would never amount to anything, I believed in my heart that I was smart and that I would succeed, and that they just didn't know the real me inside. The same thing was true in high school when I didn't go on a single date because I was shy, but I knew that if a girl would take the time to really get to know me she would like me, because I had a lot to offer.

The neighborhood I grew up in consisted of a lot of under privileged kids with attitude, most of the kids were about two or three years older than me. Getting in fights and getting your butt kicked was just a way of life. My dad had showed me how to box, so I had that going for me, plus I could throw a punch and could take one when I had it coming to me. The guys would say stuff like, "I'm going to kick your ass." I would say, "So what? I'm not champion of the world, I don't have a belt you can win from me. You're going to hit me, and I'm going to hit you and that's the end of it." That part of society

I actually understood, unlike now where kids talk about being bullied and it makes kids commit suicide, I got bullied more at home, than I did on the streets and I was ready for it. We would always go on a run like to the Sears at Five Points and the neighborhood guys would all say you would have to steal something from Sears or we are all going to kick your ass, and I was only about nine years old. So I walked out with a small bag of toy soldiers so I wouldn't get my ass kicked. I was at home playing with them and my dad walked in and said, "Where did you get that?" I said, "Mom got them for me at the store," a short time later he came back and said, "Your mom said she didn't get them for you, where did you get them?" I explained to him where I got them, and why, because I didn't want to get my butt kicked. I suppose he saw this as a fatherly teaching moment and he said, "We are going back to the store and you are going to return them, and apologize." I didn't really want to, but I said, "I guess so."

When we got to the store he said, "Are you ready? Let's go in."

I said, "I'm not going," and he said, "Why not?"

I said, "Because it's stupid, I already got away with it, why would I go in and confess? It would be like if I had stolen a hot dog and already eaten it, would I point at my stomach and confess? If you want to beat my ass, go ahead, but I'm not going inside the store."

So he did the next best thing: he took the toys in and apologized. All the way home I kept thinking how lame this was that he went in and apologized for something they didn't even know had happened. I just couldn't resist when we got home I turned my head to him and said, "Well, did you learn your lesson?" My dad was stomping mad; he was cussing so bad and stomping around the house that he totally forgot to whip my ass. He couldn't believe how fate had been so cruel to him to give him such a worthless son; those were some of the words he would say. While in the silence of my lonely room I was laughing my ass off, at how pissed I had made him and ruined his teaching moment.

Growing up my older sister Irene was big and strong and menacing, she was two years older than my brother Freddy who was four years older than me. One day the neighborhood bullies had chased my brother home; they were the ones in his age group, it was summertime at about nine o'clock at night. Irene was out in the front yard watering, when Freddy ran past her and inside the house. The ring leader was named Cesar, a local tough guy, and Irene confronted him and said, "What do you want?" He said, "We need to talk to

Freddy," and she said, "No, you don't!" He began to yell at her and said, "This doesn't concern you, this isn't your business," and she said, "My brother is my business," and she began dousing him, and soaking him with water. He was huffing and puffing, and cussing but she wouldn't stop, she would stop only for a moment and say, "What are you going to do?" He was shaking and cussing and the other two guys with him were laughing their asses off because this was a total embarrassment for them. All the while I just stood there in awe of her, of her guts and her tenacity. Sometime later my brother Freddy had to challenge one of the local bullies named Gabe who had already jumped my brother along with a couple of his friends and beat him up.

My dad could not live with any of us being a coward, so he forced Freddy to challenge him to a rematch. This took place at the alley behind our house and my dad spent extensive time with Freddy showing him the art of hand to hand combat. I was proud of Freddy because I knew in his heart he was deadly afraid, that was never the case with me because I was never afraid to throw it down. The fight took place as scheduled with like 20 to 30 people watching, almost the whole neighborhood watching, even my dad came home early from work and was peeking through the garage watching. At one point the other boy was getting the upper hand and my dad yelled through the garage, "Get him Freddy!" Soon Freddy punched the kid square in the throat and the fight was over. For weeks later the neighborhood boys would say that my dad came out and held him so Freddy could hit him, they changed the story. What this constituted was a rematch for me of sorts, I was pegged to fight Gabe's nephew Tony who was my age and at one point was considered a friend; but at this point that didn't matter we were fighting for family honor.

Tony and I squared off one fine day after school, in the same back alley behind my house, maybe not as big a crowd as before but definitely my sister Irene was watching and I wanted to do good for her. In those days most fights ended when one boy got on top of the other and pummeled him into the ground, so their whole goal was to get you on the ground face up. But I had been in enough fights to know this wasn't the case, I had done a lot of damage when I was on the ground. Some years later when I had taken a class in martial arts I learned that this was actually a tactic they used, to actually be on the ground while your opponent tries to vanquish you and you kick and strike them from the ground position up. For example, I kicked him in the shins, stomach, and even his face as he tried to approach me; I was kicking his ass from the ground up. It didn't even mater that he tried to go around me because I was spinning on my back kicking him from all directions. I'll never forget what happened next, my sister Irene started yelling, "Get up you are ruining your clothes!" and I thought my clothes? My clothes were shit to begin with. Irene screamed again, "Get up or you will have to deal with me!" I wasn't about to deal with her, so when I went to get up Tony came up and kicked me in the face to which we grabbed each other and started swinging and basically fought to a draw. So I went from a win to a draw because I didn't want to face Irene.

One of the things that I always had to do to motivate myself was watch my favorite movie about the car business—it's *Used Cars* starring Kurt Russell. The film was made in 1980 which is appropriate for me because that's about the time I went in the car business, and I've had it on video ever since it was made available. What made it impressive was that when it comes to selling cars, he knew he was the top man, just like I knew I was. The funny thing in the film is, when they have a big sale, he changes his dialogue to match different types of people. In the film, his name is Rudy Russo, but when he meets a black couple, he says, "Hey, my name is Rudy Washington." And he says, "Oh, I see you like that Cadillac over there." Then he approaches an older white couple, and he says, "Hello, mister," and the man says, "Shaunessy," and he says, "Hi, I'm Rudy O'Brian." Then he approaches a Hispanic couple, and he says, "Hello, mister . . . ?" and the man says, "Garcia," and he says, "Hello, I'm Rudy Vasquez," and he says, "Are you looking at that Chevy over there?" What's funny is his attitude; he's so positive and persuasive that people are taken back. But selling used cars is the perfect platform for it, and it's a perfect opportunity to lay it on thick and people can say, "Boy, you're acting just like a used-car salesman," and I say, "Well, that's what I am." Being a salesman is one of the few professions where you are defined by the word itself for example: a fighter fights, a teacher teaches, and a salesman sells.

If you are salesmen and you are not selling, you have to take a hard look in the mirror and say, "Why not!" That's when I look to me to give myself a pep talk, there's no greater feeling than coming home after selling a few cars and telling your wife, then you feel like a conquering hero. There's no worse feeling than coming home after two or three days of not selling, and saying, "Well, it's really slow out there." I prefer to be the conquering hero type, like being the football player that scores the winning touchdown, and he gets to go home afterward and fuck the prom queen. In the film *Used Cars,* they even had so many customers at one point that they had to get the big black mechanic to put on a suit and start waiting on customers himself. He says, "Rudy, I don't know anything about selling cars." Rudy tells him everything about selling cars in a nutshell. He says, "The first thing you do is get them in the car, because nothing sells a car like itself." Then he said, "You gain their confidence and their trust, and then you get their money." So many times in the business I'd see guys trying not to sound like a salesman, and they would even say, "I'm trying not to sound like a salesman," and I would say, "And that's why you are not selling." It would be like going to see a comedy act and the guy saying, "I'm not here to make you all laugh, but this is funny."

People know what salesmen are alike, so why not give them what they expect, so many customers would say, "Man, you're really trying to sell a car," and I would say, "Yeah, that's what I do." Or like back in the day, I would go to a club and hear a guy tell a woman he just met say, "I'm not trying to hit on you, but." I would laugh and think, that's what she's here for, and that's what you are here for, so give her a show for Christ's sake. Too many salesmen in the car business are afraid of the customer and they think the customer knows their business. When nothing could be further from the truth, they say, "This guy's a doctor," and I say, "So what? He knows how to give prescriptions, but he doesn't know what a car is worth. I'm the doctor of the used cars, and this is my world. This is how I operate. Nobody knows the true secret but me."

Finally, in the end of *Used Cars*, he wins, which is, ultimately, my goal, just like in my dreams I'm the winner, and I always win I must come out on top. To many people this may sound hokey, but this is how I envision myself in the business. "That I know a secret that not very many people do, that if I manipulate my mind to think that this is how it is; then that's how it will be." Like the scripture says, "As a man thinks in his heart, so is he."

For example, people buy shirts that say, "I survived boot camp or I survived hell week," I didn't want to be a survivor, I wanted to thrive. Mine wouldn't read I survived boot camp; mine would say, "I survived boot camp, now I own the fucking camp." Not to be too preachy but another scripture says, "Through all these things we are more than conquerors." A lot of what I did selling cars did depend on faith, for I often prayed for customers to come in, and they did. My aunt is very religious and I remember telling her once that I prayed out loud in front of everyone on the porch when a guy we called Stinky (because he smoked a pipe) had just made a really good deal. I said out loud, "Lord send me one like you did Stinky" and all the guys started laughing and to my surprise an Army Sargent pulled up right in front of me as I was pacing back and forth, and he said, "Get me out of this car, it just reminds me of my ex-wife." Stinky had made a $500 commission and I made a $750 commission in a matter of minutes after his sale. You tell me, is that faith or just coincidence?

When I was growing up in Texas instead of playing ball tag we would play with a big wad of newspapers, which when you are hit with it is like being hit with a big wad of bricks. One day when I was running up the side of one of the neighbor's house, his name was George and he "close lined me" basically he was hiding behind a bush and hit me right in the face and screamed "you're it." I picked up the paper and chased him, he was a lot faster than I was, but I caught him. I stabbed him with it and was screaming "you're it you're it!" Of course this was in the back alley that ran through the whole neighborhood and we had begun fighting. Now I stood a towering 5'2" even up to the start of high school and George was about three years older and bigger and stronger. It didn't matter to me, and soon I started getting the upper hand on him out of shear anger and guts. George actually starting getting tired and he tagged out with his cousin Mike, like wrestlers do in a wrestling match only I didn't have a tag team partner. Mike was more my size and my age, so I soon started beating the crap out of him. He started crying and yelling for George. George and he tagged George back in, this fight seemed to last for hours and I was beaten and exhausted especially with them tagging back and forth and me having to fight the whole time. There were other guys from the neighborhood watching like Raymond and Louie but nobody lifted a finger to help me, finally George was on top of me punching me, with me punching back and he was yelling at me saying, "All you have to do is say you quit, and that you give up!" I followed that with a punch to his mouth because quitting wasn't in me, even though he was beating me in punches 5 to 1.

The fight finally ended when my brother Freddy came by and pulled me out from under him and took me home. I stayed inside for a few days, and did not go out into the neighborhood licking my wounds, after about three or four days the neighborhood came to me. George and the guys he was with Louie and Raymond were on my porch. They came to ask how I was doing and to see if I wanted to hang out, as if nothing had happened. I actually thought they might want to kick my ass, and jump me again but I thought "what the hell," and I went with them. It was actually a sign of respect because I had never backed down, and I never gave up, regardless of how bad they beat me. That was the last fight I would ever have in my neighborhood. A couple of years later when I started high school a few of those guys joined the "Five Points Gang," to which I was also invited, but I refused. Through their gang wars Raymond wound up in a wheelchair for life, and one of the other guys ended up in prison, where he was stabbed and killed. As for me, I was just the chubby kid from the neighborhood, who didn't know how to quit.

CHAPTER 30
FromDodgetoLamarqueFord

Ronnie Lamarque owned the Dodge store where I worked and they had remodeled it from the ground up to a state of the art facility, but it had had foundational problems so Mr. Lamarque had a running battle with the people who had sold him the property and this turned into a legal battle. We were notified that within sixty days they were going to liquidate the inventory, and move all the operations to Lamarque Ford in Kenner and operate from their flagship store. During this process we had many sales and promotions to liquidate the inventory, but mostly the new car products which I didn't care about at all. They wanted everybody to be a team player, but I also felt that as a salesman you are not a team player, to me it is a time for individual achievement to sell for yourself, and as a commission based salesman I do not get paid to put balloons on cars or move cars around. It was easy for me to disappear when they would say we are going to have a lot party, like the moving cars back and forth, or taking them to the Ford store to get ready for the transition. What it did make me familiar with was the Lamarque brothers themselves, there were quite a bunch and they all worked in the business there was: Ronnie, as the main figure head, alongside him were Denis, Buddy, and Timmy those were the main ones. They had other nephews and nieces and such that worked at the dealership as well, but they were the main ones, and back in the day they actually had a band. Ronnie every now and then would come out with a commercial where he would be singing, "When the Saints Come Marching In." Denis's wife even recorded CDs and such, of her singing, and sold them locally.

I could tolerate most of the family, but at the time we were bringing in people like Roberto who I could not stand. The transition seemed to happen pretty quickly and soon I was working at the Ford dealership. Many of the peo-

ple at the Ford dealership had been there a long time and were very "cliquish."
Needless to say favoritism was rampant, and I was not part of the club, so I
saw my days there as being numbered. Although there were impressed by the
sales I could generate, especially the profits I brought in; I didn't have the patience to put in years of time there to be a part of the club so I was largely left
out and marginalized. The used-car department was well run by a guy named
Ray that I knew from a previous dealership. But the used-car facility itself
sucked, it was five shitty little offices and a large patio outside with a tent over
it. There was some characters there, one was named Chester a heavy set black
guy who was really funny. He was so funny that even though he had temporary
paralysis of the face, he could make you laugh with the faces he would make.
For example, he would make one of his cheeks really fat just on one side. His
favorite thing to do was when somebody was telling a story he would make the
sound from the movie *Friday the 13th* when Jason would be going after one of
the kids. I always felt bad for those kids in the "slasher" movies, here they are
trying to have sex for the first time, they have enough pressure on them, and
here comes Jason slicing and dicing them in half.

The top salesman there was a guy named Ricardo a light skinned black
guy that took himself way too seriously. I say that because he refused to laugh
at my black jokes, in fact he refused to laugh at my Mexican jokes as well.
Turns out he was not a fan of racial humor at all, even though I explained to
him I was an equal opportunity offender. But one of the things he would do
because he had been there so long was to put a vehicle on hold for days, because the managers would believe him when he would say he had a customer
coming to buy it. Then it would appear that the people didn't want it, and he
had held it for three or four days for no reason. After being a top salesman at
many dealerships I was never able to hold cars for that long, because in the car
business "money talks and bullshit walks." By most dealerships rules you have
to have money on a car in order to hold it, other than that I got along fine with
him. Another person there was a female sales person named Ashley, she was
tall and blonde and somewhat attractive with a super nice "store bought" rack
on her. Rumor had it that one of the finance managers had paid for her rack
when they were dating. She was divorced and had a couple of kids and was a
pretty nice person.

One day it was storming outside so I sat in my office catching up on my
reading and she came in to join me, she sat down and started asking me about
myself and since we had a lot of time to talk I shared a lot with her. I even

wound up quoting poetry to her, and I even think I sang her a song or two. Then after a while she looked around to see if anyone was listening and said, "I'm really getting wet, what you think we should do about it?" I said, "I don't know you can borrow my umbrella if you would like!" Then she said, "What?" and I said, "Yeah, I even have some rain gear, if you want you can borrow my jacket. I didn't realize it but she was really getting pissed, and she said, "Are you serious?" I was laughing and joking and I said, "Yeah, you can borrow my umbrella or something," and she said, "I thought you might want to buy me a drink." I said, "Sure, I got a couple of bucks do you want a soda?" I don't know where she was coming from, but I had no intention of fucking this girl. For one thing I knew if I did it would be analyzed all over the dealership and two if she was that easy, I don't know where in the hell she had been. Needless to say, I was on her shit list for a few weeks after that, oh well, besides I heard from a couple of guys in the dealership that was all that it took, a couple of drinks and you were in, in more ways than one.

I soon began looking for another place to make my income, and I started to talk to an old friend named JD. JD was running the Nissan dealership down the street, where my old friend Troy was the owner, and he been trying to get me to go work there. They were also in transition and working out of trailers which I had done before, and was not a fan of, while they built a new used-car building. So I kept JD in the back of my mind so that I knew I had somewhere to go in case I burned my bridge at the current dealership. The thing I hated worst at Lamarque Ford was the meetings, which were three times a week. It wasn't so much the meetings themselves, but that they were making you get there early in the morning when they have nothing to say. I have conducted many meetings myself, and I had learned from one of the best, my old boss Mike from Dick Poe. Mike was so good they would have him speak at National meetings for Chrysler. The art of public speaking itself is to know what you want to say, say it, and shut up. Well these guys didn't know what to say, or how to say it, and they didn't know when to shut the hell up. Needless to say, I skipped a lot of meetings, and when it finally hit five in a row that I had skipped; my old nemesis Roberto was waiting for me. He was the one that had famously withheld my check from me, at the Dodge store, because I had made more money than him.

When I arrived and was getting out of my vehicle he said that at this time they were going to fine me $50 for missing so many meetings, and what did I think about that? I said, "If you think you are going to touch my money I'm going to kick your ass, like I should have the first time you withheld my check at the Dodge store, what do you think of that?" He said, "Well, I guess if you are not going to let us fine you, then you are going to have to go."

I said, "That's fine because I have somewhere else to go, and unlike you, I have real talent. And if I were you, I wouldn't be around here while I am packing my stuff, because unlike you I have nothing to lose, and there is nothing to stop me from kicking your ass like I should have before." So sooner than I planned, I drove down the street to Premier Nissan to meet up with my friend JD.

One thing about JD is he was really down to earth for a general manager; he was a super nice guy who didn't mind working in the trenches with the troops. If anything, his downfall was that he was too nice and it was easy for people to walk all over him. For example, when I got there he cleared a space for me in one of the trailers throwing two other guys out of the space so I could have room for my stuff. Then he showed me a bunch of Nissan shirts he had bought for summer use for the salesmen, and they were really nice quality. He said I'm supposed to charge you for them but since you are not in the books yet go ahead and take a few, so I took half a dozen. JD was such a nice guy that he was trying to implement the pay plan that I had at Lamarque Dodge the first time I had met him, which included a salary and a 35 percent commission. He didn't know what I knew, that Troy the owner, would veto the pay plan so I wouldn't get paid on it.

JD said, "Just bring me some of your commission vouchers and I'll bonus the hell out of them," which he did. JD loved the Spanish radio stations, and especially the Spanish women that would come along with the live broadcasts. He was divorced and single, and loved to mingle, he would often have me translate so he could converse with the Spanish girls. He would even have me go to the radio station once a week to promote the dealership on the live broadcast; which would work out pretty well because I could give them my name and even my cell number on the air. The worst offense for JD was all the time he spent looking at on-line porn, which the company monitored coming from his computer. Troy's new found Christianity, and his wife, who was now a "goody two shoes" had people who spied and monitored JD's actions continually.

Upon my arrival I could quickly tell the stores weaknesses, one of them was Chris the used-car manager who had been fired from half a dozen dealerships around town, mostly because of stealing, his side kick was his assistant named Fred who was a down to earth real nice black guy who was really good at getting deals approved. The finance director was another story, he was a cranky old white guy named Art who I of course labeled, Art the Fart. I knew these were changes that would have to be made, but I just didn't know when they would happen and if they would involve JD or not.

JD asked me for one favor when I started, he said I know you are going to make a lot of money for yourself by selling used cars but I need to at least sell three or four new cars a month. I agreed to do this but I would mostly just sell an ad car like a new Nissan Sentra for $10,995. These were all flat commission deals that paid you a flat one hundred dollars regardless of profit or loss. I couldn't even see how they could afford to sell them for that price, because when I saw the "recap sheet" I could see that many of them were losers like at a loss of $2,000 negative profit. It was no small wonder that whenever I sold one of those new cars JD would have me go over to the new car manager to have him sign off on it because he didn't want his finger prints on it. It was a quick couple months before the used-car manager would be replaced, and in his place was my old buddy Joe, the "Italian Stallion," who I had worked with so many times before and my friend since I had first arrived in Louisiana, and I couldn't be happier. He could be counted on to produce good profits and was fair and impartial with everyone. I did know that however, JD's days were numbered; because with Troy the owner and his wife being new Christians that they would be on a crusade to clean up his pornography addiction on the internet, they had spies that monitored the internet. JD was a good guy, a funny guy to work with, and a good promoter as far as advertising campaigns and promotions to get customers in the door. I heard he was a little sloppy on the business end, but that had nothing to do with me. I had experienced for myself though what it felt like to be on the receiving end of Christians on a crusade.

When I was in Bible College I worked for UPS in Los Angeles, California and many of the guys from my school also worked there. I was a really hard worker and was really fast, I was constantly sent to different areas when they were distressed, or behind. I used to joke that they could give me two black guys in the truck that I was loading and I could keep them both humping, and they would be yelling at me to slow down, as I filled the truck with boxes. When things would slow down I would ask them what part of Watts they lived in? They did sometimes get mad and say, "I don't live in Watts." So I would say,

"Where do you live?" They would say Compton or Inglewood, all of which were notorious ghetto hoods. I used to just laugh and ask, "What's the difference?" Still I basically got along with them. My hard work had paid off and I received a promotion working in the bulk department. The plant that I worked at was the largest in Los Angeles area located at 3000 East Washington Boulevard close to East LA. The gravy job in the bulk department was that I got to ride the huge carousel around the building, and I had to know basically all the zip codes in the country, I did have a list to verify them to be sure.

There were only two areas where you picked up the bulk, tires, pipes, metal crates and wood crates and throw them into your cage. After you sorted them you would just stroll along watching everyone else work, as I would deliver them to their appropriate areas. It took 25 minutes to go around the building so even though the work was hard, it was sporadic. I spent a lot of time cruising, because the job was super easy for me, so I spent my time reading paperback novels or studying notes for school. This infuriated one of the goody-two-shoes Christians on a crusade that went to my school, his name was Mark, and he also lived in the same apartment building as I did. Mark would encourage some of the other Supervisors that would monitor our production to try to catch me in a trap for slacking off. The reality was I was one of the highest producers, as far as my production count went, so there was nothing he could do to challenge my position. A couple of times he even suggested for them to call me in for a meeting so they could grill me, and tell me not to be reading on the job. We were in the Teamsters union, so for any meeting that took place I demanded there be a union representative there on my behalf. When the union rep saw my numbers and saw that I was one of the highest producing members on the bulk team he would laugh and ask, "What is this about anyway?" They complained that I was reading on the job and that it was unsafe. I countered by saying if they can show me an employee manual that says there is no reading on the job I will gladly stop.

Mark, the supervisor that went to my school, he was there at the meeting and kept saying, "Safety first, safety first." I said well, "Have I ever had an accident, or injured anyone else while on the job?" He said you can only assume that if you are reading and you are not looking, that something can happen." He finally said, "No," but I got mad at him and yelled "just because you can't chew gum and walk at the same time doesn't mean that the rest of us can't do two things at the same time." The union rep told me to go ahead and go back to work and he would handle it from there, but it didn't end there. About a year later they called me in for another meeting and this time the union rep did not show up, and I opened my big mouth and said I would be glad to go to another department, and they transferred me. They sent me to work in the "unloading department." This was the pits, picture these trucks sitting outside in 120 degrees baking in the sun, and when you open the door dust flies everywhere. When you come out to take a break you literally look like one of those slaves from the Roman movies after working in the salt mines, the dust literally covers you face, eyebrows your ears and every orifice. This was right before my senior year and I did not plan to spend my senior year in this armpit of a job. The only good part about it was that I was working with my buddy Ron from school; he was a real good friend and a buddy of mine since my freshman year. We would drive to work together and sometimes hangout after work, sometimes he would invite me over for dinner, when his wife would cook. She and I used to date, but that was another matter and I don't want to go there. They are both really special people, because they are not bothered by such petty nonsense.

In the course of my four year history working with UPS I was probably out of work three or four times due to injuries that were mostly from my back. Because of my injuries, I had already had it in my mind that I would get my money's worth from workman's compensation, and enjoy my last few months of freedom. The great thing about being a member with the teamsters was that all you had to say was "I'm hurting" and they would send you to the doctor, period no questions asked. Just like when I was in high school and I'd be roaming the halls and they would send me to see the nurse, the nurse would take my temperature and say, "You're not sick," and I would say, "You don't know how I feel?" They would eventually let me go home. So with about two and a half months left before graduation I reported that my back was hurting and I needed to go to the doctor, my therapy was set up immediately as well as my workman's compensation pay. After about four weeks they wanted me to return to work and I said no I wanted to see a specialist, a Chiropractor.

Chiropractic treatment was basically new back then and they didn't want to approve it but they had no choice, I told them I would not return to work until I was treated by a chiropractor. It had to be one of their choosing and they chose a nice one, his office was on Wilshire Boulevard. It was just south of Beverly Hills, and his office was really nice, I would have to report three times a week for therapy. Upon my arrival and first meeting with him, I explained to him that I would have about six weeks before I graduate and return back to Texas. If he didn't mind putting me on a six-week plan, I told him, "I don't think you care. You get paid either way."

He said, "Sure, I'll put you on my seven-week plan just to be sure, and we're safe."

As graduation approached, it was time for me to handle my work situation so I went in to tell them I was resigning and they were required to give me an exit interview. During my time off when I was off on injury, I played a lot of basketball over at the apartments where I lived. Mark the righteous one; who had gone to my school and the supervisor that couldn't stand me, would come home from work at our apartments and see me playing ball. He made sure that he would be at my exit meeting, and was there and present, at my exit interview where I explained my intentions to move back to Texas, and that I would be leaving the company, and I thanked my supervisors for the job opportunity.

After that, of course Mark had to get his two cents in, and said that he would not recommend me for re-hire. He said that I was dishonest, and that I had been out playing basketball when I was off on injury and that I was getting paid from workman's comp while out playing ball. Again the righteous Christian on his crusade to set the record straight, I told him, "I'm glad you have this little job to make yourself feel important; if you knew anything about medicine you would know that I have a chronic history of back injuries that started with this company back to my first year." "Before I leave I have every right to be treated because of that, and besides that, I have no intention of ever applying with this company again, because I know that I can do better."

While back at the Nissan dealership it eventually came true that JD was fired for soliciting prostitutes from Craigslist on the internet. JD's replacement was a man named Phil. Phil had been in the area for a few years, but he was originally from New York complete with a New York accent and attitude. I immediately got along with Phil and we hit it off great, and he was familiar with my close association with Joe. He was also familiar with my vast history in the car business and he would often seek me for advice on handling certain situations. To me that's when you know a person is wise when they can ask for advice regardless of their position, or yours. They know that they can learn from someone else even though they know they are in charge. He would often walk across to the used-car building and ask me to walk the lot with him and talk about politics, sports and things that had nothing to do with the business and then he would eventually get around to talking about the business.

This was about the time that my little deaf cat passed away. Having nothing to do with the car business but everything to do with our lives, we had him for 13 years which was very few years by our standards. I was so upset that I felt I needed a few days off to process it. There was a magazine published on the North Shore named *North Lake Magazine*, and it had a section called Sinclair Loves Cats; in this section the editor would write about adventures that she and her cat had experienced on the weekend. I was sitting at home looking at the magazine pondering the life and death of my kitty when I decided to call her from the number published on the magazine. I told her that I had written a poem for my cat who had just died and I wanted to send it to her, she said that she didn't really include poems, but if I felt so strongly about it I could send it to her, and she would consider publishing it. The poem reads as follows:

FOR GRUBBY

"It was the day after, and I came home hoping to see,

His pale white body coming toward me.

But my eyes couldn't see him, try as I might.

You see, we buried my little kitty; he died last night.

When we first found him, he was so tiny he could fit in the palm of your hand.

My wife said, "We'll find him a good home, not sure just where he will land."

"Smack-dab in the middle of our hearts" is a natural reply.

He had one eye gray and the other as blue as the sky.

My kitty had a secret that soon would be made clear.

The little kitty was deaf. That's right, he couldn't hear.

He had a meow so loud it would startle you and make you jump out of your seat.

Then he would cast his pale eyes upon you and gently roll around your feet.

Through many trials and battles he had already come.

Yet he looked up to me as his father and me at him as a son.

When the time came and his illness had prevailed,

I thought to myself, *Oh my god, somehow I must have failed.*

As we held him for the last time, he sat up quickly, not wanting to let the story end.

Then we hugged him and kissed him and said we will see you again, my friend."

My kitty's name was Grubby because when he would go out and play he would come home with his pure white fur all dirty. We had him for almost fourteen years which was a short time for our standards we have had several cats for eighteen to twenty years. He had developed a blood clot near his femoral artery and after a couple days of trying blood thinners to ease the blood clot we took him to a specialist in Baton Rouge and he said that it would cost $2,000 for a surgery, and I was willing to pay, but the doctor encouraged me not to because he said that he would bleed out in the process; because it was so close to the femoral artery, so that it was best to put him to sleep. When I completed the poem and I sent it to Sinclair she called me back and let me know that it would be published. I kept copies of the magazine with me for many years and would hand them out to customers or people I knew that worked at radio stations. My buddy Juan Carlos said that girls, at the Spanish station, that didn't even know me had copies of the article up in their cubicles, so Grubby's memory lives on.

It was about this time I also met Vanessa, a soon to be a massage therapist, who was divorced and came in to buy a car with her new boyfriend. To put it mildly she was "smoking hot," and the boyfriend was a total dork. But he had good credit which is what we needed to make this deal work. Because of her current divorce her credit was not good enough, but his was exceptional, so we put the car in his name. She picked out a high-dollar Nissan Altima, and he gladly accepted the terms, and signed all the papers in his name only. Everybody was happy, I made off with a $1,500 commission and they drove off in a very nice automobile. At the present time she was going to be doing massages from her home until she got a job somewhere, and she wanted to reward me with one. My wife owned a day spa and I often got massages there once a week, or at least every other week. Her main therapist was an older Hispanic woman, which made me think of nothing but the massage itself, this was not the case with Vanessa. So a few days after the sale we made arrangements, and I went to her house for the massage. She told me to take off my clothes and lie face down on the table, and to be sure to take "all my clothes off." Of course she covered me with a towel and started my massage. Then she started telling me how her and her boyfriend were being very careful, for her, not to get pregnant and she had an adverse reaction to the pill, and now was trying various natural methods to not get pregnant. As great as she looked, and as good as she was making me feel, I was really trying not to think about her sexual activities as well. As with how most massages go, at some point, you have to turn over on your back, this created a problem, even though some would say, "Not a very big problem."

There's a story that goes why men should be great at reading a map, because only a man could look at an inch and think of it as a one hundred miles. I tried and tried to change the subject, but she kept talking about it, I don't know if she was doing this on purpose, or trying to seduce me. Part of me wanted to say, "I had a vasectomy," and she could fill free to do her thing, and the other part wanted this to be over with and get the hell out of there. I chose the latter and insisted on paying her, and I gave her a $40 tip, for a while, she called me about once a week to see if I was ready for another one. When I told my wife about it she said, "You should go back, it's so close to your work and you probably need it." My wife is a very sweet lady."

CHAPTER 31
PremierNissanandtheBigOne

No the big one does not refer to another massage (wishful thinking), I was going on my tenth year living in Louisiana and I had heard the horror stories of the storms there. I lived through a few of them, but none of the ones I had lived through were as bad as the one they described in the 1960s named Betsie, which wiped out whole communities. Hurricane season starts on June 1 of every year, and every year the weather forecasters predict so many storms, so naturally, everyone worries when they hear of a tropical storm on the horizon, fearing that this may be the one that finally buries Southeast Louisiana. For my wife and me, we had already learned how to get through them; even the hurricanes that we went through were not that bad. We lived in Covington, LA and north of I-12, which was a "volunteer only" evacuation area, so naturally we didn't ever evacuate. We had it down to a science, as to how we would prepare for the lack of electricity was we would fill both bath tubs with water, and the washer as well, because when the power was out our water well pump would not work. Then we used about twelve ice chests, and I would buy about sixteen bags of ice, and we would prepare to put our food in there from the refrigerator. My wife always had a good supply of candles around the house, and we would have plenty of batteries and flash lights and that was it. We could cook our food on the grill in the backyard and calmly wait for things to get back to normal. We knew that as situations would improve I would be super busy because people would have insurance money to replace cars lost in the storm. At the same time my wife's business would also be booming, because people would go there seeking to de-stress from the storm, and purchase massages and other spa services.

It was around late May of 2005 when we planned a trip to El Paso to visit my wife's parents, we had even planned to take them to Albuquerque and Santa

Fe, NM to see the sites and enjoy nicer weather. Upon our arrival in El Paso we noticed that her father's health was not good, he had a heart condition for a few years, and he even had a pace maker, but he did not look good at all, he looked close to death. He had plenty of health insurance, but was somehow not getting the care he needed, so we decided to intervene and take him back to Louisiana with us to get him the care he needed. I gave up my seat on the airline to Dora's mom, and we bought her dad a ticket and she flew back to Louisiana with them. Before that I hired a U-Haul and selected many of their personal items that they needed and attached it to the blazer I had given them. I hired one of the neighbor's sons to help me drive it up to Louisiana; I would pay him, and fly him back. This was going to be an adventure for us, because we didn't know if they would be staying with us for only a little while, or if we would need to move them up there permanently. Fortunately our house had plenty of room, it was over 2,800 square feet and they would have their own wing. They would stay in our guest bedroom that was next to the fitness room.

I immediately signed the up for the all-Spanish network on TV and they were all set. Next was to find a source of treatment center for Mr. Guzman, and we chose the Heart Hospital in Lacombe, LA. They had six heart specialists on staff, and they gave around the clock, excellent care as we checked him in for an extended stay. They discovered that he had excessive fluid in his lungs, so much so that they had to draw it out with a hypodermic needle. This was done twice daily, for the first three or four days of his stay. Then they decided on a new pace maker for him, because the old one was not functioning properly. His medical treatment in El Paso had been so bad, that they suggested an AIDS test on him because they didn't know why his feet were swelling up. After a couple of weeks he was released back into our care, but I had to take him constantly for check-ups and follow up visits. Fortunately at work I had produced enough when I was there that Joe my manager, and Phil the general manager, said I could be on the C-Shift, all that means is that, "when you see, me I'm there." I could come and go as I pleased without any restrictions.

My previous observation of the finance department was correct, and soon the cranky old Art the Fart was replaced. His replacement was Lou, a jolly older guy who was Lebanese, and he had suffered a partial paralysis on his face. Lou was very efficient, and he got immediate responses to our finance deals, just as you're supposed to. I used to mess with him about his face, and I would say, "Don't give me that look." His face was all pushed to one side, as if he had half a mouth full of marbles. I even used to tell him like the show on

TV, *Inside the Actors Studio*, I would say, "Show me comedy, show me sorrow," and then I'd say, "You are giving me the same face for everything." He would finally just flip me off, and tell me to get the fuck out of his office. He would call me Samson, because I was always trying new stuff to grow my hair, but at this point I had already given up. My wife would see actors on TV with a full head of hair and say, "See, they are older, and they have a full head of hair." I would remind her about actors like Ed Harris, Woody Haralson, and John Travolta who had all the money in the world, and still and no hair. As time progressed, we got through most of the summer without incident, as far as the storms went, that was until late August 2005.

It was about August 25, when a tropical storm was on the horizon that would soon become hurricane Katrina, the big one. We prepared for it in the usual way and I remember it was on a Saturday and business was slow, because everyone in the world was watching the weather and waiting to see which direction the storm would go. Because storms have a tendency to change direction and turn around, that was the case with this storm it looked like it was going to hit the Florida panhandle or Alabama coastline. It must have been five o'clock when I decided to leave work, I went to the store and the store looked like in the movies, when all the shelves are raided, and hardly anything was left. It all seemed so surreal, because everybody knew that the big storm was on the horizon.

As evening progressed, it became evident that it was not going to Florida or Alabama, but it was heading straight up the Louisiana shore line to New Orleans and its surrounding areas. As Sunday arrived it was truly the calm before the storm it was clear skies, no wind, and warm temperatures, it would make you think the whole thing was a mistake except for the weather forecast. Storms are rated by categories and Katrina was rated to be a 4 or 5 one of the strongest ever. That night after about ten o'clock you could hear the winds pick up and it seemed to go on for about 16 hours, with the wind getting louder and louder and stronger as time went on. I watched the weather channel until the power went out, which was at about 1 a.m. So now it's late August, pitch black, with no power, and no air conditioning, and I didn't know how my in laws would handle it. We quickly lit our candles, got the flashlights ready and tuned into the a.m. station which gave updates of the storm.

We had our little portable radio, with tons of batteries to keep us updated on the storm. It had been reported that many of the locals in New Orleans had fled to the superdome and the convention center hoping to find relief from the storm, I immediately knew that was a bad idea. The poor people that went to these places hoping for relief soon found that they wound up in a large public area that also had no electricity, only now they were with thousands of people, some of which had bad intentions. They began raping, and robbing the weaker ones, a true "Darwinian" society, where only the strong survived. As the storm progressed, I heard much about some of the massive flooding in the low lying areas, we were excluded from this, because we were on high ground. But the wind was nearly unbearable; I will never forget the sound of what 140 miles per hour wind sounds like up against your house, with trees, and limbs flying everywhere. We lived next door to a vacant lot, and I could hear the trees falling as if King Kong were over there knocking them down. Miraculously most of them landed on each other forming a sort of Tee Pee, only one of them landed on the roof of our house, and another landed on the side of the house, ripping off the electricity panel, making it harder for us to get electricity when power would become available.

I began patrolling the house, we had our 2 dogs in the garage with one cat, and three cats underneath our bed; and of course my in-laws huddled in their room, I checked on them constantly. As daylight approached I heard on the radio that prisoners had been released from the jail, because they also had no power, and experienced flooding there as well. This was not only in New Orleans, but also in surrounding areas, and they did not have anyone to watch them or contain them. Now I not only had to worry about my home and family, but I had to worry about them coming to our side of the lake and the risk of them looting and robbing and taking what we had. So I immediately loaded my dad's M1 rifle and began standing watch hoping for the best, but preparing for the worst. I heard later that we were supposed to have a couple of windows cracked open, to let the air circulate so that the house doesn't become a vacuum, I think what spared us was the doggie door in the garage. I had acquired a new car at the dealership before the storm and left my Blazer there, it was a 2004 White Lexis IS300 which was like brand new and only had 10,000 miles. We couldn't go anywhere because there was branches and debris all over the driveway but I was determined to take my in-laws to get something to eat and get them out of the house, and especially out of the heat.

That morning as the storm was blowing passed us, I paced back and forth in the living room looking at our huge picture windows, waiting to see if a tree would break through them. My mother-in-law kept coming out of her room as well, and I would shoo her away, and she said, "I'm over eighty years old and I can see whatever I want." So she sat down, and together we watched all the trees and debris flying into our huge windows. We had a bamboo tree that had been growing since we moved there ten years before, it was huge and it was soon leaning to its side whirling like a propeller with chunks of bamboo hitting the ground and flying into our windows, yet not a window broke. All the trees were swaying, the winds were howling, with trees and branches flying everywhere. To think that the worst part of the storm had already passed us. Fortunately, the windows we had were thick, double paned glass windows. As the storm passed that Monday afternoon and things got quiet again, I realized that everybody was in shock; my in-laws refused to eat or drink water. My father-in-law finally got the hint and decided to eat, but my mother-in-law was severely dehydrated, so I began wetting towels and throwing them at her face. She kind of got mad and told my wife "look he's treating me like a little kid." The evening wore on and things seemed to calm down, and we were able to go outside and grill to eat, there was not much else to do but sit back and hear the radio or read books by candle light. We opened all the windows, and did our best to catch a breeze, but I sat diligently, near the front window with my gun ready in case any looters came up the driveway. The authorities had installed a curfew in all areas, including the one we lived in St. Tammany Parish (Louisiana is divided into parishes instead of counties).

We had wanted to go to my wife's shop to check out the damage there, but we couldn't because the Police had blocked it off due to the flooding, her business sat right next to the Tchefuncte River. Once we were able to check on her business, we discovered the building had running water there, because the city had water and the plumbing was working, so we were able to go there to take showers. After a few days we also discovered that the roads were open to go to Baton Rouge, so once we were able we drove there to the airport and we bought tickets for my in-laws to fly them back to El Paso. The soonest flight they could be on was on the following Saturday. The remainder of the week was spent driving to Baton Rouge every day, if nothing else to have the air conditioner and look for a place to eat, or a store to buy supplies. I'll never forget the first restaurant we went to, it was an all you can eat buffet; keep in mind all we have had to eat was sausage, and crackers, after having grilled whatever chicken or fish we had to grill the first day or two. I remember my father-in-law looking at me saying that he had eaten two pieces of steak, he was so proud that he could put that much food away. He and I both ate like condemned men, enjoying their last meal.

My wife insisted that I take her to a nail salon to do her nails, because according to her they were a disaster. This salon was filled with fumes, chemicals, and overweight black ladies talking to who knows who on their cell phones. There's a saying from an Earth, Wind and Fire song that says, "I heard a voice out in the crowd, saying nothing and talking loud." I remember telling my wife afterward, "if that was my lot in life to be stuck with one of those fat black women, I would switch sides and go play for the other team," I would go get me a clean little white boy in the French quarter or something, in other words I would rather be gay then a slave to one of those black women. We often made it back from Baton Rouge just in time to go shower at my wife's spa, which was carefully guarded by the sheriff's deputies, who would flash their lights at us, showing that they knew it was us.

I had become more secure with our surroundings at home, mainly because the National Guard had appeared at the Target center near our house, giving out supplies and MRE's and they began to patrol the area, so that there was an armed presence there. Our good friends Keith and Angie lived in Denham Springs, which was very close to Baton Rouge, and they had been very helpful in helping me get a generator and other necessities. As Saturday approached, my wife became more and more at ease, knowing that her parents would be going back to El Paso and leaving this desolate area that had become our home. There were no direct flights to El Paso, so they would have to take a connecting flight through Southwest, this would be a problem because they spoke very little English. I scheduled them to ride as handicapped passengers, so that a wheel chair attendant would take them from one gate to the other. As it turned out they barely made it on time for their connecting flight.

We had gone to eat dinner with our friends Keith and Angie in Baton Rouge, my wife was desperate calling the airline, and her parents to make sure that they made the connecting flight. She finally got a hold of an attendant that said they barely made the flight; they were wheeled down just as they were closing the door for the flight to leave. At dinner my wife's face was glowing, she was so happy that her parents didn't have to struggle with our surroundings anymore. I kept telling her how pretty she looked and she was embarrassed because I was saying this in front of our friends, that night as we drove back from Baton Rouge we drove by her shop and guess what? The lights were on. She immediately went out to inform the sheriff that we would be staying the night there, after spending a week without air conditioning, or electricity we would now have both, and from then on we would be spending our time there, her shop was like a little house.

There are signs that describe Madisonville, Louisiana as being "scenic" and that couldn't be truer. The river bank was lined with tress and Spanish moss hanging everywhere. Every scene that you looked at was like out of a movie, or a famous painting that describes beauty by a waterfront. Keeping in mind that my wife and I were from the desert of El Paso, Texas we didn't want to take for granted the beauty that lay before us every day. The only thing bad about South Louisiana and the water front was the mosquitos; they rival those of the jungles in Mexico because of the humidity that exists there. In Louisiana everything grows, my wife actually thought she had a green thumb because of all the plants she had grown, when in reality, I've joked that you can eat an apple and throw the core and grow a tree out of it. After Katrina, we even started growing some strange grass that was blown in by the wind, we had like an 8×10 rug of grass that was shear and soft like a putting green on a golf course. So I put a couple of holes in it and made it my 8×10 putting green.

There are two unmistakable sounds that I experienced living in Louisiana, one is when the power goes out; this is not exclusive to just hurricanes it can be in rain, or any strong storm, fall, winter, summer it didn't matter. Summers were the worst, it could be storming outside and then you have the unmistakable whirring sound of finality. That means your world is about to change and all you can hope for is that they have the problem fixed in the next six to eight hours, so that you can have air conditioning again. Some people including one of my neighbors have these huge generators that power the whole house and cost about $12,000, but I wasn't about to do that. In contrast one of the greatest sounds in the world is when the power comes back on; it's like a reverse whirring sound, and it's like everything coming back on. You have your ceiling fan, air conditioning everything on all at once, and it's four in the morning and your thinking "AHHHHH." Being a former boat owner you can equate it to owning a boat, they say the best day of your life is the day you buy a boat and your second best day is the day you sell the boat. I sold my boat in 1999 when the Lasik eye surgery first came out, and with the funds I had my eye surgery.

My wife's shop stood right near the bank of a river, and you could stand on the front porch of her shop and see the river, it was right near a boat crossing, where barricades could come down and block the traffic so that the boats could pass by. One of the most familiar and pleasant sounds that we would hear was a horn blowing signaling that the bridge would be opening and the traffic would be stopped. This really worked well for us with the business, because we were able to hang banners outside the building; so as cars were stopped they had nothing else to do but read our advertisements of our specials. The property was over 100 years old and it was built up four feet off the ground, so that it was highly unlikely to flood, the style is what they call in New Orleans a "shotgun house." This meant that the house was divided by a hallway with different living areas on each side, and this floor plan accommodated my wife's various different spa treatment rooms. The back of one side of the house was the kitchen area and the other side was a restroom with a shower, so we had all the comforts of home, but I had to clear out every day so she could treat clients.

I myself was unable to go back to work until they repaired the Causeway Bridge and even then only with a permit. Soon my boss Joe faxed me a permit so that I could go with him and see the dealership and examine the damage. There is such a survival mode in south Louisiana when a storm passes, that when you see each other the normal greeting was "how'd you make out in the storm?" They could see that you survived, but they want to know how you made out, it didn't matter if they were strangers at the super market, or friends from work it was always the same. I know people died during the storm and I don't make light of that, but I just knew it would not be me; a house up the street from ours about seven houses away completely blew up. Three or four trees landed on it, and it blew up the gas line as if a bomb had exploded, but thank God nobody was home.

I've never envisioned my own death, but I think about it like Michael Corleone did at the end of *Godfather III*, he was sitting in a chair watching the sun set with his dog at his side and he just collapses. In reality, I've faced the possibility of death many times, one with my nearly fatal car accident; or diving in the Bahamas with sharks, even once while diving in Bora Bora. I thought I would have to square off with large Moray Eel that was following my wife around, because she had accidentally worn her diamond earrings, we just happened to be 60 feet below the surface with nowhere to run. Once we were even confronted by a pack of wild dogs on a beach in Bora Bora when I ran at them, instead of running away from them, my wife thought I was crazy but my theory was that if you show fear they well smell it and attack you; so I figured if you take an aggressive approach they will fear you and they did.

When I arrived at the dealership the new general manager Phil, who I barely knew, was offering me money as an advance because he was afraid I would go work somewhere else like in Baton Rouge. It took about another week to ten days before we could inhabit our building and start selling cars. All total I would owe the dealership about $12,000 before actually going to work, because every time he would see me, Phil would offer me money just to keep me in the loop.

Back in our neighborhood survival was in full bloom, with the sound of chain saws and trucks rambling up and down the road doing repairs. We still didn't have power at our house because I still needed to repair the electrical box that had been torn down on the side of our house. I had hired a company to remove the huge tree that had landed on my roof, I think it was called removeatree.com. We made out good with the insurance company though because we were given about $3,800 to fix the roof and I got a guy to do it for about $1,000. In the process I also found an electrician to fix the box outside and the house, and then it was just a matter of getting a hold of the electric company to come and turn it on. There were very few restaurants open but the ones that were, were jam packed at lunch time. There was a wing place not far from my house that was open and I went there one time at lunch time and saw three CLECO trucks there, that was the local power source for our electric company. So I went in and started looking for the guys that worked there, hoping I could bribe one of them to come do my house that was only three blocks away. They began to tell me that they couldn't accept any money to go, but they had to go in order of what jobs were given them.

I explained to them that it had been days since I called in so there was a work order somewhere, so it would not be like they are violating protocol. I said if I can't bribe you with money, could I perhaps offer you some beer or whiskey. I started to walk away, and one guy told me "I could go for some beer," I said, "Come on over then right after lunch;" I gave him my address, and wound up giving him a case and a half of beer my mother-in-law had bought. It wasn't long before we had power and things were looking up again, and it wouldn't be long until I would be going back to work. I still needed a lot of work to do at the house and the fence still needed to be fixed so that my dogs would be safe, I was so scared the neighbor's large dogs would hurt them. A large tree had fallen on the side of the property on the fence and rather than dragging it away we decided to use it as a part of the fence, for at least the time being because our small dogs could not get over it. We were fortunate that all we suffered was wind damage being that we were on high ground; wind damage is easy to repair, a few shingles here and a tree there.

My wife's car did get destroyed however, as it was totaled from a tree hitting it, we learned afterward that we could have taken it to the Target parking lot about half a mile away and left it parked there like many others did to avoid it getting smashed by trees and such. We practiced this later with other storms that followed after Katrina and it seemed to work because none of our other cars ever got destroyed. The car that had gotten totaled was a Mercedes 260 that we had bought in Dallas at a dealership called Texascarsdirect.com. So since there was a shortage of cars in our area we decided to look there again. As things appeared to be normal at the house, until my wife then brought home four more of what she called her "spa cats," which meant we now had seven cats and two dogs. With so many cats around the house it wasn't long before a cat would just show up. Then we were forced to deal with them, and some of them were mean like alley cats, that we would have to trap and let them go on another side of town. Every one of our pets was a foundling, and as long they were nice and polite we gave them a home. Our main dog was a beautiful border collie named Tiffany we named her after the Blue Dog portraits; our other dog was a Chihuahua mix that we named Chi Chi the Chihuahua. They stayed in the garage where they had heaters and air conditioning and a doggie door to the outside. But every now and then my wife would bring them inside and let them visit with us while we were watching TV.

One evening when we were watching TV and Chi Chi curled up with my wife on the couch and she said, "He's such a sweet little dog how could anybody just kick him out and let him wander around like that?" About that time I went to pick him up and take him back to the garage and he showed me his dark side, he showed me his fangs and began barking and growling at me, I started laughing and said, "There that's why, now you know why somebody was content to let him go." Even one of the more docile cats named Puffy attacked Chi Chi one time because Chi Chi must have showed him his fangs and dark side. Puffy was huge and easily outweighed Chi Chi. Puffy was grabbing him and clawing him with Chi Chi yelling bloody murder, our dog never did that again to Puffy. All this was served as a part of the calm before the storm because I knew that when I went back to work it would be like a war zone.

CHAPTER 32
BACK TO WORK

Years ago I visited with my cousin Chris to our first Dallas Cowboys game in Dallas, Texas, I've been a cowboy fan for most of my life. As we checked out the stadium and took in the whole event my cousin asked me what I thought, and I told him it was like dying and going to heaven, because everyone was wearing the Dallas blue and everybody loved the Cowboys. Being a car salesman in South Louisiana during post-Katrina it was much the same way, imagine a world where everybody needed cars and everybody had money to spend. The only difficult part was dealing with the imposed curfews in that we had to close before it got dark. But believe me the hunt was on, it was like being a lion in the Serengeti watching the antelope run; it wasn't a matter of if you were going to get one it was a matter of which one did you want. My approach was a slow deliberate type, I could deal with more people than one at a time; but it had to be on my terms, I refused to run around like a chicken with its head cut off. I think of it like the story of two bulls sitting on a hill watching a herd of cows, one is older and one is younger. Upon seeing the cows, the younger one screams, "Look at those cows, let's run down there and fuck one!" The older one says, "Slow down, son, let's walk down and fuck all of them." As for me, I didn't care about selling three or four cars in a day, it was about the profit, because we got paid on the profit, not on the number of cars we sold.

Our owner was my old buddy Troy, who I had worked with on several occasions and he owned all the Premier dealerships in the area which were: Premier Nissan, Premier Chrysler Dodge, Premier Honda, and he still owned Toyota of New Orleans which did not carry the Premier name and it was also no longer in the hood where I used to work. They had designed a state of the art facility in New Orleans East. I've always known Troy was a slick operator and he didn't disappoint me, soon after Katrina he was on a plane to Washington, DC to try to obtain federal funding for his dealerships. I was told he came back with approximately 16 million dollars to help supply cars to the storm ravished area. Just as the sales and profits were about to grow post-Katrina Troy and many other dealers decided to improve on their own profit, "The Pack" has been around for as long as I've been in the business. The pack is a guarantee of profit for the dealer, in the old days it was about $400 to $500, for example if a dealer takes a car in for $7,000 then $500 would be added on automatically and the salesman would start to make a profit after $7,500. As the profits were going to grow, many dealers including Troy increased their pack to $1,000 or even $1,200 further guaranteeing their own profits. Whereas, if a salesman was willing to fight for their profits, like I was, you are making even more money for the dealer. The only place where this was not a factor was when cars were taken in under $3,000, which is what we flocked to get. Cars that were taken in for that value only had a $200 pack and they were sold "as is," and they didn't require any service work on them. After the storm, trucks or SUVS in particular where at a premium because everybody needed them for clean-up work.

I remember waiting on a doctor and his wife because the wife was going to start up a landscaping business, unlike most salesmen I did not care that he was a doctor, he was no better than I was, I was a professional in my field just like he was in his. I showed them an older Ford pickup that we had taken in for $2,000 and I priced it at $7,999 it was clean, but it had about 160,000 miles, which didn't matter on a pickup. You have to understand this was a "dog eats dog" world out there at the time and people would practically kill for a pickup truck, and I had to fight off other salesmen just for the keys. So they started trying to negotiate with me, and the husband even said, "Isn't it true that the more profit you sell it for the more money you make on commission?" I said, "Well, really, that has nothing to do with it, right now it's all about supply and demand, obviously we gave more money for the truck then other dealers did, and if we gave more then we need to sell it for more." Then he said it again trying to be clever, regarding that if I sold it for more than I got more in commission. I turned to him with a straight face and said, "Isn't true that if I go see you as a doctor you make more money the more shit you find wring with me?" He said, "Well, it's not exactly like that," and I said, "So if I go see you and you write me a prescription, you will make the same as if you perform surgery on me?" The wife could see where this was headed so she intervened, and said, "Look, tell your boss I'll pay $7,000 for it." The end result is I wound up making a $2,000 commission on a $2,000 truck, is this great country or what!

There were some new characters at our dealership because some of the other premier stores where not up and running yet. One of them was a tall thin black guy named Sean; he loved to hangout in my office even though I would always kick him out. He was really intelligent and even had a degree in biochemistry, and I would ask him what the hell he was doing selling cars, because he wasn't that good at it. He was smart enough to know when I was baiting him, telling him my black jokes just to see if I could make him mad. For example I would say what do you call a black man in a suit? The defendant! Or I would say, "What are the three things you can't give a black man? A fat lip, a black eye and a job." Or he would come in and say, "I heard there were four murders in New Orleans last night," because things were still pretty bad. I would immediately ask him, "Yeah, but were they black or white?"

He would say, "Black," and I'd say, "Well, that's just nature's way of cutting down on crime." He sometimes got upset and said, "What do you mean by that?" and I would say, "What do you call a black woman getting an abortion? A crime stopper." My friend, Joe, the manager, had loaned this guy Sean a car, and I found out later that he and his girlfriend were sleeping in it because they had nowhere else to stay. There was so much money to be had that the federal government even had this program called the "road home program," which I didn't take advantage of, but I wish I had. Where people like Sean could apply because they didn't have anywhere to stay, and the apartment he lived at was gone, he soon received a check for $25,000 from the government. He took the money and moved to Houston and worked at a chemical company that sent him back to New Orleans to test the water. They paid him a nice salary to go back and test the water post-Katrina. I remember telling him the same thing "is this great country or what?"

Another person of interest was Ronea, a female salesman who had worked at Toyota New Orleans, she was very capable and professional, and she and I became friends for a long time. She was in her late forties and attractive, but we were strictly friends and never thought of anything else. She would call me whenever she had Spanish customers she needed help with or even when she had difficult customers that she was struggling to close the deal. I would help her close them and we would split the commission. Ronea and I would remain close associates for many years to come. Two white guys

286

named Glenn that were easily distinguishable one was a guy in his midforties who was a stone pervert, I mean this guy had pictures of his step daughter on his cell phone, and not the good kind. This guy was so bad he would get on Joe's computer when he wasn't there to look at porn, not knowing how closely monitored those computers are. He was finally let go when a female salesman reported him after walking into Joe's office and seeing him watching an X-rated movie. She went to tell Phil the general manager, and he walked in and terminated him.

The other Glenn was a classic moron, this was a short time after the movie Million Dollar Baby came out, and I named him Danger, after the retarded kid in the movie. To top it off, he was from St. Bernard's Parish, where I joked for years about their constant incest abuse. I used to joke that he should be a poster child, and they should have his picture on a bill board up in St. Bernard's saying, "Stop the madness, incest should be a crime, and stop dating your sisters." He was one of these people that got in this business after Katrina because he thought he was good at selling; when in reality he was selling cars because people needed them regardless of his talent. Joe had me close so many of his deals and split the commission that it wasn't even funny, and he started crying saying that all his deals were being spilt, when in reality he couldn't close them, and would have had nothing if not for the help.

One day he had a huge profit deal with Spanish customers and he could not close them and I had just gotten to work, Joe called me aside and said this deal is so big that I'm only going to pay you on the amount you raise them. For example, if I raised them the price of $3,000 then that's what I get paid on it. I wound up raising them over $5,500 so I made a little over $2,000 commission. It was easy because I just raised them $200 a month on their payment. I told them they would be paying the vehicle off in less time, what the fuck did they know? They couldn't read English. That was a $12,000 plus profit deal; it was like a whole other car. The customers constantly came back to fix the radio, or some other problem which I made Danger handle, because he made most of the money on our deal. I used to make fun of him so much that I actually felt bad one time; he came to work so happy because he found out his fiancé was pregnant and I said before I congratulate you I have to talk to you about something very important. I called him into Joe's office and closed the door and there was only Ronea, Joe and I. The two important questions I had to ask him were: Number one," are you related to her? Number two; have you actually had sex with her?" After he turned all colors, he dutifully answered the questions that yes he had had sex with her, and no they were not related. Only then did we congratulate him.

There was another character named Tommy, this guy had to be a product from incest, he had to be, this guy was separated from his wife; but she would always come by and visit him, and they had to be related because they looked exactly alike. We would walk into Joe's office and watch them as they argued on the porch and I would say, "Could you imagine them fucking those two?" Since they were separated they often argued, I heard one tell the other "you're stupid, and then the wife said you're stupid!" I felt like going out on the porch and saying, "Now, now you are both pretty stupid." But the most comical thing he had was a lisp, where he talked like Daffy the Duck, the old "Suffering Succotash." Joe would call me in to take over a deal for him, and I would tell him to tell me in detail what went on, just to listen to him, and he would say, "Thiess guy was looking for a pickup, but he didn't like the ones we had, so I told him, 'How 'bout an suve. Nethan makes a really good suve.'" After a couple of minutes of listening to him explaining, I would be laughing so hard I could hardly go talk to the customer, and Joe would yell at me and say, "Get the fuck out of here, and go talk to the customer yourself." He would finally realize he couldn't take the abuse and started his own business where he would repair windshields; there he said he was destined to make a fortune, a very small fortune. Last I heard he was living at a half-way house after getting in trouble for beating up his ex-old lady, or sister, whoever she was.

As you know by now one of my favorite topics is the black salesman, I think it humorous that it's one thing for them to promote the black myth, but it's quite another to actually believe it. A guy I worked with named Brian had a girlfriend following this time, post-Katrina, when we were so busy and he found out she was cheating on him with a white guy. He was devastated, not only by the fact that she cheated on him, but also about the fact that it was with a white guy. I began telling Brian just because you guys promote all that shit about your sexual powers, it doesn't mean you have to believe it; she was obviously looking for more than what you had. This was the same guy that had said before that he played football for LSU but we later found out that he was one of the flag dancers with the band, so he had a habit of lying to himself. Even worse he would not get rid of her, he would not throw her out of his apartment, he was determined to win her back and even hooked up a GPS to her car so he could track her all day. The rest of us were busy selling cars and making money while he was busy tracking her and calling her to see where she was, to see if she would lie about it. Later he found out she was pregnant and everyone told him he should get a paternity test; but he was too proud to do that, he just kicked her out and wound up paying child support, even though she was sleeping with like three or four other guys.

During this period after Katrina we were so busy, I remember waiting on an older white man named James and he started telling me that he has been to other dealerships and when he would go back they had already sold the cars; so what could he do to prevent that because he was looking for a car for his wife. He had landed on a late model Nissan Sentra and I asked him if he was driving the car that he planned on trading he said yes, so I did a "loaner agreement" for it and with my bosses permission I put him in the car, driving it so he could go show it to his wife. He was ecstatic that he was actually driving the car, and that no one else could drive it, and he called me a couple times to tell me that he was excited and bringing the wife back to make the deal. That evening when he returned we made that deal and he even picked out a car for himself, and the next morning he brought his daughter in to buy her a car, so I sold him a total of three cars for a total of about $3,600 in commissions.

One day one of the guys ordered some pizzas for the New Car department next door and I just noticed that the pizza delivery girl had an old car that she was driving, and she had parked near the used car lot, and as she was getting ready to leave I followed her out to her car and started talking to her about it. She told me that within in a few days she was expecting a check for $5,000 for her road home money from the storm, and she was planning on buying another car. I asked her, "What if I could hold your check for about a week and you could pick out a car to drive home today?"

She quickly walked the lot and picked out a nice Nissan Altima fully loaded with a sunroof and leather interior. She said, "Do you think I could get this one?"

I said, "We can sure find out," and I took her inside and started her credit application. As it turned out, she had really good credit and certainly qualified for that car, especially putting $5,000 down on top of her trade-in. So I did the same thing, I let her drive the car since she had to go back to work delivering pizzas while I got her paperwork ready; and I got her approved through the bank. She was a nice, chubby little Hispanic girl, which I didn't think anything of but Brian was after her, looking for redemption from the one that got away. I told him when I finish the deal you can do whatever you want with her just don't tell me about it. That evening I completed her deal and made myself a $1,500 commission and she couldn't be happier. A few days later she brought in her boyfriend, or ex-boyfriend whatever, to see if I could help him get a pickup truck. Upon seeing her bring the boyfriend Brian said, "Do you want me to help you with that deal, I've been going out with her." I said, "I told you that if you went out with her I didn't want to know anything about it; and you don't want to know anything about my business, and this is my business." As it turned out she had to co-sign for the boyfriend for him to qualify, while I made another $1,000 commission.

In the car business people are constantly trying to steal each other's sales, they call it "skating." The problem is that most salesmen don't know how to protect themselves or their customers. In the modern era one way of securing salesman protection is to log the customer in the computer by entering the customer as their client including their name, address, phone number and the car that they were interested in. By rule at most dealerships this protected the salesman for seventy-two hours if the client came back and purchased a car from another salesman they would be entitled to half of the commission. The problem was that things were happening so fast after Katrina that most salesmen didn't have time to log the customer properly. Often the customers were bounced from the New Car building because they didn't qualify, and came over to the used-car building. Oftentimes, this was the case with myself, when I approached customers that had been qualified from the New Car side they would tell me that they were not qualified to buy but were just looking. Such was the case with Mary, a young black girl in her twenties, with her child and young sister she told me she knew she didn't qualify; but that if I would be so kind, she could drive one of the Nissan Altima's just to see what it felt like. I told her I would let her drive the one she liked the best; just one test drive and just one car, if she promised to tell me the whole story when we got back to my office.

I let her test drive a nice cranberry red Nissan Altima and then when we got back to my office she began to tell me the story. She began telling me that she could easily afford the payments and had $4,000 to put down but that her credit was unworthy because of a recent divorce. I took out a sheet of paper and told her start telling me the names of people you think might qualify as a co-signer for you. First she said her Dad, and then her Mom, and then she stuck with her Mom but she said her Mom lived out in Lulling, Louisiana which was about 45 minutes from Metairie, which was where the dealership was. I told her to call her Mother if she was home, and she said, "Yes, and that she was off because she worked nights." I asked her if she would be willing to give me the credit information over the phone. As it turned out her Mother was credit worthy, and I got on the phone with her and told her what she need-ed to bring as far as paperwork, a recent paystub and a phone bill. I explained to her Mother that we would be going to pick her up in Lulling in about an hour in the new car, so she was to have all her paperwork ready. After we drove to Lulling to pick up the Mother she asked, "So am I going to be co-signing for her?" I said it's "like a co-signer, but you will be buying the car in your name, because if we put your daughter's name on the title; then the bank will not approve it, but you yourself have already been approved." As usual she wanted a few minutes alone with her daughter to explain the ground rules, how she would have to make the payments on time, etc.

Upon seeing me walk next door to the main building where the finance office is, the New Car salesman saw me with the client that he had before, and he went crying to the manager. He complained and asked how could I be selling her a car when he was told she didn't qualify, and why wasn't he getting half of the commission because he had logged her as a customer earlier that day. Well as it turned out he didn't log the Mother, and she had a completely different last name, and she was the one buying the car, so it's like you say in baseball, "You're out!" I had made another $4,000 profit on that car and a $1,500 commission proving once again that I know how to swim in shark infested waters.

The other thing I was very protective of was my used-car lot. As long as I was there I wouldn't allow any new car salesmen to run across and grab any of my used-car customers. It wasn't uncommon for me to go out there after they approached one of my used-car clients, and I would say, "Excuse me; he sells new cars how can I help you out here?" The new-car salesman would go back to his building pointing and complaining. Such was the case one day with a young Hispanic man named David, he tried to approach two young men as they got out to look at trucks on the used-car lot, the same thing happened I yelled out "he sells new cars how can I help you over here?" The same thing happened, David turned tail and went back over to new cars as I began talking to the men, the young man was looking at a nice late model Toyota pickup, which he didn't qualify for, he didn't have bad credit he just didn't have enough credit and would need someone to co-sign for him. I did the same thing I always did; I took out my sheet of paper and made him list all the people he thought might co-sign for him. We tried his Father, Mother and even his sister but none of them qualified.

The young man said, give me some time and I'll work on it and come back within a couple of hours. A couple of hours later he told me he was bringing his Grandpa in as a co-signer and he had good credit. That evening upon meeting the Grandfather he asked me how long I had been selling cars and I told him; and he said his Grandson had been to three or four places and they were not very nice to him after he did not qualify. He said he was extremely pleased that I had been so polite and cordial to his Grandson; he asked me what the total cost of the car was including tax, license and registration. Once I gave him the number he took out his check book and said that he was going to pay for it in full, that he would loan his Grandson the money that way he could pay him back with zero interest. Once again for very little effort I made a $1,000 commission, within that year the young man David, the New Car salesman had become a finance manager, and we actually became pretty good friends. He used to kid me all the time for taking that deal away from him; of course I would give him my Godfather answer, "that it wasn't personal, it was only business."

I seldom had to get rid of salesmen, like I had to back in the old days, but every once in a while the situation arose. It was a cocky young white kid that they had hired to sell used cars. One day I was parking a car up front just as a customer arrived and I began talking to them. I didn't noticed that the young kid had made his approach to go talk to the customer; so when I went in to get keys from the key machine he said, "Hey, I was on my way to talk to that customer." I said, "I guess you were but it's first come first serve." As usual, it was the case with me, if someone was going to be pissed off at me anyway, I would go ahead and make the deal, which I did. Of course being a young boy full of testosterone, he told me that if I ever did that again he would do such and such. I said, "You don't have to worry, it's not going to happen again," and he said, "Oh really? You promise?" I said, "No, it's not going to happen again because you're going to be out of here. All I have to do is say the word, and you will be out of here on your ass in no time."

Since my manager, Joe, was at lunch, I went over and found Phil, the general manager, and told him this young punk was threatening me; Phil calmly walked over and told him to pack his shit and go home. When Joe came back from lunch, he was shocked and said, "If you're going to fire my people, you could at least have a replacement ready." The kid went on to work at one of our other stores, the Kia store, and on occasion, he would come to our lot to check out our cars; when he would look at me, he would look at me like one would look at a neighbor's dog that had bit him, with awe. That look alone was priceless and worth the price of admission to me.

There's a parts department entrance very close to the used-car side of Premier Nissan, one Saturday morning I saw an old car pull up to the parts department and a young lady got out, and like the song said she was built like a "brick house." Her name was Katy, and she was looking for parts to fix her old car which was a Nissan but the department was closed due to inventory. She was driving an older Nissan and asked me if I thought she could qualify to get a newer one. As it turned out she was a bar tender and had worked most of the night, but she needed to get her transportation problems fixed. She wanted to try something sporty, and something with a standard transmission. She didn't know how to drive a standard, but asked if I would teach her. She picked out a Toyota Celica a sporty green one, we drove it back behind the park, and lucky for me she had a hard time getting the gears in place; and she wasn't wearing a bra, so lucky for me I had to lean over and help get them in place. As it turned out she could not master the gear shift of a standard transmission, but fortunately for me it was one of my more memorable experiences ever, because I got an eye full of her ample breasts. I admired the fact that she was such a good sport about it, to do for me as I did for her, many women in that situation wouldn't want a guy "ogling" her chest like I did. We went back to the dealership and found her one with an automatic transmission and her Dad co-signed for her. We were both very happy. She worked at a very popular beach themed bar within a couple blocks of Emeril's restaurant in downtown New Orleans. She constantly invited me to parties and promotions at her bar.

I had my own way of protecting the customers, one that I learned many years ago when I was at Dick Poe. My way of protecting myself with customers was to do what you call "low balling it" for example if the customer was going to leave I would say if they were looking at a car that was $12,000 I would tell them "what if I could get you that car for about $8,000?" "I'm not saying I can but if I could would you buy it then?" This is an art form, and rare in this day in age, like I said but I learned it many years ago and I learned the right way to do it. If you do it just right, then the customer wants to deal with you, and only you, not anybody else. Oftentimes I would get a call from a customer that had been in the dealership when I was not there and tried to get that price and no one else could do it. This works exceptionally well for people that won't give you their information, their name and phone number, etc. This also works well if the customer had a trade-in, I would do the same thing. If they had a car, they felt was worth about $2,000 I would say what if I could get you about $5,000? I would also give them my patented answer when they'd call me and ask if I could do this and I would say, "I don't know if I can do this or not, but I will try and give it my best shot."

When they'd come in, I could look them in the eye and say after my manager penciled the deal saying we couldn't sell it at that price, I would say, "I would if I could, but my manager won't take the deal," so I'd blame it on him. In reality I really would sell it for that if my manager wanted to take a $2,000 loss on the car, that's up to him. I would still have gladly filled out the paperwork; he just didn't want to do it, so I really wasn't lying. If we could not agree on a deal and the customer was still leaving, I would leave them at their last offer. For example, if my boss's offer was at $12,000 and they were at $10,000, then I would say, "I only know for sure it's not 10,000, and we know he wants 12,000, so somewhere in between, there is deal."

Oftentimes the customer would ask, "Would they take $10,500?"

I would say, "Are you offering $10,500 now?"

They would say, "No."

Then I would say, "Well, let me know if you are ready to offer 10,500, and I'll make the offer for you."

Then they would call me and say, "Okay, we are ready to offer $10,500."

And I would say, "Well, you have to come in."

They would get mad and say, "But we were just there."

And I would say, "Yes, but it's like a contest where you have to be present to win."

When they would come in, my boss would pencil them at $11,800. If they were smart, they would negotiate between the 10,500 and 11,800 but often, people weren't that smart. I realized this is why many people hate car salesmen, but I played it to a tee like an actor playing a role, and I knew my role, and I played it really well, way better than they ever knew their role. Oftentimes people were mad with me and still bought the car, because it made sense to them—like an attorney creating reasonable doubt, I would guide them as to which way they should go.

One time way back in the day when I first started selling used cars at Dick

Poe an old man named Wendell had trained me, and trained me well, and I had become his protégé in selling cars. I was dealing with an older black gentleman and his family, as he was trying to buy a car for his daughter. I had a scripted way of presenting an offer, and I did not vary from it. Every time the customer increased their offer I would write it down plus tax and license and have them initial it. The old man was getting frustrated and would start walking away saying, "Tell them I'll go $8,000," and then he would get up and start walking out of my office. I was getting upset because he was not following the protocol that I had set up before him. The next time he did this and said tell them I'll pay this much and started walking away I stood up and yelled, "Sit down!" He turned around and glared at me, and I said, "That's disrespectful for you to keep walking away, I understand if you don't want to buy the car, but if you are going to negotiate the right way then you need to sit down and we will both do it the right way." The man said, "I apologize" and he came back and sat down and we finished the deal. While they were in the finance office doing the paperwork another salesman showed me the man's picture in the newspaper. He had recently retired from the Army at Fort Bliss as a two star General. All the salesmen were impressed including Wendell that I had succeeded even though I yelled at him.

I understood it perfectly even though the man was a General, he understood what it meant to follow a chain of command and to take orders, even though he was used to giving them. This did not make me over impressed with myself, but with the system, and I believed in the system. In all the successful years I had with selling cars, there have always been young men who would ask me what I did to become so successful. I would tell them three things: believe in what you are doing, understand what you are doing, and practice what you are doing. Aside from that I would say, "Find a system that works and doesn't vary from it." I refer to sports where every sport has fundamentals, it doesn't matter if you are swinging a baseball bat, shooting a basketball or throwing a football if you do it the same way every time you will be successful. When it came to selling cars I never let a customer's attitude influence me, whether they were upset, anxious or in a hurry it doesn't change the way I conduct my business.

The first month post-Katrina I made about $35,000, that year I finished up making about $145,000 a couple years following that were equally as successful I made between $150,000–$165,000 each year. My wife and I enjoyed the fruits of this; and took vacations to the Bahamas and our favorite was to

Destin, Florida which is in the Florida panhandle, and only about four hours from where we lived. We would go to the Hilton Sand Destin which is a lovely hotel, with a great spa. It's not just a spa but if you get spa service, you get to use the locker room which consists of a spa within itself. It has its own pool and hot sauna where you can control the steam of the sauna, and when you step outside there are ice cold towels waiting for you. If you go into the pool, there is a Japanese water flow system that fills up and then pours the water over you. Or you could just walk around the locker room and watch sports on the TV's and eat from the various trail mixes, and fresh fruit they provided. The first time I went there I didn't realize that I had left my wife at the beach for over two hours while I enjoyed the spa which is called Serenity Day Spa. After I told her about it, the next day she left me at the beach for over two hours while she enjoyed it. Destin offers many of the great enjoyments such as fine restaurants with great sea food, concerts and even a Jazz festival once a year. It's one of our favorite places to go to in the US, if not the world.

Of course for real entertainment we were only forty-five minutes away from downtown New Orleans and the French Quarter. Every week was like a new adventure a restaurant was opening or re-opening a celebration of the coming back of New Orleans, with the whole world cheering us on. Every spring there is a Tennessee Williams festival, he was the author who made famous, "The Street Car Named Desire" featuring Marlon Brando. On Sunday at the end of the festival, everyone gathers at a hotel in the French Quarter where the men scream to the ladies in the balconies "Stella," and there is a contest held to reward the winner. One man even came out on the local news because when it was his turn he yelled out "Fema" instead of Stella, because everyone was still waiting on their "Fema" money. This was very popular because of all the struggles the people were having with the Federal Emergency Management Association. Just like in New Orleans our good times were rolling and you would think they would never end. But like anything else it has to come to an end, but we enjoyed at least three full years of prosperity following Katrina.

CHAPTER 33
MY MOMMA

In 2007, we still enjoyed much of the prosperity of the post-Katrina boom era. That year on October 23, my mom passed away; she was living in Tulsa, Oklahoma, where one of my sisters and her daughter lived. I had been to visit her that summer because I knew she had heart issues and I wanted to see her before she got worse. She needed a stem put in her heart and my Nieces husband was a doctor, and he could have easily done it but she didn't want any kind of surgery. It would have been a simple procedure, not a serious invasive surgery, but she would have nothing to do with it. When I was very young my mom had suffered from mental illness which in those days they had called it a "nervous breakdown."

It was in the early '60s and much of the news centered on the Cuban missile crisis followed by the Kennedy assassination. Many of my fond memories took place before then, when she would let me skip school and stay home with her. We would drink coffee and watch I love Lucy and listen to her records. One of her favorites was Bobby Darren, and it became one of mine as well, she used to crack up at me trying to sing, "Mack the Knife." Years later when I returned from college to visit she gave me that album to keep for our memories and I still have it to this day. My mom was very musical and taught herself to play the guitar, and she had a beautiful singing voice, which many people think I inherited from her. Because she was not around much, most of my childhood was spent with my aunt and my Cousins. When she wasn't home we often spent time travelling to Big Spring, Texas where the state mental hospital was located. In those early days of treating mental patients much was made of the use of shock treatments as therapy. The electrodes are placed on the sides of their temples and the patient is literally shocked into forgetting painful memories. Unfortunately they forget many memories altogether, and quite often my mother would sit there and have a recollection of a memory that had been long lost, and I would just listen to her as she expounded on something that she had just remembered.

My older sisters would never admit to this, but they were never kind, or friendly to her in her mental state. They often treated her as a non-entity, someone that they really didn't have to deal with because she was not well; I hated them for this and often wanted to kick their asses because of it. Especially when my brother died in Vietnam in 1969, she had lost her son, and there is no pain like a mother losing her son, yet they didn't feel the need to comfort her as I did. Years before that at one point my dad was contemplating on divorcing her, and I heard him speaking to my aunt and Uncle at the house while I was in the living room asleep with my Cousins. He was talking real serious, like this was the end, and he was going to finalize the divorce and proceed with his relationship with his girlfriend. I woke up and went to the kitchen and he began telling me that they were going to divorce and that my brother and sisters were all going with him and that I should to. He said, "If you come with me you will have everything you need;" inside I laughed to myself as I thought, "what hypocrisy, you're going to start giving me something that you never did before." I told him, "I have everything I need now," and I heard my aunt say, "Praise the Lord."

I told him, "Since no one is going with Mom, I better go with Mom."

My aunt told me, "You can always stay here, and I told her, "That's what I'll do, Dad, I'll stay between here and with Mom." I must have been about ten years old. From that day forward I never heard anything about a divorce, or a pending divorce.

My high school years were equally troubling because my mom and dad had no relations, my dad would go out drinking all night. So I would wake in the middle of the night hearing my mom yelling for me to come save her because my dad was drinking and making advances on her. Naturally I would sit there with my dad and try to calm him down, and when that wouldn't work, I would have to wrestle with him until he passed out. My dad would go drinking with a pocket full of money, sometimes a $1,000 or so. This was money I was never privy to so if he gave me an exceptionally hard time on any given night I might roll him for $40 or $60 to make it worth my time. He may have been drunk but he was no fool, he would wake up the next morning and say I'm missing some money. When I was older and used to go to the bar with him, I would see how much money he would leave on the counter. He always knew how much he had, and if the waitress took more than she should have, he would be after her complaining.

But during my high school years and when I was trying to calm him down he would often throw punches at me, which made me tougher and able to take it. He never hit me in the face, though he always hit me in the body, and I never once thought to lift a hand to him because he was my dad. One time I thought I had him completely calmed down, I even had my mom's room locked and he sat on one sofa and me on the other, and I saw him nodding off, he stood up suddenly and side kicked the door breaking the lock, the door knob everything even part of the panel that holds the door.

That's not all, he would come home and start complaining that we used the phone too much, so he would cut the phone lines, and he would even get mad at my sister and threaten to ruin the car he bought her, which was an old Fair lane. Once he got so mad he thought he would ruin the motor of the Fair lane, so he went out there and started moving stuff around under the hood. One of my Cousins was staying over, and it must have been a Friday night, at about 2 in the morning. Once he would get the hood open, I would run behind him and shut it down almost catching his finger. We lived on a busy street and even at one point all the neighbors would come out laughing at the comedy because as soon as he would get the hood open, I would run over and slam it shut. He finally got tired and went inside, but he was still causing a lot of trouble. I got so tired of all the trouble he caused that I tied his shoelaces together; my cousin laughs about it to this day, how my dad woke up cursing in the middle of the night, because I caused him to fall when he would get out of bed to go bother my mom. The worst thing he did however, out of everything was bring drunks home with him. I'd hear strange voices in the middle of the night and strange footsteps because I had trained myself to know everybody's walk, so if I heard strange footsteps, I would get up. Sure enough he would be in the kitchen or living room with some drunk showing him his guns, and of course they were loaded. How dangerous was this? Taking some stranger home with you, with all that money you carry around with you, and handing them one of your loaded guns to admire? When I would come into the room he would introduce me, and I would say, "Yes, and you have to leave now" and I would pick up one of the guns and hold it in my hands, so they knew I wasn't drunk and I knew how to use it. My dad would get mad and say, "This is my house and this is Jim" and I would say, "I don't care I have sisters here, and I don't know this guy from Adam," he can come back when you are both sober. I usually earned their respect especially with me holding a gun, and they would immediately leave.

As the years past and after my dad's death, my mother had moved to Oklahoma. She seemed less and less in touch with reality, she had been through a lot with her medications and mental illness and treatments over the years. But I did spend that week with her that summer before she passed which made it somehow worthwhile. As I mentioned she had a heart condition and would not receive the stem surgery to correct it. It was at this point where they knew her death was unavoidable, so Hospice would go visit her, her Hospice representative just happened to be a retired preacher. He would always ask her and remind her if she knew Jesus, just to hear her confess it, and she would say, "Yes, I sure do," and he would say then I'm going to sing a song for you. Then he would sing, "When the roll is called up yonder, I'll be there." There was a point in the song where you can insert someone's name and he would say and "Maria will be there." After she passed, and it was time for her funeral, my sister asked this man to sing that song at her service, and it moved me to tears.

CHAPTER 34
THE BATTLE OF MY LIFETIME

Mental illness is prevalent these days, more and more so because of the popularity of depression medications, that along with Cialis commercials. I often hear these commercials and they talk about the side effects I think, "shit I'd rather have the disease when the side effects are: death, stroke, blindness, diarrhea etc." I never had a fear of becoming mentally ill like my mother; it's just something that never did occur to me. My oldest sister, Irene, tells a story that when my dad was explaining my mother's mental illness to her, my brother, Freddy, and my sister, Offie, he said that "one in four people have mental illness and there are four of us here, so one of us could have it." My sister Irene turned to him and said, "Well, it's not me dad, so you don't have to worry." My brother, Freddy, also followed saying, "Yeah, Dad, you don't have to worry about me I am sure I don't have it." That only left my middle sister, Offie, who started crying saying, "I must have it. It must be me." We talk about it and always get a kick out of it.

The year was 2008 and business was still good but the dark clouds were on the horizon. Mine came in the form of a twitch in my left hand, my finger would move like the little kid in the film "The Shinning" when he was speaking to his imaginary friend. I thought nothing of it and even joked about it with my wife and her massage therapist, when I would go and receive a massage at her spa. The other dark clouds on the horizon were the looming of the economic crisis, and the threat of Obama winning the election, both of which caused me great anxiety. It seemed to hit me like a ton of bricks, everything at once. I began stressing over the bad economy and not sleeping, only getting three or four hours a night of sleep. Then I would wake up early in the morning at about four am and my left hand would twitch uncontrollably, my wife would even wake up and hold it for what seemed like hours. After she had her own battle with depression before, my wife thought I might be having the early signs of depression and I should get checked out. All I knew was that I had extremely high anxiety and shortness of breath, and I felt like I was walking a tight rope without a net. I often had the visualization of being on a ledge of a tall building, knowing that at any moment you could put your butt up against the wall and fall to your death. All the while I still had to go work and put on a happy face, and have a positive attitude and do my work and sell cars and guess what? I was still doing the job, and doing it well.

By now my old boss Joe, the Italian Stallion, had left after having an argument with Phil the general manager. I was stuck with the new guy named Oscar and the only good thing I could say about him was he was Hispanic and from Honduras, he was a good natured guy, but he was dumber than a sack of rocks. He was so absent minded that he would forget to write the "liner ads" that go in the Sunday paper. Every week the dealership would run 25 to 30 liner ads in the newspaper, these are to entice people to call and come in. So Phil the general manager commissioned me to start writing them. I said that it would be fine with me, I said, "But you know I'm going to put my phone number on about half of them to ring directly to my cell phone." So this became my salvation as the economic crisis loomed and sales slowed down, because people were afraid of what the future might hold. My phone still kept ringing with people still looking for cars, so I was often the only one selling any cars. This brought a lot of envy for Oscar since he knew what I was doing, and he would go complain to Phil, and Phil would say no "I want Richard to keep doing it; he's doing a fine job."

As my anxiety got worse, it became more and more obvious to my wife that I was battling depression; I had lost about 20 lbs. I couldn't eat or sleep and was constantly obsessing over the news, the stock market and the economy. Also our savings that we had been saving from my wife's 401K and IRA were heavily invested in the stock market which was losing money dramatically. She located me a therapist to see in our area in the city of Mandeville, this is the type of therapist that can only counsel you, but not distribute medicine, and it was a joke from beginning to end. As I went over my feelings on how I couldn't eat or sleep and how I was obsessing over everything all she did was sit there and make faces and say, "Oh, that' s terrible are you working?" I said yes I sell cars, toward the end of the session she said, "I don't know how you can wait on any customer and possibly sell in your condition." I explained to her that I was still the top salesman because when I am with a customer I go into acting mode and I'm like an actor playing a role I would be laughing on the outside, while crying on the inside. At the end of the session she had the nerve to ask me if I felt any better. At this point I had nothing to lose so I told her, the only thing that might make me feel better was that I found someone more fucked up then I was. She said, "Whatever do you mean?" She was shocked, and I said, "I didn't think it was possible but you made me feel worse, that anxiety that I feel of jumping or falling off a building, if I was there now I would probably go ahead and jump."

My wife determined that my condition needed more serious attention, so we contacted River Oaks Hospital which is in Jefferson Parish, about half an hour from my place of work. I had to take a day off and go there to be completely evaluated and start taking medication, and I began receiving treatment there. My treatment would involve meeting every morning at eight o'clock for one on one sessions and group therapy, at first they recommended I check into the hospital, but I wouldn't have any part of that. That was for people who had tried to commit suicide. So my days consisted of being there at eight o'clock in the morning with a session lasting till noon Monday through Friday, this also included lunch that is if I could eat anything. From there I would go to work, and try to put on my happy face and sell cars. I must admit at that point I did become scared that I was touched with the mental illness my mom had. I already had my fill of anxiety, and now I had even more to deal with thinking that I might be going nuts. I had a lot going for me though; I had hope, a loving family and a loving wife. When my friends like Alex and my cousin Chris found out about my struggles; they would call me, and encourage me. My older sister, Irene, would say that I could overcome this, but mostly it was my wife who supported me and never stopped believing in me. We would often go to dinner near her spa and I couldn't eat, and after two or three bites I would be full, she would say something like "you're not enjoying your dinner." I would say, "How the hell can I enjoy it when the stock market lost 300 points today?"

As I grew more familiar with the people in my group therapy I began to see how hopeless a lot of them were. Some were living at the hospital and when the therapist would ask them what their goals were for the day some would say, "I'm going to write letters, or take a nap or go for a walk." When it came to my turn I often said, "Fuck, I have to go meet customers, answer irate customers on the phones, and deal with my asshole managers while trying to make $100,000 a year." My only solace was I was still doing well at work and I would go see my General manager Phil with request forms and get advances of $2,000 or $3,000 and I would easily cover them just like I had done after Katrina. He finally asked me if I was gambling or losing money at the track or something, and I would say no I just feel more secure having more money in the bank.

In one of our group sessions they talked about developing a "coping mechanism" to help you deal with the times you have the most anxiety whether it be a thought or mantra, or a scripture something you can repeat to make you feel more secure. I didn't even know what they meant until it was on a Wednesday, and they passed a little globe around to each individual to ask them to describe what you would change about your world if you could. The reason I knew it was a Wednesday was because I said I would immediately hit the Powerball, and Powerball's were drawn on Wednesday. As I said the words everybody said, "Yeah, that would be great," and soon as they were nodding their approval. I began to realize about what I had said, and I retracted and said, "Do you know what? I have hit the Powerball, I have people who love me, and care about my well-being and that's worth more than gold." The therapist looked at me and said, "That is a coping mechanism and that's what you need to think about when you feel despair." Another time during the session when it was my turn to speak after hearing everyone's lame expectations of what they were doing for the day, when it was my turn to speak I stated, "I don't even know what I'm doing here, I am not in despair like most of them here I help people like my family, my sisters, my in-laws people who need me I'm not the one that needs help." The therapist told me "right now you do need help," and I told her, "Well, not for long. Believe me, I won't be here for long because this is not me I hate being here, I hate being like this and I refuse to be a victim of anything including my anxiety."

It seemed like I turned a corner from that point on, and I wasn't there much longer, I ran into a male nurse in the hallway and he had heard what I said, and he said I should start working out again that I looked like I was pretty fit; he said that exercise and perspiring creates endorphins in your body that makes you feel better and helps get rid of the anxiety. I had reinstated our membership at the health club and began working out again. When I was finally released from the program the therapist said she was amazed by how quickly I had gotten better, it had only taken me eight weeks to recover from what they term as clinical depression. The most telling factor to me was that my wife noticed that I was able to laugh and joke and sing for her again. When it was all said and done I had finished the year as salesman of the year again for the dealership, not bragging, but this was perhaps my finest hour because I had overcome so many obstacles, but mostly in my mind. I had often slept just two or three hours a night before going to my treatment, and when I slept, I often had the worst nightmares you could imagine. I once dreamed that our cats were outside in the front yard being roasted by homeless people about to eat them.

My friend Ronea who worked with me often tried to get me to eat because I couldn't stand food or the sight of food, sometimes we would go to a drive through restaurant to order take out, and she would hold my hand because it was shaking so bad due to my anxiety levels being so high. Yet even with all that I persevered, and would but I have to put a smile on my face to greet customers and close deals. I didn't make what I had been making the past few years in mid six figures but I still managed to make $118,000 while battling my depression. Even though I had recovered from my depression the pain that was in my left wrist was unbearable and that was the hand that was prone to twitching. So when I saw an acupuncture business, near my dealership that was on Veterans Boulevard. I decided to try it out.

It was an old doctor from China whose name was Doctor Woo. His Father had once been the chief physician to the emperor of China. He didn't speak any English, so he had a girl there to interpret for him as he examined me. He practiced what I now realize is Iridology, this is where the Doctor looks into your eyes and can tell what's wrong with you, so the young lady told me, "the Doctor can help with the pain in your wrist with the acupuncture." But she pointed to my left side of my head behind my ear and she said, "The doctor said you had a stroke on the left side of your brain and you need to see a specialist for that." I thought yeah right, they had already told me I had to drink a bunch of their nasty tea to help me and I thought it was just their way of trying to sell more tea, so I put it in the back of my mind. It did help the pain in my wrist with three or four treatments of the acupuncture; it wouldn't be until later that I would discover what I would need to treat the suspected stroke that I had suffered.

Soon my wife and I began planning our twenty-fifth wedding anniversary; it was to take place in our home town of El Paso with all our family and friends. It would be on June 19, the date of our wedding anniversary and also my wife's birthday. It would take place at my uncle Mando and Aunt Irma's house, which had a very spacious backyard. The music was performed by our good friend Victor who was the husband of Alicia, my wife's maid of honor at our wedding. My best friend since grade school Alex was there with his wife, Liz, and many of our close family and friends would also be in attendance. It was a joyous event for us, and our pastor, Brother Mac, renewed our vows. He was also the one who married us twenty-five years before. Brother Mac's real name was Paul McKeacharen, and his wife's name was Christine; as it turns out, their wedding anniversary was also the same day. I had attended the same Bible school he had, Life Bible College. When he and his wife attended there she also played the organ at Angelus Temple, the founding church of our college in Los Angeles. Being around him sometimes made me regret not going into the ministry since I had studied for it, I had my own reasons for not going into the ministry. One of the main ones was the principle of tithing which is when you give 10 percent of your income to the church, and I found no scriptural basis for it. Everybody would always bring up Old Testament examples but at the same token they would want to be a New Testament church. To this I would reply, "If you want to be a new-testament church, sell everything you have and give it to the church as they did in the book of the Acts of the Apostles.

The other thing I sometimes feared was how easy it was to fall into the trap where women throw themselves at you. In my own experiences going to Bible College it was often a challenge to some women to see if they could seduce you; to others it was a way of reaching out because you touched them emotionally and spiritually, in ways that they are looking for a release. You hear about all these controversies with churches were there is adultery and marital affairs, I thought I had a better chance of keeping clean if I wasn't in the ministry. Regarding our anniversary, the best comment or complement that I heard was how happy my wife looked. Whether it was at the event itself, or looking at the photos taken afterward, everybody commented on how happy she appeared. I always heard that if a man claimed to be the world's greatest lover, he should at least have the capacity to make one woman feel loved, and happy. I was proud that I had at least accomplished that, and as long as I could continue to make her happy, at least that part of my life would be fulfilled.

While on the previous subject of infidelity, there was a good friend of mine while I was in college, his name was John. We sang in choir together, both of us singing tenor, we stood side by side (and he was involved in his own controversy while we were in college). He was well-known and respected, and his parents were school Alumni and served as missionaries for the Four

Square Church. It seems that while we were on tours which we did every year visiting Northern California and Oregon representing the school choir, he had become friends with a young lady in the group; which no one thought anything of because they were always talking as friends. But it was soon revealed that they had been carrying on a torrid affair, and both of them were forced to leave the school in shame, mostly because he was married at the time. For me personally, though I see the wrong in it, I think that there are a lot worse things that people can be involved in, since these are matters of the heart. You hear of situations where pastors embezzle money from the church or molest young people, or where they out right swindle parishioners by claiming certain projects need to be created for the church. When I debated going into the ministry I thought that if I had to pound the pulpit by asking for money, I knew that I could do a heck of job, which was evident by my sales ability. In my heart I knew I could not treat my faith in that way, there are things that I still consider as sacred, I could play tricks when it came to selling cars, but not with the ministry.

CHAPTER 35

FOURDEALSTHATCEMENTEDMYLEGACY

It was about this time that my friend and manager named Joe, "the Italian Stallion," made his return to the dealership at Premier Nissan. He had previously had a run in with the Phil, the general manager, and they had since patched things up. This was great for me since I now had a manager that actually knew what he was doing. Joe saw to it that I received some benefits even though he couldn't pay me a salary, and I was no longer writing the ads. He saw to it that I received all calls or inquiries from "cars.com" that were directed to our dealership. It was his first Saturday back and I had an appointment with a man named Gene, who was interested in a Frontier pickup that we had advertised on cars.com. He had been shopping at other dealerships and had been told that his trade-in was worth $5,000. It was a 5 yr. old Mitsubishi Diamante, which were not very popular. The problem was that he owed $7,000 on it and was therefore upside down. Some Saturdays start out kind of slow, so I wanted to make the most of my opportunity and maximize this sale. I did a thorough demonstration of the Frontier pickup and was satisfied that he was convinced to purchase it.

I then took an unusual course to further demonstrate the value of my truck; I had Joe make me a book value sheet which gives the wholesale value with all the options of the vehicle we're selling. This form normally accompanies every transaction which is bank financed. I showed him this form to explain the great deal on the truck he was buying. Then I explained to him because of his situation where he owed more on his car than it was worth, that it would be to his benefit to let us certify the vehicle through Nissan. This certification comes with a 5 yr., 100,000 mile power train warranty and it also enables us to finance more money on the vehicle since it is certified. In other words, most banks usually lend 120 percent of the vehicle value, but on a Nissan certified car, Nissan will finance 140 percent of the value with approved credit. I told him that I would have to charge him $695 to certify our car, but our real cost was only $300. Then I had Joe the manager appraise his car and he actually gave me $6,000 for the appraisal value. Then I went and told the customer that because of the great deal we were giving him on his truck that I could only allow him $4,600 on his trade. With my creativity I had just increased the profit by $1,700 on an advertised vehicle that normally carried only a $1,500 profit margin. So now I had increased the profit to over $3,000 thus maximizing my commission potential.

But I wasn't through yet, I explained to him that because of the great deal on my truck we wouldn't need as much money down as the other dealers had told him. The other dealers had told him he needed $3,500 to $4,000 down. But we were able to get him approved with only $2,000 down because we were certifying the vehicle. He was a very intelligent man and I laid it out for him that way so that his analytical mind would understand it. Then the real kicker came in and he turned to his wife and said, "What do you think, honey?"

His wife was a petite blonde who had hardly said a word during the entire process, but she spoke now. She said, "If I can be frank, I'll say one thing. I think they're fucking you!"

He said, "Honey, they laid it all out for me."

She said, "Yes, but they are charging you for this and that, and I just don't like the deal."

Now it's been my experience that most "white guys" will do what the wife says, so when he asked for me to leave the room so they could talk in private, I expected the worse. So I went and hung out in Joe's office, which was very close to mine, and I just waited.

After a few minutes, the man poked his head in and said, "Okay, come on back."

When I went back to the office, I said, "What are we going to do?"

And he said, "Let's finish the deal. I sent her home."

As it turned out, they had come in two cars, and she had gone home in her own car to wait for him. When we pulled the man's credit, he had an eight hundred credit score, which helped matters even more. His credit was approved before we even got to the finance office.

After he took delivery of the vehicle and left, Joe called me to his office and said, "How in the hell did you make $3,300 profit on a vehicle with a $1,500 markup?"

I proceeded to tell him and explain the part that he had not heard from his office. Joe and I have known each other for a long time and have been good friends, but this, perhaps, was a moment of revelation to him—that he turned and told me that I was the best salesman he had ever seen.

Another way that we would get leads through the dealership was what we called "bogus lead ads." This gives people who think they have no shot at getting approved on credit, but at least it gives them a chance to apply. So we'd get twenty to twenty-five applications a day and Joe would pass them out to the salesmen. This was a slow day during the week, like a Wednesday, the application I received was from a woman that lived two hours away and possessed a 400 credit score. Not only that, but she was interested in a Nissan Armada, the most expensive vehicle that we sell. Not having anything else to do, I decided to give her a call. It didn't help that she also had a trade-in that she owed $4,000 more than it was worth. After I introduced myself over the phone, I said, "Tell me something good like that you have 7 or 8 or $10,000 to put down. She said, "No I do have $2,000 to put down, but I may have a co-signer." So I said, "Tell me about your co-signer." She proceeded to tell me she had recently married a man with excellent credit and he might co-sign for her.

I said, "Call him and ask him if I can call him and get his credit information over the phone and call me back." After a few minutes she called me back and gave me his credit information. The man did have excellent credit; he also didn't have a car in his name. My natural instinct was to see if she'd be willing to let the car she had go back to the bank, and just buy this one outright. She said, "I don't want to ruin my credit." I told her that her credit was pretty well shot, because she had a 400 credit score. She said, "Her husband would only sign if she agreed to trade in her car." So I pieced the deal together, and even Joe thought it was a total waste of time to submit the deal to finance. Because even though the man had superior credit, it was not enough to overcome a $4,000 deficit on the trade-in with only $2,000 down, and one where we could still make a profit. I asked him to humor me because he wasn't doing anything else, so we sent it into the bank. The bank gave us a qualifying amount that they would finance. Based on what he perceived her trade to be worth and the

$2,000 down we would be making a $1,500 profit. Joe explained to me that I would have to put it in the husband's name only and I said, "No problem, I will get them in today."

I called the woman and congratulated her and told her to bring in her husband, her trade-in and her checkbook. Keeping in mind that they were 2 to 2 ½ hours away, I expected them at about 7 or 7:30. I believe in fundamentals, and for every sale you have to sell the product first. I've seen too many salesmen put the cart before the horse and start selling the financing before selling the product. I had the vehicle cleaned, it was silver Nissan Armada with leather and sunroof and all the toys. So I brought it up to the front and let them take a nice long test drive before I went over any finance details. When we sat down in the office, I asked for his driver's license and insurance.

The wife said, "What about mine?"

And I said, "I'll get to yours in a minute." I then had to explain that all the transaction would have to be in the husband's name. But the good news for her was that we were taking her vehicle in trade thus freeing her up from that responsibility. The husband got a little angry and asked why we didn't explain this over the phone. I said, "Two reasons, one you wouldn't have come in, and two I can't very well show you the numbers over the phone. "Then I explained to him another part of good news that even though the bank was asking for another $2,000 down, that I was going to be able to take his check and hold it for thirty days for that additional $2,000. So he exclaimed, "Do you mean we have to put $4,000 down?" I said, "Yes, but only $2,000 now and a $2,000 check that we will hold for thirty days." He said, "I don't know we'll have to talk about this." I said, "Fine, you all talk and I'll leave the room, but remember how much you love her, and you all are newlyweds, and at some point you probably said I'll do anything for you honey." After a few minutes, they called me over and said, "Okay, let's do it." By my getting the extra $2,000 down, I had added that $2,000 to the profit thus making $3,500 gross profit instead of $1,500. My goal was always to make a $3,000 profit because it makes me at least a $1,000 commission.

The next deal was far less complicated, but still a defining moment of my sales career. It was during the winter on a cold windy, and gloomy, rainy Saturday. This was the kind of day that was hardly worth opening the doors for, even for a very successful Nissan dealership. The store had sold three new cars, and two used cars, for very little or no profit. It was near the end of the day, for me anyway, about six in the evening or so, when I received a call from a young lady looking for a car. I could tell by the sense of humility in her voice that she was not very picky in her quest for a three-thousand-dollar type of "transportation" car. I learned over the years that many people really wanted you to take their money; they just wanted you to give them a good reason.

After obtaining her call back information, I phoned her back and told her about a clean older Buick that I had just received as a trade-in. I told her about the car's good qualities, a solid engine, good air conditioning, and heater. I also told her some negatives, such as no radio, dents, and a broken head light. I shared this with her to maintain credibility, and a sense of honesty, but I told her for the amount of money she was spending she could do a lot worse. She said that she and her girlfriend would be taking a cab, and would be arriving shortly, and not to worry about the radio, she had one from her old car. When they arrived we went for a short test drive through the park nearby, and she could hardly wait to give me the money. I sold them the car for $2,950 and a profit of $2,500, I had made more money on an old "hooptie" than the entire dealership had made on all their other sales combined. I had managed to make an eight-hundred-dollar commission on one the ugliest days of the year, I also closed them on the fact that this was an "as is sale" and I never expected to see, or hear from them again. I remember they were so happy "making out" on the show room floor, waiting to do the paper work; as I went home early, once again the envy of all the other salesmen who said I was "so lucky."

On another occasion, through our bogus tip line I received an application from an African American lady named Rosie. Thank God Rosie had no trade-in, but she had really bad credit. She had a very good job with verifiable income and could provide proof. I went through my usual spiel and asked her if she had 7 or 8 or $9,000 to put down, because based on her credit she hadn't paid anybody else. It turned out; she had $8,000 to put down. There is a saying, that you never tell a "bogue" that they are approved. (A bogue is someone with very poor credit.) So following up with that, I told her we had several banks that would consider her on the right vehicle only. She was a single Mom with four kids and had designs on purchasing a vehicle with a third seat, like a Nissan Pathfinder. She also liked the Nissan Murano but it only had room for only five passengers. By now we had a program that was designed to inform us as to which vehicles of your inventory you could sell on a payment basis like this, and make the most profit. The program automatically gives you the top five vehicles in your inventory that would allow you to make the most profit. The Pathfinder she chose was number five on the list, which meant we could only make a $2,500 profit using her $8,000 down. My manager Joe was happy with that, she was happy with that, and her kids were really happy with that. The only one that wasn't happy was me. I kept thinking that with $8,000 down we had to be able to make more money than that. Joe my manager was telling me "finish the deal, go ahead and go on to the next one." But I kept thinking about number one on the list, which was a Hyundai Santa Fe, which would make an $8,000 profit. Just before we went to the finance office for the Pathfinder, I stopped her and showed her the Hyundai Santa Fe. In fact, she liked it a lot, it was a champagne color and it had leather with a sunroof and low mileage. I also explained to her that Hyundai carried a warranty up to 100,000 miles and the vehicle only had 13,000 miles.

As we went to the main building to wait for financing, there is a list where you have to wait your turn for finance. Since there were three or four people ahead of us, I decided to pull the vehicle up and let her drive it while we were waiting. When we came back from driving it, Joe began paging me on the intercom, and asked me what the hell I was doing.

I told him, "I was trying to switch her to the Hyundai so we could make more money."

He said, "Go ahead, but if we lose this deal, I will be really pissed."

I told him, "We're not going to lose anything, because I already had her money on the Pathfinder and if nothing else, we would at least sell that." Now with the little time we had left before going into finance, I explained to her how much better off she would be with the Hyundai. At this point I would have told her anything, I would have told her the world was flat to get her to sign for the Santa Fe. I told her how much sportier it was, how it had a better re-sale value, and a better warranty than the Nissan. She agreed with me but she finally said, "That they barely fit in it, meaning her and the four kids."

I finally told her, "Yes, but your oldest boy is seventeen, and he's going to be wanting his own car pretty soon, and after you get this vehicle and establish your credit, you'll l be able to get him one to go to college with and sign for him." Although she could have accomplished the same thing with the Nissan she agreed to switch to the Hyundai Santa Fe. For Joe it was just a matter of switching vehicles in the computer and the book value sheet as well. For me, it went from making a $2,500 profit or an $800 commission to making an $8,000 profit or a $2,800 commission. I did have to throw in a couple of oil changes and a free detail, but oh well, it was worth it.

CHAPTER 36
MY HEALTH ISSUES

The year was 2009, the local sports team, the New Orleans Saints were having an incredible season on their way to winning their first ever championship. You can imagine how everybody's attitude was soaring with the positive vibe that came with every victory. In the midst of all this, while I was walking the lot one day it was almost as if I had a blowout on my left foot. Being in the car business, that's the only way I can relate what happened to me. As I was walking, it suddenly became unbearable to put any weight on my left foot just as if I'd had a flat tire. I limped around the rest of the day and soon got my things and went home early. I soon began seeing a doctor near my home in Mandeville Louisiana. He recommended a procedure called an Osteotomy. In this surgical process the bones of your foot are broken and reset in such a way as to form a corrective measure. I researched it online and even got other opinions, mostly from a podiatrist. The podiatrist wanted to do a similar process but rather than breaking the bones, he wanted to fuse them creating a virtual stump of your foot. I knew a gentleman who had this procedure and was not very happy with the results. So I chose to go with the Osteotomy and which meant I'd be off my foot for 6 weeks total before I could start physical therapy and bring it back to working order.

I spent a lot of time at home reading and watching football, biding my time before I could get back to work. It was grueling and exhausting, wondering how it would be and how well I would recover. Before the year ended, I was able to return to work, albeit on a limited basis. My boss Joe continued to funnel the leads from Cars.com to me so that I could set appointments and not have to chase customers across the lot. Of course they used me for closing Hispanic customers for other salesmen. I also became the "go to guy" for any mission impossible type of deal.

One such was a crazy lady named Judy, she had not only called Joe, my used-car manager, she had also called Timson the new car manager and she had even called Phil, the general manager. She was after the elusive great deal, as she put it, on a Nissan Altima. She wanted a dark color, like a charcoal gray or black, low mileage, sunroof, and other specific options. She was referred to me when the general manager Phil came over to the used-car building and gave me her information; we had a brief meeting, with Joe, my used-car manager. Not only was she "a special client" but she was a referral from Troy the owner, it appeared she went to church with Troy's wife and required special care. She became my project for about a week until I found her the right car. Since I had more or less adopted her as my client, she felt it necessary to call me three or four times a day and even text me on Sundays when the football game was on. When I found her the right car that she could fall in love with, she insisted on having a good deal.

I had to use psychology on her and explain to her that a good deal was a state of mind. I had learned this long ago from Wendell; my first used-car manager, who taught me how to sell used cars. I shared with her that there were cheaper cars to be had; and those were "good deals." But for her to be satisfied, she would have to receive a fair deal on a car that fulfilled her desires. Therefore, when I presented the figures to her, where I was making at least a $3,000 profit, this included certifying the car for her through Nissan so that she would have a 100,000 mile warranty. I made it evident to her based on the law of supply and demand, that this was the best we could do. I learned long ago that when dealing with such a client, you have to present your figure and stand fast. Even though she complained and wanted another three or four-hundred-dollar discount, I knew that if I gave an inch I would blow the whole deal. After she complained about the price, I explained to her how satisfied she was with the car itself, and two or three years from now she would not remember three or four hundred dollars, but how happy and satisfied she was with the car. I thought I might have to live with her for a while so I made sure I made at least a thousand-dollar commission, but to my surprise she signed the papers, and took delivery and I never saw her again.

Meanwhile my foot was healing ever so slowly, when I first went back to work I began using my walker then I started using my cane longing for the day that I could walk normally again. There's an old saying, "If I knew I was going to live this long, I would have taken better care of myself." When I think back on my early years in the car business, when I worked at Dick Poe Chrysler in

El Paso, I used to haphazardly jump off the wall by the used-car building to be the first one to go get customers. As I hobble around on my one good foot, I would think about all the times I did that and how it might have contributed to my current situation. For as long as I can remember, I've struggled with fallen arches and have been fitted with custom orthotics at least half a dozen times.

I have may have mentioned this before, but I despise selling "new" cars, I've always said that the best thing about a new car, is that it eventually becomes a "used" car. However, beggars can't be choosy and since I'd become the new problem solver in the dealership, I became fair game for also closing new car deals. So one day Timson, the new-car manager, called me over to interpret for him with some Spanish speaking new car customers. They had leased a Pathfinder the year before, and had recently had an accident with it; but during the process they had let their insurance lapse so that the accident was not covered. The vehicle had about $1,800 worth of damage, but they had maintained a good credit status during the process, and they had also recently renewed their insurance. They were afraid that their accident could affect their status with the bank because it was a lease and not a purchase and they wanted to know if they could trade the vehicle without the bank knowing about the accident. This of course was possible, but Timson and I played it like were doing them a great favor. I had to pick out a new Pathfinder which carried a $3,500 rebate which was more than enough to cover the damages of the old vehicle. When I put their paperwork together along with their applications, I asked them how much they would be willing to go up a month to solve their problem. Their reply was fifty dollars to sixty dollars more a month, which I told them would not be sufficient. I ran the figures with Timson where I would at least be making a $3,000 profit and they would have to go up $110 a month in order for this to work out in my favor.

I don't know why but customers always say they don't want to pay for a car for "long terms." Without fail; I would tell them the story of the man who went to the doctor, and he was only given six months to live. When the doctor found out the patient couldn't pay the bill, he was given another six months. The Spanish customers were soon shaking their heads saying no, they couldn't possibly afford that, even though I explained to them the bank had already approved them for the $110 a month increase. I also explained that the bank used a debt to income ratio based on their current bills, and they would not approve them if they could not afford it. Not only that, but I told them they would have to make the first payment up front and they had 10 minutes to decide before the bank closed, and if not we would be forced to let the bank know about their accident without having insurance coverage. I left the office and within 5 minutes they were waving me back telling me that they would do it. The managers and other salesmen always got a kick out of hearing about the tactics I used, but I never felt bad, I think of it like a war of attrition, it's either them or me. I would often even ask my wife if she felt bad about all the people that I would nail on a car deal, and she would just say, "If not you, somebody else would do it and you might as well get paid for it."

That year ended and I didn't make my traditional 6 figure income, it was more like $75,000. Just when I thought I might be recovering from my foot with little else to worry about, a funny thing happened. My left hand began to twitch more and more, oftentimes shaking uncontrollably. One day when I was working on a sale with Joe, my manager, he asked everyone else to step out of the room, he closed the door and said to me "Have you ever been checked for Parkinson's Disease, because my dad had visible tremors like that and he went and saw a neurologist and it turned out that he had Parkinson's, and he was given medicine to help control the symptoms." He said he was just telling me for my own good that I should research it and maybe see a doctor. I soon came in contact with a doctor close to my home and after he analyzed me he said he was pretty sure I had Parkinson's but he wanted to order a brain MRI. When the results of the MRI came back, he told me I had a stroke on the left side of the brain. I remember I told him that the Chinese acupuncturist, Dr. Woo, had told me the same thing just by looking in my eyes. He was amazed at the doctor's ability to know all that just by looking in my eyes; nevertheless I was now forced to deal with the fact that I had Parkinson's on top of my foot injury. Fortunately for me, I had purchased a long term disability policy about ten years prior to this and at some point I felt like I would have to use it. I never in my wildest dreams felt like I would be physically unable to perform my duties as a salesman, in a business that I had thrived at, and I loved so much, but I was faced with the reality that time was drawing near.

When I visited my neurologist, I explained to him that I had purchased a long term disability policy and wondered if he'd be willing to sign off on it. He said yes but he said he recommended I apply for social security benefits first because they took 90 to 120 days to respond. Whereas the other policy I purchased would respond immediately within 30 days. I was sensing that this would be the plan I would take to end my long and illustrious career as a car salesman.

CHAPTER 37
WINDING DOWN A GREAT CAREER

You wouldn't think a lot could happen in ninety days, but believe it or not, I was visited by many repeat customers during this time. The first was Alberto, a Mexican national that worked for an off shore oil company. There are many off shore oil companies in Louisiana, and they pay quite well. Alberto was a professional diver who had suffered an accident while working off shore; he had been sucked in by the current and forced underneath the ship and thrown to the other side. If you know anything about diving, you'll know that an abrupt change in your body from shallow depth, to a deeper depth caused the "bends." In Alberto's case it caused a bubble to form in his brain, and he could no longer work. He'd been given a partial settlement of a couple of hundred grand on his way to a generous settlement of over 4 million dollars. When he came to see me, he was driving a five- to six-year-old truck and wanted to upgrade to a Nissan Titan. The first deal he did was rather abrupt as he saw a black two door Titan that he fell in love with immediately. We spent a lot of time talking since I had experienced recent injuries, as did he.

Needless to say I made a six-thousand-dollar profit on him. He was so happy that before the month was over, he brought his wife to buy another car for her, and we made an easy five-thousand-dollar profit on her as well. Before my time was over, he would come back and trade the Titan truck I sold him this time for a new four-door Titan fully loaded with leather and sunroof. This time I made an eight-thousand-dollar profit on him. My sales were not as frequent as before because I couldn't get around as well, but I tried to maximize each sale with pure profit potential. Since I had no particular time to be there, my friend Ronea would call me to see if I was on my way yet. She would sit on customers and save them for me because she knew I was on a mission for making profit, and she could make more money splitting a commission with me than she could on her own. This was more easily accomplished if they were Hispanic customers and she did nothing but demonstrate the car, pull their credit and babysit them without giving them prices. Then I would arrive as a hero to give them the "best deal," of course that was the best deal for us, not them.

During this time, I also had to go to physical therapy sometimes in the morning before going to work. One day a lady was receiving treatment next to me, and she started talking about a friend of hers that had visited Egypt. I said, "I've also visited Egypt, my wife and I went years ago." She said that her friend had tasted a rare delicacy, camel burgers. She asked if I had tasted them, even though I hadn't I said, "Oh yes, they're great." I asked her, "Did she tell you about the camel toes?" Both of the physical therapists stifled their laughter, the woman was probably in her late sixties and had not heard of the term. She asked me "are those a delicacy, and how are they prepared?" I said, "I'm not sure, but they can come out very thick and juicy." The one therapist that was working on me was turning all red with colors trying not to laugh, and the other one was already cracking up.

She asked, "What else can you tell me about them?"

I said, "Evidently they are hard to clean, because sometimes they still have a little hair on them. And sometimes they can carry a pungent odor, but you know what they say."

She said, "What's that? Once you get past the smell, you've got it licked." The therapists had to take a short break to gather themselves while the lady was wondering what the hell was going on.

One afternoon I came across a young guy wondering aimlessly around the used-car lot, he said he was just looking and had already been approached by two or three people. I said, "I don't care about that, come on in let's take a few minutes and talk." He said his name was Aldo; he stood about 5 feet tall and looked like one of the characters from the "Snuffy Smith" comic strip. He told me what he had already told everybody else, that he'd only been six months on his job, had no credit and only a thousand dollars to put down. I said, "Don't worry about that, write down the names of three people that might co-sign for you," which he did. Then I gave him a piece of paper and pen and told him to go write down the stock numbers of his three favorite cars. Of the three cars he picked, the one with the most potential was a Mitsubishi Galant, it was not terribly expensive and we owned it cheap according to the book value. Then I sat him down and asked him about his potential co-signers. I asked him which of the three of them had the best credit in his opinion. He said his mother was the most likely choice, but he said that she was mean, and if she didn't like me that it would be no deal. I said, "What have we got to lose, we have a fifty-fifty shot, either she likes me or she doesn't," so I asked him to call her. After he tried in vain to explain the deal for a few minutes, I told him to hand me the phone.

I've always been proud of my phone skills, but even I must admit this was a masterful job. I spoke about her son as if he were a young apprentice of mine, with a bright future ahead of him. I went on to explain to her that it was our job to set him in the right direction. I told her it was my responsibility to guide him through a deal that would make sense; and all she had to do was merely loan him her signature for this one time only. When she began asking about the car and for me to describe it to her, I said the next best thing to do would be to go take it to her. Fortunately she lived about 15 minutes away, and when we picked her up she was impressed with the automobile. I must say she was equally impressed with me, because I was calm and polite and not pushy or aggressive. She even phoned her husband from the driveway, and said that she would be going to the dealership to co-sign for her son. When we arrived at the dealership I pulled both of their credit reports, his was just as he said, and he had no credit. And hers was just as he thought, excellent. When my boss Joe and I put the deal together, we realized that I could make a twenty-five-hundred-dollar profit with just his $1,000 down. But as with anything in life, I wanted more. So as I was putting all the paperwork together, and Aldo and his Mom were bonding nicely in my office, I went back and sprang the news on her. I told her in order for this deal to work for the best possible results they would need another $1,500 down. This would make the payment more affordable for him, and easier for the bank to approve it. She was in such a good mood by now that she went with the deal, so I made my $4,000 profit instead of $2,500. This is an improvement from a $700 commission to about $1,300, and with everybody happy.

Before my 90 days were over Aldo had his car stolen and it was determined by the insurance company to be a total loss. Fortunately, the two payments that he had made during that time gave him sufficient credit to purchase another car in his name only. Good thing, because by then he had pissed off his Mom, and had been thrown out of the house, he didn't have as much buying potential as he did with his Mom but it was sufficient to get a car. This kid became a real groupie of mine, he would often come spend a couple of hours in the morning, drinking coffee and telling other customers what a great salesman I was. He even found out that I was from El Paso and took the new car that I sold him on his vacation to visit El Paso just to see what it would be like to visit my home town.

On another occasion I had to go to physical therapy on my way to work, I carried a banana with me, my Nook reader and my cane. I usually had enough time to eat the banana before starting my therapy, but in this case they had a new young blonde assistant in her early twenties. She immediately greeted me and began to bring me toward the back to start my therapy. She saw that my hands were full, and said, "Do you want me to hold your banana for you?" I was shocked and surprised and she began to turn red realizing what she had said. Then I said in a loud voice "boy this is a friendly place!" and Shaun the head therapist looked up at me waiting for my next comment. Then I said, "This young lady just offered to hold my banana for me" loud enough for everyone to hear. Patients and therapists alike all began laughing and carrying on. The poor girl was so embarrassed, that Shaun came and took over for her to work with me.

There was a tall attractive woman named Racy; and she worked for a finance company, she would call on our dealership to solicit business. When I met her I flirted with her and told her "she was like a tall drink of water." I offered her a banana, as I told her that climbing her would be like climbing Mount Everest. As she started to eat the banana I asked her if she knew the difference in a single woman or a married woman while eating a banana; she said no. So I showed her; I said a single woman peels it normally and brings it up to her mouth. A married woman peels it first then; I grabbed the back of my head and forced it down onto the banana. Then I asked her if she was married or not. Her face flushed red, and she went to Joe's office to finish eating her banana. After that she never accepted another banana from me again, but she did send me friends of hers to buy cars from me.

Later when I arrived at work, Joe my good friend and used-car manager, who is terribly homophobic, sat in his office with Ronea and two other salesmen and a box of brownies. When I arrived I went in and let him know which appointments I had coming in that day, I turned to walk away ignoring the brownies, and Joe said, "Wait, don't you want a brownie?"

I said, "No, I want your brownie." He began yelling and screaming, "There you go again with that homo stuff, I'm not gay." The more he yelled the more everybody else laughed at his extreme reaction.

Sometime toward the beginning of my 90 day resolution, I met a Puerto Rican couple whose last name was Gomez. We got along quite well despite the wife telling me how Mexicans and Puerto Ricans don't get along. She asked me to explain my position on what I thought about Puerto Ricans. I told her that the main difference between Mexicans and Puerto Ricans is that my ancestors were given a rake and a shovel and the opportunity to earn their way into America. Whereas Puerto Ricans had been coddled and babied and allowed to live a halfway existence between Puerto Rico and the US while reaping the benefits of both. In other words; "they get to have their heart over there and their belly over here." She began extolling to me the virtues of Puerto Rico, the country itself and how beautiful it was. She told me how since my wife and I like to travel, my wife and I would love a trip there and appreciate its scenic beauty. After carefully thinking about it, I said, "There would only be one problem with visiting Puerto Rico."

She said, "What's that?" and I said, "It's full of Puerto Ricans."

In spite of our differences, I ended up selling them a brand new $35,000 Nissan Quest van. I mentioned before how I hate selling new cars and I was only able to make a $300 commission. To top it off, they had multiple problems with the vehicle. And because new cars are so conscious of customer service, I had to give them loaner cars while theirs was being repaired. As luck would have it, before my ninety days were up, someone did them a favor and stole the vehicle from them. So they came back and purchased a used one for $25,000, and I was able to make a nice $1,500 commission, justice had triumphed.

Another day when I arrived at work Joe, my used-car manager, and three salesmen were all staring out the window of Joe's office. It had tinted windows to protect the glare from the sun, but also customers could not see what they were looking at. I walked in and said, "What's going on?" Joe said, "Look at that," as they ogled a woman in a short white skirt walking around the used-car lot with her husband and another salesman. Every time she leaned in to look inside a car, you could practically see through her skirt, her well defined butt. They seemed an odd pair, her young vivacious body and him an overweight long haired guy with glasses. So as the other salesmen commented "Have you ever seen an ass like that?" I said, "No, and hers isn't so bad either" as if they had been looking at his ass instead of hers. Joe and the salesmen came unglued saying, "There you go with the gay stuff again," but of course I'll do anything for a good laugh.

It seemed almost surreal but my time was drawing near, the waiting period went through on my social security benefits, as well as my other disability policy and it was time to call it a career. My friend Ronea planned a going away party for me and we had cake and refreshments and plenty of well-wishing cards to commemorate my early retirement. I never knew how to react to people treating me warmly, since I often treated others so poorly. But as with anything, it's a matter of perception. Perhaps when I thought I was treating them poorly, I was just showing my competitive nature, which most people in the industry understood. I've never been one to fish for compliments, but Phil, the general manager, Timson, the new-car manager, and Joe my friend and used-car manager all commented that I was the best they'd ever seen. I only wish I had more time to really show them what I could accomplish.

CHAPTER 38

IN CONCLUSION

It was in the late spring of 2012 that I officially retired from the automobile industry. After that I spent my days exercising at our local health club called Pelican Athletic Club or exercising with my Parkinson's exercise group at East Jefferson Hospital. I did all I could to learn all about my disease, through classes and symposiums, and of course, I started working on this story. At the beginning of my story, I spoke about an article I had saved for many years from the *LA Times*, where it spoke of men and women in the field of automobile sales, having the true entrepreneurial spirit of American business. This has never been truer in my mind, and this story is as much about my fellow salespeople as it is about me. I pay tribute to all those who have endured the blistering heat of asphalt lots in the middle of summer or the dreaded cold winds of winter, while trying to supply a good living for their families. If you're like me who has ever been on a test drive with a crazy customer who actually wrecked the car they were trying to buy or followed a customer home at ten o'clock at night to look for the title to their trade-in, this is for you. To all those who thought they had seen and heard it all, I had a customer tell me that they needed to consult the internet before making a decision to buy a car. The first time someone told me that as their reason to wait another day, I said to them, "Sure, you consult the internet while I go home and ask my refrigerator if it's okay to sell you the car."

Some may say that I romanticize too much about the industry, but I can tell you in a descriptive manner how the sun set appeared at every car lot I ever worked at. Not only that, I can search the archives of my mind and tell you what each lot looked like at the beginning of the day, the middle of the day, and at closing time. Maybe it's because I had so much hopeful anticipation for what each day would bring. I loved the sound of the phone ringing, that it might be a worthy prospect on the other line. As the sun was setting, I could often see cars angling toward the lot, and I knew they would soon be pulling in to explore the wonders of my used-car lot. With each sunset brought the hope of that evening's business and future sales for me.

In the film *Used Cars*, Rudy Russo, played by Kurt Russell, had to give the eulogy for the old man Lou, the dealer, who died on the back lot of a heart attack. For various reasons, they chose not to bury him in the traditional way, but instead to put him in his favorite car and lower him into a pit that was in the back lot. The car hung from a cable, while Rudy, Jeff, and Big Jim, the mechanic, stood ready to lower him into the ground. Rudy lifted his head up to the sky, which was already raining, and he said, "A good man had gone over the curb for the last time. Lou, we can't give you a headstone, but we will keep your name up in lights and will keep the finest overhead weather-resistant banners flying over the lot that carries your name. Ford, Chrysler, and General Motors shall be your epithet as you go to a place with a clean inventory, low discounts, and high-volume selling. Amen." I often thought someone should say that at my funeral, as the mariachis play music in the background.

A good friend of mine, Hector, worked with me way back in the day at Dick Poe Chrysler, and on weekends, he played in a band for various bars and taverns around town. As with most bands, they were followed by several groupies. He had one such woman who was his regular sex partner. On one occasion, he was having sex with her standing up behind the building in the back alley. This woman had one particular defect, and she had one leg longer than the other one and had to wear a special platform shoe. So as he was having sex with her, he told me he began to get bored with the same old thing. Just then he reached out with his foot and kicked her platform shoe away, as she stumbled and kicked in the darkness trying to recover her shoe; he claimed that in those thirty-five to forty-five seconds, it was the best sex he had ever experienced in his life. Most people would ask, "Is that a true story?" But a car salesman would never ask that question. They would just appreciate it for what it is, "a good story." I was a car salesman for over thirty-two years, a damn good one.

The End